SIGNS OF STRUGGLE

by

John Carenen

Neverland Publishing Company
Miami, FL

This book is a novel and a work of fiction. Names, characters, places, and incidents either are products of the author's imagination or are used fictitiously. Any resemblance to actual events or locales or persons, living or dead, is entirely coincidental and should not be considered real or factual.

Cover Design by Joe Font

Library of Congress Control Number: 2012950511

Printed in the United States of America

ISBN: 978-0-9826971-60

www.neverlandpublishing.com

This novel is dedicated to my loving,
long-suffering, and patient wife,
Elisabeth (Lisa),
for her steadfast encouragement,
wise suggestions, and brilliant insights.

I could never have completed
***Signs of Struggle** without her.*

Prologue

"Thus a dark hue moves ahead of a
flame over a sheet of paper,
as the whiteness dies away before
it becomes black."
- Dante's Inferno, Canto XXV

Karen O'Shea and her daughters expected a good time in Atlanta. They were excited about going Christmas shopping that Saturday morning.

Waiting for the girls to come downstairs, Karen fixed herself a cup of Earl Grey tea. It smelled good. She blew lightly across the surface, took a sip, and gazed out at the bird feeder beyond the kitchen's bay window. The tea warmed her chest.

A brown thrasher scrounged for seeds below the feeder. Karen studied the bird. Brown thrashers were beautiful if you looked closely. Rows of brown specks flung across a white breast, rich chocolate feathering with white wing bars. Sharp, pointed beak. Karen had identified thirty-one birds on her Peterson Field Guides Eastern Birds checklist. "Thirty-two," her husband, Thomas, had said, "if you count me, a common loon." She smiled at the memory.

She gazed beyond the fence behind the house, the branches of the maple trees stark and bare. A sudden gust of wind shook loose three bits of color; red, yellow, and orange leaves, last remnants of a spectacular autumn. The leaves drifted to the ground.

Karen set down her tea and took an onion bagel out of the freezer, nuked it, pried it open and spread cream cheese on the steaming halves.

Michelle came into the kitchen first, an eighth grader with dark good looks and a flashy smile. Effervescent and energetic, she looked forward to the crowd and the crush of the mall in Atlanta. She headed for the cupboard, pulled out a box of Fruit Loops, and dumped the cereal into a big bowl. "If I keep eating stuff with lots of preservatives, I'll live forever," she said.

Gotcha, the family's brindle and white English Bulldog, rumbled into the room, sat in front of Michelle, and looked up.

“No bites for you, Gotcha," she said. "This is *my* breakfast. You're doomed to failure if you expect me to feel sorry for you. I have a cold heart, pupper."

The Bulldog tried to look underfed. She stared at Michelle until a handful of colorful bits of cereal fell to the floor mat. Michelle sat down at the small table by the bay window and poured milk over her cereal. Gotcha ate the Loops, snorting and slurping. A thin smear of slobber remained where the cereal had once been.

Annie came into the kitchen. Tall, blonde, and lean like her mother, Annie strode to the cupboard and pulled out a box of Life cereal, read the label to be sure, and took the bowl over to the table. Karen grabbed her bagel and tea and sat down with the girls. Annie had started in on her cereal.

"Michelle’s up front on the way in and I'm shotgun coming home," Annie said. “That way, I'll be able to keep Mom company so she won't fall asleep at the wheel and kill us all," she continued, winking at her sister. Mom took the bait.

“I have never, ever fallen asleep at the wheel,” Karen said. “I don’t even get drowsy." The girls made eye contact with each other and grinned. Mom was half right.

They finished breakfast, aired Gotcha, and left the house. They drove through town and onto I-75 North.

"Where'd Dad say he was going today?" Annie asked. "Albany?"

"Augusta," Karen said. "He's got to tell a potential client there's no deal."

Michelle said, "Why can't he just give the guy a call?"

"Your dad likes the man. He didn't want to tell him over the phone."

"Speaking of Dad," Michelle said, "let's not forget to bring him something to eat."

"Such as?" Karen asked.

Michelle said, "How 'bout jelly beans? He inhales Jelly Bellies."

"He'd flip out," Annie replied.

It was cold for early December, and the sky was dark and slate gray, even darker north of them. "Looks like we might have some weather ahead of us," Karen said, "but I'm sure we can drive through it."

They passed Macon. Annie read a book. Michelle and Karen talked about Michelle's friends. The O'Shea's left Macon and McDonough behind, quickly approaching Atlanta.

A semi-trailer truck, southbound on I-75, was drawing closer as the O'Shea's Highlander approached Atlanta. Ricky Damon, behind the wheel for twenty-one hours straight, was sleepy. He had drunk three cold beers, the third one to cool his throat after the joint he'd sucked in half an hour before. Now, he was sleepy again. His eyelids drooped. The beer slipped from his right hand and fell to the floor of the cab, waking him. Ricky saw his truck drifting left from the fast lane. Someone had abandoned a Mazda Miata and he was going to hit it. A curse burst from his lips. The small car served to launch the truck over the low concrete median divider and into the northbound traffic.

The eighteen-wheeler flopped down on the O'Shea's Highlander like a blind spaceship, its hot underbelly pinning the SUV and disintegrating the family, their beauty broken and crushed in a bloody bed of safety glass chips and razor-sharp metal, diesel fuel, and grease. Then it all hissed and exploded in towering flames with thick black smoke curling upward into the heavens.

Thomas O'Shea stopped by the Thrifty Flower Shop on the way home from Augusta and purchased red roses for his wife and daisies for the girls. He would be home first, and it would be fun to have the flowers waiting for his family.

When he pulled into his driveway, the Georgia Highway Patrol was waiting.

Chapter One

"No one ever told me grief felt so much like fear."
- C. S. Lewis

All I want is peace. All I want is to be left alone with the privacy and quiet that goes with it. So I gave myself the gift of a leisurely drive in the countryside. What could be more benign?

I needed time to recover from my Georgia-to-Iowa nonstop road trip and two days of fruitless house hunting in Rockbluff. I needed cheap therapy, and a late springtime wandering in the hill country seemed like a good idea. I thought it just might work better than counseling, pharmaceuticals, or maybe even a cold six-pack.

I had left America's Best Bulldog, Gotcha, perched on her pillow back in the Rockbluff Motel, our home the last three days, and escaped into my country cruise. That's all I wanted—a drive in the bucolic backcountry—something I'd often enjoyed before the move to Georgia. Something good, back when I had a family. Before the troubles came. Before a lot of things. So I took off, leaving Gotcha to catch up on her beauty sleep.

The May morning was glorious as I meandered down gravel roads, weaving through dense stands of hardwoods alternating with fields of fertile farmland. Thick pigs wallowed in fresh black mud, and grazing dairy and beef cattle concentrated on generating more butterfat and bigger briskets. Living industry; blood and breath.

I drove randomly for a while, serenity at every turn. But then, on a blind curve, I met a speeding, skidding, silver Corvette that nearly ran me off the road. I couldn't blame the driver. Hard to improve on springtime and sports cars. I glanced in my rearview mirror and saw the 'vette disappear into its dust cloud behind me.

I continued, rounding a gentle, deep-shadowed bend, and slowed to a stop to admire a mailbox seated squarely on a brick column. I had time. The surname "SODERSTROM" was calligraphied on the side of the mailbox in the midst of flashy cardinals, burly blue jays, and pink wild roses. Good Iowa name. Not many Soderstroms in south-central Georgia.

Just then, a movement in the shadows caught my eye. I glanced up into a tunnel of shade produced by the oak-lined lane leading away from the mailbox. And there she appeared, tall, blonde, and full-breasted, emerging quickly from the shadows. A sprinting screamer, bloody and berserk.

And her face? Fear and terror, and agony of some kind. Edvard Munch should have painted her instead of the sexless being in "The Scream." He would've sold more t-shirts.

My highly-cultivated selfishness took over and I paused, wondering if I could escape and avoid whatever problem was pushing that woman toward me, closer and closer. It would be so easy. I wanted to leave, free of any duty, responsibility or moral compunction to help someone else in pain. Her problem, not mine.

My decision bounced around in my mind like lottery ping-pong balls waiting to be plucked. I froze. I muttered to myself, pounded my palms on the steering wheel. I knew I was going to do that which I did not want to do.

The woman loomed twenty yards away, fifteen, closing fast. Too late for my escape. Maybe I had let the decision be made for me by deliberate dawdling, linked together with its sluggish brother, procrastination.

I slammed the shift to park; killed the engine, stepped out of my pickup truck onto the gravel, pocketed my keys, my blood pressure in my ears, beating out a regular rhythm of "dumb ass, dumb ass, dumb ass." I looked up into the sky and silently asked, *What am I doing here?* No answer. Imagine.

I was reminded of the poem by A.R. Ammons, "Coward," herein completely recalled: "Courage runs in my family." I should have split.

The woman, lithe, long-legged and swift, ran beautifully and with purpose, her footspeed driven by some revulsion back there, at the farm. She drew quickly to me, her bulging breasts fighting for freedom under her pale pink t-shirt. I took two steps toward her and then the woman, shrieking words I could not understand, a kind of gory glossalalia, smacked into me in an awkward embrace. I staggered back, repositioned my glasses, and simply held her, overcoming my urge, even then, to flee.

I wanted peace. Now this woman took it away, falling into my arms and covering me with blood and pulp, screaming words I finally understood: "Where are they?! Where are they?!"

I shuddered, even in the growing heat of the day and with the warmth of her panting body pressed against me, almost enough to make me overlook the goop now pasted on my chest and arms. The tormented expression on her face would have stopped my heart a few months ago. Not now.

I drew my head back and looked at her. The congealing bloodstuff smeared her arms, up to her elbows, and splattered on her tight t-shirt and light blue jeans. I pulled back my head a bit in distaste. I do not have the gift of mercy, unless it is directed toward myself.

She trembled through our grim embrace. I took her shoulders and pushed her to arms' length and looked into her face to try to stop her panic, to give her a stable point of reference, her stunning blue eyes wide and filled with fear, and comprehending more than I could understand. Her outstretched hands and forearms, slick with spilled life, reached out to me as she sobbed convulsively. Then she pulled me tightly to herself again and I said, "It's okay."

I am beyond stupid.

If only I had kept my moronic mouth shut. What I really should have done was pretend I had been blinded by the sun, or got a gnat in my eye, and kept driving. Now it was too late for that self-serving wisdom.

She did not appear to be hurt. She ran too quickly, embraced too powerfully, screamed too forcefully and wildly. Suddenly, chest heaving, she pushed hard away from me and looked at me as if I were insane. It made sense. After all, I had just told her, "It's okay."

She looked wildly up and down the road and shouted, "Where are they?!"

"Who?" I blared back.

"The ambulance! I called nine-one-one minutes ago! Oh, Jesus, where *are* they? Help my husband! Help *me*!"

"I'll help you!" I shouted.

She turned instantly, like a filly startled by a snake, and sprinted back up the shaded lane with its enormous oak trees grown together into a canopy over the gravel road.

I pursued her, the gravel shifting and crunching under my shoes. I could not keep up with the athletic twenty-something. I am older than I used to be, ten pounds over fighting trim, and decades from street fighting, athletic competition and military service.

The passage of time exacts a toll, and at that moment, as I pretended to be a sprinter in order to catch up to the bloody beauty, I felt a hot twinge and heard a wet, popping sound in the back of my right leg, up near my butt.

I'd blown out my hamstring, my biceps femoris, but I wasn't going to baby it (too much pride in the presence of the young woman). The pain nauseated me, so I modified my stride, continued on, surprising myself that I could still move at all, slinging my bad leg along and following the woman. I heard approaching sirens.

"Help's on the way!" I shouted. She ignored me, racing another thirty yards into the farmyard toward the thing on the grass, where her sprint became a stumble, a stagger, a stop. She sank to the ground, wailing, keening in unspeakable agony just beyond where the machine had skinned her man.

I managed to lurch forward a few more yards. I stopped and

stared. The John Deere tractor and giant green rotary mower it pulled had angled away, driverless, and nosed into a ditch, engine still chugging as if it had not eaten enough.

I heard myself whisper, "Oh, my God."

The machine left behind two things. One part, knees down, was human, intact, although blood-splashed. Blue jeans and heavy work boots somehow escaped the mower's sharp blades. The body above the knees had been flayed, as if set upon by an army of angry razor blades intent on slicing away clothes, skin and muscle, deflected only by a bit of bone here and there. The back of the skull, shoulder blades and ribs glistened wet and white in the sunlight. The buttocks were gone, sliced away. Pieces of blue shirt and red flesh were everywhere. I could smell the blood.

That thing on the ground before me had been human only minutes before, fearfully and wonderfully made. I had seen men who'd stepped on land mines. This was worse.

I forced myself to look away from the dead man and turn to the new widow, collapsed on the freshly-cut green grass a few yards away, slumped against a weeping willow tree. That wonderful smell, the rich, redolent glory of cut grass, would never again be the same for her. Maybe not for me, either. Sirens screamed up the lane, promising help for her, relief for me. Let someone else restore order to chaos. I would leave it all with the locals and have a cold one. More than one. A blessing both ways. They were trained in tragedy. I am merely experienced. I did not even know these people, this young woman, her shredded husband.

I could go away and be alone again.

An EMS (Extra Messy Situations) vehicle, lights flashing, siren wailing, roared up and skidded to a stop in the farmyard. The siren cut off in mid-shriek, a short "WHOOP!" that ended abruptly. Directly behind the emerging vehicle, a charcoal mini-van stopped. A young woman opened the driver's door and eased out. She had short red hair and wore a dark green t-shirt, baggy black Umbro slacks and running shoes. She rushed to the woman on the ground. She made eye contact with me. I nodded, and she turned back to the woman now quietly fallen against the willow.

The EMS team came up, saw what was on the ground, and slowed to a walk. One of the men ran over to the tractor in the ditch and killed the ignition, then returned. The men approached me, their eyes on the thing that had been a man, until all three of us just stared at the bottom of the victim's Wolverine work boots.

"What happened?" The EMS tech looked like someone who rode jet skis all weekend. The nametag over his shirt pocket read, "Schumacher."

"I don't know," I said. "I was driving by and she was running down the lane, covered with blood, screaming."

Schumacher suddenly staggered away a few steps and threw up into a ditch. I turned to his partner, "Aldrich" on the nametag. I asked him about the lady from the mini-van.

"She's Molly Heisler, pastor's wife," he said.

"Who's the bloody lady?"

"Wendy Soderstrom. Her place, but she's not from around here."

"You know the family?"

"Yeah, went to school with her husband, Hugh," Aldrich said. "Played football together. Conference champs last two years. Heckuva linebacker."

"She said it was her husband."

"Hugh? God Almighty. I was afraid of that. Good Lord," Aldrich whispered. "I was hoping it was one of the hired hands, I mean, since it had to be somebody. Big farm."

"Maybe you can get the pastor's wife to take Mrs. Soderstrom out of here, escort her to the hospital. She's got to be in shock. It looks like she tried to pick him up. Do they have any children?"

"No, but they were trying," Aldrich said. No secrets in rural Iowa.

Schumacher stumbled back to us, looking sheepish because his humanity had overcome his training. Nothing to be ashamed of. He rubbed his mouth with the back of his hand. Organization and process began asserting themselves. I looked around to keep from looking at Schumacher. He didn't need eye contact. Not now.

The two-story Soderstrom farmhouse, big, square, and white-framed, boasted a broad front porch furnished with a swing hung from the ceiling and a scattering of Adirondack chairs, weathered gray. Good place to kick back at the end of the day. A gray stone chimney dominated one end of the house. Secured high up on the chimney, a big, wrought iron letter "S" announced ownership. Green shutters. A small satellite dish perched on the green-shingled roof. Frilly white curtains framed the windows, upstairs and down.

The farmyard included three white barns with green roofs and a wide, open-faced garage housing trucks, tractors and machinery. White grain silos stood like bleached Pringles potato chip cans. Evidence of wealth everywhere.

The wind picked up, soughing through the trees. Pretty sound. Peaceful. I looked at the sky. Storm clouds building, thunderheads rolling in from the west. I wiped the sweat off my forehead. A sudden, rough breeze drove back some of the sick feeling I was fighting from my aching leg. I took a deep breath, closed my eyes. I'd rather have pain any day over nausea, but when I have both, I can be irritable.

We stared at the body. Schumacher turned away. "Better get a body bag, John," he mumbled.

"Looks like he fell off the tractor and got run over," Aldrich said. "Size of that mower, man, what's left of him, musta bled to death in seconds. Exsanguination. God Almighty, Gene, this is terrible," he said. He edged toward the body as Schumacher brought the body bag.

The two men snapped on latex gloves and walked over to the dead man. Hugh. They hesitated, then expertly, reverently, placed the remains in the bag, zipped the envelope shut, positioned themselves at each end of the heavy brown vinyl container, and lifted. They lugged the body to their vehicle and swung it inside, grunting in unison. They peeled away their gloves, dropped them in a bio-waste container just inside, and slammed the doors shut. Aldrich was weeping.

Schumacher edged over to the women and said something to Molly Heisler, who had positioned herself so that the young widow was shielded from the moving of her husband's body. Heisler nodded and stood, then helped the other woman to her feet. The women, hanging onto each other, struggled to the passenger side of the mini-van. Heisler opened the door and helped the other woman inside and shut the door, then scrambled around to the driver's side, seemingly unconcerned about getting blood smears in her spiffy van. Good for her. She drove off.

The EMS truck, silent and somber, followed the van down the lane.

I took another deep breath, felt better as the nausea backed off just a little, and looked around the farmyard, admiring the obvious pride of ownership. The wind kicked up again and the first drops of rain, big and thick, typical prelude to a toad-choking downpour, began to pelt down. The clouds broke open with a booming clap of thunder that made me jump, and heavy rain slammed into the farmyard. I didn't seek shelter. I just let the rain fall on me, soaking my t-shirt. It felt good, cleansing, cool, like a sweet shower. I took off my glasses, lifted my face to the sky, and closed my eyes.

I heard tires crunching on gravel. I put my glasses back on and looked.

A white car with "Rockbluff County Sheriff" stenciled in green on the front door crawled up the drive and pulled to a stop in the driveway. The cruiser's headlights glowed and the windshield wipers arced back and forth. The driver killed the lights and engine and got out. The wipers stopped in mid-sweep.

The young man, big and beefy, maybe a tight end in college, slipped into his raincoat and pulled on a black baseball cap with "RCSD" across the front in yellow letters. The snug raincoat made him look shrink-wrapped. He strode over to the bloody grass, meeting me there. He said, "This is worse than I thought when they called it in."

His blue eyes, squinty against the rain, studied the lawn, streaking now, like faint pink ribbons trailing away from a girl's hat. He turned and looked at me, offered his hand, and said, "Stephen Doltch, Deputy Sheriff."

"Tom O'Shea, unfortunate passerby." It was like shaking hands with a bear.

Just then lightning lacerated the sky, the heavens cracked wide open with window-rattling thunder, and buckets fell.

"Terrible accident," Doltch yelled through the cloudburst.

I shouted back, "What makes you think it was an accident?"

Sometimes I like to stir things up just to see what happens next; besides, Doltch's observation seemed like a pretty quick analysis of the situation. Not that I disagreed, but my leg hurt and nausea nudged my guts. I wanted to leave, and here's a young deputy, supposedly inured to presumptions, making judgments already.

He looked at me as if a banana slug were emerging from my left eye socket. "What else *could* it be?"

I shrugged, trying to appear disinterested, uninvolved. I looked around. I rubbed the back of my aching leg. "Suicide? Farmers have high suicide rates."

"Not Hugh," Doltch said, his voice loud. Another shaft of lightning, farther away, then a distant rumble, rain letting up a little. "Too much to live for: Wendy, this farm, children someday, season tickets on the forty at Trice Stadium, forty rows up. No, sir, this wasn't any suicide. Besides, I don't think anyone would do himself in this way. My God."

So the dead man was an Iowa State guy. Talk about a string of bad luck. First the football team, now this. I said, "I knew a guy in college who killed himself by drinking a beaker of hydrochloric acid."

"This ain't no suicide."

"Murder?" Forever picking. Wise guy. *Provocateur*.

"Murder?" The young lawman grimaced. "Jesus, Mary, and Joseph, where do you get murder? Everybody liked Hugh. Good grief. You obviously aren't from around here."

"Actually, I am." Faint flash of lightning in the next county east, thin thunder following. I pushed my glasses up on top of my head and wiped the rain from my face, took my glasses in hand and ran a fingertip across the lenses. I put them back on. I felt suddenly cold on a warm spring day. "I am about to buy a house. As soon as I find it."

"That your truck back up the lane?" he asked.

"Yes, sir."

"Very nice."

"Thank you." The new, four-door pickup was a failed attempt to help me get my mind off my dead family. An attempt to buy a change of pace back in Georgia. Still, it is nice, a luxury I can easily afford after selling my half of the business; collecting on insurance policies; selling the house, furnished; selling the lake house, also furnished; selling the ski boat, and closing out our checking and money market accounts. My liquid assets nudge well into seven figures with more than my toenails on that million-dollar line.

The truck, a big V-8, is very fast, and I have driven it out to the top end, sometimes in the middle of moonlit nights on remote Georgia blacktops. With the headlights off. Slowing when I thought maybe a dog might wander out in front of me. Some farm kid's pet. No fear for me, however. After all one's greatest fears have happened, what is left to fear? I looked back at the deputy as he began to speak again.

The deputy said, "Georgia plates. I ran them. No problems, but they still aren't Iowa plates, if you get my meaning. You're still a stranger."

"In a suddenly strange land."

"I don't appreciate a wise guy right now, Mr. O'Shea. Hugh Soderstrom was my friend."

"Sorry. I didn't know him."

"Your loss." A challenge in the statement, gone unanswered. No reason to.

I nodded my head. "I guess so."

Doltch looked at me, searching for sarcasm. Another time. "I understand Chuck Aldrich was the first person here."

"Besides Mrs. Soderstrom, that's right."

"Mind if I ask you what you were doing here?"

"Do I need a lawyer?"

Doltch smiled a little smile. "You are not a suspect; not even a person of interest."

"If it's an accident, there aren't any suspects, or persons of interest." Wiseguy again. Doltch picked up on it. His little smile went away. I rubbed my leg just below my butt. The rain continued, somewhat abated. Like it was tired, or had seen what was on the ground and slowed for a look before moving on. We both stood there, listening to the sound of gentle rain pelting into the earth. "To answer your question, I was just out enjoying a drive when I bumped into all this," I said.

Doltch hunched his thick shoulders against the rain, reached inside his gray, opaque raincoat, and fished in his shirt pocket until he produced a pen and notebook. Technology stampede. "I'd like to ask you a couple more questions."

Instantly, the rain stopped, as if to listen to my answers. Just like that. We both looked up. The sun came out. Perfect growing conditions which drive the economy of an entire state. The world smelled fresh and clean.

Doltch asked routine questions. No edge at all. He did not ask me if I saw or heard anything unusual. It was an accident and would be reported as such, although he had yet to ask the only witness what she saw. He finished in ten minutes, leaving me stunned over his zeal to get to the truth.

I must confess, though, it did excite me to see a law enforcement professional at work. It's a natural rush no television crime show can match.

When the questions ended, Doltch said thanks, strode over to his cruiser, opened the rear door behind the driver's side, pulled off his raincoat and tossed it in the backseat. He slammed that door, opened the driver's door, scrunched in behind the wheel, turned his baseball cap around backwards, and began writing on a clipboard. He finished writing, placed the clipboard onto the seat next to him, and pulled the door shut. Then he left, nodding soberly at me as he drove away, tires wet on the gravel.

I hobbled back down the lane to my truck, opened the door, and slid inside, lifting my right leg and swinging it into a position on the floorboard in front of the accelerator. It felt like someone had stuck a hot ice pick in the back of my leg, then wiggled it around. My nausea was gone, gradually replaced by significant discomfort. Now it was tightening up. Oh, joy. I started the engine.

For a moment I just sat there, soaked to the skin, staring at that beautiful mailbox, but seeing the face of Wendy Soderstrom. The cloudburst had washed away the gore she'd pressed onto me, but I didn't have any trouble remembering it felt like that gelatin that oozes out from around the circumference of the meat in a can of Spam just opened. Only warm.

Maybe it was time for the Iowa Tourism Board to revise their ad campaign. Maybe they could entice visitors with a come-on, something like, "See Iowa! Four beautiful seasons! Friendly people! Gorgeous, bloody women screaming down lovely country lanes!"

Maybe not.

After a while I dropped the truck into gear, performed a loose, three-point turn in the smushy gravel road, and headed back the way I had come. Clearly time to have adult beverages, a little reliable chemotherapy to smooth me out through the next little while. Time to think, my least favorite activity these days, next to messing around with the cell phone I hate and refuse to use.

Chapter 2

"Every man should believe in something: I believe I'll have another drink."
- W. C. Fields

Back at the motel, I asked Gotcha if she wanted to go out. She declined. So I took a quick shower, swallowed four Advil, then two more, and changed clothes. Even after seeing all the gore out at the Soderstrom place, I wanted food. I burned up a load of calories hugging the bloody lady, sprinting up the lane, fighting the pain of my hamstring, and holding back my sarcasm with "CSI Rockbluff" star, Deputy Stephen Doltch.

So I decided to forage for food after providing Gotcha with a jumbo Milk-Bone to tide her over. Her sloppy, wet munching sounds followed me across the room and out the door. She sounded like a Shop Vac cleaning up an oil spill.

The Grain o' Truth Bar & Grill commands the west side of the Whitetail River at the edge of a business district cuddled alongside the river, north of a double arch limestone bridge. Beautiful bridge. Unique. Centerpiece of the town's identity. Just today I saw it as part of the town's logo on the side of the EMS vehicle and Deputy Doltch's cruiser. I guess it's an official bridge. Iconic.

I had noticed the bar and grill the day before and made a point to see what it offered beyond its interesting name. The "Grill" part drew me. And "Bar" produced a certain existential appeal, too.

A dozen vehicles hunkered down in the sunny parking lot, but one, a mint-condition pearl-gray '51 Packard, stood out among the Asian sedans and assorted pickup trucks with bumper stickers extolling the virtues of DeKalb Corn, Lutheran marriage, and Iowa football.

I parked and ambled toward the entrance, gritting my teeth as I concealed my limp, and crossed the slate patio. I pushed through the solid-core oak door. Subdued lighting and air conditioning greeted me inside.

In the background, the jukebox offered up Carmen Quinn singing "Stardust." I needed, in addition to food, something nice, something soothing, and Carmen delivered. Nice surprise. I expected to hear "Bubba Shot the Jukebox Last Night."

An old, sunburned, string-bean of a man sat in a window booth, watching me. He wore a white t-shirt with a green Celtics tank top over it, camouflage Bermuda shorts, orange elbow and knee pads, and red socks. No shoes. A pair of black in-line skates were plunked down on the bench at his side. In front of him, a skid-marked white bicyclist's helmet with a peeling Cubs decal rested next to a half-empty pint. His wispy white hair sweat-stuck to his bony head, and he nodded at me and lifted his beer in salute.

"Horace Norris is the name," he said, smiling through the gap in his front teeth.

"Thomas O'Shea, sir."

"With that name, then, it's the top o' the mornin' to ye at The Grain o' Truth Bar & Grill, sir!"

It wasn't morning, it was early afternoon. I replied, "And the rest o' the day t' *you*." I was in no mood to quibble over niceties like time reference errors. I'm Irish; the niceties often escape my countrymen and me, especially after dark.

The old man shifted in his booth, like a cat wiggling its backside before it pounces on prey. Then he lowered his voice, looked around conspiratorially, and said in a stage whisper, "I'm dyin'."

I didn't know what to say to that, so I replied, "Aren't we all, now?"

Horace Norris smiled. "And ye can't stop me."

"Nor would I try, without your permission."

The old man grinned thoughtfully and nodded his head. "I can live with that!"

I nodded, smiled, and looked around.

There was a decent lunch crowd in the place, but the establishment's U-shaped bar, an ornate mission oak monster complete with a gleaming brass rail, drew my attention. Carved wooden shelves and an enormous mirror backed the bar, and on the walls a variety of old neon beer signs presented themselves, including one for Pickett's, no longer made in Dubuque or anywhere else, to the deep sadness of connoisseurs.

Wooden booths along the walls, two antique pool tables and several tables and chairs rounded out the furnishings. In the back a standard red "EXIT" sign glowed and, nearby, a lavender neon sign reading "rest rooms" in elaborate script decorated the wall. Tiffany lamps, or more probably their replicas, hung low over the pool tables and throughout the place.

The presence behind the exquisite bar commanded my interest. Taking in my conversation with Horace Norris stood a man, thick and strong looking, wearing a loose black t-shirt with "IOWA" across the front in block gold letters. I approached the bar, sat on a stool, and scrutinized the hand-written menu on whiteboard over the mirror behind the bar. The bartender acknowledged my presence with a nod of his head, but said nothing. He put down his Wall Street Journal.

"Beautiful bar."

"Thank you," he said, his voice a deep baritone, rich and rumbling.

I ordered the Specialty of the House, the Loony Burger, a 12-ounce ground round burger on a Kaiser roll. French fries included. The man silently prepared the food, working efficiently at the grill and deep fryer. When the meat sizzled and the fries bubbled in the hot oil, he returned to stand before me.

"What would you like to drink, Mr. O'Shea?"

I ordered a Three Philosophers, not expecting him to have it. The bartender produced my favorite Belgian ale, popped the cap, and handed over the bottle and a frosted tulip glass. He said, "Excellent choice for a hot day." I poured the liquid, leaving a one-inch head, drank it down, and set the empty glass on the counter. He gave me another and I polished it off, too. A minor buzz edged into my head. Empty stomach syndrome combined with 9.8% alcohol.

"You call it the Loony Burger because one has to be crazy to order that much?"

The bartender, handsome in a rough way, my age, not quite as tall, inclined his head just a tad. His t-shirt hung loosely from thick trapezius muscles inserted into the base of his skull. He did not have a neck. The sleeves of the black t-shirt were tight. I noticed when he came back from starting my order that he wore black jeans and a black belt with a small turquoise and silver buckle.

His black and silver hair was combed straight back and gathered into a short, flat ponytail. Black eyes under thick salt-and-pepper brows scrutinized me. The man's hawk nose made him look menacing, although the eyes were merely intelligent.

He said, "I named it after *me*. It is my creation. It is my business. Loony Burger lacks dignity, but enjoys twisted commercial appeal. It works. I sell many Loony Burgers. Chance to sell out to big businessman from Waterloo for serious wampum. I declined. He envisioned chain. He calls every year with ever-growing offer."

"You named it after yourself?" The man nodded solemnly. "You're an Indian."

"You have a steel-trap mind. Custer could have used you."

"So what's your name, and don't tell me it's Burger," I said. "I've been there, and I know a German when I see one."

A hint of humor passed across the bartender's visage, either at what I had said or the name he was about to provide. His eyebrows danced independently of each other, giving his craggy face an aura of interior conflict.

"My name is Lunatic Mooning," he said, his rich voice adding luster to his name. The Loony in Loony Burger is short for 'Lunatic.'"

"'Lunatic Mooning'?" I said to myself. He turned away and attended to my order, then brought the Loony Burger on a large, thick porcelain plate in one hand and, in the other hand, a green plastic tray lined with waxed paper overflowing with French fries. In the background, Nat Cole was singing about how, when he falls in love, it will be forever.

I looked at the man, selected a fry as thick as a hot dog, dunked it in a coffee-cup sized stainless-steel vat of ketchup shoved in next to the fries, and placed it in my mouth. It tasted good, fresh, clean. An excellent French fry seasoned with lemon pepper and garlic salt. Crispy on the edges. Outstanding. Good to be hungry.

"So, tell me about your name," I said, picking up the Loony Burger with both hands.

"My mother, slave to Indian myth and tradition, named me after the first thing she saw after I was born. She gave birth to me in the state mental hospital in Mt. Pleasant, looked up, and saw a lunatic mooning her for all he was worth. Not a common name. I happen to like it."

"Lucky for you your mother didn't look out the window and see a squirrel with diarrhea. Otherwise you might not have liked your name so much." I took a bite of the burger. Delicious.

The big Indian, his gaze intense and dark, looked at me, nodded slowly, and said, "Ugh."

I finished chewing my first bite and swallowed, nodding in satisfaction. I took another bite of the burger. The inside of my mouth smiled and sighed. Thick, succulent meat with some kind of sauce I'd never tasted before, plus honey mustard and crisp dill pickle chips. Understanding the extent of my hunger, I ordered another Loony Burger, hold the fries. Then, "As long as I'm being nosey," I said, "tell me about the name of your establishment."

"With pleasure," he said. "Good beer is made from good grain, and there is a grain of truth in every good beer. One grain of truth I have acquired after several good beers, often realized, is this: I don't like people."

Sensing a trap, I said, "But that's the exact wrong reason to open a bar, isn't it? Bar owners are gregarious, enjoy social interaction, want people to know their name. Haven't you ever seen *Cheers* re-runs?"

"Every man should engage in work that affirms his beliefs, and I have done so. I have strong beliefs, which once were mere biases but are fast becoming convictions, about the ultimate distastefulness of man. I opened this bar to prove it, and I haven't been disappointed. The Grain o' Truth. Everybody reinforces my predisposition about how unlikable people really are."

"What about Horace Norris over there, he seems like a great old guy."

"Sometimes it takes a while. Most people do not immediately reveal their character. There is a veneer behavior that makes real behaviors difficult to discern. With Horace, time will tell, as it does with everyone. Especially politicians."

I paused, thinking about what Lunatic Mooning just said. Then I asked him, "So, you don't like me?"

"I *won't*," he said simply. "But don't take it personally. It's just information." Then, "Perhaps another Three Philosophers?"

I nodded and said, "Even though you're not going to like me, I still would like to ask you a question. Bartenders are famous for being veritable founts of knowledge spanning the breadth and depth of the human experience."

"You have the gift of discernment," Lunatic Mooning said.

I told him I was looking for a house and some land, and described it. I wanted a unique house, solid construction, private, ideally on land with trees. A nice view from an elevation. No nearby neighbors. A place to heal, if that was going to happen, but I left out that part. Mooning listened intently, and when he served the third ale, surprised me.

"There is a man who has such a house, Mr. O'Shea," he said. "His name is Gunther Schmidt, and he built a house on the bluffs south of here, before you get to Guttenberg. The land is more than you want. Fifty or sixty acres, mostly timber and rock. He might break it up for you if you only want part of it." Mooning leaned forward a little and put his hands on the bar. The hands were thick and broad, more like a pair of catcher's mitts.

"Gunther builds strong houses to last. Exceeds code on everything. Uses four-by-eights two feet apart, copper wire and copper pipes, screws in hardwood floors instead of nailing them, countersinks the screws and hand-cuts wooden pegs to fill in. Even the sub-flooring's oak. He takes pride in what he does. You will see eagles from that place."

Eagles? I paused. "And the house is available?"

"It will be very expensive, but a bargain," he said, looking directly into my eyes.

"He must be a wealthy man," I said, my curiosity piqued by the possibility of eagles at such a place. I had never seen an eagle in the wild.

"He's on the verge of bankruptcy," Mooning said. "People don't want to buy quality. He built three homes in the last four years, all on spec, and sold only one, which keeps him from starving, but not for long. He envisions an idea for a kind of house he would like to build, and he builds it for the satisfaction. The man has no mind for business."

"So who bought the house he did sell?"

"Who do you think?"

"Oh," I said. I took a deep drink from my glass. Since the deaths of Karen and Annie and Michelle, I drink too much. I admit it. I tell myself I will cut back. I've been telling myself that for eighteen months now, and I mean it. I can go days without, but prefer not to. After all, it's not like I'm inflicting harm on my family.

The third Three Philosophers tasted even better than the first two, smoothing me out. Of course, it was working on my mostly-empty stomach. I dug into the Loony Burger for a while. Then I said, "Sounds like there might be something likable in Gunther Schmidt after all, which would, of course, destroy your biases. You might as well close down the bar, or revise your thinking. Sounds like he possesses strength of character."

"Nobody likes a failure," Lunatic replied.

"If he's such a failure, where does he get the capital to build the houses in the first place? Where does he get his construction loans? What banker would loan him money?"

The big Indian snorted. "A banker who happens to be his father-in-law. The house I've mentioned is his last. He's not going to ask anyone for another dime. He's thinking about going to work down in Dubuque, at the meat-packing plant. A steady paycheck and benefits look pretty good to a young man with a pregnant wife, with child for the first time, even if it does mean driving to Dubuque five or six days a week."

"You know, you're sure talkative for an Indian," I said, half in jest. "I thought all Indians were laconic."

"Most are. I'm Ojibwa."

I laughed.

"I believe I got you," Mooning said.

"I believe so, my Ojibwa acquaintance. Now, is Gunther Schmidt in the phone book?"

"No, but his name is, under 'Schmidt, Gunther,' and also in the Yellow Pages, under 'Builders and Contractors, Schmidt and Sons.'"

"He has sons? I thought his wife was pregnant for the first time."

Lunatic shrugged his bowling-ball shoulders and said, "A romantic gesture. A hope deferred. A prophecy yet unfulfilled."

I worked on my burger for a while and silently thanked myself for ordering that second go-around. Then, since I didn't have my cell phone, I slid off the stool to head for the pay phone on the wall back by the bathrooms, wondering why restaurateurs have such a predisposition for placing listening devices near public toilets.

"Something wrong with your food?" Lunatic asked, the edge of challenge in his voice.

I stopped. "No, why?"

"You're moving away pretty fast."

"I'm going to call Gunther Schmidt."

"You can't reach him by telephone."

"You just said his name was in the phone book."

The big man behind the bar shook his head sadly. "I did, but his service was disconnected for non-payment. You are impetuous. You need to gather more information before acting."

I returned to my lunch and plopped down hard on the stool,

totally at the Ojibwa's mercy. I finished my ale and pointed at the glass. Lunatic provided a fresh Three Philosophers and whisked away the empty glass, replacing it with a clean one. Three ales gone, another to go. I took another bite of the burger, chewing slowly. A near-religious experience. "So how can I get in touch with him to take a look at the house?"

"You can find him in here most evenings. Not a very likable trait, especially with his family getting ready to grow and not having much money left, especially to spend on beer. But a man in that kind of pain needs a few beers now and then, so I only sell him three Millers from the tap and send him on home to Julie."

"A troubled man needs those three grains of truth."

"Assuredly."

Lunatic looked over at Horace and then poured a fresh pint of draft Heineken's and took it over to the old man, who reached up and patted the bartender on the shoulder and thanked him. Just then, three older men came in together, dressed in expensive golf clothes, and took a window booth.

The men said hello to Lunatic as they settled into their booth. One, a bald man with a good start on a beer belly, said, "Oh, *garçon*, three Specials and a pitcher of Bud Light, and make it snappy." The other men laughed.

"Coming up," Lunatic said, coming around behind the bar. He set to work and soon the food was cooking. He poured a pitcher, put three glasses on a tray, and served the men. None said thank you. One said, "And another pitcher when you see this one getting low. Bud Light."

Lunatic ignored the man and came around behind the bar. I hoped he would never look at me with that same expression on his face.

"So the best chance of running into Gunther Schmidt is to come here in the evenings?"

"I congratulate you on your uncanny ability to process information."

"I accept your congratulations. My self-esteem is soaring like an eagle," I said. Mooning rolled his eyes. I said, "I'm staying at the

Rockbluff Motel for the time being. I was wondering, since you've already found the house I want, if you could recommend something a little more commodious in the short run."

"Harvey Goodell is a regular customer. What's wrong with his motel?"

"Nothing. I just don't want to stay there much longer. I'd like to spread out a little bit. Is there a bed and breakfast around?"

"There's a bed and breakfast across the river and down to your right, near the high school."

"Thanks. You do, indeed, know all," I said, poking the last ketchuped French fry into my mouth.

"You're better off at the motel," Lunatic said.

"Why?

"The bed and breakfast is called The Serendipity Bed and Breakfast and that should be your first clue. The rooms are filled with doilies, afghans, doll collections, and knick-knacks. The only TV station you can get is The Home and Garden Channel. One overnight and you'll be saying 'mahvelous' all the time. Lady who runs it, Margo Dweibling, is pleasant, in the superficial, insipid manner of a Chamber of Commerce intern."

"I'll stay at the motel," I said. "By the way, if Gunther comes in some night and I'm not here, would you give me a call?"

"I'm not a personal services guy."

"Well then, I guess I'll be in here tonight for sure," I said, and turned to my Loony Burger.

Lunatic grunted and left to take another pitcher of Bud Light to the three men, who were talking about their afternoon's golf game. I emptied my glass. When he came back, I ordered a Heineken, just to clean my palate, drained it, and slid down off the barstool, feeling much better than I felt driving away from Soderstrom's Rendering Works. I left enough money on the bar to cover the cost of my food and drink and a twenty-dollar tip and hobbled for the door, saying to Mooning in passing, "By the way, I like your Packard. She's a beauty." I nodded at Horace Norris and left as the big bartender picked up his newspaper.

I sat in my truck for a moment before starting the engine. The alcohol felt good, blunting the morning's craziness. One more would be even better, I thought, an even six-pack, but I would be returning to The Grain o' Truth in a few hours, and then I could self-medicate a deeper deadening.

I drove back to the motel, suddenly needing a nap.

Chapter Three

"A woman can look both moral and exciting...if she looks as if it was quite a struggle."
- Edna Ferber

Hours later, in my motel room, I sensed a presence even as I slept, a feeling of scrutiny. I woke up. Gotcha was on the bed, staring at me, her face a few inches from mine, her Milk-Bone breath brushing lightly across my face. Her signal. She wanted to go for one of her rare walks. I have learned from experience that when Gotcha wants a walk, she cannot be deterred.

I swung out of bed and checked the time. I had slept four hours. I stretched and yawned, my fingertips seeking out my right hamstring, marginally better. I got rid of my beer, ate four more Advils, headed for the door. Outside, I opened the front passenger's door of our truck and Gotcha jumped in. We drove downtown. I parked on this side of the Whitetail River, the energetic stream that divided the town, connected by that picturesque bridge. We got out and walked toward the bridge.

At its midpoint, I paused and looked around, enjoying the steady hurry of clear, deep water tumbling and rushing southward over the spillway like praise songs in worship, and then on downstream where a handful of scattered boulders broke the otherwise smooth surface. Gotcha waited at my side. I turned and looked north. A few yards upstream a restaurant on the east side of the river spread out and over the surface of the water, a redwood deck with potted plants offering open air seating. I wondered if they had a bar. In the warm sky I observed a cloud formation that resembled the offensive line of the 2005 Iowa Hawkeyes.

"Well, Gotcha," I said to the Bulldog who stopped and looked at me, "I've had three days of boredom living out of a motel room, and one helluvan interesting morning. I vote for boredom. How 'bout you?" She returned my gaze and blinked.

We crossed the bridge and turned right, down a street that cut through a middle-class neighborhood of solid frame homes with screened-in front porches. Gotcha rumbled along, leashless, under voice command, brilliant dog. Soon, we were at the high school.

Rockbluff High School, a two-story, block-granite building emptied out for the summer, rose near the banks of the Whitetail River. A broad, sloping lawn extended down to the water. Carefully-tended flower beds, groupings of holly bushes, and several red maple trees accented the campus. Smooth, white, pebble-gravel walkways wandered off in different directions. Redwood picnic tables, green trash cans with beige plastic liners, and a statue of the Red Raider, RHS's team mascot, completed the grounds. The Red Raider appeared to be, based on his hypertrophied musculature and aggressive facial expression, fueled by steroids.

Gotcha led the way down to the water. Inspired by the passing of liquid, she squatted. The river slapped softly against the bank. Far downstream, I could see frothy rapids; upstream, the limestone bridge. Gotcha wandered off to an uncut area of tall grass and weeds and hunkered down. She looks like a football center when she does that, ready to hike the ball. She finished and came to my side. We turned back to the school, crossing deserted parking lots, maneuvered around a corner of the building, and nearly bumped into a woman and her dog.

The lady, petite with short blonde hair and looking like maybe she ran too much for someone in her 40's, stopped suddenly. She wore Bermudas and a baby doll black tee that showed off her light hair. Nice figure. Good proportions. Skimpy sandals completed the outfit. Her toenails were painted bright red. I'm sure there's another name other than red on the bottle. "Classic Carmine" maybe, or Annie's favorite, "Matt Adore Red." *Oh, Annie.* I swallowed hard.

The woman's right hand fluttered to her face and she said, "Oh, you startled me!" She had blue eyes Karen would have called periwinkle. Her dog, one of those trendy little Jack Russell Terriers, bristled and lunged, held back by the woman's firm grip on his leather leash. Gotcha wiggled her little corkscrew tail and sat down next to me, prompting pride.

"Sorry," I said. Then, "I like your dog." Which was true. Just not my style. Too noisy. The only thing noisy about Gotcha is her snoring, and even that is soothing.

"Thank you," she replied, working to control the dog. "Milton!" she said firmly, tugging hard once. The dog quickly sat beside her, eyes alert on his owner. "Your dog is very nice, too. English Bulldog?"

"Yes, she is. A bit big for a female, but we didn't buy her for the show ring. We bought her to be our family dog," I said, looking at Gotcha to avoid staring at the attractive woman. The personal information had slipped out, and now I couldn't retrieve it. An opening I regretted immediately.

"What's her name?"

"Gotcha."

"I love it!" the woman laughed, smiling at Gotcha. "She's very well behaved. Do you hear that, Milton?" Then, turning away from her dog, "Please excuse my poor manners. My name is Olivia Olson, 'Liv' for short. I teach English here at Rockbluff High."

"Thomas O' Shea."

"Nice to meet you, Thomas. You're new in town. Welcome to Rockbluff."

"How...?"

Liv smiled. "Small town. Everyone knows everyone."

"I should have thought of that," I said.

A smile lit up her face, an engaging, honest smile. "Since this is a small town, and we all know you're new, you might as well come clean with your origins," she said.

"I grew up a little downstate, in Clinton. And you?"

"Right here. Born and raised. Went off to Cedar Falls to get educated and came back here right after I got my M.A. and started teaching, which was many, many years ago. Previous millennium, in fact. My students love to hear my stories about when I was young, shortly after the earth's crust started to cool."

"I don't think it was too long ago," I said, smiling. She looked fit and energetic, an ex-cheerleader on Surge? I wanted to get out of there and was mad at myself for extending our chat.

Sometimes, at night, dreaming, I think I'm sleeping with Karen, and when I wake up without her beside me, it breaks my heart. For months I was not attracted to women, my libido in solitary confinement somewhere. Maybe Peoria. I would look at females with nice figures, like Liv Olson, but look at them as if I were considering the conformation of a purebred Chesapeake Bay Retriever at the Westminster. I thought I was dying.

She said, "You're very nice to say so, but believe me, it was a long time ago. So where's your family? Will they be joining you when you get a house?"

I was stunned for a moment, but only a moment. Her question was not unexpected. I had made provision for it, so what did I expect?

"You said you acquired Gotcha to be your family dog. I just thought..." her voice faded. My stomach knotted. That will never go away, no matter how often I pray it will. Like St. Paul's thorn, a permanent thing.

"I did say that, didn't I?" I said, scrambling. "It's true, but I've lost my family, and, um..." I muttered, looking at my hands, then Gotcha, then the ground. I regrouped, sought Liv's eyes. "They were all killed in an automobile accident a year ago last December, in Georgia. My wife, Karen. My daughters, Annie and Michelle. So I don't have a family any more. Just me and Gotcha now."

"Please forgive me," Liv said, her periwinkle eyes suddenly

moist. "I am so sorry," she went on, "I noticed your ring. I was just trying to be..."

"I know. It's okay. You were just trying to be friendly. It's okay, really." I forced a quick smile to help her out. "No harm."

"I'm sorry for being so emotional," she said, her saddened eyes never leaving my face. "It's just that there is so much that can happen to people. Your terrible loss, and now our community loses a wonderful man, you probably heard about it, Hugh Soderstrom, horrible accident on their farm this morning. His wife a young widow."

"It was on the news," I guessed. "A tragedy."

"Yes, it is." She dabbed at her eyes with her fingers. "In any case, it was nice talking to you, Thomas, and I'm glad you've come to live among us. Hope to see you and Gotcha again sometime. Forgive me."

"Nothing to forgive. It was nice talking to you, too. And very nice to meet both of you," I said, my smarmy façade oozing all over the place. I started off and Gotcha swung into step, her distinctive rolling gate proving her pedigree. Olivia Olson took off toward the river with Milton, tugging on the leash to get him to stop admiring Gotcha's figure and get going in the right direction.

Disgusted with my slip into pathos, my strong conservative ancestry reminded me emotions were not for men from Iowa. After all, Marion Morrison, aka John Wayne, was from Iowa.

With my leg acting up again, we tramped back across the bridge and to our truck. At the motel I took a long shower with plenty of hot-hot water directed to my aching hamstring, ate another half-dozen Advil, stepped into a change of clothes, and watched ESPN. Gotcha took a nap, a month's worth of exercise completed. I buttoned off the television and left to shuffle the mile and a-half to The Grain o' Truth. I decided to force my leg to get better by not driving.

It was well after six when I arrived, part of a growing crowd. I smelled steaks and onion rings cooking. Mick Jagger was singing "Under My Thumb" and two couples danced a loosey-goosey freestyle, improvising, light and laughing.

I approached the bar and took the only unoccupied stool

between two young couples, the women seated on either side of me. Each ignored me and I thanked God. No demand for small talk, charming *bon mots* or the projection of a persona. Each woman leaned forward to listen to her young man. Talk of the future, talk of tomorrow. Easy lies.

Lunatic Mooning appeared. “If you stick around, you’ll see why so many people come from London, Paris and Vienna to spend their nights in Rockbluff.”

“No doubt. It does feel like it’s starting to throb a little.” *Like my leg*, I thought. I took in the small crowd. Tony Bennett's turn on the jukebox. “I’m a little surprised at their taste in music, however. A bit retro.”

“My place. I stock the jukebox. I try to educate. I want to make a difference.”

“Methinks your place is a gold mine, my Ojibwa acquaintance.”

“I do okay, plus it reinforces my...”

“...belief in the ultimate distastefulness of man,” I said.

A half-smile came to Lunatic’s face. “Your short-term memory appears to be intact. Now, what can I provide you, a Three Philosopher’s, or would you like to order something from the menu, or both?”

“I’m hungry and thirsty, so I think I’ll have a Loony Burger and a pitcher of Corona, if you don’t mind. You’ve got something going with those burgers.”

Lunatic turned to a lady behind the bar and said, “One Special and a pitcher of Corona for our patron, Rachel.” Then he turned back, gestured at Rachel and said, “Rachel, I’d like you to meet Thomas O’Shea. Thomas, Rachel Bergman.”

Rachel vigorously wiped her right hand on her apron and reached across the bar and we shook hands. She had a good, earthy smile. Her dark hair streaked with gray and braided close to her skull made her look efficient. Fifties. Sassy. I liked her face. We exchanged pleasantries and she provided the beer, turned away, and set to my order.

I said to Mooning, “I don’t suppose Gunther Schmidt is here tonight, is he?”

"Not yet. He's overdue. But he is also random. Feel free to stick around, shoot a little pool, hit on some women. Kick back. He might show."

"I believe I'll do some of those things," I said.

I spent the next hour finishing my food, shooting enough pool to improve a little, and eavesdropping on conversations. I chose not to hit on women, although one, somewhere in the confusion of her late 30's, did smile at me every time I looked her way. I tried not to look her way. Too old to be a boyfriend, too young to be a daddy sub. I longed for Karen to walk through the door.

Gunther Schmidt showed up at eight-thirty. Early 30's, powerfully built with a little paunch, red-blonde hair long and curly in the back, and a beard, darker than his hair. Schmidt wore stained, faded Levi's; worn work boots; and a navy blue t-shirt with a chest pocket torn loose and floppy at one corner. He looked like "The Spirit of October," albeit anxious and defeated, looks that did not suit him. I glanced over at Lunatic, who nodded.

I waited until Schmidt sat down at the bar and ordered his first Miller's draft, then edged over and sat next to him. He did not look up. He studied his beer, perhaps wondering when the grain of truth would appear in the amber liquid.

"My name is Thomas O'Shea, and I need to buy a good house. I understand you build them."

Schmidt turned his head and looked at me for a long time, as if he were searching for a clue that this was some kind of joke set up by a cruel drunk. We shook hands. His were thick and hard. "Gunther Schmidt," he said, his voice soft and reedy, a surprise.

"The houses I have seen for sale around here are overpriced, poorly constructed, or unimaginative. The others are already occupied. Would you be willing to show me one you have built?"

Schmidt smiled ruefully. "I show only to discriminating clientele. Just ask Moon here."

The big Ojibwa stood before us, polishing a shot glass, biceps bulging in his shirtsleeves with the rotation of his forearms. Mooning watched Gunther finish his Miller's and handed up another, fresh from the tap in a clean glass.

He took away the first glass, wiped away a condensation ring on the bar.

Gunther went on. "Trouble is, there's only been one discriminating buyer, and there are three more houses." Lunatic smiled at their shared joke. I offered to buy dinner, and Gunther accepted.

We ordered cheese nachos and a large meat lovers' pizza with extra cheese, picked up our drinks and found a booth. An hour and a half later Gunther agreed to show me the house Lunatic Mooning spoke of.

We looked at the house the next morning, Thursday. That afternoon we agreed on a price for the house, and all fifty-three acres of the land, that was more than I ever paid for personal property in my life. The next afternoon over a late lunch at The Grain o' Truth Bar & Grill, with Lunatic Mooning and Horace Norris looking on from a distance, I wrote a check on my new First Bank of Rockbluff account. I slid it across the table.

Gunther studied the check as if it were written in Farsi, looked up and said, "This is less than our agreed-upon price, Thomas."

I withdrew my billfold and splayed it open on the table while Gunther analyzed the check. I said, "One thousand less, but I thought I could make up the difference in cash. Thought you might want to take your wife out to dinner and a movie tonight."

Gunther said, "Thank you. I appreciate that."

"The check is good, of course, but it's late in the day and the bank doesn't always recognize transactions immediately, especially one of this size, even though I let them know ahead of time it was coming."

"I'll bet my father-in-law is happy to have you as a customer," Gunther said, smiling.

"He did not object to my opening accounts."

And so we finished, meeting with a real estate attorney three days later to attend to all the legal details. I owned a house and Gunther Schmidt recorded his second sale. He left the bar with money and reason enough to forget about the packing plant in Dubuque and begin vigorously marketing his other two houses.

Lunatic Mooning seemed to bask in the satisfaction of being behind it all.

I am pleased with my house, deep in the woods seven miles from town. A private place. A retreat. An authentic Craftsman, with room upstairs for guests if I ever have company, God forbid. Bedroom and master bath plus a powder room downstairs, along with a study with built-in bookshelves, and a well-designed kitchen with an island. Plenty of room, but not so big that I'd feel like “a marble in a shoebox”—one of Karen's sayings.

The same afternoon, after I wrote Gunther's check, I bought linens and beginner groceries. Then I bought all my furniture in one store. I call it “eclectic.” Karen would have gagged. To the satisfaction of all, the people at Feinberg’s Furniture accepted my cash bonus for immediate delivery. Kitchen appliances came with the house. Nice ones. Stainless steel with black trim.

I called my ex-partner and asked him to go ahead and ship my books and a few other boxes to me, stuff I didn’t want to let go of. Pictures, mainly. And some crafts things my girls had made for me: a black t-shirt with “Dad’s A Stitch” appliquéd on it, a Three Stooges poster, a sampler showing a morbidly-obese man preparing to eat a huge piece of pie and “A Waist Is A Terrible Thing To Mind” written in flamboyant cursive along his protruding belly.

Gunther thought of everything. The property includes an artesian well and modern windmill, so I will never want for water that is sweet and clear, filtered over time through earth and limestone and shale. The windmill generates electricity, and the home is heated by a fuel oil furnace more efficient, Gunther said, than the Ebola Zaire virus.

A deck juts out from the back of the house providing a splendid view of the Mississippi River valley in the distance, the Whitetail River valley closer. That first evening, while thickset young men moved furniture in, I took my evening meal of fast food and Heineken’s out on the deck and ate, standing, enjoying the vista falling away far below me to the distant river. I now had a beautiful place where I could live alone, reinforcing my bedrock selfishness.

And then I saw an eagle, diving and plunging as it played on a rising thermal, exultation in the air. For several minutes it played, then, gloriously, another, smaller eagle appeared, approaching the first. Together, they swirled around each other, darting and swooping in a *pas de deux* that had me holding my breath, my attention riveted on the display before me.

Then, to my amazement, the two enormous raptors joined talons and fell away to the ground, locked together, breaking loose at the last moment before striking the earth, then gliding away together into the distance. Transfixed, I stared at the sky long after they left. I knew I would have to talk to the Ojibwa about this.

I also knew that, at some point, God would show me what to do with the rest of my life. Or not. But for now, with this place, I am self-sufficient and determined to live a very private life. I have solitude, a beautiful hardwood forest that creeps up to the very edge of my new home, and plenty of good beer.

"This is enough for now," I said to myself, wondering what was waiting for me after "for now." A cold beer, then another, provided the immediate answer.

Chapter Four

"When anger rises, think of the consequences."
- Confucius

My first night in my new home, I dreamed about a filleted farmer and his hysterical wife and eagles and a big Indian, and I woke up in the dark just before dawn, wide awake and not as disoriented as I should have been. I knew where I was. And why.

I pulled on Levi's and a light sweatshirt, set Mr. Coffee to work on a twelve-cup pot, and padded out on the deck. Gotcha rose with a groan from her tuffet and followed me, sniffing the cool morning air.

Far below I saw a scattering of yard lights from small farms that peppered the area. A faint glow came from the north, where Rockbluff, the city that never wakes, was sleeping. I wondered if Liv Olson was sleeping in the nude. I shoved that thought aside, wondering where the hell it came from. Then I brought it back. Gave it life and breath. I surprise myself. After months with no carnal interest in females, and months more of recovery, I was wondering if Liv Olson slept in the nude.

I also wondered about something deeply theological. Did Karen in Heaven know that I just thought about slipping into bed with another woman? A whole new category of guilt was available to shoulder its way into my life. Damned if I think about a naked lady not Karen, damned if I act on it. But a saint if I ban the thought completely from my mind and think about kittens and butterflies. So much for sainthood.

There is, however, that beacon of hope beckoning from deep within my psyche. For the first time in a long, long time, I am definitely noticing a woman. A specific woman. Maybe I'm not dying after all. If that's not recovery, what is?

Gotcha stood at one corner of the deck, staring at the little side gate that led out to the property.

Bulldogs do not typically whine or cry or bark when they want something. They usually just stand and stare at what they want until their owners respond to vibes so powerful they cannot be ignored. I let her out. She chunked herself down the four steps and lumbered off. With no neighbors closer than five miles, and Gotcha's limited range, I did not worry about her wandering far. Not a particularly active breed, Bulldogs nevertheless keep track of their source of primo dog food, pricey treats, and tuffets. They are not stupid.

I went inside and poured coffee into my jumbo Harley-Davidson mug, added a couple of glugs of cream, tossed in three tablespoons of sugar and stirred. I let it set while I reached for the pain meds, tossed four Advils down, grabbed my Bible, and hobbled back out on the deck rubbing my leg and watching the sky lighten up enough to read by.

The glory of a rich red and purple sunrise kept interrupting my Bible reading, so I set it aside and simply enjoyed my coffee and the dawning of the day.

Sometimes I wish I would just die peacefully in my sleep and wake up in what Dietrich Bonhoeffer called "the true country." I could avoid the stabs of pain that I know in my heart are going to pierce me for the rest of my days. Every time I have a sharp memory of Karen or the girls, there it will be. I don't like to think about that truth, so I try to avoid it. Beer helps, of course.

When friends and acquaintances asked me if I was going to be all right, I had to just smile and say, "I don't think so." Not the answer well-meaning people wanted, but the truth. The last seventeen months have borne out my diagnosis. However, I now live where people won't ask the question.

Bonhoeffer said, exactly, "Christians are ambassadors of the true country." For some reason, that gives me comfort; it shifts my focus to the fact that life is a mist and quickly leaves us, and then the adventure really begins. In heaven or in hell. Yes, the real estate people are right: it's all about location. Likewise, I realize I'm a lousy ambassador for that "true country."

Friday morning was in full bloom. Time to turn on ESPN and check out the baseball scores. My team for decades, the Red Sox, won, giving them two of three from the Yankees. In the Bronx. Good way to start any day with the Forces of Light and Goodness prevailing over The Evil Empire. Tonight it's the lightning-fast Rays.

Hungry now, the package of burritos, lonely in the freezer, did not appeal to me, nor did anything else in the house. Loony Burgers for brunch did, so I headed for the door, called Gotcha, gave her a Big Dog Milk-Bone, and left as she shuffled over to her tuffet at the foot of my bed to enjoy her treat. I locked the door and left.

Walking out to my truck, a sense of guilt washed over me, guilt driven by my lack of activity the day before. After all, there had been a period of several hours spent napping when all that I had done was stumble on a scene from hell, meet a collection of escapees from a parallel universe, and bought a house. I didn't count the purchase of furniture as productive time. Anyone can do that. Not much to show for my seventy-two hours in Rockbluff. *Sluggard.* I shrugged it off, vowing, as I drove into town, to do better in the future.

Entering Rockbluff, I slowed and found myself admiring the older homes, mostly Victorian with gingerbread trim, some with widow's walks. Ostentation abounds. Other homes were stolid frame or brick Colonial mansions. No brick ranch homes in sight like in the south, where bricks were cheap and ranch homes proliferated like lies at a political convention. The street reminded me of Summit Street in Iowa City, where upper middle class families had lived for generations in subdued elegance.

I did not expect to see the man lying face down in his front yard, motionless.

What is it about this town? And why am I the one who keeps stumbling onto stuff? And why do I never learn to give in to my natural disinclination to help?

I stood on the brakes and screeched to a dead stop, shifted the truck into park, set the emergency brake, and left the engine running in case I had to rush the collapsed man to the hospital.

In for a penny, in for a pound, I thought, as I pounded across the street and, forgetting myself, hurdled the low, ornate wrought iron fence hemming in the big yard. My right hamstring yakked back and I gasped, but landed solidly on the lawn. I limped up to the man's side, fighting off nausea once again. Before I could kneel down, the man in the grass spoke.

"Keep movin', pilgrim," he said, remaining motionless.

What? I started to bend over, stopped again when the man spoke once more.

"Go *on*, pal, I'm okay, I'm just fine. Tourist," he muttered under his breath.

"But..."

"I'm not kidding. Bug out. You're going to tell me I'm face down in the lawn, right? Like this had occurred without my knowledge? Jeepers. Leave me alone."

"I've never seen anyone in your position before who didn't need help," I said, straightening up halfway and moving a couple of steps to the right to better see the man's face, which was mostly in fresh green grass that did not yet need mowing. I put my hands on my knees and leaned a little toward the man and peered.

"Leave me alone!"

"Well, if you're sure you're okay..." I said, fully standing up, knowing I sounded stupid. I do that a lot. Just ask Wendy Soderstrom. The man in the grass pounced on my words.

"Is there an arrow in my back? Is there a rattler on my ass? Do I have a sucking chest wound?" he asked. "If not," he went on with exaggerated patience, "buzz off."

He was wearing tan Bermudas with no belt, old Converse low-cuts without socks and a green golf shirt soaked with sweat down the middle of the back and under the arms. Calves like kegs rose from thick ankles. A high school football star twenty-five years ago. Maybe a letterman at Luther College.

"Why did you call me 'tourist' just now?" I asked, looking at the man, perhaps thirty pounds overweight and a little soft looking, tan, with male pattern baldness eating his hair. A pair of sunglasses lay in the grass nearby. He remained motionless.

"Because only a tourist would stop," he intoned. "Anybody local knows I'm perfectly fine when I'm face-down in the grass, or hanging over the fence, or collapsed on the front steps. Go."

I relaxed a little, rubbing at the fire in the back of my right leg. I said, "Who are you?"

"Arvid Pendergast. Lutheran Brotherhood. If you'll wait an hour or so, I'd be happy to review your insurance portfolio. What's your name?" he asked the earth.

"Thomas O' Shea."

"Doesn't sound Lutheran to me."

"Reformed Druid," I said. Pendergast snorted. I couldn't tell if it was derision or appreciation.

"I wouldn't be wasting my time with you if you hadn't stopped, O' Shea, much as I hate to admit it. Most tourists use their cell phones to call nine-one-one if they can remember the number. The rest just drive on into town and tell the Sheriff or Fire Department that there's a stiff in a yard back up the road."

"But why are you doing this?" I asked, shifting my weight to my left leg.

"It's none of your beeswax," Arvid said, "but since you had the courtesy to become involved with what looked like a possible tragedy, a singularly rare response these days by the way, I'll tell you."

"I appreciate your largesse."

Arvid chuckled, moving his head a little. Then he returned to relative immobility.

I felt a little peculiar carrying on a conversation with someone face down in his lawn, dead or catatonic, but it was an improvement over an afternoon with the Soderstroms. I looked around the sprawling yard. Ancient oaks, a few maples, and a singular birch provided patches of shade. If I were going to collapse on purpose, I'd do it in the shade.

Arvid said, "I was musing one day on the back porch," he began, "and it occurred to me it would be a horrible shock for Clara or one of the girls to find me dead someday, crumpled at the refrigerator, collapsed on our bed, or face down in the yard. So, being one in the helping profession, as it were, and also one to try to prevent undue grief befalling my family when I do pass on, I decided I would practice croaking, so that, when they do really find me dead, it won't be such a big deal."

"Impeccable reasoning."

"That's right, worry-wart. And, for the last three years, I've been practicing dying so, when any of the ladies see me, they won't faint from the shock. I let them know ahead of time at first so when they found me practicing they wouldn't experience any psychological scarring, and I've been doing it ever since, whenever it strikes my fancy."

"So these collapses are spontaneous?"

"Since the first couple-three. Don't want to stifle the creative impulse."

I wiped my sweaty forehead and surveyed Arvid's abode, an immaculate three story white Victorian with lemon yellow trim, a wrap-around porch, and brick sidewalks leading up to the front porch and around toward the back.

In the front yard, maybe an acre, I saw two bird baths and several bird feeders. "How long do you plan to practice this time?"

"It depends."

"On what?"

"Until I'm good and ready to quit. What I do is a kind of 'performance art' and I am the artiste. I am led by a macabre muse."

"But you're not prepared to stifle that muse now?"

"No! *Now*," Arvid said impatiently, as if speaking to a small child, "I've afforded you a thorough explanation of my activity. Will you please go? If my wife comes home and sees you talking to me, the practice will have been futile, all for naught, and I will not be in a very good mood. I hate to waste an otherwise perfect fatality."

"May I ask you another question?"

Arvid muttered something into the root systems of the grass. "You just did ask another question. What you should have said is, 'May I ask you a question after this one?' But you didn't. I won't penalize you. Go ahead, shoot. And be glad I'm in such a condescending mood today."

"Don't people talk about you, avoid you in the supermarket, move to a crowded booth when you walk in The Grain o' Truth?"

"Truth is, smarty-pants, people seem to like it. Gives them something to talk about. And, an added bonus, since my motives are altruistic, sales are up. Seeing a corpse every now and then makes people think. I've been a member of 'The Million Dollar Round Table' every year since I started dying on impulse. Never was before. Life is good in America when you're willing to sacrifice a little."

"What a country."

"That's the gospel truth." Arvid watched a fat black ant walk across the shaft of a blade of grass and disappear into the undergrowth beneath his chin.

"I'll quit bugging you and go on my way now. See you later," I said.

"Not if you're a tourist you won't," Arvid muttered, snorting, working at snorting. Maybe the ant was interested in one of his nostrils.

"I'm not a tourist, I'm a new resident." I stretched my back and put some weight on my right leg, turned away, and hobbled down to the wrought iron gate, opened it, stepped through onto the sidewalk, and closed the gate behind me. "So," I called back to the man in the yard, "I'm going, feeling really dumb talking to an amateur corpse."

"Artiste!"

"See ya!"

"And if you do see me and I'm not upright and mobile, leave me alone," Arvid said, his raised voice muffled by the plant life pushing up against his face.

"I'll leave you as you fell!" I shouted, crossing back over the street, climbing behind the wheel of my truck, and heading on into town.

I parked in the nearly-empty lot at Lunatic's place. I had just stepped onto the slate front porch and reached for the door when a silver Corvette, filmed with dust, skidded into the parking lot and lurched to a stop, the engine killed by the driver's misuse of the clutch. A lean young man, late twenties, shaved head, earrings, lunged out of the car and started toward me. He held something in his hand, and as he drew nearer, I noticed that it was a Pittsburgh Pirates baseball cap. He popped it on his head and turned the bill backwards.

He wore jeans, a sleeveless red t-shirt, and cowboy boots. Several tattoos decorated his thin arms. I turned to go inside, heard the man running up behind me.

"Move it!" he muttered. I stepped back. He rushed by me and bulled his way inside. A tattoo of an elaborate cross graced the back of his neck. The smell of whiskey was strong.

I drifted inside, nodded at a stunned-looking Horace Norris, and edged over to the bar, not quite as hungry as I had been. The kid sat on a stool at the bar, so I took a seat around a corner from him, both to keep distance and to observe.

Moon moved over in front of the young man and put his hands on the bar. "Larry, I'm sorry about your brother. He was a good man."

"You sayin' I ain't a good man, Injun? What would you know about it?"

Mooning raised an eyebrow, said, "I liked your brother, that's all. I am sorry he's dead. What can I get for you?"

"Everyone acts like Hugh was some kind of a saint or something, which he wasn't. If you only knew. Now, gimme a pitcher of Bud Light and a glass, and shut up about my brother."

Lunatic looked at the man for a moment, then filled his order. The Ojibwa's eyes had changed. Somehow blacker, more intense. Almost glittering.

Larry said, "I bet you'd throw a party, drinks on the house, if I got run over by a mower."

"Hugh was a good man. You aren't."

"Mighty good at judging people, aren'tcha? So easy when you're perfect, right?"

Larry poured his pint glass full and chugged the contents, refilled the glass, looked around. At me. "What are you staring at, Pops?"

I wondered about "Pops," first time ever I've been called that, but I just said, "Sorry. I didn't mean to stare. It's just that I might have seen you before. Recently," I said, thinking more about his silver Corvette than its driver. Someone had had to be behind the wheel the day before.

"I doubt it. I ain't never seen you. You're new around here, am I right?"

"Yes," I said, "I am. Too bad about your brother. I'm sorry for your loss."

"Ain't no big deal, dude," he said. He drank down half his beer and looked around the bar. His gaze came back to rest on the big Indian. He jerked his head at me and said to Lunatic, "See, the man over there has some manners. Common decency. But you gotta go judging people."

Lunatic Mooning said, "A great writer once wrote that the truth doesn't change according to one's ability to stomach it."

Larry glared at Moon and then threw the half-empty glass at the Ojibwa bartender, who dodged. The glass shattered on the bar behind him, breaking several glasses, beer and foam spraying. When I looked back from the damage, Larry had a stiletto in his hand.

When Lunatic came up from his crouch, he was holding a pistol grip, pump action, sawed-off shotgun. He chambered a round, and pointed it with one big hand at Larry's chest. Larry froze, his eyes spitting hatred. At that point my appetite was completely forgotten, but I was suddenly very thirsty.

Mooning said, "Larry, most people I shoot don't begin to smell until after they're dead, but you're clearly the exception. One more step and you'll be the latest addition to my compost pile. Now get out and go on and don't ever come back in here again. You can do your drinking at Shlop's. I am sorry about your brother, but as for you, well, you're just plain sorry. Now go, and stay gone."

A stream of curses spewed from Larry's mouth. Lunatic said, "If you throw that pigsticker, I'm pulling the trigger. Swear to God. I'll survive. You won't. I said leave and don't ever come back. You may leave the knife here on the bar."

Larry looked around, his eyes bloodshot and mean. He looked at me. "What you lookin' at, jerk?"

"I think you have supplied the operant word," I said.

Larry looked confused. "Don't mess with me, man. You'll be sorry. I'll take you out in a heartbeat. I'll remember you."

"Same here," I said, my heartbeat jacking up.

There was more invective from Larry, who stabbed the stiletto into the bar, spun off his barstool, and strode out the door. No one said anything until a big engine roared to life outside, tires squealed on parking lot blacktop, and sound receded.

Moon put the shotgun back out of sight, carefully wiggled the stiletto loose from the bar, then stashed it out of sight. He ran his fingertips over the place where Larry had planted the knife.

"You have now met Larry Soderstrom, the brother from the dark side. Sorry I could not introduce you two formally. A social faux pas I will forever regret."

"He appears to have issues."

"He is a stinking mass of putrescence. And that's on his good days. The wrong brother died."

"You knew Hugh, I guess."

"He put to the test my theory on the ultimate distastefulness of man. An anomaly."

"What about his wife, Wendy?"

"Jury's still out. How did you know her name? Oh, you must have seen it on the news."

"I met her, sort of."

Mooning's eyes locked onto me with serious interest, and I wasn't sure I could be comfortable for very long with that look. He said, "How?"

"There you go with that Ojibwa talk again."

He cocked his head and did not smile.

"I was there. Just before EMS pulled in. And Molly something, a preacher's wife."

"Molly Heisler."

I nodded. "I saw Hugh on the ground. The tractor had run off into a ditch. The engine was still running."

Moon said nothing for a full minute. Then he said, "Larry was out there too?"

"I met a silver Corvette on the road just before I rounded a bend before the Soderstrom farm. I was admiring the mailbox when I saw Wendy running down the lane, blood-soaked. I tried to help. Too late. How many silver Corvettes do you have around here?"

The big Ojibwa bartender looked at me, tilted his head toward the front door. "Just that one." Then he turned to the mess and began cleaning up.

Chapter Five

"I'm not greedy, I just want the land next to mine."
- Anonymous farmer

Horace Norris piped up from across the room, "That's the most fun I've had since the Hawks beat the Heels in the Dean Dome. Now, that's entertainment!" he said, laughing and shaking his head. He took a long slug from his beer, smacked his lips in deep satisfaction, grinned and said, "When I can enjoy a cold beer and good food and watch Moon face down a second-rate hoodlum, there's nothing more I can ask for in the day. So I say to you, Mr. O'Shea, the top o' the mornin'."

"And the rest o' the day to you, Squire Norris."

Horace was wired. "It is sooo satisfying to see good triumphing over evil, experience prevailing over sickening youth, and all that. So rare these days." Horace lifted his beverage high in a wobbly salute, spilled a little down the outside of the pint and onto his hand, ignored it, and said, "My compliments, gentlemen."

Moon rolled his eyes. I nodded in Horace's general direction.

"You know," Horace said, "if he'd taken Moon out and got by you, I would have finished him off myself. You need to know I got your back."

"I know you do," I said, "and that's a comfort."

Horace nodded and reached for his food. Then he looked up and said, “Moon, great quote from Flannery O’Connor.” He turned back to his food and I turned back to the bar, impressed.

I said to Lunatic, “That pigsticker was a surprise."

“He keeps the stiletto in his boot. It wouldn’t have surprised you if you were from around here.”

“So tell me about Larry.”

“He is not Evil personified. He’s not as intimidating as I think Evil in the flesh would be. He’s about two or three notches below that due to his physical and mental shortcomings,” Lunatic said. “I am not, as you may have noticed, a talkative man, and to tell you about Larry is not a quick thing,” he said, his baritone radio announcer’s voice somber.

“Good thing you’re Ojibwa and not laconic.”

Mooning looked like he was about to smile, fought it off. “Larry Soderstrom is what you palefaces call, in the precision of your rich therapeutic professional vocabulary, a ‘wacko.’ He’s rich, lazy, corrupt, and an embarrassment to his family.”

“He is Hugh Soderstrom’s brother, though, isn’t he?”

“Larry is that. Hungry yet?"

"I am. Two Loony Burgers and a Diet Coke."

“Going on the wagon?"

“Good question. Come to think of it, the answer is no. Switch out the Diet Coke for a Samuel Adams Boston Lager if you have any, please.”

"If I have any? There you go again with that. You should know better by now," Mooning said.

I like to tweak Mooning, implying his inventory of beer is insufficient for my sophisticated palate. He set the burgers on the grill and started the fries, then poured and placed a dark pint of Sam Adams on the bar in front of me.

I said, “Moon—may I call you ‘Moon’?” The big Indian paused, nodded. An inroad extended. I took it. “Moon, I was the first person on the scene. I came upon Wendy, screaming and covered in blood and running down their lane. She had called EMS but they weren’t there yet. I stopped.”

"The news on the radio did not mention you," Moon said.

I shrugged. "So tell me more about the family."

"Hugh and Larry's parents died ten, eleven years ago, but even then I think they knew the younger son would turn out badly. But nothing like he is today, a nearly perfected piece of crap. Inherited half of Soderstrom Farms, which is slightly less acreage than Connecticut. Rents out his half so he won't have to work, spends the proceeds on wine, cheap; women, also cheap; and song, mostly Heavy Metal. Nothing from him would surprise me."

I tasted the beer and asked, "And Hugh got the other half."

"Yes. Hugh Soderstrom loved the land and worked it well and smart, revered the Christian version of The Great Spirit, seemed to delight in his wife, hoped for children. Always bailing Larry out of what we in Rockbluff euphemistically call 'scrapes'."

"Did Hugh come in here?"

"Regularly. Brought Wendy in after a day of shopping, or for random lunch breaks. Treated her well. Adoration is the word that fits."

"What about her toward him?"

"Love, I think, but not as fervent. Many marriages consist of one person loving the other and the other allowing it. That's the feeling I had about them, and that's not to put her down. She was very nice, very polite, witty."

"So when did Larry start screwing up?"

"Right after his parents died, he started to drift, then ran completely off the tracks. I hate to show leniency toward his behavior, Thomas, but having a brother like Hugh was impossible to live up to. So he just gave up and didn't try. Decided to be his own person, you might say. Followed the line of least resistance. He had the added benefit of wealth to cushion his fall."

Moon moved away, put my lunch together, brought it to me. I finished my beer and another appeared. Moon said, "Sheriff might want to know about the silver Corvette."

"Deputy Doltch told me it was an accident. Couldn't be anything else."

"Probably was, but I have trouble with Hugh falling off his tractor. It doesn't make sense."

"What's the sheriff like?" I asked, digging into my food.

"Nice guy, tough, but a little too willing to discuss situations instead of bringing a forearm up under the chin," Moon replied. "Sees himself as part of the new wave of law enforcement professionals who get to the root causes of crime while invoking minimal reminders to the lawbreakers which, in my opinion, encourages them. Prides himself on a low crime rate, but that's not much to hang his hat on. This is a nice town with people who respect the law. If it were up to me, there'd only be one report to make if Larry came for me, and that would be from the Rockbluff County Coroner."

"You're kidding."

"I'm not, and Larry knows it."

"How does he know that?" I asked.

The big Indian leaned forward, resting his elbows on the bar in front of me, the muscles of his chest rolling and merging into thick biceps and shoulders and brawny forearms. "Because I told him a long time ago I would kill him if he ever started with me." Moon's eyes looked darker somehow. "He knows Chief Justice appears only when the intent is to be used."

"Chief Justice?"

"My shotgun."

"Wouldn't a forearm up under the chin be an effective deterrent to Larry?"

"For most guys, yes, but with Larry, it would only persuade him to retaliate in some gutless way. That knife is a good example, and he usually has a box cutter in his other boot. My Mossberg," Mooning nodded in the general direction of under the counter, "is not a prop."

"Well," I said, picking up my beer and lifting it toward the bartender, "I don't want to get too emotional about it, but I was glad you cooled him off."

"Emotions are deceptive, unreliable," Moon said. "I just want to keep my business enterprise under control, and Larry was way over the line."

"It's a relief to know you run a tight ship." I studied the vintage electric Hamm's sign on the far wall, a classic depiction of a northern waterfall in the woods, the bright blue water looking as if it were actually tumbling over the rocks. The sign had to be at least forty years old. I finished off my Sam Adams and held up my glass again. "The possibility of violence always makes me thirsty. Dehydration from sweat breaking out all over my body in anticipation of my becoming an injured bystander," I said. "Plus peeing my pants. Two more Sam Adams will facilitate my recovery from emotional trauma."

Moon straightened, strode partway down the bar, reached into a cooler underneath, and pulled out two bottles. He popped the caps and set them up, pouring one into my empty pint glass.

"You didn't piss your pants, Thomas. And I doubt you broke out in a sweat. You did not appear to be concerned."

"But I was a little more focused than usual when Larry pulled out his knife."

Lunatic just shook his head. "Food okay?"

With both hands, I picked up my first Loony Burger and bit into it. My taste buds had a dancing party in my mouth as I chewed and swallowed. I drained half of my third beer. Moon watched me, amused.

I said, "The food's okay. By the way, may I just call you 'Loon Moon' for short?"

"No."

I savored more of the Loony Burger as Moon studied the nick in the bar, running his finger back and forth on the blemish. He was scowling. I finished my beer and poured the next one, and on impulse I told Moon about the pair of bald eagles, and how one had been diving and rolling for several minutes, and then the other had joined and the two huge raptors had locked talons and plunged together.

Moon's eyes took on a deeper interest. He stared to the point of my discomfort, but I did not look away. I was afraid if I broke eye contact, it would be an insult to the Ojibwa, and Moon would put down his head and charge. The mission oak bar would be only a brief barrier.

Finally, he spoke. "You have lost loved ones."

I flinched. I had never mentioned Karen or Annie or Michelle. And even though I had mentioned my loss to Liv Olson, and this was a small town, I didn't get the feeling that Lunatic knew yet.

He said, "The bald eagle, my people call him *'Mi-Ge-Zi,'* is sacred. Everything about him is sacred. He went, on his own, as an emissary to The Great Spirit long ago, flying to The Creator's world beyond the sun, because he had heard The Creator was going to destroy my people for doing that which insults the universal harmony established by The Great Spirit.

"Mi-Ge-Zi intervened for my people, who were then known as the Anishinabe, and asked The Creator to send teachers to show us how to live respectful lives. They were called Elders, and helped restore the Anishinabe, also called Chippewa, to harmony in the universe. My people believe what you saw are the spirits of those you have lost, communicating to you that all is well with them in the world of The Great Spirit. It is a rare thing to see, and a most rare thing for you—a white man—to see."

I heard the faint, soft tumble of the Whitetail River outside, behind and below the building. I heard a car go by. Moon's narrative, although based upon a belief system other than my own, was to me a confirmation of what I felt to be true. A comfort, and I held onto it. Every little bit, you know.

"Who did you lose?" he asked, his voice soft. There was keen interest in his eyes.

"My wife, Karen. Both daughters, Annie and Michelle. Killed in an auto accident in Atlanta. A year ago last December. Annie was sixteen, Michelle twelve."

Moon nodded. "I am sorry," he said. "It is a sad thing to lose one's woman and children. You have no other children?"

"No."

"Why are you in Iowa?"

"Born here. Raised here. No reason to stay in Georgia. Just wanted to get back and regroup in the peace and quiet of small-town Iowa, home of suspicious farm deaths and nutbergers who fake death in their front yard. That kind of thing."

"You met Arvid."

"Strange bird. Yeah, Iowa's been pretty swell to me since I got back here, just a few days ago, actually. Just super peaceful."

"It is a good place," Lunatic said. "A beautiful land."

"Thank you for telling me about your people, and what the eagles mean," I said.

Lunatic nodded, asked, "When will you acquire another wife?"

"Shortly after I win the Nobel Peace Prize. The time for another wife has passed," I said.

"You do not look old. You do not act old. Your chest is deep, though not as deep as mine; your arms are large, though not as large as mine; and your stomach is flat."

"And not as large as yours," I said, craning my neck in an exaggerated attempt to see over the bar. Moon's stomach was flat, too, but also thick. Maybe a forty-four. Mine is a thirty-six, despite the beer. Used to be a thirty-four. Smaller frame than Loon Moon.

He ignored the jibe, said, "Also, I must say your neck needs some work. How many winters have you seen, forty, forty-two?"

"I have seen more than forty winters, less than sixty, oh Wise One." The Chippewa looked surprised, then shrugged his shoulders as if the information were irrelevant. He said, "There are some women nearby who would make fine wives. The women of Iowa are fair, with fine breasts and strong thighs, although they have too much education and do not keep their ideas to themselves. Also, some are too thin. They exercise and starve themselves to look good for men who would rather have some appropriate plumpness. Nevertheless, there are opportunities. I will look for you," he said.

I had finished my first Loony Burger. "Don't worry about me, Moon, I will find my way, and right now my way does not include romance." Liv Olson came to mind just then. *Hmmm*. I munched on my fries. I finished my beer.

"I said nothing about romance. I speak of marriage, white eyes."

"Been there, done that, got the joy and the beauty and the t-shirt," I said. "I do appreciate your concerns for my love life, however."

"I accept your rejection."

"Are you married?"

"Not the type."

"Girlfriend?"

"Plural," he said.

"Where? In the back?" I stretched and stared toward the back door.

"Wherever I go. Vulga, Monona. City girls. They have sisters."

"But not for me," I said.

"You are an enigma, O'Shea," Lunatic said.

"And you are Ashinabe, Moon, not to mention Ojibwa and Chippewa." I stood, grabbed a napkin from the bar, wiped my mouth, and asked for a doggie bag for my second Loony Burger. Lunatic produced a white Styrofoam box and placed the second burger inside. He closed the lid and secured the little tab to hold it shut.

"I think it's time to visit with the Sheriff. I thank you sincerely for the insights into the story of Mi-Ge-Zi." My use of the Anishinabe word pleased the bartender. "See ya later."

"Yes, see you. By the way, do you think Larry was somehow involved with what went down out at the farm with his brother?"

"Does Beyonce float?"

I waved and turned to leave and nearly bumped into Horace Norris, who had appeared behind me. His old eyes were moist and calm. He said, "I'm sorry for your great loss, sir. It's a sad thing." Then he turned and shuffled back to his booth and his beer as I shouldered by the double doors and strode into the sunlight.

Chapter 6

"Iron sharpens iron,
So one man sharpens another."
- Proverbs 27:17

I decided to hoof it to the Sheriff's office eight blocks away and leave the truck in the parking lot. It was already warm, ninety degrees according to the Hawkeye State Bank time/temperature sign. No sense in waiting for it to get hotter before going to meet The Law. The opportunity to field test the effectiveness of mega-doses of ibuprofen on my thigh was another motivator. And a short walk would let me grab a closer look at Rockbluff's downtown. I set my Styrofoam box in the truck.

Twenty yards south of The Grain o' Truth, my curiosity was tweaked by Mulehoff's Earthen Vessel Barbell Club and Video Rental across the street. Having a lifelong interest in places where people pay good money to publicly hurt themselves, it was worth a look. An old yellow Pinto wagon with a gray-primer driver's door drove past. Its tailpipe hung from a bent coat hanger, and made metallic farting sounds as it went by. I crossed the street.

The combination of gym and video rental reminded me of businesses back in Georgia, sprouting up like fresh stinkweed everywhere. Laser eye surgery and funnel cakes in one place, fertility clinics combined with hot air balloon excursions in another. My favorite example of capitalism's spirit in the Deep South combined a barbeque joint and dog grooming emporium, raising questions about the menu and the Department of Health. But I'd learned that loose licensing and a bit of grits graft can work wonders.

The storefront of Mulehoff's looked like the aftermath of two architectural approaches running headlong into each other. Old brick and cheap, warped exterior paneling butted heads against blocks of opaque glass and a single Doric column by the front door. In a previous life, the enterprise might have been a neighborhood grocery, or maybe a tanning salon before that. I thumped the Doric column as I went by, confirming my guess that it was plastic and hollow (a little like me), and pushed through the glass door. Once inside, the air conditioning whispered up against me. Refreshing, soothing, like a kiss from a best friend's girl. Not too cold.

The inside walls were concrete block painted green and gold. Scattered across the open floor space were benches and barbells, racks of solid dumbbells, and exercise machines. The abundance of good, familiar equipment was impressive. I meandered to the far end.

The video store was situated in the right rear corner. Movie posters of current films were taped to the back wall. Vampires feasting on busty *ingénues*, scenes of explosions, and top stars in heated liplocks returned my gaze.

A cash register sat on a display case that featured muscle-building food supplements, Earthen Vessel t-shirts, and bodybuilding magazines. A cooler the size of a tipped-up coffin and filled with water bottles and multi-hued sports drinks hummed softly against the back wall next to the posters. Powerlifting trophies, adorned with little silver statuettes of bulging men in frozen flexings, posed on a shelf next to the cooler. Probably the proprietor's. Instant credibility.

I looked back at the workout area that comprised ninety percent of the room. Five men and two women in their twenties and thirties pumped iron, accompanied by good-natured chatter and encouragement. The men wore tank tops and Umbros; the women, brightly-colored thongs over iridescent tights, and tees over sports bras. The men tossed brief, insouciant glances in my direction. The women ignored my entrance after a quick size-up. I was old enough to be, given opportunity and lack of self-control in high school, their father.

A man sporting a short, salt-and-pepper beard muscled bench presses on a wooden lifting platform in the middle of the gym. He finished a set of five slow, smooth repetitions with an Olympic bar loaded with four forty-five pound plates on each end, 405 pounds counting the bar, which bent slightly under the weight, then bounced and clanged when the lifter racked the barbell.

I have never even attempted to do one rep with that much, and this man, in his fifty's somewhere, had done five easily. He sat up, rubbed his gloved hands together, and looked around. When he saw me, he got up, stepped down from the platform, and ambled my way.

He wore a green t-shirt, black sweatpants, and gray New Balance cross-trainer shoes. He oozed power. Like a friar's tonsure, curly gray and silver hair circled his balding pate. He bobbed along on the balls of his feet, moving like an amiable bear on street speed. I put up my hands as he approached.

"You *look* friendly," I said. He laughed a peculiar, high-pitched giggle that immediately put me at ease. Most people that big and strong are docile, like bullmastiff dogs, understanding their strength. Good thing.

"Mike Mulehoff," he said, peeling off his right glove and offering a handshake. The grip was not for the faint of heart.

"Thomas O'Shea."

He looked me over. "Bodybuilder?"

"No. I just work out to delay decay."

Mulehoff smiled, revealing a gap between his top front teeth. I nodded at the bench in the middle of the room. "I couldn't do one rep with four-o-five."

"You could if you worked out here. I guarantee it."

"You sound like an entrepreneur."

"Naaa, I'm Scandinavian," he deadpanned, "and trying to make a couple of bucks on the side to supplement my meager teacher's income."

"What do you teach?"

"History, Dubuque Senior High School. Down the river a ways. Know it?"

"Used to," I said, "a long time ago when I attended Clinton High and used to bang heads with the Rams in the old Mississippi Valley Conference. Nice campus."

"That it is. I like it there. Good kids."

"Nice gym," I said. In addition to the weights and machines, the place offered a complete array of treadmills, recumbent bikes, and elliptical trainers. "No tanning booths? No Day Care?"

"I'll add them in when membership hits two thousand."

"May you never reach that number."

"That's the way I feel, too. You want to give us a try? A free week and a t-shirt if you buy a monthly membership. You ought to consider us. Unlimited workouts. If you want music, bring your own iPod and keep it to yourself. No television sets. Tell you what, if you can bench two hundred pounds once with a three-second pause, I'll give you a free month. If you can push the poundage, you can't lose."

"Thanks, but I plan on buying my own equipment."

Mulehoff shrugged, then assessed me. "You don't look familiar. You live around here?"

"I'm new in town, and I live south and east of here, on a bluff. House that Gunther Schmidt built a few months back."

"Oh, so you're *that* guy! Okay, now I understand," he said softly, nodding his head slowly. "So, welcome to the Greater Rockbluff Metroplex, future sight of the Winter Olympic Games."

I smiled and nodded and started for the door. Mike's voice interrupted my flight.

"It's okay to work out by yourself, but you might do better here. Scripture says 'iron sharpens iron.' If you can bench two hundred with that short pause, you can save money and still have people to work out with, or not. No one will bother you if you choose to work out solo."

I went back. "I guess I have nothing to lose. Do I have to sign a waiver in case I blow out my shoulders? They're creaky."

"I think I can trust you not to sue."

Already in t-shirt and jeans, I walked over to an empty bench, set an Olympic bar on the rack, and slid a pair of forty-five pound plates on my end of the bar as Mulehoff did the same on the other end. I sat on the bench and swung my arms across my chest a few times to loosen up.

"That's two twenty-five, you know. You only have to do two hundred."

"If I'm going to win a free month, I want to remove all doubt," I said.

Mulehoff grinned. "I'll spot you." He moved to the head of the bench.

I laid back and scooted up. Then I reached up to the bar, gripped the cold, gnarled metal at shoulder width, popped the bar off the supports, steadied it, then slowly brought it down to my chest and held it there.

"One thousand one, one thousand two, one thousand three. PUSH!" Mulehoff shouted.

I pushed. The bar went up smoothly and I racked the weight, took a deep breath, and sat up. Sharp pain yelped deep in my left shoulder, but I didn't mention it.

"Congratulations, Thomas!" Mulehoff said. He seemed genuinely pleased. "Not bad for an old Clinton High River King."

"Thanks. I'll be in Monday morning. What are your hours?"

"Open every day except Sunday, six AM to ten PM. And no additional charge for the subtle and sophisticated ambiance. But, changing the subject just a second," he said, folding his thick arms across his deep chest, "were you in The Grain o' Truth just now?"

"I was."

"I thought I saw you go in. I was looking out the window between sets and saw Larry Soderstrom leaving a couple of minutes ago. Looked perturbed. What happened?"

"Moon did not like Larry's attitude and told him to leave. Larry pulled a knife, Moon pulled a shotgun, Larry left."

"A little free advice, Thomas. Avoid that guy. He's bad news. And if I had been Moon, I might have just gone ahead and taken Mulehoff's Initiative, someone pull a knife on me." He pulled off his other lifting glove, the Velcro cherking with the movement.

"Mulehoff's Initiative?"

"When I really want to do something, I just go ahead and do it. Calling it Mulehoff's Initiative makes it sound more philosophical than carnal. So who else have you made friends with in Rockbluff, besides Larry Soderstrom?"

"I don't know about friends, but I've had conversations with Lunatic Mooning. I met Arvid Pendergast, and bumped into Horace Norris, Rachel Schoendienst, Harvey Goodell, Liv Olson."

"Horace is a trip, isn't he?" Mulehoff asked rhetorically, laughing and rubbing his hands briskly with the white towel draped around his thick neck. "You need to sit down with him sometime and get to know him. Did you know he has terminal cancer?"

"He told me he was dying."

"Prostate got to him, but so far it's the slow-moving kind. Might have years and years left, but he's not going to count on it. He does the roller blade bit, occasionally skydives, does snowmobiling in the winter. Squeezing out every bit of life available. Who else have you met in our metropolis?"

"I wasn't formally introduced," I said, wondering why I was giving Mulehoff so much information about me other than the fact that I liked him right away, "but I did run into Wendy Soderstrom yesterday, at their farm, and Molly Heisler, Deputy Doltch, a couple of EMS guys. Schumacher and Aldrich, I think their names were."

"You were out there when Hugh was killed? Are you kidding me?"

"I was driving by right after the accident. Tried to help. Too late."

"What do you think happened?"

"I don't know. I guess I'd like to know how Hugh Soderstrom ended up under that rotary mower. I think I'll share my questions with the Sheriff. That's where I was headed when your sign caught my eye."

"He'll listen to you. He's fair. I'm sorry you had to bump into something like that so soon after moving here. It's not perfect, but Rockbluff's a good place to live."

"Well, I gotta go. Maybe my new buddy Larry was up all night drinking because of what happened to his brother. I can understand that. He just needs to take his anger out on something more appropriate, like the heavy bag, or some deadlifts. Maybe a twenty-mile hike."

"Larry's up all night drinking most nights, Thomas. He doesn't need an occasion. You might say the wrong brother died yesterday."

"You're the second person today who's told me that."

"I doubt the observation will stop with two," Mike said, holding his hand out again, "I'd be happy to be friends. The first of many, I suspect. And if you want to rent a movie..."

We shook again. "Thanks," I said, then turned and left the gym, striding back outside and into a day where sweat would be cheap.

I waited for a John Deere tractor to pass, one of those green and yellow *Jurassic Park* monsters sporting tinted glass air-conditioned cabs with heavy-duty sound systems, refrigerator, and handball court. The driver, from his position behind the wheel ten feet up in the air, nodded. I nodded back and crossed the street, wading through a blue cloud of diesel exhaust.

I continued on toward the Municipal Building, thinking about Mike Mulehoff's open offer of friendship. One doesn't make new old friends, but one can make new friends who might become old friends down the road a ways. And then I remembered my new friend had overlooked my free t-shirt.

Chapter 7

"And we're so by God stubborn
We could stand touchin' noses
For a week at a time
And never see eye-to-eye."

- Meredith Willson, "Iowa Stubborn" from The Music Man

On First Street, the businesses all seemed to be thriving. Probably due to the plentiful, free angle parking, a Chamber of Commerce stroke of genius for those who equate parallel parking with surprise colonoscopies.

No malls for Rockbluff. And no boarded-up storefronts of small businesses that always show up around the malls, ubiquitous as rusty weight benches on the front porches of single-wides. I lingered in front of the Rockbluff Opera House, a refurbished brick edifice that attracted first-rate, second-tier entertainment, according to the "Coming Events" handbill in the glass case out front. The blues *chanteuse* heading our way in August I had actually seen on a PBS Special, and a Minneapolis production of *Wait Until Dark* was scheduled for September.

I'd expected a harmonica contest and maybe Elvis impersonators, or perhaps a "Battle of the Accordions," but then, that's a problem Iowans face: Always expecting bad stuff, hoping for good things, and stunned off our butts when those good things happen. Then, we go back to feeling inferior. The Puritan Ethic in bib overalls.

Iowans are well versed in politics, wrestling, and fine arts. Hard to beat that, especially when you match it up with no crime, average life span of 123 years, and the nation's highest literacy rate. But pride would be a character flaw. So we're always sure someone better will jump up out of nowhere and send us, collectively, to the woodshed for much-deserved self-flagellation. "Pride needs its comeuppance" is in Latin on the Great Seal of the State of Iowa. You can look it up.

Next door to the Opera House stood the limestone and glass Rockbluff Community Library and Media Center, new since 2004 according to the brass plate mounted on a granite boulder next to the book drop. Libraries are a cold pint of beer to curiosity's panting thirst, and, based on the dozens of cars and pickups in the parking lot, the locals were busy reinforcing their literacy rates.

It felt like the temperature had gone up three degrees while I admired the new library, so I decided to just accept the heat and allow myself the simple pleasure of taking in a hot day. No point in fighting the inevitable. Iowa summers are as humid and sticky and close as a tight t-shirt after an hour on an elliptical trainer, but they are worth it. They make autumn worth waiting for. It was late May, and I was already looking forward to the next season, and humbly grateful that I had something to look forward to for a change.

The sharp pain in my left shoulder had progressed to merely aching now, to go along with my sore right hamstring: Perfectly-balanced discomfort that provided me with an upright posture as I approached the mid-town bridge.

It occurred to me that simply dropping in unannounced might be welcomed by a sheriff who, no doubt, had very little to do. According to a brochure in the motel lobby, Rockbluff employed eight law enforcement officers for the entire town and county. Eight. Of course, the population of the entire town and county together was just under 14,000 people. This "Serve and Protect" reconfiguration took place two years ago when, for fiscal reasons, the Rockbluff Police Department and the Rockbluff County Sheriff's Department merged. Several police officers retired or took early retirement, and two were absorbed into the Sheriff's Department, which had the higher jurisdiction in county law enforcement protocol.

I tramped over the Whitetail River at the bridge and marched up the brief knoll to the courthouse. On the right side of the solid granite-block building, there was a retro sign—a weathered wooden finger pointing down a flight of time-smoothed stone stairs. "Rockbluff County Law Enforcement Center" was positioned just below the finger. I descended and entered through a glass door straight ahead of me.

I went in with trepidation (my next dog will be named "Trepidation"), fighting a life-long discomfort in the presence of law enforcement types. I have never been convicted of any crime, civilian or military; have never committed any act that made me more ashamed than any other act I've committed; and have never, ever broken a law that, given the unique circumstances of the situation, didn't need to be broken. Still, I'm not comfy with cops.

Two officers looked up, one, young, deskbound. The other officer stood in front of his desk, reading something; a report perhaps, or news of a suspicious yard sale. The man was lean, tough-looking, and about forty years old. He was tall, at least six-five. He studied me when I moseyed into the office, then looked back down at the paper in his hand. "PAYNE" was printed in white block letters on a black plastic nametag pegged over his right breast pocket, just like the one Deputy Doltch displayed at the Soderstrom farm. A badge was over the other, protecting his heart. His uniform was crisp, and why wouldn't it be? How much sweat can one work up ticketing kids riding double on a bike? Or shooting rabid bunnies?

"What can I do for you?" he asked without looking up.

The other officer was too young to be serving and protecting anything except maybe his high school cheerleader girlfriend. His name, according to the tag, was "Lansberger." He was blonde, tall even while sitting, and squared away. I wondered how in the world Rockbluff came up with all these law enforcement people who could make spare cash modeling for Land's End.

"I'm Thomas O'Shea," I said, walking over to Payne and shaking hands.

"Harmon Payne," he said, his voice deep and neutral, his handshake firm, his eye contact direct. "That's Deputy Preston Lansberger."

Lansberger and I nodded at each other.

"Just a second," the Sheriff said, turning to Lansberger, "Call Doctor Elmendorf and see how Wendy's doing, will you?" The deputy began punching numbers into the land line telephone on his nicked-up wooden desk. The Sheriff looked back at me.

"You didn't come in just to introduce yourself."

"No. I want to provide observations about the situation with Hugh Soderstrom."

Sheriff Payne took a pen from his pocket, sat down behind the desk in an old green leather swivel chair that squeaked, ignored his computer, and dragged over a yellow legal pad. His right forearm revealed a globe & anchor tattoo with USMC beneath it. He said, "Have a seat. Talk to me."

I sat in an oak banker's chair and told Payne what had just happened at The Grain o' Truth. He scribbled on the thick pad with "Samuelson's Hy-Vee" lettered across the top. I mentioned that Larry appeared to be drunk.

"Nothing new for him. He's been on one kind of intoxicant or chemical burn for a long time. I'm no fan of Larry Soderstrom. Far from it, but maybe this time he had a reason beyond finding nothing worth watching on HBO."

"His brother."

"Terrible accident. A man doesn't fall under a rotary mower, especially a heavy duty job like Hugh was pulling, and live to tell about it. Same thing happened four years ago down in Maquoketa. Little boy riding with his dad. The fender broke off and the boy fell under.

"Dad grabbed the little feller's hand, he was eight, but he slipped away and the big tire of the tractor ran the length of him and the mower finished the job. Dad went nuts. Tried to pick up his son. Couldn't pick him up. Ran into the house to get his pistol to kill himself but a farmhand beat him to it, stopped him. Spent the night in a padded room in Iowa City. Later, he got himself some counseling, but he still hasn't fully gotten over it. Might drive me to drink, too."

"I understand. I was there. At the Soderstrom's. Just before EMS showed up."

Payne gave me a look of skepticism, then rummaged quickly through some notes on his desk, found a report, scanned it, and looked with at me with new interest. "I guess you were. Sorry, didn't make the connection right off."

"I guess when it's just an accident it doesn't matter whom is whom."

"I apologize. I should have noticed."

"How's Mrs. Soderstrom?"

His chair squeaked again as Payne leaned back and looked at Lansberger who had just hung up the phone. "How's Wendy?"

Lansberger said, "She's wiped out, but she's strong. Doctor Elmendorf will take care of her."

"That answer your question?" Payne asked.

"Yes, that's good." I continued to be underwhelmed with the police work, but I was impressed with Payne's apology.

"Tough way to start out married life," Payne said, leaning forward again, the chair groaning.

"I heard Hugh Soderstrom was a decent man."

"Yes. And now there's another big adjustment for his wife. Mighty young widow."

"Another big adjustment?"

"Oh, you know, life on the farm for a city girl. Davenport. Alone a lot," Payne said, relaxing back into his squeaky swivel chair. "Used to the city."

" I've got something else to report."

"What's that?"

"When I was out driving, just before I saw Mrs. Soderstrom screaming for help, I met a car that was going pretty fast."

"It's a country road."

"It was a silver Corvette." Payne cocked his head just a little. "And I noticed that Larry Soderstrom was driving a silver Corvette today. Many like that around here?"

Payne started to say something, stopped, said, "Who was driving? Get a tag number?"

"Nope, I just think it's interesting, a silver Corvette leaving the neighborhood of the Soderstrom farm right after the accident. In a hurry."

"Might've been going for help," Payne said, his response lacking conviction.

"Anything in the paperwork about Larry?"

"No."

I shrugged and stood. Payne did, too. He said, "I guess I can have a conversation with Larry. Can't hurt."

"Might help," I offered brightly, choosing to be chipper.

"Anything else?"

"A friend of mine, former Green Beret, used to say, 'Don't ask the question if you can't stand the answer.' I guess you can stand the answer. I think Hugh Soderstrom's death seems a little suspicious." Fun to push people a little. My obnoxious side flexing a bit. Nothing else to do.

Payne grimaced, then sat down heavily in his squeaky chair and beckoned for me to be seated again. Lansberger was grabbing his hat and leaving, but it was clear from the scrutiny he gave me that he had heard, but did not believe. It's one thing to be a skeptic; that's usually cool. But stupid has yet to be cool. Payne said, "Go ahead, Mr. O'Shea."

"There are several things," I said, pleased to notice Payne was taking out his pen again. "First, I can't believe Hugh Soderstrom fell off his tractor and got run over. He was young, and most farm accidents in Iowa are tractor turnovers with men in their sixties and seventies, and older. That's common knowledge. Second, he was a gifted athlete, according to the EMS guy, I forgot his name. Aldrich I think it was. What in the world would make him fall off his tractor?"

Payne looked like he needed an antacid pill, but he was paying close attention to what I was saying. He scribbled something on his legal pad and looked at me.

"The questions that Deputy Doltch asked me were designed to prove a bias toward accidental death. For Pete's sake, he never even asked me if I had seen anything out of the ordinary, and I was the first person on the scene, except for Mrs. Soderstrom.

"Anyway, I was not impressed with the investigative prowess of your deputy. Seemed like a nice guy. Wouldn't even consider if the incident was anything other than an accident. Practically took my head off when I suggested maybe it was a suicide."

"Hardly enough there to make us investigate suicide, and besides, who would commit suicide that way? And not much to go on for a homicide investigation, for that matter. Mrs. Soderstrom said he just fell. Eye witness. Stranger things have happened. Farming is damn dangerous."

"I've always had a problem with just letting things go, Sheriff. I don't want to cause any trouble, but what if Larry Soderstrom was out at the farm that morning? Did Mrs. Soderstrom say he was?"

"No."

"Well, there you go," I said, leaning back and stretching my legs out in front of me, ignoring the twinge in the back of my right thigh. "If she said he wasn't out there, but Larry was driving the Corvette I saw, what was that? A coincidence?"

"No, sir. It's a problem, O'Shea," Sheriff Payne said, a bit of steel in his voice. "A problem for me, not you. I'm going to go find Larry Soderstrom, and I'm going to interrogate him. I'll get to the bottom of it. Thanks for coming in." He stood. So did I.

"Thanks for listening," I said.

"Now, unless you have some other bit of information to share with me..."

"I'm gone," I said, wanting to get out of the way after having done my civic duty. I turned and left, out the door, up the worn limestone steps, and into the hot summer day. I sat down high up on the steps of the County Courthouse where, based on pedestrian traffic, nothing was happening.

I sighed and rotated my head from left to right, front to back, enjoying the cracking sounds and release of pressure. I dug my fingers into my neck muscles. I rolled my shoulders, removed my glasses, rubbed my eyes with the palms of my hands. Slipped my glasses back on. Looked up.

From the height of the courthouse steps I could see most of Rockbluff stretching out from north to south, embracing the steady waters of the Whitetail River like lifelong lovers. Beyond the town, easily in sight, stretched carpets of corn and soybeans springing forth from fertile fields, silently generating wealth. Rockbluff was oozing commerce and well-being, but it seemed like maybe some secrets were starting to ooze out, too.

I smelled freshly-cut grass, the heavy scent of the slow-moving river, and the heat of searing sunshine. The breeze shifted, and the sweet fragrance of luscious lilacs came to me, a heavy perfume I could almost taste in the heated air.

It somehow didn't fit that Hugh Soderstrom was dead in this place, and under peculiar circumstances, and the lively exchange I had witnessed just minutes before in The Grain seemed out of place, too. And yet, Ann Frank's quote came to mind: "Look around you at all the beauty and be happy." I decided to try, and this was a good place for it. Sitting alone in the sun on the stone steps of the County Courthouse, I looked out over the clean, clear waters of the Whitetail River, where even now several boys in inner tubes were drifting downstream like bugs on leaves.

And at that moment, just for the hell of it, I decided to attend the funeral of Hugh Soderstrom, taking place tomorrow.

Larry Soderstrom might be there, and then Payne could interrogate him and I could find out how that went. Besides, I could check out the pastor. My friend and pastor back in Georgia, Ernie Timmons, had called and nagged me once already about finding a local church , and I had just kept putting him off, mainly because my first day in Rockbluff was a Sunday and I was exhausted from driving straight through from Belue, Georgia. And a second Sunday was still two days away. Ernie could be a pest.

I stood and looked around again and realized maybe my expectations had been a bit ambitious. To have expected everything to go according to my plan, especially where there were flesh-and-blood people, was naïve, but I had to admit, except for the situation at the Soderstrom Farm, my sore leg, and aching shoulder, I was in pretty good shape. Time to count my blessings and leave the rest to Sheriff Payne.

I stretched again and descended the steps of the County Courthouse. The sign on the Hawkeye State Bank read ninety-five degrees, high for late May. Ambling along Bridge Street toward the river, my hamstring let me know it was still there, but at least it wasn't shouting. More like snickering at my advancing age and reluctant healing.

At the peak of the bridge I waved back at some sunburned kid draped into a black inner tube, the last one in the group of adventurers I had seen from the courthouse steps, laughing in delight as his tube approached Fisherman's Dam and its gently-sloping, twenty-foot spillway. His friends had already negotiated the giant slip-and-slide, and were now turned around and encouraging him to enjoy the ride as well. He picked up speed and began shrieking louder, and I realized it was not a sunburned kid. It was Horace Norris.

"What are you doing down there?" I laughed, calling loudly to the old man.

"Better question! What are *you* doing up *there*?" Horace repeated, shouting over the sound of the spillway. "That's Thoreau!"

And then he was passing beneath the bridge, waving with both hands and laughing out loud, head thrown back, purely gleeful, slipping beneath the bridge and over the smooth face of the dam's spillway and on again downstream for more adventures. I wondered where I could acquire an inner tube.

I turned and headed for my truck back up the street in Moon's parking lot. Seeing Horace, I knew I needed to get out more and meet people, and what better opportunity than a funeral in a small town?

Chapter 8

"They say such nice things about people at their funerals that it makes me sad to realize I'm going to miss mine by just a few days."
- Garrison Keillor

Hugh Soderstrom's funeral took place at Christ the King Church. I parked two blocks away. It was as close as I could get. Once inside, I smiled and took a program from a desiccated little old man whose white shirt collar was two sizes too big for his skinny turkey neck.

I entered the sanctuary and sat on a gray metal folding chair in the back because the pews, choir loft, and the balcony were bulging with mourners. It reminded me of the crowds of married grad students at the "All You Can Eat For $5" lunches at the Pizza Inn in Iowa City when Karen and I were first married.

Lunatic Mooning sat in the choir loft, wearing a suit, charcoal gray; shirt, white; and tie, black. Oh, those flamboyant Indians and their penchant for colorful ceremonial costumes. I caught his eye. He nodded, looked away.

I looked at the program printed on stiff gray paper. Symbolic. A pen and ink drawing of the church on the cover. Inside left, Hugh

Soderstrom's birthdate and date of death, and the fact that The Reverend Dr. Ernst VanderKellen would be officiating.

Inside right, a brief biography of the deceased. Hugh earned twelve varsity letters at Rockbluff Community High School, participated in Future Farmers of America and 4-H, and reigned as Senior Class President and Homecoming King. He graduated from Iowa State University, married Wendy, served four years' active duty in the Air Force. Then he came home to work the family farm when he wasn't flossing after every meal.

He was twenty-eight when the machine ate him, three years older than Wendy.

The old college senior-freshman attraction. Reasonably mature guy, drooling idiot sorority girl.

The Soderstrom family came in, Larry leading the way, Wendy leaning on his right arm. I watched the shattered family proceed. With the exception of Wendy and Larry, they all looked like people of the land, strong, weathered, and prosperous; resolute in their grief. People to whom pain is a normal part of life to be endured and accepted, like drought and hail, tornados and floods. Loss a part of life, defined by the details of miscarriage, stroke, and accidents that mangle and kill.

More family came in, parents and aunts and uncles, I guess. I only paid attention to Wendy, her lovely face tear-streaked; and Larry, who looked bored. Probably thinking about little girls and how to get them in his van, if he had one. Would you like to see my puppy? They walked to the front of the church and sat in the first row.

The Van Dyke-bearded Pastor VanderKellen entered the platform from a side door, strode manfully to the pulpit, sable vestments swaying, and provided a glowing eulogy for Hugh Soderstrom. When he finished, he came down from his heights to personally shake hands and whisper what had to be inspiration and comfort to each member of the immediate family: Hugh, Wendy, and an older couple, probably Wendy's parents. The common touch, as it were. The populist preacher. The pandering pastor, maybe fishing for a small bequest.

After VanderKellen spoke a very long time to Wendy, he gave

her a lingering look that did not exactly define "chaste." Résumé-builder for an aspiring televangelist?

He then swept back up to the pulpit where he pronounced a solemn benediction in his best preacher voice, stentorian, rich and rumbling. The men from the funeral home, professionally somber, appeared and slowly, reverently, guided the casket back down the aisle, staring straight ahead. The family followed.

I shouldered my way past several people so I could be on the aisle when Larry came by. The bereaved brother nodded and said "God bless" to people who reached out to pat him on the shoulder or shake his hand as he passed. He looked as if he were in pain, either that or trying to suppress raging flatulence. Then he saw me.

His somber facial expression transformed into a glare, and it hurt my feelings. I was going to give him the kiss of peace until then; so I merely leaned over, looked him in the eye, and said, "I *know*." Then I winked and leaned back.

I think he would have killed me on the spot except for the unfortunate restraints placed upon him by the reality of all those pesky witnesses. Wendy, on his far side and sensing anger, looked up, followed his eyes, found my face. And I found hers.

Put simply, Wendy was tan and beautiful. Shoulder length curly hair, the color of cornsilk, and large cerulean eyes that revealed a deep, intelligent aspect. At the farm, distracted, I had not noticed their striking color before. But now they looked back at me, alluring, hypnotic. I forced myself to drop eye contact and look at her chest.

Her extraordinary figure could not be muted by her simple black suit. With regard to Wendy, everywhere I looked there was temptation to fantasy.

And now she was left alone to carry on except for the manly ministrations of her brother-in-law, Saint Lawrence of the Dubious Comfort. I looked back up at her as she passed by. She returned my gaze, nodded, said, "Thank you," then looked again to the back of the church and the doors that would lead to the limousine, the ride to the cemetery, and a future that must have, just a few days ago, seemed rich and promising, but now was bleak and barren, as if saturated with Roundup.

The relatives passed by quickly, sunburned men in ill-fitting suits and dull neckties, and able women in simple church dresses. And, of course, The Reverend Doctor, a righteous vision in his opulent vestments. Ushers dismissed the rows of mourners from the front of the church on back. Sheriff Payne looked at me as he left. By the time I limped outside, the hearse was pulling away, followed by cars with headlights burning, cars filled with solemn, good people proceeding to the grave. Like all of us.

In the midst of all the Crown Vics and SUVs, a chocolate-brown Jaguar XKJ pulled away to join the single file of vehicles filled with the grieving on the brief journey to the hungry, open mouth of the earth, waiting to swallow up the remains of one who had worked the land with joy, and now would be entombed by it. I wondered about the Jag's driver, but then I heard my name called.

It was Payne, standing at the bottom of the church steps. I joined him and said, "You wanted to talk to me, Sheriff?"

"I do, Mr. O'Shea. When you dropped by my office I forgot to ask you something important," he said, looking me directly in the eye.

Eye contact to Iowans is key. If an adult does not give eye contact when he's talking to you, he is probably from Minnesota, holding something back or twisting the truth. If a child withholds eye contact, she is lying, and probably has kinfolk in Wisconsin. I looked at him and said, "Ask away."

"What are you doing in Rockbluff?"

"Hiding out."

"What are you hiding from? What did you do?"

"It's more like what I didn't do, Constable," I said, thinking back to Georgia.

"I don't understand. Help me out here."

"I didn't die in the car wreck, and that's why I'm here in Rockbluff," I shrugged. "Simple is as simple does."

"Let's get a bite to eat," he said, starting down the steps. "I'll buy."

I agreed to meet him at The Tenderloin Tap, which seemed more like a name for a risqué dance than a restaurant. "I'll have a question for you, too."

The Tenderloin Tap is one of those institutions that have existed forever in small towns, never changing their menu, steadily generating profit; long, narrow and parallel to the street with a counter and stools on one side and rows of booths along the big windows on the other. There is at least one in every village, fighting off inroads from fast-food joints. Local cholesterol always tastes better than cholesterol from national chains.

The Tenderloin Tap's neon beer signs offered a kind of comfort Ronald McDonald couldn't. I joined Payne in a booth, sitting across from him and glancing out the window to the quiet street. I guessed everyone was at the cemetery.

We ordered from a perky high school girl in a green-and-white uniform who appeared with a pad and pencil. Payne ordered the chicken fried steak, peas and corn, and coffee. I ordered the House Special, a 16-ounce Conestoga Tenderloin, hold the veggies, and a Heineken.

"Veggies are awful good for you," pronounced our waitress, whose name was, according to the cursive over her ample left breast, "Bernice." I didn't think people named girls Bernice anymore. She added, "No extra charge. You get two. They're awful good for seniors." Payne stifled a laugh and looked away.

"Two steaks? You said I get two? I don't think I could eat two steaks."

"Two veggies, silly! Two veggies are included in the price of the entrée."

"Bernice, didn't you ever stop to think that meat is nothing but vegetables compressed over time, and a whole lot better tasting? The steer ate the green veggies, and I eat the steer. It's all there. Eliminates the middle man."

Bernice's face fell. She said, "That's icky," and left. Payne was shaking his head. In a moment, Bernice reappeared with the Sheriff's coffee, my Heineken, and a glass.

"Classy joint, bringing me a glass without my having to ask," I said after Bernice left. I poured the beer. I took a long drink. Funerals make me thirsty.

"Tell me more about the car wreck in Georgia," Payne said.

I did, but I left out the details, left out how the driver of the 18-wheeler heading south on I-95 must have dozed, drifted left, onto and over the abandoned Mazda Miata on the shoulder. I left out the part from the eyewitnesses, how the truck had come down in the northbound lane. On top of my wife and daughters, exploding everyone into a crushing fireball. I left that out. No point. Just the facts.

He nodded. "I'm sorry," he said. He sounded sincere. "I hope you can regroup here in Rockbluff. It's a good place to live."

"Thank you," I said, remembering Mulehoff's identical sentiment. "I'm looking forward to settling into the fatal farm accident capital of the western hemisphere. I have a question for you. With Hugh being dead, might there be some financial benefit to Larry?"

Payne stopped stirring the three packs of sugar he had just dumped into his coffee and looked at me. "You sure don't tiptoe around the tulips, do you?"

"Not my style. See, I don't think Larry's a stellar guy, and people who aren't stellar do horrible things, especially when enough money is involved."

Payne went back to stirring his coffee, studying the light brown liquid, as if he expected a Sports Illustrated Swimsuit Model to rise from below the surface. A battered white Ford F150 pickup truck passed, driven by an old man whose hair matched the paint job. Two kids, a boy and a girl high school age, drove by going the other direction in a red Mustang convertible. Top down. *Ah, youth*. The Sheriff finally looked up from his coffee, started to speak, stopped when he saw someone approaching our booth.

Bernice, a platter of food in each hand. Fast service. Probably big bins of sustenance under red lamps in the back. She left our food and disappeared.

Payne picked up his utensils, set them down again. "You've almost put me off my feed, sir, and I was so looking forward to a friendly chat. Helps digestion. So, you think Larry murdered his brother for money?"

"Yep. More bucks for the lifestyle. It's logical the parents would have set up the estate like that: One son dies, it all goes to the other, just to keep it in the family."

"Actually, I think it might be something like that, me being a professional information-gatherer in a small town, but so far, there's no evidence to support your theory."

"Maybe not, but some interesting coincidences. So, since I have nothing but time on my hands and you're busy, I'll check it out. My hunch is, if you look at the estate plan and the will closely, you'll see that I'm right. The surviving brother gets the bulk of the estate. That would guarantee Soderstrom Farms remains Soderstrom Farms. And Shazam! Up jumps a motive. Nothing new under the sun."

"How do you know so much about estate planning and distribution of assets?"

"I read a lot," I said.

Payne cut off a piece of chicken, stabbed it with his fork, and put the morsel in his mouth.

"Another thing," I said, "when Larry was leaving the church just now I spoke to him. I said, 'I know' and I thought he was going to spit."

The Sheriff looked like he was in pain. "What's that supposed to mean?"

"Whatever Larry wants it to. I could have meant that I know what he's going through, or, if he has a guilty conscience, he could take it to mean that I know what he did. Judging from his reaction, I'd have to say he didn't take comfort from my remark, which beckons me down the path of suspicion."

The Sheriff chewed his food and shook his head, clearly a coordinated guy. Point guard in high school? He said, "Do you want me to arrest him now, or may I finish my lunch first?"

"Be as cautious as you want to be, but when I get an insight like this, it's almost always accurate. Course we can't arrest him now—we've got to get some evidence first."

Payne's eyes brightened. "I never thought of that! You do read a lot!"

"Touché," I said.

"Mr. O'Shea, I have had more than one run-in with Larry, and I can tell you that, just because he's a nefarious individual, it doesn't mean he murdered his brother." Payne returned to his food, eating deliberately and with serious purpose.

"Okay, so who was the guy driving the Jaguar XKJ?"

Payne stopped eating and very deliberately wiped his mouth with his napkin. He said, "Jurgen Clontz, Junior, the richest man in northeast Iowa."

"Real estate."

"How'd you know that? Oh, the 'MYLAND' vanity plate. Of course," Payne said.

"Where'd he get his money in the first place?"

"Family."

"A rich daddy, huh?"

I waited for his response while Payne completed his meal, wiping down the plate with half a roll that remained and popping it in his mouth. He pushed his plate to the side of the table and Bernice swooped down and took it away. We turned down apple pie.

I ate. The meal was good. Fast food home cooking. I wondered how long my steak had been sitting under a lamp. It didn't matter, it was tender, fork-cutable.

Payne went on. "There's pretty strong evidence, great word there, evidence, that his grandpaw parlayed winnings from high stakes poker games, running moonshine, and smuggling Canadian whiskey during Prohibition into a fortune in cash and land. The old folks say that in the twenties private planes used to fly into Rockbluff County with gangsters and high rollers from Chicago, Kansas City and Omaha, big landowners from all over the Midwest, to play a little five-card stud game every Thursday night through Sunday afternoon. Fortunes won and lost. There's supposed to be a hidden airstrip in some valley up there in the bluffs somewhere, but I've never seen it."

"That proves it's hidden," I said. The Law ignored me and continued.

"Old man Clontz's son took over from there and, through pure genius, and I have to give him credit for it, built even greater assets through all kinds of commodities trading, building shopping malls, and he even had a piece of the Chicago Bulls just before they got Michael Jordan. Sold off his share three years later. Considerable profit.

"From that, Jurgen Junior, Jaguar dude, took over the business when Daddy fell to his death on a hiking trip during a family outing up in Baraboo—actually just Jurgen and his dad were on the hike, the rest of the family was back at the lodge—which raised questions that went away very quickly, which raised even more questions from my perspective. Anyway, Jurgen Junior inherited the gift. Owns enormous chunks of property. Crazy about land. With his dad and grandpaw, it was a game and a challenge. With Junior, now," Payne said, shaking his head, "it's more like a sickness."

"Why do you say that?" I asked between bites of my Conestoga Tenderloin.

"It doesn't make him happy. Always wants more. Seems pretty miserable most of the time, even with his Armani suits, which come in real handy here in Rockbluff, you know, at the Grange meetings and tractor pulls, and the Rolex and private jet and so on."

"The hunger that can never be satisfied," I said.

"Yeah, that and he's always asking people to sell their land. Sometimes he asks nice and sometimes he's a little pushy for this part of the country, if you know what I mean. If a man doesn't want to sell, he doesn't want to sell, but Jurgen won't take no for an answer. Course, some people who said no in public later said yes, perhaps under duress, in private. And then moved away with their money."

"Makes me wonder," I said.

Payne looked at me. His eyes were somehow different, more serious than serious. "One other thing."

"What?"

The tall officer rose, leaving money on the table for our food plus a nice tip, and grabbed his hat. He looked at me and said, "I've never come face to face with any cannibalistic serial killers; but other than that possibility, Jurgen Clontz is the only person I've ever met who is capable of giving me the willies."

Chapter 9

"Christianity might be a good thing if anyone ever tried it."
- George Bernard Shaw

I spent the next week getting used to living in my new home, determined to back off from questioning people and to let Payne do the heavy lifting. I drank beer and wine, forgot to go church shopping, and re-read everything written by Ron Rash. I caught up with the Red Sox and wrote out several routines to try at Mulehoff's. I needed to get back into good, hard condition, but frankly, I wasn't motivated. My daily three-mile runs on the blacktop road at the bottom of my drive temporarily assuaged my guilt.

Saturday afternoon, the next-to-last day in May, I nearly jumped out of my skin when my cell phone sounded off to the tune of "Three Blind Mice," the Stooges theme song. It was Ernie Timmons, my pastor in Georgia, and the second phone call I'd had since moving. Both from him. We had exchanged a couple of e-mails, one from me when I bought the house. So he wouldn't worry. I traced the music to a stack of newspapers on a kitchen counter, the black umbilicus to the charger a major help.

"Found a church yet?" he asked.

"No, have you?"

"So when will you?"

"Not yet, Ernie. Good to hear your voice."

"Do I need to send a church planting team up to Iowa, Thomas? You know I will if the Lord leads me."

"The Lord leads you where you want to go, it seems to me," I teased.

"We can all say that, can't we? 'The Lord is leading me to be a missionary in Congo.' And then, when we find out they have green mambas and folks who hate whitey, we say, 'The Lord's leading me to start a strip club in Reno so I can minister to exotic dancers.'"

"Sorry the strip club didn't work out, Ernie. So, how are things in Belue?" I asked.

"Bleak. You left, remember?"

"Vaguely. How're Jan and the boys?"

"Pretty good. She wants you to come by for Italian tonight. The boys, too. Can you make it?"

I laughed. "I'm afraid I'd be late. Rain check?"

"Sure. Always."

"Thanks, I do appreciate it as long as you use Stouffer's lasagna. Jan's a terrible cook." This was a running joke between us. Jan is a glorious cook. Her last name before Ernie ruined her was DiBella, and she learned her way around the supermarket and kitchen before she could reach the knobs on an oven.

"Your house is a mess," he said.

"How would you know?"

"Because I know that it is not good for man to live alone, and you be livin' alone, bubba. You need to pick up your clothes and wash them, take the trash out, tidy up. Run the vacuum. Dust."

He was right. Before the accident, I did all of those things. And I did them for Karen because I loved her, and for the girls, so they could see that a guy can clean up after himself.

After they all died, I found myself being a slob for days on end, and then I would suddenly do everything, including cleaning out the lint filter in the dryer. But my heart wasn't in it. My heart was buried in a cemetery in Belue.

"What else, Ernie?"

"Why haven't you found a body of believers, Thomas?"

"I'm looking," I lied. "Besides, I hate church shopping."

"A necessary evil," Ernie said. "Do you even have churches in Iowa? I've read somewhere that Iowans need missionaries more than the lost in the Sudan."

"Why is that?"

"They think to themselves, 'We're good, salt-of-the-earth people and we do good things. That should be enough.' No problems with sin rearing its ugly head."

"Pride isn't a sin, is it?" I asked.

It was quiet for a moment. Ernie was thinking. I could tell he was going to bring up something serious.

"Any more thoughts of suicide?"

"Ernie, why don't you quit dancing around the issue and, you know, come right out and say what's on your mind?"

"Any more thoughts of suicide?" Over the last few months, he had asked often.

"No. They're gone. I've progressed from wanting to kill myself to not wanting very much to live, to just trying to find something to look forward to."

"Do you still have the shotgun you pushed under the sofa when I dropped by after the accident?"

"You know I do, and you also know it's only for sentimental reasons. Dad gave me the gun when I turned twelve. That Stevens .410-.22 over-and-under is a classic."

"I keep seeing that shotgun poking out a little from beneath your sofa."

"The shotgun was for you, in case you dropped by and said, 'The Lord won't give you any more than you can handle,' or, 'He'll make you stronger in the broken places.'"

"Some of those things are true. He will give you more than you can handle. That way you'll have to turn to Him for help."

"Yes, but the timing of that advice is crucial. So each day, I say, 'Your will, Lord, not mine.' Sometimes I even mean it. Anyway, I'm doing okay on my own."

"So, since you're doing okay on your own, we can stop praying for you? It takes so much of our time to cover all the bases."

"No, don't stop. I can't, you know, pray for myself right yet."

"Okey-dokey."

When Ernie stopped by for the second straight day after the accident, I had taken out the old Stevens and put a shotgun shell in the chamber. I had done it the night before, too. But this time my thumb was on the trigger and the barrel was in my mouth. It didn't taste very nice—metallic, with a thin essence of oil. I couldn't come up with the proper wine to go with it, even though I thought and thought about it.

That's when the doorbell rang. That's when I put the gun under the sofa.

"Are you hiding in your new house all day and all night?" he asked.

"No. I've joined the Elks, Lions, Moose, Rotarians, and Kiwanis clubs, and I'm taking lessons in macramé, stenciling, gourmet cooking, and financial planning. I've joined the Rockbluff Choraleers (a men's barbershop quartet), and I'm working part time at Momma's Little Blessings Daycare. I've been here two weeks, Ernie! Two weeks! And, yes, I realize I've been dragging my feet."

"Are you staying in the house all day and all night?"

I told Ernie about the farm accident.

"Maybe you should stay in the house all day and all night."

He has nice ways of asking forgiveness, for a pastor. I told him about Lunatic Mooning and The Grain o' Truth Bar & Grill.

"Why don't I come up and you can buy me a beer?"

"You should, and I will, but you've got to give me some more time."

It was quiet for a moment. Ernie said, "You're not okay, are you?"

"Not yet, but I am not going to kill myself. What would I do the day after? Sheesh. Listen, Ernie, I looked lustfully at a woman a few days ago. I stared at her butt."

"A hopeful sign! If God could use Balaam's ass, he could use that woman's derriere."

"You're a sick man of God."

"Thanks. You're in our prayers every morning, man. Don't forget it," he said, and clicked off.

Just hearing Ernie made me think back to life in Belue. Annie had dated Ernie's son, Matt.

I pulled two Coronas and a frosted mug out of the refrigerator, then grabbed a bag of chips and a plastic tublet of shrimp dip and meandered out to the deck. I did not see eagles.

I drank both beers while standing on the deck looking out toward Wisconsin, and then I took the empties inside before I touched my food. I grabbed a six-pack and three singles and cruised back outside. Gotcha had been in the yard but now she wanted up on the deck. I swung open the little gate and she joined me. She looked at my beer, then back at me, so I got out her terra cotta beer bowl and poured half a Corona for her. She went to work, slurping and slopping, amber bubbles emerging from around her pendulant chops.

I continued to drink beer and eat chips and dip. Training table fare. When the chips disappeared, I ate roasted almonds scavenged from the pantry. More beer washed down the residue from the almonds. My face was numb, and then I closed my eyes as I stretched out on a deck lounger.

A light rain woke me. Drops pattering on my face. Dark out. I looked around bleary-eyed through wet glasses, sat up, and stood. I stumbled, drifted toward the sliding glass doors I'd left open. I accidentally booted an empty bottle and sent it scooting across the deck. It shattered against the side of the house. I shuffled inside, slid the glass door shut, and aimed straight for the kitchen cabinets.

I took out a bottle of Myer's Rum, poured about four ounces into a juice glass, and drank it down to get rid of the stale beer taste and clean my palate for sleep. Then I turned out the lights and stripped down to my undies. I gave Gotcha, who was in her recliner, a kiss on her wrinkled forehead, and wiped her foamy mug with the towel on the arm of the recliner just for that purpose. Then I tumbled into bed.

A throbbing head and a mouth tasting like stale rum helped me wake up the next morning. I swung my legs out of bed, put on my glasses. I hesitated, stood, and sat back heavily onto the bed.

"I'm not hung over," I said to Gotcha, looking up at me from her giant pillow on the floor at the foot of the bed. "I'll be just fine in a few minutes." My head hurt. My hair hurt. I tried again.

In the bathroom, I took inventory of my appearance and discovered that I looked old. A quick glance down at my stomach before I remember to tighten it revealed truth I did not particularly want to acknowledge. I realized I would have to step up my running to accommodate my drinking. Not a good thought.

I'm a big guy, and I've benefitted from years of weight training. My body looked decent this morning, but I did notice a few gray hairs on my chest, and my face had crow's feet around the eyes from years of laughter, now gone, and smile lines from the corners of my mouth to my nose. Karen and my girls put those there. My neck hasn't gone turkey-fleshed yet, but there is a helping of silver in my hair that was once black. I like the silver. I've earned it. There's a little sag between my eyebrows and eyelids. Nothing that cosmetic surgery couldn't cure, if I wanted it.

Gotcha stood behind me in the bathroom, watching. "Next time I'll shut and lock the door, Miss Nosey," I said. She stared at me. "I'd think, after all I've done for you, you'd cut me a little slack, so back off!" Gotcha stayed put, her large brown eyes on me. She seemed a little judgmental for a mere dog, but there wasn't anything I could do about it. She's all I have.

I turned on the hot water in the shower, slipped out of my underwear, slinging it unsteadily with my foot toward the dirty clothes hamper. The briefs and t-shirt landed on the hinged top of the hamper, which gave way. The clothes fell inside.

My shower took a while, the water as hot as I could stand it. Then I began to back off the hot water until the spray was only warm. I shampooed, then held my face up until it practically touched the fixture, the surge of water drumming into my face. Then, abruptly, I shut off the water, stepped outside, and toweled off.

After shaving, I downed four Extra Strength Tylenol with a glass of water, and padded into the bedroom. I slipped on a pair of briefs that were snug at the waist; a plain, gray XL t-shirt, and one of my two pair of faded blue jeans. Flip-flops completed my ensemble.

I made an eight-egg omelet, fried link sausage and bacon, micro-waved a double serving of hash browns, poured myself a tall glass of whole milk and took the food out on the deck, sliding the door shut so Gotcha wouldn't follow me out and cut her feet on the broken beer bottle. The day was clear and the sky was blue and it was not yet hot. When I finished eating, I swept up the mess on the deck, took Gotcha with me down to the mailbox where the Sunday *Des Moines Chronicle* was waiting, bagged in plastic on the white gravel.

I did not know until then that it was Sunday.

We walked slowly back to the house. Inside, I gave the panting Bulldog a Large Milk-Bone, looked at the clock on the computer. Ten AM. I decided to go to church.

I changed into my best clothes; a pair of khaki's and a dark blue knit shirt. Shoes and socks. I said so long to Gotcha and headed for town, grateful for the overcast morning, determined to attend a church, any church, feeling guilty after Ernie's comment and knowing Karen and the girls would have wanted me in worship.

When I pulled into the parking lot of the first mainline denominational church I saw, I noticed people going inside who were not cheerful in their countenance, and who did not seem interested in a stranger, even though I nodded at several people.

In any Belue, Georgia church where a new face might show up, swarming handshakes, greetings, questions, and information would transpire immediately. I could do without the questions, but I had hoped to at least be welcomed.

Inside the narthex of the large, limestone church, I found a table stacked with pamphlets and bulletins. I took a bulletin. At the back of the church, where dark walnut double doors opened wide, an usher offered his hand and said, "Good morning" as if it were a chore. Inside the sanctuary, I noticed that the back half was filled, the front half vacant. Maybe a hundred people, more or less. With no other choice, I crept to the first available pew feeling everyone's eyes on me.

I endured a service that took fifty-five minutes with an Order of Worship that included two hymns sung as if each note had to be extracted from amber, an anthem provided by a choir of grim-looking people, a sermon which included a brief quote from the Bible, and an offering, to which I contributed a hundred dollar bill for the fun of it. There was no reading of the Gospel, and I needed that. I craved a message with grace as the centerpiece.

The worship service was quiet, a kind of verbal chloroform. Had there been a rat licking flour in the basement, I would have heard it. To my relief, the Benediction arrived just before I would have started screaming.

The quiet of the service disappeared when earsplitting organ music burst forth at the end of the service as if The Bride of Dracula were at the instrument, committed to making it impossible to carry on a conversation. I jumped a foot when the organist blasted the first note.

I hoped to escape through an open side door, but I found none, so I plodded through a few minutes of worshippers' skimpy smiles, perfunctory nods, and mouthed greetings followed immediately by averted eyes and rapid pivots away from me. As the last person to enter the church and therefore the last to leave, I was the final lamb to speak with the pastor, a man older than I, sporting a paunch and a shock of gray hair, combed straight back, used car salesman style. Finally face to face with the pastor, we shook hands and the shepherd said, "Your first time at our worship service?"

"Yes. Good scripture in your sermon," I said with unassailable logic.

"We do hope you will come back," the pastor said, glancing at the parking lot.

I said, "Thank you," then resisted the urge to sprint to my truck. By the time I reached the parking lot, everyone else had left. I have learned over the years that good churches tend to have people arriving early and staying late, carrying on conversations with fellow believers on the steps and in the parking lot. My truck looked lonely as a well-proportioned girl at a fashion show.

I didn't want to go home, so I decided to just drive around and see what might strike my fancy for lunch since The Grain o' Truth was closed on Sundays.

Driving over the bridge, I again noticed the restaurant with the deck jutting out over the river, the one I saw when Gotcha and I took our walk. People were scattered about the deck, chatting, eating, and watching the Whitetail River flowing by. It looked inviting, friendly. I parked and walked up to the entrance.

The restaurant, Blossom's Bistro, churned with clientele. Two people left as I pushed my way inside. Immediately, a well-tanned, blonde, blue-eyed young woman with perfect white teeth, not yet employed by FOX News, came up to me and asked, "Deck or booth?" I wondered if Lansberger was her last name.

"Deck, please."

She smiled, turned, asked me to follow, and out we went. Her uniform consisted of khaki, loose-fitting Bermuda shorts and a bright orange golf shirt. She wore her hair in a ponytail, and it bounced joyfully as I followed her to the wide double doors, propped open, that led out to the deck. She turned back and asked, "Are you meeting someone, or are you alone?"

I said, "Quite alone."

"We're very informal here, so feel free to find a place and I'll send someone to take your order. We have a salad bar and a light lunch menu on Sundays. I'm Beth Gustafson," she said, "and you're...?"

"Thomas O'Shea." Beth grinned, tilted her head, and was gone. I plunged ahead into the bright sunshine, looking for a place to sit. A voice stopped me.

"Mr. O'Shea?"

A woman's voice, pleasant and soft. I glanced around and started forward again, and then she said, "Thomas? I'm over here."

Liv Olson sat at a little round table with two chairs in the corner of the deck above the Whitetail River. She smiled and mouthed a silent "hello" and waved me over.

I said, "What a pleasure to be new in town and see someone I've already met. Makes me feel more at home."

"I'm glad!" she said, and smiled.

"Are you waiting for someone?" I asked, then quickly, "Not that it's any of my business."

"No, I just decided on the spur of the moment to wander down here. Blossom's is usually kind of fun, the day is drop-dead gorgeous, and my stomach was growling. So here I am. I just got here, too. Grabbed the last good spot."

Liv Olson was dressed in white walking shorts and a pink sleeveless blouse, both of which made me want to look at her. A lot.

"Would you care to join me?"

"I was hoping you'd say that."

She smiled and pushed the empty chair toward me with her foot. I noticed brief sandals, bright pink toenails, shapely, tan legs. Her casual nudging the chair my way made me smile. I took the seat. She looked so good I found myself trying not to stare.

"Your first time here, G.I.?"

I laughed. "Yes. Pure impulse. Went to church and decided I didn't want to cook for myself, so I took a little excursion and here I am. I like this place."

"Me, too. I come down here every now and then, and have never been disappointed. Where'd you go to church?"

In a neutral tone, and with a poker face, I told her.

"How'd you like it?" A little smile played on her lips and an eyebrow went up.

"That's a loaded question, especially in a small town. I step on the wrong toe here and someone down the street yelps."

"Well. Let me unload it for you then. It's a terrible church. On a hot day without air conditioning its fervor for Christ might ascend to the level of lukewarm."

"I thought it was just me and my critical attitude. My spiritual gift."

Liv's laugh was rich and deep. "I went there twice and came away thinking if those folks have Jesus in their hearts, they ought to inform their faces."

The waitress appeared. She looked like the younger sister of Beth Gustafson. Maybe all of twenty. No bumps in her life so far. She was a little bubbly, but she explained the options pleasantly, asked if we were prepared to order or if she should come back. I told her five minutes would be excellent. I turned to Liv.

"What would you suggest?"

"Everything's good. Extraordinary salad bar. Menu is solid, too. I like their blackened redfish."

"Sounds good, but I'm more in the mood for salad. My approach to nutrition hasn't been exemplary lately."

"Can't go wrong with the salad bar."

The waitress, who had introduced herself as Ellyn, returned. "Are you ready to order?" she asked.

"The lady would like the blackened redfish..."

Liv said, "The lady, and thank you for that, has changed her mind. Woman's prerogative. She'd like the salad bar."

"Two," I said, and Ellyn left after taking our drink orders: iced tea for both of us.

"I just thought it would be nice to go through the salad bar with you. You look nice, and this is pleasant, and besides, I can offer expert commentary on the various choices. Let's go," she said, and I came to my feet and held out her chair for her. "Salad bowls are at the bar," she said, winking.

I could not remember the last time a pretty woman had winked at me, but I did know this: It had been too long. I was happy to follow Liv.

Chapter 10

"There's a difference between beauty and charm. A beautiful woman is one I notice. A charming woman is one who notices me."
- John Erskine

Everyone seemed to know Liv Olson. They smiled and nodded or waved from across the room. And still another tall, blonde girl, obviously one of her students said, "Hello, Miss Olson!" and gave me the once-over.

When we arrived at the salad bar, I said "After you."

"Thank you," she said, and we began working our way along the stainless steel containers under the Plexiglas shields and bright lights. "That's good, and that's good," she said, pointing at various options along the line. "That cheese is local and wonderful, and the salad dressings are made from scratch by Blossom himself. I like the bleu cheese, but suit yourself."

We customized our salads and maneuvered our way back onto the deck, once again Liv nodding and speaking briefly to people as we passed. Two of the women looked at us and glanced at Liv as if to solicit an introduction, but it was not forthcoming. We returned to our small table at the corner of the sunny deck.

I held her chair and she scooched in. I sat, smiled at Liv and said, "I'd offer up grace but I guess you could say I've backslid a little."

She smiled. "A regular experience for me. And most of us, I imagine."

"Yes. Anyway, I just forgot. To bless the food," I quickly added.

"Are you a religious man, Thomas?"

I took a small bite of salad, mostly cubed ham and shredded local cheddar smothered in bleu cheese dressing, chewed briefly, and said, "The roots of my faith go back to a church in Clinton, where I went as a child and young man, although I wasn't much for faith back then. I thought I was too intellectual. Shows how dumb I was."

Liv chuckled. "Lots of dumb intellectuals."

"Anyway, years later I wised up a little."

"HEY, LIV! THOMAS!"

The voice interrupting us came from below, and slightly upstream. Horace Norris, again floating down the Whitetail River in a big inner tube, was waving his skinny arms. He wore a bright yellow t-shirt with "I-O-W-A" in black, block letters across the chest. Baggy chartreuse swimming trunks, big blue-mirrored sunglasses, and that Cubs baseball cap completed his ensemble.

"Mr. Norris, great to see you!" Liv laughed, standing and waving vigorously.

"Looking good!" I said after coming to my feet for a better look.

Horace held up a twenty-ounce bottle of Hamm's and grinned. "It's a great day to be alive and celebrating the last day of May! Tomorrow let's get together and celebrate the first day of June! Behave yourselves now, you two!" He coasted on by Blossom's and headed under the right arch of the limestone bridge dividing the town.

We sat down, laughing. She said, "I've known Mr. Norris all my life. He was a teacher here, then a principal, and finally, superintendent. Retired from the school system about eight years ago. A good man. Never married. Threw himself into the life of the community. Now, since he's been diagnosed, he seems to be throwing himself into life itself."

"I've had a few short conversations with him at The Grain o' Truth. He seems happy," I said.

"He is that. So, what do you think of Lunatic Mooning, Thomas?" she asked, raising her eyebrows.

"Well, I haven't figured him out. You know, that 'inevitable distastefulness of man' stuff he likes to pontificate upon. For someone who has a pub to affirm his negative beliefs about people, he seems like he might be a soft touch."

"He really is a softy. Always helping people out. Likes to hire people who've made bad decisions and then help them get straightened out. I love the big guy, truth be told. We go back," she smiled, taking another bite of salad. "Just don't let him get away with the noble savage routine. Or the fractured syntax. The guy is a well read, astute businessman, and an individual with very strong feelings about right and wrong."

"He told me he wasn't married. True?"

"I think so. Rumor has it he has various intoxicating women of all colors and ages stashed in small towns spanning northeastern Iowa, southeastern Minnesota and southwestern Wisconsin."

"I wouldn't doubt it," I said.

Ellyn came by, asked if she could clear our dishes, received permission, picked them up, and then asked if dessert might be an option. Before I could answer, Liv said, "Thomas, I'm still hungry."

"I was going to say the same thing," I said. "As good as it was, salad doesn't cut it for Sunday dinner." I turned to Ellyn. "Dessert options?"

There were several, and Liv settled on something called Chocolate Epiphany. I ordered cherry cheesecake. "This will take care of my chocolate craving for the next two weeks," she said. "After this, I hope I can get into my bikini. It's hot enough."

Liv in a bikini. Something to think about. Maybe a string bikini. *Be still, my heart*. There I go again, but I'm not telling Ernie.

"We did have salads, remember," I said, "and there is protein in chocolate."

"There is that," she said, "and I love you for saying so."

"I read a study somewhere claiming women actually have a physical need for chocolate to maintain their equilibrium and sense of well-being."

"I have no doubt about the validity of that study."

The desserts arrived and we consumed them in quiet pleasure with minimal conversation. Ellyn brought the check, I took it and left the tip, then escorted Liv to the front door, where the cashier waited. After I paid, we stepped onto the sunny street.

"Thank you, Thomas. That was a wonderful treat. You made my day," she said, touching my arm.

"My pleasure. May I give you a lift home?"

"No, but thank you. I think it would be wise to walk after scarfing up that Chocolate Epiphany. I walked down, so a walk home would be good."

"May I walk you home, then?"

"I'd like that," she replied. We began walking.

"Thomas, since you decided to come back to Iowa, I'm curious why you didn't move back to Clinton. Home town, all the reasons for returning to something you know." We walked past bungalows and neat, two-story frame houses.

"Most of the guys I hung around with in high school have scattered. One's in New Mexico, several in Chicago, one in Des Moines. This is close enough. I still keep in touch with e-mails."

"Any old flames?"

"Actually, I keep in touch with a couple females I didn't date, just out of friendship. I missed a class reunion a while back and this one girl, woman, was telling the attendees that she'd heard I was dead. No one seemed to be able to refute it, so when I heard about her comments through a rather circuitous route, I sent her a letter informing her that I, despite rumors to the contrary, still existed."

"You and Mark Twain."

"Me and Mark Twain. Good company."

We stopped walking. "This is it!" she said, providing a sweeping gesture toward a small, one-story brick cottage. A white picket fence, a gate and a rose-bedecked arbor over the gate framed the front yard. Flower beds flourished. A neatly edged sidewalk split a recently-mowed, tidy yard. A half-dozen steps led up to a brief porch. Big windows gave the house an open, airy look.

"I like your home," I said.

I wondered if she would invite me in, and felt a sudden tug of fear that she would.

"Thank you for a nice time," Liv said. She extended her hand and I took it.

"And thank you for a nice time, too. Oh, and by the way, I meant to ask you, where do *you* go to church?"

"Here and there as the Spirit moves me. Usually, if Pastor Heisler is preaching, I drop in at Christ the King, up the street, north of here."

"I was there for Hugh Soderstrom's funeral."

"Oh, well, then you know why I'm not enthralled with the good Reverend Doctor VanderKellen. I think he's a priss and a gadfly. He just has an attitude of superiority that I can't abide. I take fleshly pleasure in thinking about how pride goeth before the fall. I am an evil woman and I look forward to his fall. Forgive me."

"Who's Pastor Heisler? Assistant Pastor?"

"Yes, and he's very good. If Carl's not preaching, I go other places, sometimes out of town, combining a Sunday drive with a worship service in a new place."

"I guess I'll need to check out Christ the King, then, when Reverend Heisler is conducting. Well, I'd better let you go. I hope to see you again. Soon."

"Me, too. Have a nice Sunday!" Liv said, giving me a hearty squeeze on the shoulder. "Good muscle there," she said, smiling, bopping my shoulder with her fist. Then she opened the gate and closed it behind her before she headed up her stairs. In the interests of rehab, according to my spiritual advisor, I stole a glance at her lovely backside, waited until she disappeared inside, then turned away.

I still didn't want to go home. And I was suddenly sorry she hadn't invited me in, and almost as suddenly, a little guilty about being sorry she hadn't invited me in. I wondered if I were going to be conflicted about women the rest of my life. I walked back to my truck and drove home.

Chapter 11

"It takes me a long time to lose my temper, but once lost, I could not find it with a dog."
- Mark Twain

Monday morning I slept in, and when I got up, I dressed and took Gotcha on a long, lazy walk on my land. Gotcha, never big on long walks, seemed surprisingly eager.

The woods were cool. The leafy abundance of big trees blunted the heat, and the wind rustling through the treetops improved the comfort index considerably, bringing hope for a mild summer for those given over to delusions. Iowa summers sear the flesh and addle the mind. They'll make a rattlesnake pant.

Gotcha's ears perked up every time she heard the underbrush scurrying of some squirrel, chipmunk, or released Burmese python. She knew she could catch them, but I could tell she also felt it beneath her dignity to chase little woodland creatures. When the wind paused, I heard the sound of an airplane, then a distant truck on a blacktop road, its tires whining on the hot pavement. Sunlight filtered through the green lacework of the treetops, and the earth breathed its timeless fragrance of fertile summer. May slipped into memory on this first day of June.

I thought about Wendy Soderstrom and the transitions before her, a time of sorting through Hugh's clothing to trash it or donate to charity, a time of reading insurance policies and Hugh's will, a time of taking stock of finances with lawyers and accountants. A time of confronting "after," of adding and subtracting, and always coming up empty no matter what the numbers said.

Returning from our walk, I heard the distant and vaguely-familiar rumbling of a big engine. We picked up our pace. I had not had any visitors, in fact, had not invited anyone to stop by. I'd paid for privacy.

The woods thinned near the house, and it was then I spotted the silver Corvette slowly approaching. Larry Soderstrom and I made eye contact through his windshield.

The car stopped, twenty yards away, engine chugging. Gotcha and I stepped out onto the fine white gravel of my drive. I started to say something, but he gunned the engine and the car lunged forward, spewing gravel, snapping pieces of rock into the underbrush behind him.

The car was coming straight toward me, and before I could decide whether to hold my ground and call his bluff or jump out of the way, the 'Vette skidded to a stop, the sharp front edge of the vehicle two feet from my shins. Gotcha scattered back into the edge of the woods, wisely protecting my flank.

I walked around to Larry's window. "I don't remember inviting you out here. This is a private drive."

Larry laughed. "I don't give a crap. I just came out to tell you I don't appreciate you settin' the Sheriff on me."

"What does that mean?"

"It means Payne's lookin' for me, wantin' to ask questions about my brother's accident, and I understand you're the one that told him I know something about it."

"All I said was that I passed a car like this one that day at the farm," I said, leaning forward and patting the hood. "Do you have a reason to be so touchy?"

"You ask a lot of questions about stuff that don't concern you. My advice is to fuck off."

"Larry, I was out at the farm that day. Got there before anyone else except your sister-in-law. Her report did not mention you, so that makes me wonder what you were doing out that way. That is, if it was you."

"Back off, Pops. Stop poking your nose where it don't belong."

"But I'm curious."

Larry scowled and gave me the finger. "I said back off, and you will, if you're as smart as you think you are. I'd hate to see you have an accident."

"My goodness," I said. I fluttered my hands to my face and in my wimpiest voice said, "I do believe I have been *threatened*."

"No threat. Promise. Go watch *Green Acres* reruns. I ain't warnin' you again."

"Why are you so uptight about a few innocent questions here and there? Hiding something?"

Larry's scowl grew into a glare. "Back. The. Fuck. Off. I'm not playin'. I could kill you now."

"Not without a weapon." The blood was pounding in my ears now, but I hoped I looked calm. I didn't expect him to bring up a handgun the size of a kitchen appliance and point it at my chest, but he did.

"I can take you out this minute. And then I'd shoot that ugly, chickenshit dog of yours over in the bushes just for the pleasure of it all."

"Yes, you could, but in the meantime, would you like to put that gun down and step out of your car and see if you can back up your threat without a pistol?"

If anything ignites my temper, it's someone threatening me or my family. And since Gotcha's my only family, Larry Soderstrom had just done it.

"You heard me." He put down the howitzer and jammed the low-slung car into gear, whipping through the turnaround circle. Then he roared away, kicking up chalky dust and loose rocks.

I called Gotcha to me and rubbed her silky ears for a while. Then we went inside. She slurped water and flopped down on the floor in the study and promptly fell asleep, her belly spread on the cool slate, her hind legs splayed out like a frog's, her tongue comfortably flopped out. I fixed myself an egg salad sandwich and a beer and shuffled out onto the deck. I dropped into one of the Adirondack chairs and put my feet up on the matching footstool and ate lunch. It was late afternoon when I finished.

I had other, more nuanced questions to ask Larry if he hadn't left in such a snit, so I decided to take the initiative and go find him without consulting Payne, who would order me not to. Maybe Larry'd ask me to forgive him and we could hug and have a beer together.

Or maybe not. I tidied up, left Gotcha sleeping on the floor, and drove into town.

Business was brisk at The Grain o' Truth with the evening crowd drifting in as the sun slipped lower toward Strawberry Point. I ordered a beer from Rachel and stood sipping until Lunatic was free. The big bartender glided over to me and said, "You can sit down and drink your beer if you want to. I know you respect me, but don't feel as if you have to stand on ceremony, oh favorite of Mi-Ge-Zi."

"What is 'Shlop's' and where is it?"

"Was it something I said?"

"It always is, but that's not the issue." I finished my beer. "I'm looking for Larry Soderstrom, and I thought that might be a good place to start. You mentioned Schlop's as an option for him last time he was here."

"Why are you looking for him?"

"He came out to my place today and pointed a big handgun at me."

Moon looked at me for a full minute without speaking. Then he said, "Larry has a few glaring deficiencies in his repertoire of social skills. Are you going to guide him to remediation?" He turned away for a moment, poured a pitcher of Budweiser, and placed it on the tray of a waitress, a tall bottle-blonde who looked like she had a history. He called her "Trudy." She left with the order and he turned back to me.

"I just want to ask him some questions about the accident at the farm. You know, innocuous stuff designed to precipitate male bonding. This morning he was reluctant to chat."

"Ugh," Moon said, his face impassive. He seemed to be

ruminating about whether or not to give directions. “Okay, white eyes, you can find Shlop's Roadhouse out on High Road. I know, I know,” he said to my raised eyebrows at the name of the address. “Go back outside to Main, head south to Bridge, cross, turn left and follow Iowa Street north out of town. You’ll go by Christ the King Church on your right just before the road curves to the right. A sign after that portrays a biker momma in a suggestive pose on the back of a Harley, and she’s pointing with her bare, well-formed leg down a gravel road flaring off to the left. That’s High Road. Shlop's Roadhouse is the only building on that road which is, prophetically and ironically, a dead end.”

“Thanks. I believe I’ll go take a look. It won’t hurt to ask a few questions.”

“It might. I hope your health insurance is paid up, because Shlop’s can be hazardous to your physiognomy. First sign of trouble, abandon your self-image, desert your sense of courage, and boogie right on out of there.”

“If I need help, I’ll give you a call.”

“No, you won’t.” The Ojibwa turned away to put an order for two pizzas in the oven. He returned and said, “Because under circumstances in which you might need my help, they won’t let you get to a phone.”

“Thanks for the warning.” I paid for my beer and headed for the door.

“Take your cell,” Moon said.

“I hate cell phones,” I said.

I followed Lunatic’s directions and quickly came to the sign he described. The biker momma on the back of the Harley was well endowed, and oblivious to modesty. Her nude leg did indeed point off to the left down a dirt road. The sign said “Shlop's Roadhouse.”

The direction of biker momma’s big toe led me down the road. Half a mile later, I came to Shlop’s. The enterprise was off the road to my right, housed in a modest, unpainted cinderblock building without windows or curb appeal. A variety of neon beer signs, some functioning, were nailed to the outside walls, and a dented steel front door was propped open by a mangy stuffed lynx poised on a chunk of wood, the work of a taxidermist influenced by controlled substances and a hatred for felines. An olive green Army blanket hung over the door, ostensibly to keep out the larger flying insects.

I pulled into the rutted dirt parking lot and parked alongside a half-dozen pickup trucks and a pair of big Harleys.

Shlop's mildly-pitched roof was covered with tarpaper and randomly placed tires to keep the wind from peeling it off. Because of the fetching exterior, I felt compelled to go inside, anxious to see whether the ferns were artificial, if the sushi was any good, and whether the string quartet approached my lofty standards.

I had seen similar places, some even less sophisticated, but that had been decades ago and not in the United States. Providence suggested I consider my next step.

"You're too old for this kind of place," I said out loud. I felt a tug in my gut as I stepped out of the truck, locked it, dumped the keys in my pocket, and strode toward the droopy Army blanket.

Inside, I paused, allowing my eyes and nose to adjust to the dark and the stink of stale beer and cigarette smoke. Directly across from me a long bar backed by a Dutch door led into a well-lit kitchen. Booths lined the walls, and a dozen or so Formica-topped tables with molded plastic aqua and orange chairs were scattered about. A pool table and two poker tables were set off to the side. No poker players yet, but two men were shooting pool. The sound of the balls clicking was nearly drowned out by the juke box, where Willie was singing about someone always being on his mind. The floor was filthy linoleum of no discernible color or pattern, peeled back in some places and chipped away in others.

The lighting came from bare blue or red light bulbs screwed into cheap metal fixtures ringing the walls. Overhead, stained ceiling tiles sagged, pink fiberglass oozing out around the edges. Wiggly strips of flypaper, displaying their catch, hung from the ceiling tiles' support runners.

A handful of men inhabited the bar, none of them Larry Soderstrom. A female stood behind the bar. At first glance, she looked like Cher on Human Growth Hormone, except she had silver hair. Maybe a wig.

The men were all ages, grouped in two's and three's and, without exception, fat. None of them had sleeves on their shirts, and they looked like beached fish as the pale skin of their round faces and plump arms reflected the lights. Three women, white trash wannabes, distributed themselves among the groups of men. Two lone drinkers occupied opposite ends of the bar. Generally speaking, the men in the establishment were dressed like bikers, bubbas, and bums. The women had "turbo slut" written all over them.

I walked up to the bar, every eye in the joint on me. I told Cher I'd like a beer. She was adorned in a short pink tank top without the benefit of an appropriate undergarment, and low-slung, greasy black jeans. Her belly was bare, and a color tattoo of a large, bloodshot eyeball surrounded her navel. Because of her lack of abdominal definition, the eye looked puffy and sore, as if it had been in a fight. I wondered if it would follow me around the room.

She shoved a cold bottle of Schlitz at me, no glass. I said, "Ah, my beverage of choice. You must be clairvoyant."

"No, I ain't," she snapped, tilting her head back and running her hands through her hair. "This color's natcherl."

"Forgive me," I said, taking the beer and giving her a fiver, which she kept. I realized that Shlop's reminded me of a bar I had frequented in the Philippines, when I was stationed Temporary Duty at Clark Air Base a long time ago. A rat had run across the bar then, spilling my beer into my lap. A friend grabbed the rat as it scampered by, bit off its head, spit it out, then threw the headless corpse of the rodent against the mirror behind the bar and snapped at the astonished barkeep, "You need to clean up this place!" I wished that same buddy were with me right now, but he had disappeared into Costa Rica ten years ago.

"Would you like a menu?" the silver-maned bartender asked sweetly. I nodded. She turned away.

I took a pull from the sweaty bottle and had barely swallowed when two of the men arose from their tables and approached. My heartbeat picked up. *You really are too old for this*, I reminded myself.

When the men reached me, one sat on the stool to my right, and the other took up residence immediately to my left. Each leaned a little toward me, crowding in. I felt like a Dodge Neon between a pair of gravel trucks.

"Evening, gentlemen. How ya doin'?" I asked.

The men said nothing. They just swished the beer around in their bottles and stared at me. They smelled bad and their breath was worse.

"You're that new guy, ain'tcha?" the lady behind the bar said, handing me a menu and hooking her thumbs into the empty belt loops of her low riding jeans.

"At my age, how new could I be?" I smiled. They didn't. Advantage, regular patrons. "My name's Thomas O'Shea, Miss…?"

"Steele, with an 'e'," she said. "First name's 'Bunza' with a 'z'."

"But her name ain't none a your business, bub," the land mass to my right said. He did not sound as if he were trying to get to know me or manifest, in any way, the gift of hospitality. In fact, I thought with some alarm, he sounded a little adversarial. I was becoming less joyful by the minute.

On the left, a voice from an old mine shaft, said, "What else you wanna know, slick?"

I took another slug of Schlitz, swallowed, not tasting it. "Actually, I was wondering if you could tell me where I could find Larry Soderstrom. He came over to my house this afternoon, but didn't stay for the lovely English teatime I had prepared. I was wondering if I had done something wrong, of if he feared a lack of marmalade for the crumpets."

"You ought not be askin' questions 'bout Larry," Mineshaft said.

"So, where can I find him?"

"That's your last question for the evenin'," the man on the right said, drawing himself up and turning slowly toward me.

Ever the wiseass, I said, "Wanna bet?" and it began.

Chapter 12

"You only go around once in life,
So grab for all the gusto you can."
- retro Schlitz Beer commercial

Mineshaft grabbed my shoulder, spinning me so that we were facing each other. Figuring his move wasn't preparation for a hug, I called on dormant skills to bail me out.

I grabbed the neck of my own beer and backhanded the bottle across the nose of the landmass behind me. Shards of glass and beer bounced off the man's face as he yelped in pain and surprise. He slipped halfway off his stool, spurting blood from his broken nose and his eyebrows. He moaned and brought both hands to his face. This took maybe two seconds.

I ducked and grabbed the long neck of my victim's bottle, still on the bar, and brought it down as hard as I could, tomahawk style, on the bleeding man's forehead. The bottle exploded in beerspray and bloodsplatter. Sometimes they don't break, especially if they have beer in them. It's not like in the movies.

He dropped to the floor, loose-limbed and slack, as if his muscles had gone liquid. The fallen man's pal clamped onto me from behind in a sweaty, smelly bear hug, pinning my arms to my sides. I snapped my head back to pop him in the nose, but the man's face was buried in my back above the shoulder blades. Mineshaft grunted, his breath bad enough to divert a comet. I wondered about his stamina. Instant power, yes; continued power, maybe not. I felt elated over being able to even up the sides so quickly, at the same time wondering if the establishment's habitués would provide them reinforcements.

I twisted hard to my left to try to break free. My lower left arm was now pressed against Mineshaft's soft, fat abdomen, so I could rotate my hand against the flab until I acquired a significant grip on the biker's future offspring. Then I did my best to make jelly of his jujubes.

The bearhugger, head buried between my shoulders, screamed something unintelligible, but he did not let go. He did let up a little. Why the man continued with his approach, I will never know, but his resolve chipped away at my confidence. Was I dealing with some kind of mutant? The need for the biker to escape my grip was obvious, but he did not make any attempt.

Why do people loop poisonous snakes around their necks, tease sharks from flimsy aluminum cages, and goad 400-pound tigers in zoos? My best guess is stupidity. I squeezed again, focusing all my strength into my left hand, determined to overcome stupidity with agony. It had to work. And it did.

The man's grunts shifted into a truly impressive single-note shriek, which reached an altitude that, frankly, surprised me, not to mention the patrons of Shlop's Roadhouse. Mineshaft let go and doubled over, covering his crotch with both hands. This, of course, left me free to retaliate. In anger, I might add.

I took his head in both my hands to steady him, pulled down hard, and brought my knee up into his face. I let go as I connected, allowing him to drop to the floor as his friend had, helplessly woozy.

Fueled with righteous indignation, I considered challenging anyone else in the place to come forward, but wisdom overcame adrenalin. I was breathing hard, and I felt ashamed about it, but did not notice anyone who looked ready to tease me about being out of shape. I leaned against the bar and said, "Bunza, may I have another bottle of Schlitz, please?"

No one moved. No one laughed. They went back to whatever they had been doing before the battle. Just another night at Shlop's?

Miss Steele silently pushed toward me the menu already on the bar, a laminated and folded sheet with a cover displaying a smaller version of the motorcycle momma road sign. Apparently the publicist for Shlop's Roadhouse was up to speed on the importance of consistency in advertising.

I opened the menu. Shlop's offered barbequed beef, pork and chicken; burgers; fried fish; chicken fingers; buffalo wings; fries; pizza with a variety of toppings; fried cheese; chili, and a plethora of additional treats, mostly fried. Shlop's also offered domestic and imported beers, soft drinks, and wine coolers.

"Surprised, ain'tcha?" Bunza said, smiling.

"Yes," I said, shaking off the beads of beer scattered across the menu. "I thought people just knew what you had, and then ordered."

"Most do, but you're a newby. What'll it be, then?"

I heard a noise behind me, glanced back at the two breathing throw rugs.

"They won't bother you again. Shlop don't allow no fightin' in here."

"So, what was that that I just experienced?"

"Well, there are exceptions, but that there you had was more of a tussle, not a real fight. Normally, Bob and Ray are fine. I don't know what got into 'em. Most fightin' goes on outside or down the end of the road by the dumpsters, and they know it. I expect them to just get up and leave soon's they able. Crystal!" Bunza shouted. I jumped a foot, the decibel level of her voice capable of penetrating Cheyenne Mountain during an alert. And from such a petite thing, too.

A girl emerged, skinny, early twenties with no hips or confidence, but well-scrubbed with intelligent eyes peering out from under her sprayed-in-place carbon-black hair. She looked like one of the group home kids Karen and I once worked with in western North Carolina, only older, abused and neglected, smacked around and ridiculed, dropped out and skill-free and ready to take on the world, and not all that surprised, just sullen and bitter, when the world defeated them, taking away their dreams of a double-wide, a Trans Am, and a satellite dish all financed by minimum wage lifetime jobs.

"Clean up the mess, willya, hon?" Bunza said sweetly, her voice soft and pleasant in direct contrast to the phlegm-lifting shout from mere seconds earlier.

Crystal nodded and left and returned with a broom, a dustpan, and several big, heavy rags, which took care of the majority of the mess. She disappeared and appeared again with a damp mop that completed the job after she rolled each of the groaning men a couple of rotations away from their point of impact. The floor that resulted from Crystal's efforts was several shades lighter than the floor around it.

"Now she's going to have to mop the whole thing at quitting time, just to make it all the same shade," I said.

"You got that right, cutie," said Bunza. "But that's okay, because we ain't done the whole floor since Reagan was president."

At that point, Landmass sat up on the floor, one leg straight out in front of him, the other bent at the knee. He was hugging the bent knee. Then he touched his face and felt the blood and looked at his shirt and looked at his hand and then glanced around until he saw me. There was no fight in his face, only swelling and blood and little pieces of glass. There was, however, sudden recollection, and fear.

He rolled to his hands and knees, grunting, staggered to his feet one leg at a time, keeping an eye on me as if I were going to whale into him again. He lurched over to his friend and began dragging Mineshaft out of the bar, backing his way out until they disappeared through the army blanket.

"Now what will it be?" Bunza asked, wiggling her eyebrows in a manner that I feared was intended to be seductive.

I glanced around Shlop's while I considered my order. Maybe Larry would show up. I looked back at Bunza and ordered fried mozzarella sticks and chicken fingers with fries. And another beer.

"No charge on the Schlitz," Bunza said, "on account of

environmental issues for which we accept limited responsibility." She smiled sweetly, then turned and shouted through the half-door that led to the kitchen, "Ordera fried sticks and hendigits, Max!"

She turned back to me. "Anything else?"

"Hendigits?"

She looked sheepish and just shrugged her shoulders in response. "Shlop's word."

I said, "Bunza, do you know where I could find Larry Soderstrom? Does he come in here? If he does, are there any nights in particular that one could count on him appearing? Where does he live if I can't find him elsewhere?"

"You ask a lot of questions."

"I have a thirst for knowledge."

"You talk funny, too."

"A symptom of the aforementioned affliction."

Bunza laughed and shook her head, arching her back. Her nipples strained against her pink tank top like living Binkies. I averted my gaze after I'd seen enough. She said, "Any other questions?"

"You haven't answered my first batch." Outside, the reverb of a big bike cranked up and then another engine throbbed into life. Faint, shouted threats followed, then revving of engines, followed by fading motorcycle noise.

Bunza said, "When I have all your questions, I'll think about 'em and answer those what I can."

"Two last questions before you make your selections," I said. "Who is 'Shlop'? And, is 'Bunza Steele' your real name?"

She squealed with delight, rolled her eyes and clapped her hands and I, ever victim to her vocal stimuli, jumped again. I could not get any more used to her fortissimo than I could grow comfy with a taser going off in my Fruit of the Looms.

"I *knew* you'd ask me that question!" she chortled in triumph. "Everbuddy does."

She placed her hands palms down in front of her on the bar as if to calm herself. "My birth name was 'Brandy Steele' with an 'e,' but after I got older and bigger and I got into workin' out, Shlop said

I should legally change my name to 'Bunza' Steele, because they are. See?" Stepping back from the bar, she turned around. Over her shoulder she said, "I'm wearin' a thong so's not to break up the picture."

Her slick Levi's were as one with her epidermis. Bunza looked over her shoulder at me and moved from one foot to the other, allowing the opportunity to see how a butt changes shape. She then stood flat-footed, feet a little apart, and flexed her gluteus maximus *en extremis*. They truly appeared to be buns of steel, or at least reinforced aluminum.

"So," she said happily, turning around to face me, "Shlop got his lawyer to change my name, and he did it 'pro boner,' which means 'for free,' and that should answer one of your questions, shouldn't it?" She looked very pleased with herself, and I wondered how many times she had gone through her routine for others. Not that I was jealous.

"My name change was done so I would have somethin' unique when I start rasslin' pro, with Shlop as my manager, of course."

"Of course."

"I've been pumpin' iron and Shlop's been showin' me some holds, and when I save up enough, I'll be going down to Atlanta to rasslin' school to get me goin'. Also," she said, acting as coy as her profession, environment, and appearance would allow, "I might be goin' to medical school to be a brain surgeon. Shlop says that women what use their figures in the entertainment industry sell more tickets if they're *intellectural*," she said, emphasizing the word she pronounced imperfectly to prove that she was. "That's why strippers who go to law school get more Franklins pushed into their panties."

Properly educated, I breathed deeply, relieved when my order showed up on the cook's counter. Bunza fetched it and brought it over. It actually looked well prepared. I began to eat.

I dipped a mozzarella stick into the little bowl of sauce and took a bite. It was good. Greasy. Bunza said, "I don't know where Larry lives, but he comes in here several nights in a row, sometimes by hisself, sometimes with his friends, and sometimes with some of the wildest-lookin' women I ever seen."

She leaned over the bar in a confidential pose when she told me about the women. When she tipped forward she displayed a cleavage that might have led to another name change, but after a quick glance downward, I gritted my teeth and made eye contact.

"So, when was the last time he was here?" I asked.

"Lunchtime."

"Today? He was in here for lunch today?"

I finished the cheese sticks, asked her where Larry lived. The best she could do was, "Somewhere out in the country in a fancy place," and wave toward the door. The jukebox cranked up. Some guy was singing about keeping his six-pack cold by putting it next to his ex-wife's heart.

She pushed off to wait on some customers who had drifted in. I ate my hendigits and shot a couple of games of pool by myself. When two more hours had gone by without Larry showing, I bade good night to Bunza Steele and left.

I felt a little better about being productive. I had been slothful lately, but after my meeting with Larry and my evening at Shlop's, I was making better use of my time. Would God be proud of me? Would Ernie? Karen?

For the first time in a long while, I just wanted to go home and go to bed. So I did, knowing I'd be sore in the morning. A tussle can do that to you.

Chapter 13

"Do not envy a man of violence, and do not choose any of his ways. For the crooked man is an abomination to the Lord; but He is intimate with the upright."
- Proverbs 3: 31-32

My evening at Schlop's Roadhouse left me introspective—something I try to avoid. What was bothering me was that about halfway through the brawl I realized I was enjoying it. The violence is coming back to me, and I am embracing it. And Schlop's wasn't the first time since I'd lost my family, either.

On my way out of Georgia, heading for Iowa, months after the accident that took my family, and just as I was being sucked into Atlanta traffic on I-75/I-85, a kid in a red pickup truck pulled even with me, mouthed an obscenity, and cut in front of me. We nearly collided, but I stomped the brakes, swerved briefly on squealing tires, and threw black smoke from the rear of my vehicle. I dropped in behind the kid as traffic behind me scattered like illegals during an ICE raid.

The kid, blonde with a wispy beard, wore a black knit cap pulled low despite the warm spring day, and a black tank top over a skinny upper body. He flipped me off again and laughed as he surged ahead in the south Atlanta traffic. One of his bumper stickers suggested what his fellow motorists could do if they didn't like his driving, and the other was an epithet directed at people not from the South. That would be me.

When the red truck exited, so did I.

I followed him down the ramp feeding into the central city, the driver apparently unaware he was being tailed. I trailed the pickup truck into a parking garage near Underground Atlanta, and took a meter stub from the machine. The red truck curled on up to the top level, from cool shadows into warm sunlight. Gotcha was up, wide awake from the turn signals and the truck's slow movement, eagerly looking out the window.

Now that there were just the two of us on the rooftop, the kid stabbed glances at his rearview mirror as he parked bumper against a wall. I pulled in behind him and blocked his truck, jumped out and strode up to him. He looked irritated, opening his door and starting to get out, fearless facing the old guy. "What's your problem, dude?"

"Your bad driving and worse manners. Your obscene bumper stickers. You." I was trembling, but my voice was low and calm. I knew better ways.

"Up yours," the kid said, starting to get out.

I struck quickly, palm smacking hard into the kid's forehead, snapping his head back and sitting him down. He blinked, muttered a curse, started out again, contempt on his face. Ready to go, box cutter in hand.

I struck again, palm lower this time, flush on the bridge of his nose. A crack and sudden rush of blood followed. He slumped, blood streaming down his chin onto his tank top, his lap. The box cutter was not in his hand anymore.

"Oh shit!" he said. "You busted my nose!"

I leaned forward, hands on knees, my face one foot from his. "Be courteous in traffic from now on, and remove those bumper stickers."

The kid looked at me, fear was in his face. I liked that. He said nothing at first, then muttered, his voice nasal and wet, "You're nuts, man."

"Don't forget what I said." I pulled back my hand, he flinched, ducked back.

I turned, got in my truck, cruised down to the street, paid the minimum fee, and eased back into traffic. I turned onto Peachtree Street until I found an on-ramp, and then once again streamed into northbound interstate traffic, moving fast.

And that was that. I thought it was a one-time thing. Until my set-to at Schlop's.

Now, the morning after my tussle I was hurting, my ribs in particular. And I had slivers of glass in my hands, so I ran cold water in the sink, dumped in ice, and soaked one hand at a time, drawing the glass toward the surface, removing the slivers with tweezers.

After a shower, I took stock of my situation. Sure, I had stumbled onto a suspicious death, raised a few questions here and there, experienced a death threat, and been assaulted in a bar. It was the Chinese curse: "May you live in interesting times." But it had to stop, and the best way to do that was to butt out and let Sheriff Payne do his job. I want peace and privacy.

I stayed home more, ran extra miles and worked out regularly at Mulehoff's. I lunched now and then at The Grain. I called Payne randomly and left messages, nagging about Larry. The few times he returned my calls, he always said, "I'm working on it, Mr. O'Shea, now leave me, and it, alone." And so it went.

Every single day I thought about calling Liv Olson. But I did not.

Gotcha and I strolled in the woods in the cool of the mornings after my runs, enjoying the lay of our land. We took breakfast on the deck and messed around with a tennis ball—a boy and his dog. Gotcha likes to pin a tennis ball in her front paws, then get a grip with her teeth on the cover somehow, and peel it off. Scary when you think if you were someone she didn't like and she had you down between her paws.

If I didn't go down to Moon's place for lunch and my five-beer limit (drinking a six-pack might signal a problem), I'd fix myself something at home, have a few cold ones, nap, get up and read for a few hours. Maybe watch some television, and call it a night. Over the next two weeks I bought groceries a couple of times, stocked my pantry, stopped by the bank. Saw Arvid collapsed on his front steps and honked (he did not respond), and worked out hard eight times.

I did not see Larry. Neither did Payne. Once, in the evening and on impulse, I drove out to Schlop's and asked Bunza if she had seen him, and she said he had been in around midnight the night before with a "funky looking girl, no more'n fourteen."

One night I couldn't sleep. I watched the Red Sox edge the Royals in ten innings in Kansas City, then *Baseball Tonight* on ESPN, and still I wasn't sleepy. So I gave Gotcha a giant Milk-Bone and drove into town. It was midnight. It was something to do.

I crossed the double arched limestone bridge and parked in front of Bloom's Bistro, closed down for the night. I began walking, looking in the windows of the shops there on the east side of the Whitetail River. After a while, I crossed over the river and strolled through old, established neighborhoods nestled in darkness among big, leafy trees, looking at houses and wondering what the people inside were like. Did they love each other? Did they harbor petty offenses? Were they happy? Did they have nightmares?

Walking the silent streets after dark in a small town is one of life's great therapies. There is time for peaceful reflection, or just simple strolling without worrying about being mugged. I finished my walk sometime after one. I went home and slept soundly.

Three nights later, again unable to sleep, I hung out in The Grain, nursing beers and chatting with Horace until he left. Now, just past Last Call, it was only me, an older couple finishing off a pitcher, Rachel, Moon, and a couple of men I didn't recognize.

The big Indian beckoned me over to the bar. "You seem to be of great interest to those guys at the table by the front door."

I turned and looked. The two men looked down and began talking.

"They were here last night, too, and the night before. Seemed to be waiting for someone, sipping their beer and looking up every time someone came in the front door. When you came in tonight they quit looking."

"If they were sexy women, I could understand." I rotated part way back so I could talk with Moon while checking out the strangers. One man was in his 20's, chunky build, beer gut, camo t-shirt. His matching pants were the kind with big pockets on the sides of the legs so, if he wanted, he could quickly reach in there for a ham sandwich or a Snickers. He had curly dark hair and needed a shave. The grunge look had moved on and left him behind. I thought of him as Porky.

His thirty-something pal looked tall even when sitting down. He wore Levi's and an orange Miami Dolphins t-shirt. His head was shaved. So was his face. He looked at me with small eyes over a nose that had been broken at least once. He looked away.

I finished my beer, paid up. "Keep an eye out, Thomas," Moon said.

"Sounds painful," I replied, leaving. The two men made a point not to look at me as I left.

I still wasn't tired so a stroll by the river seemed in order. I toodled down the street and started across the bridge, drawn by the soft shushing of water slipping over the spillway. I was just about midpoint when a car approached from behind. I turned and saw a black Jeep Cherokee stop before crossing. Someone got out and slammed the door shut. It sounded loud over the black water in the quiet night. Peculiar place to get out.

It was Porky. He began walking toward me. The Jeep gunned across the bridge, passing me as I jumped over the curb onto the crosswalk to keep from being run down. It was Flipper, grinning, and not a pleasant grin. He pulled over across the river, got out, and deliberately closed his door. He commenced strolling back across the bridge toward his companion, toward me. My scientific mind calculated stimuli, and I concluded that this might not turn out well.

What was it about this town?

When they were each about fifteen feet away, they stopped. Porky was rocking back and forth on the balls of his feet. He displayed a white, doughy belly not completely covered by his camouflage t-shirt. Why have a six-pack when a pony keg will do?

The other man was, as I suspected, maybe six-four, lean. His broken nose suggested he might be a sucker for a left hook. He smacked his right fist into his left palm, over and over.

Of course, I trembled.

I wished I could just go home, absorb a couple of cold Coronas, use my Jennaire to grill a pair of kolbasi, slather horseradish mustard on them, catch the West Coast baseball scores, and go to bed.

"We're gonna kill you," Porky said.

"That's against the law," I said.

"Fuck you," he said.

Slowly filling with adrenalin and rage and welcoming both again, I said, "You might be more convincing if you were in better shape. And if you weren't so stupid. If you want to sneak up on someone after dark, black is the preferred color of professionals, but your white belly would give you away." I wanted to stall the inevitable, yet, at the same time, provoke them. Make them forget their plan. Make them make mistakes. Maybe make them teedle in their panties and run away. Maybe not.

Flipper, the tall guy, said, "Neither one of us needs to sneak up on you. We gotcha without it. And why aren't you afraid of *me*? You should be."

I turned and looked at him. "I'm not afraid of you because you're with him. Look, I got about a hundred and sixty bucks I can give you now and save us both unnecessary pain. My ego is not tied up in this. I just wanted to grab a little air and watch the river go by."

"You're gonna wish you could grab a little air in about five minutes. It's gonna be mighty hard to come by," Flipper said, "with a knife in your ribs."

"We're supposed to take you out," Porky said. Flipper told him to keep his stupid mouth shut.

"It's the truth, and it don't matter if he knows it 'cuz he's gonna be dead," Porky whined.

Flipper shrugged his shoulders and spoke the generic, "Whatever." And then he produced a knife that looked like it would be useful if one were preparing to skin a wooly mammoth.

He said, "You know, he's right, it don't matter what you know 'cuz you're gonna be fish food. The two guys who jumped you at that bar a while back'll be blamed for your death because you whupped their sorry butts and they wanted revenge. It's all pretty simple. And your hunnerd and sixty bucks is gonna be ours anyway."

I realized they were serious. *What did I ever do to them?* I wondered, and how did they know about the scene at Shlop's? I asked them.

"We got paid to know things, paid to take you out," Flipper said.

"Satan never sleeps," I said.

"I don't know about that," he said, "but you can ask him yourself because in a few minutes you're gonna get to meet him."

"No, I won't. God loves me."

"God ain't gonna be no use to you, and you ain't goin' nowhere, 'cept into the river, dead," Porky said.

Okey-dokey, I thought. *If that's the way you want it.* I began drawing into myself. "In that case, I feel sorry for you two. Overmatched, and you don't even know it." Truth to power. A little psy-ops.

Porky laughed. "That's rich. You the one's gonna die right now, man, 'cuz you ain't dealin' with a coupla Rockbluff boys no more."

Where was Sheriff Payne when I really needed him? "Oh, so you're hired muscle, maybe from as far away as Dubuque?" I could tell by their reaction that I had guessed right. "So why are you going to kill me?"

"You're too damn nosey, pal," Flipper said, "You might screw up a good thing."

"You'll never get away with this. Use your coconuts. There's probably eight people watching us from behind curtains and writing down your license number. The law should show up at any moment, and even if they don't, you won't get out of the county before you get stopped and locked up."

"You wish," Porky said. "Jeep ain't got no plates, ain't nobody watchin' from no windows, the cops are someplace else, and you'll be dead and unable to identify us."

"Sounds like point-counterpoint," I said, fighting back the funny taste in my mouth. I hate it when that happens. Rambo would be ashamed of me.

Flipper came forward, closing in. Porky took the cue and then they rushed me.

Rage came like a gift, and I cheered its arrival. My best chance to survive was to focus on the tougher guy first. Break him down, demoralize the other.

I faced the tall man. He was wearing running shoes, so when he closed and reached for me, I grabbed his knife hand, pushing his arm up and away from me. I spun sideways, ducked low, and stomped down viciously with my heel on his instep, breaking his foot. He shrieked, released the knife, and fell. I kicked the knife and it skittered away.

I dropped to my knees and thrust my right hand at the man's face, digging my thumb into one eye and my middle finger into the other. Then I wrenched hard. One eyeball prolapsed immediately. The other eye squished. This took just seconds. He went down, moaning.

Porky lumbered up behind me, so I went flat and rolled. He tripped over me, grabbing thin air and cursing, falling to the street, scrambling up and coming back at me fast. I came to my feet and chopped at his windpipe and missed, striking his cheekbone. He pivoted and kicked me hard in the face and I realized I had made an amateur's mistake—underestimating my opponent. My glasses flew off. For a person with 20/120 uncorrected vision, it was a fate worse than being stabbed.

I ducked away from a second kick. My nose was numb and tingly and runny with blood. Some teeth felt loose. Without my glasses, my vision was blurred. But my fury was focused.

Porky blindly charged again, cursing. But he never reached me. He seemed to rise up into the air, like Enoch, without moving a muscle. *What?* I figured God had come to my aid, then I realized it was just some big person. I squinted in the dark and saw that that someone had him by the crotch and throat and was lifting him overhead, then slamming him sideways on the stone parapet, driving him into the rock.

I heard ribs break and rejoiced as the man cried out in agony. Then, in the distance, I heard sirens. Too soon. There was still much to do.

I looked for my helper, saw him loping back across the bridge to the east side of the river, heading up the street and into the shadows. I turned back to Porky, struggling to his feet, all humped over, protecting his broken ribs. I walked up to him, spun sideways, and kicked in the outside of the man's left knee. Porky went down again, screaming, grabbing at his knee.

The sirens were much closer now on the west side of the river, so I hurried and grabbed my portly assailant by his greasy hair and bounced his face off the side of the parapet and released him, now unconscious, to the sidewalk.

His buddy was muttering incoherently, and when I turned to see why, I noticed him trying to reposition his eyeball back into the socket. "You should wash your hands first," I said. He fingered his dangling orb, confused, listening, afraid. Sightless, he turned his face in my direction.

I walked over, picked him up by the back of his Dolphins shirt and the back of his jeans, and staggered to the side of the bridge. "You need to cool off," I said, and dumped him into the Whitetail River. I'm a catch-and-release guy. Environmentally sensitive. Green to the core.

He screamed on the way down, splashed loudly, and then began flailing at the water. I shambled over to Porky, picked him up, hoisted him at arms' length overhead and, staggering under his weight, started for the side of the bridge.

My uncorrected vision identified Sheriff Payne walking quickly toward me, a backdrop of flashing blue lights jazzing the night. "Better not, O'Shea," he said. I stopped, breathing hard, strength starting to desert me, arms quivering. "Set him down," Payne said. I dropped the thug with a thud. Payne turned toward the patrol cars and made a gesture with his hand across his throat and the sirens stopped.

I shuffled back to where I thought my glasses might be, afraid I'd never find them in the dark. But a bit of flash from the cop cars glinted bright blue off titanium frames. I picked them up. Without them, there would be no point in life. How would I find the beer? I slipped them on and looked in the direction my helper had run. Nothing but empty street. I returned to the company of the constable.

"Well," I said in a thin Irish brogue, breathing hard, "if it isn't himself, the Sheriff of the City and County of Rockbluff, come to converse. And what brings you out this fine evenin', sir?"

I was panting, wanting to put my hands on my knees for a while and recover, embarrassed again by my lack of conditioning but feeling good about my strength. I touched fingers to face and felt stickiness. I did it again, unable to keep my fingers away.

Payne looked at me, strode to the side of the bridge, and shouted directions to officers to get downstream and recover Flipper before he drowned. EMS arrived and drove onto the bridge. I didn't recognize one of the men, but I exchanged looks with Schumacher. He gave a little half-grin and went to work. They removed Porky and roared away, sirens starting up again, a chorus from chaos.

Now, shouts from the spillway. Flashlights stabbing tubes of light into the night. Deputies splashing, retrieving the other punk and getting him into another EMS vehicle. It hurried off, slinging red light on dark buildings, siren piercing the peace. The Sheriff looked at me. "You've been busy this evening."

"Idle hands are the devil's workshop." My fingers found my face again.

"I wouldn't want you to be bored. You might get into mischief," Payne said. "Let me take a look at your face."

I held up a hand. "My face is fine, given my genetics and age."

"It doesn't look so fine to me."

"*Ad hominem* attacks will get you nowhere."

"Where you need to go is Rockbluff Community Hospital. Know where to find it? Maybe I should drive you."

"Thanks, but I'll pass. Besides, if it gets out that I go running for help every time I get a boo-boo, I could be in trouble. Someone might try to pick on me."

"Since you're in such fine fettle, then, perhaps you can answer a few questions," the Sheriff said, leaning against the side of the stone bridge, "like, what happened here? You better have a good reason for what you did to these poor tourists."

"What's a 'fettle'? And is there such a thing as a 'poor' one?"

Payne gave me a look, slowly shaking his head.

I told him what happened. I stopped puffing and felt better about that. "By the way, Sheriff, where were you all night? I've been walking the streets hoping I'd see you so I could find out if you ever check your messages."

Payne straightened, stretched, looked up and down the river. "I got called over to the hospital to check on an alleged rape victim. Woman not from around here, shook up, tearing at her clothes, begging for a shower. We offered, she declined. Finally calmed down. They're keeping her overnight for observation. Questions in the morning.

"As for you, some citizen called me on my beeper and said there was trouble on the bridge. Did these boys tell you why you ticked them off? I'd like to know," he said. "Professional curiosity."

"These wimps told me I've been asking too many questions, that I might screw up a good thing, that someone hired them to shut me up. Say!" I said, snapping my fingers, "do you suppose Larry might know who's behind this?"

"Just because they said they were hired to kill you, and then they tried to kill you doesn't mean Larry hired them, necessarily."

"There must be an element of jest in there somewhere. Maybe even a fettle."

It was quiet now above the river, except for the soft tumbling of water over the spillway. No cars, no shoppers, no activity except for the two of us on the bridge. A very pleasant evening if you factor out the attempt on my life, but who am I to be picky?

Payne said, "Yeah, I'm kidding. But these guys on the bridge tonight, you say you've never seen them before?"

"I've seen the type. Semi-pro muscle."

"I think you surprised them. They obviously underestimated you. O'Shea, you're something, a 'type,' your word, my pappy talked about when he regaled me with stories about tough guys."

"What type is that? Handsome, erudite, chick magnet?" My mouth and lips and nose throbbed; my face felt enormous.

"You're a 'manhandler,' and I don't mean that soup they used to advertise on television. You must have been something twenty years ago. I saw the tail end of your fight here tonight, and you manhandled those two guys, throwing them around, just flat out wreaking havoc. There's lots of tough guys in this world, but you have a style."

"I had help, Sheriff."

"And who would that be?"

"God," I said, wondering about the man on the bridge with me, now gone, "and to Him be the glory. And please call me Thomas."

"Can't argue with that, Thomas. But besides your hand-to-hand combat skills, I noticed that you can take a shot and not be deterred."

"I try to avoid those, but I am getting older. Diminished skills."

"So," Payne said, leaning forward and dropping his voice conspiratorially, "why didn't you *kill* them?"

I smiled and it hurt. "The Good Book says thou shalt not kill. But it doesn't say thou shalt not maim. There's such a thing as righteous anger. I prevented those guys from committing murder. Mine. It's a ministry I have just begun here in Rockbluff, Aggravated Assault Capital of the Midwest."

"Well, it has been since you arrived," Payne said. He started to say something else, but his pager went off. He retrieved the number, strode a few yards to the far side of the bridge, reached into his cruiser, made a call. Then he walked back to me.

"Larry called to confess, right?"

"No, that was the hospital. The 'rape' victim waited until I was gone, then gathered up her things, walked briskly and with composure out of the hospital, flashed the bird to everyone on the graveyard shift, and disappeared into the night."

"Those guys are smarter than I thought. The tall one did say you guys were someplace else."

"You're a paranoid schizophrenic, Mr. O'Shea, but maybe not this time."

"Sheriff," I said, and he held up his hand. I stopped.

"Call me Harmon."

"Harmon, let's face this heavy dose of circumstantial evidence. In addition to what I've already related, these goons tonight told me they were going to kill me and a couple of guys from Schlop's were being set up to take the fall."

Payne interrupted. "I know about your fight at Schlop's."

"I'm sure you do. Small town. Anyway, now this 'rape' victim makes it obvious. I think you'll get more information from these guys when you talk to them in the morning. By the way, you got guards posted to keep these two safe? I don't think their boss would like them being in custody, and with your waterboarding skills, it could get dicey when they spill their guts and tell you who paid them."

"I've ordered a couple of auxiliary deputies at the hospital, each with a sidearm and a shotgun. I'm also putting out an APB on Larry. In the meantime, I'll see about getting a search warrant for his place and revisit the scene of Hugh's accident. When I have the paperwork in hand, I'll give you a call. This is beginning to smell to high heaven. Now, why don't you get your non-injuries checked out and go home?"

"I'll go home right now if it's all the same." I resisted the urge to touch my face. "By the way, there's a knife back there somewhere on the bridge. Theirs. You might want it for that evidence thingy we talked about over lunch."

Payne walked slowly back along the bridge, paused, then bent over and using two fingers, picked up the knife. He came back, showed it to me. Hunting knife. Seven inch blade, surgical steel. Bone handle. Lots of those around.

"One other thing," Payne said as we walked off the bridge together to his car.

"And that is?"

"You got any weapons, any firearms?"

"Nothing serious any more, just a Stevens .410-.22 over-and-under. From my innocent boyhood, a gift from my father for my twelfth birthday."

"I'd load it and keep it handy. Since the semi-pro muscle failed, maybe their employer will hire someone who provides full-time discouragement. If Larry's the employer, he will be able to tell them where you live."

"And where I live is where I'm going. Good night."

"If you'd like to go with me when I take a look at Larry's house, you're welcome, but only as an observer. I don't expect to find anything I can use in court, but I might stumble onto something else. Even a blind pig finds an occasional acorn."

"Good luck," I smiled a little, turning away to study the river so the Sheriff wouldn't see my pain.

"You, too." I heard him get into his car. The cruiser pulled away. During our conversation someone had taken away my sparring partners' Jeep.

I watched and listened to the black water slip smoothly over the spillway as it had for well over a century. I wanted to put my face in the cool water for a while. Bits of light danced on the smooth surface, and it was beautiful. I walked off the bridge, retrieved my truck, and drove home. There were no other vehicles on the road.

Gotcha was happy to see me, begging for a Milk-Bone. I gave it to her, then she stood at the door until I let her out. In a minute she was ready to come in. She likes air conditioning. She flopped down on her tuffet on the floor at the foot of the bed. She does a stellar job of taking frequent naps so as not to be too tired to sleep when it's time to go to bed for the night. The dog is smart.

I opened a hallway closet door and pulled out the Stevens, slipped it out of its case and retrieved two boxes of shells. I loaded a .410 shotgun shell and a .22 Long Rifle into their respective chambers, snapped the weapon shut, and sat down in a chair next to my bed.

After a minute, I stood and closed all the plantation shutters, locked the doors, grabbed two cold Heinekens from the refrigerator, held a bottle on each side of my face for a while, and drank them both.

I checked my e-mail. There was a message. Ernie. A brief note, the kind sent when he was tired and at the end of his day down in Belue, just before going to bed, the kind that prompted a short reply. There had been several since I moved, always checking.

We had once discussed a synopsis for *A Tale of Two Cities* in the movie section of the local paper's television listings. It read,

"Urban drama." Two words for a classic. From that point on, we competed to see who could be the most succinct in reviewing movies, and other communications. *Field of Dreams* became "Rural drama." We appropriated the truncated approach to our e-mails.

Ernie's message:

How you?

My reply:

Active.

I had been in Rockbluff one month.

Chapter 14

"I'm a loser,
I'm not what I appear to be..."
- Beatles

I dreamed about fights, rivers and, briefly, my daughters. We were making popcorn in preparation to watch one of the old Muppet movies—I did not know where Karen was in the dream—and we were laughing and teasing each other and looking forward to the treat—a movie and buttered popcorn with parmesan cheese, garlic salt, and lemon pepper sprinkled over it. Annie called it "toxic waste popcorn." A tradition.

When I awoke, I was disoriented. The dream had been real, vivid, in color. Alive.

Then I understood. I wept. So sue me.

"I wish I could get back in that dream," I said out loud. I sighed, rubbed my face, and yelped. My face felt unfamiliar, bigger, painful. I swung my body out of bed. I made more noise than usual upon arising because Gotcha opened one eye and closed it, frantic with worry, yet never breaking the rhythm of her soft snore.

In the bathroom, I flicked on the light. When I saw my reflection I laughed, which hurt, and I laughed again, which hurt some more. I looked like an inept prizefighter the day after a few rounds with the young Joe Frazier. My lips were fat; my left eye purple, black, green, and nearly swollen shut; and a bruise on my forehead resembled the tread of a boot. With my thumb, I gently wiggled three teeth loosened from the kick. Not too bad. They would tighten up and survive.

I took a long, very hot shower, directing the spray onto every aching part of my body except my face; then I dressed. I skipped shaving. I shuffled into the kitchen, grabbed a Diet Coke, and headed for the front door. Then I stopped, returned to the bedroom, picked up the Stevens, and hastened out and down the half-mile drive to my mailbox, studying the woods and the road ahead. At the mailbox, I withdrew the *Des Moines Chronicle* and started back.

Halfway home, I remembered the other man on the bridge, my helper. Lunatic Mooning? Who else could it be? Dark out, no glasses, it could have been Sasquatch for all I could tell. But Mooning knew about the two thugs—he had warned me about them. When they left, he must have put Rachel in charge and walked down to the bridge, intervening when he thought it necessary. But would he ever own up to it?

Breakfast was quick; three heaping tablespoons of creamy peanut butter dipped one at a time into a jar of Iowa honey, a frosted strawberry Pop Tart at room temperature, a handful of salted cashews, and several glugs of whole milk straight from the jug. I chewed everything on the right side, sparing my loose teeth on the left.

I brushed most of my teeth, mouthwashed, and ran a comb through my hair. Cleaned my glasses. The right lens had a little scratch, but I could call my optometrist in Belue and have extras overnighted. I let Gotcha outside and let her back in. After grabbing my weapon, I dumped a handful of mixed shells in my pockets, snagged another Diet Coke, and left as Gotcha jumped into her recliner for her morning meditations.

The Grain wasn't open yet, but the pearl-gray Packard was in its familiar spot. I walked around back to the door that led to

Mooning's office and peered in through a lone window. He was at his computer. I pounded on the door. He finished a few clicks on his keyboard and the screen went blue. He looked up. He let me in.

"What happened to your face? It is more interesting than usual," he asked.

"You saved my ass last night, didn't you?"

"When I cut off your beer, perhaps. Not likely, though, given your capacity," he said. His eyes were dark, impassive, curious. "Of what do you speak, if not that?"

"I saw you on the bridge last night, taking out the guy in the camo outfit, you know, one of the guys that followed me out the door when I left."

"I remember them leaving after you left. I gave it no more thought after that. I heard on the news this morning about an altercation. Two men in custody and hospitalized. You must have acquitted yourself well, considering *you* are not hospitalized, although you might explore that option. Your rambling suggests head trauma."

"You were there. I want to thank you."

"You mistook someone else for me. It was dark. Your glasses were knocked off."

"How did you know my glasses were knocked off?"

"Your right lens is scratched. It wasn't when you left. Simple logic. Something else you might explore. What happened?"

I smiled, winced. "You know what happened."

"Humor me. Pretend that I speak not with forked tongue."

I rolled my eyes. Even that hurt. "Okay." I spilled the details, emphasizing my outside help. "I gotta go now. Anyway, thank you."

"You have resources for a CAT scan. I recommend it." He held up his hand with three fingers extended. "How many?"

"Eight," I said, and left.

Three cars occupied the parking lot at Christ the King Church. I figured the Cooper belonged to a lay worker, the Camry was the church secretary's, and the third, a silver Mercedes sedan, The Reverend Doctor Ernst VanderKellen's. A muddy yellow mountain bike leaned against the building behind a well-tended bed of purple and pink flowers. Karen could have told me, but I think they were petunias and snapdragons.

Inside, an office to the right side of an expansive foyer beckoned. I went inside. Two women working. One, a teenager. Cooper girl. The other, in her fifties, sported short white hair with lots of spikey thingies. Camry woman. She studied me over the top of half-glasses. Her expression might have been mistaken for stern, but her face reflected humor and sense. I liked her immediately. Both looked surprised, and then I remembered what my face looked like. I addressed the woman.

"I was wondering if Reverend VanderKellen might be available to speak with me for a few minutes, please?"

The girl stared, but the older lady walked quickly to the counter that separated her from visitors. The closer she came, the more I realized this was a beautiful woman.

"You are?" she asked.

"Oh, sorry. Tacky manners. I'm Thomas O'Shea."

"Good morning. I'm Eleanor Bixby, and this is Julie Dreusicke. I hate to be forward, but you look like you could use the services of a doctor."

"Thanks, but I'll be fine. I'm a quick healer. I am here to see Doctor VanderKellen, though. Maybe he'll fix me up. Would that be possible?"

"Doctor VanderKellen does not usually tolerate walk-in appointments, but I think he'll make an exception if I lead the way," she said. *Does not "tolerate" walk-ins?* "I'll take you back to his study," she said, coming around the counter. "I'll be right back, Julie."

"Nice to meet you, Julie," I said to the girl, who smiled. I turned back to the older lady. "Thank you."

"You're welcome. Follow me."

We walked down the hall and took a right into a short hallway marked by a sign on a wrought iron arm sticking out over the top of a heavy wooden door. It read "Pastor's Study" and, on the oak door, a brass sign was screwed in that read, "Reverend Ernst VanderKellen, D.Div."

I pointed at the D.Div. and said, "I always thought that stood for someone who made great Christmas candy."

Eleanor, enduring my attempt at humor, smiled patiently. She knocked on the door. Three short raps, military style. Eleanor waited, looking at her shoes, hands together in front of her. Ten seconds later, the resonant voice of The Reverend Doctor Ernst VanderKellen boomed out, "Enter!" He sounded annoyed.

Eleanor opened the door wide enough to stick her head in and announce, "A Mr. Thomas O'Shea to see you, Doctor VanderKellen," and stepped back. She gestured for me to enter, the gesture exaggerated by a faint flourish. She gave me a quick look, then beat it back down the hall. I stepped in and closed the door.

The Reverend stood from behind a desk that could have served as a handball court except that it was mahogany. He did not come around to greet me; instead, he gestured to one of two chairs situated in front of the desk. The chairs were upholstered in blood red leather with brass studs. I offered my hand. VanderKellen reached across the desk and shook briefly, a look of recognition in his face, then released my hand as if it were sticky. The bearded Reverend Doctor was dressed as if golf were happening soon. His clothes fit his lean physique. He sat down and indicated I should do the same.

"What can I do for you, Mr. O'Shea, other than recommend a physician?"

"I just had some questions, and I do apologize for my appearance. I assure you, assuming this is a confidential conversation, it was not self-inflicted."

"Oh, I know how it was inflicted," VanderKellen said, stroking his Vandyke beard. "Small town. Word circulates, even if it isn't gossip. I hear you emerged victorious in the altercation," he said, eyeing me.

I realized Ernst was the kind of preacher who liked to make people feel uncomfortable. I returned the gaze without smiling. Liv Olson was right.

VanderKellen went on. "You were in attendance at Hugh Soderstrom's funeral."

"You have quite a memory." The church had been packed, but my rugged good looks must have stood out.

"What did you think?" he said.

"What do you mean?"

A friend of mine, a former Green Beret down in North Carolina, once said to me, "Don't ask the question if you can't stand the answer." I decided to give Dr. VanderKellen a pass.

"Oh, I thought it was just fine," I lied.

"Anything stick out in particular?" he asked, leaning back in his elegant leather chair and dropping eye contact to examine the fingernails on his right hand.

"Well, I thought your Doc Div robes were cool."

"Doctor of Divinity," he corrected.

"Yes. Doctor of Divinity. I think the embroidered scarlet Latin crosses on each side of the front were stunning, yet not overstated, shown to benefit by the basic black of the vestment."

VanderKellen shifted his eyes from his fingernails to me, his look intense and probing. "And did you notice the scarlet piping around the black velvet panels and doctoral bars?"

"I did. Quite impressive, actually. Got my attention as you approached the pulpit."

"Good! Yes, yes, you understand the importance of visual presentation," VanderKellen said. "I doubt anyone else in attendance understood the significance of my robe. They didn't even understand my old, Geneva robe. Most of the locals would only reference 'Geneva' as that lake in Wisconsin."

"Your doctoral vestment is a big step up," I said.

"I ordered it a while back, and it happened to get here the very day Hugh Soderstrom died. Good timing, one might say."

"One might."

"Notice anything else, Mr. O'Shea?" he asked, his gaze locked on my face.

While I tried to think of some other innocuous observation, the good Dr. VanderKellen rose abruptly from his desk and strode over to a beautiful, arched window that looked out on a woodsy neighborhood, and behind that, a backdrop of rugged bluffs. He began slowly rocking back and forth on his toes, seemingly lost in thought while I tried to come up with another observation.

Several expensively framed diplomas adorned the wall on one side of the window, and on the other side various awards, commendations, and photos of the man with other presumably important people I did not recognize. There were no family photos.

On each side of the study, books filled built-in bookshelves. A large sofa and coffee table, two wing chairs, and an end table with a pale blue porcelain lamp completed the furnishings.

I heard a truck go by on the street behind the church. There was a clashing of gears and then the truck backfired. VanderKellen flinched, then turned away from the window to face me.

"Can't come up with just one more observation? You seem reasonably bright, but your appearance does belie that."

"The flower arrangements were special," I said. A fail-safe topic.

His face brightened. "I did that. My doing. You are perceptive, Mr. O'Shea. Did you notice that my tie was accentuated by the dahlias?"

"Totally escaped me. My powers of discernment obviously failed."

Dr. VanderKellen offered a brief, artificial smile, as if he were riding along on a float with other grandees during a town parade and I, a street urchin, had waved at him. "You said you had questions for me?" he asked.

"I did, but I believe they have fled my mind," I said. "Thanks, anyway."

"In that case," he said, returning to his side of the mahogany handball court, "I have much to do this morning."

I stood. "Thank you for your time."

"You're welcome. I'll be happy to meet with you another, less frenetic, time. Good day, Mr. O'Shea. Oh, and I'd have a physician take a look at your wounds. There are several excellent plastic surgeons in Iowa City." He sat down and began shuffling through a sheaf of papers in front of him.

"I think plastic surgery was an option *before* the rumble," I said.

VanderKellen did not respond to my wit, so I turned and left his office as he called out, "Please close the door, Mr. O'Shea."

Responding to my inner adolescent, I left it open.

I retraced my steps and found myself in the domain of Bixby and Dreusicke. They looked up and smiled. I said, "Thank you for working me into the good pastor's busy schedule. I appreciate that."

"You're welcome," Eleanor said. Then, before turning back to her work, she said quickly, "Would you like to meet our Assistant Pastor, Carl Heisler? He's in, and he loves to talk to people without appointments."

Eleanor was up to something. I could feel it. The day was becoming brighter, and I could feel life pushing its way back into me. Besides, Liv Olson said good things about Heisler. I said, "I'd love to. Thanks."

"Follow me," she said again. I did. We came to an office with a sign that read, simply, "Assistant Pastor." In various colors. In crayon. A child's hand. The door was open just a crack and I could hear Harry Chapin music. Eleanor stepped just inside.

She said, "Thomas O'Shea, Carl." *Carl?* She stepped back and said, "He's all yours," smiled, and left.

I went in. Mostly windows and books; a mess. A sandy-haired, angular young man who looked barely fourteen slouched behind a desk piled high with books, newspapers, and empty Diet Dr. Pepper cans. On the edge of his desk a glass jar quarter-full of peppermints sported a peeling Minnesota Twins decal. The young man jumped to his feet and accelerated across the room, right hand out.

Tall and lanky, he wore faded khaki's, running shoes, and a white t-shirt with a picture of Michael Moore in a tutu. Under Moore's picture was written, in block letters, "JESUS CAN REDEEM ANY HISTORY." Heisler's blue eyes made me think of the word "merry."

"I'm Carl Heisler, and what in the world happened to you?"

We shook hands, Heisler's big and strong. I said, "The metaphor is 'speed bump in an industrial park.'"

Heisler laughed. "Great, but that can't be the explanation. What happened?" I told him about the fight.

"I heard about it on the news this morning. I should have made the connection. They gave your name. What was that all about? And what can I do to help you?" Heisler dragged forward a pair of folding metal chairs and sat down in one, offering the other. "Can I get you anything to drink? I'm going to get a Diet Dr. Pepper."

"I need a beer, but I'd be happy with what you're having."

"Excellent." He sprang to his feet and disappeared out the door. I looked around the cluttered office where sports equipment and boxes were scattered. Several posters adorned the walls; one of Jerusalem, another of the New York City skyline with the two World Trade Center towers smoking from the terrorists' attacks, and still another of Kirby Pucket catching a ball as he crashed against an outfield wall.

Behind his desk, slightly askew, hung a framed diploma from Luther College, and another, from a seminary I couldn't discern. An Honorable Discharge from the Marine Corps and a certificate naming Carl Heisler as an All-American in NCAA Cross Country kept the diplomas company. He came back with the soft drinks.

"Hope you don't mind drinking from the can," he said, handing me the soda. "I can get you a glass and ice if you'd like."

"This is fine. Thank you."

"You're welcome," he said. He flopped down in the chair next to me. "Now, wha'sup?"

"Eat Dessert First."

"Eat Dessert First? You wanna talk about Cherries Jubilee?"

"I once saw a t-shirt in a shop in Abingdon, Virginia that read, 'Life is Short: Eat Dessert First.' I would have bought one, but they were all too small," I said, smiling and instantly remembering my hurting face.

Carl smiled too. "Poignant revelation. And this relates to...?"

I decided to go for broke. I told Carl what had happened, from Wendy screaming in my arms right through to the attempted murder on the bridge last night. Carl raised his eyebrows, stood, stalked to a window, and gazed outside at the church parking lot. He turned away from the window and said, "What do you think happened? And why?"

"I think Larry killed his brother, probably for the money that will likely become his inheritance. Greed's always been a strong motivator, especially when you mix in booze, drugs, gambling, and sex. Too bad for Wendy. I'm glad your wife was able to get out there so fast that day."

"Molly mentioned you. She said God had sent a kind man at that exact time. She did not know who you were, had never seen you before. Said you might have been an angel."

"Those guys on the bridge wouldn't say so."

"You ever notice that every time an angel is mentioned in the Bible, there's always an admonition from the angels to the regular folk to 'be not afraid'? It ain't because angels are little chubby cherubs with wings and curly blonde hair. Would you piss your pants if an overweight baby showed up at your house? Angels are awesome, fierce looking, filled with God's power, and highly capable individuals no one in their right mind would mess with. So you haven't disqualified yourself by putting two tough guys in the hospital. They probably deserved it. So, what's Sheriff Payne say about all this?"

"He said he'd look into it. I think he's suspicious."

"Well, duh!"

"I trust him to do a thorough, careful job of finding out the facts. He wasn't all that inquisitive to start with, but his activity on the case has increased since all these coincidences have reared their ugly little noggins. He's getting a search warrant for Larry's house, wherever that is." I took a slug from my cold soft drink. It tasted good.

"In the meantime, maybe you can tell me something about the Soderstroms, or people who might be useful in helping me get to the truth about what happened that day."

"Why don't you leave it to Sheriff Payne? He'll do a great job, really."

"Payne might, but his cohorts don't impress me much. Besides," I said, scooching forward to the front of my chair, "I am taking this personally. Larry Soderstrom threatened to shoot my dog."

"That's despicable!"

"You must have a dog."

"Why wouldn't I?"

"Tell me what kind, and I'll immediately be able to know a lot about your character."

"We have a Bullmastiff. His name is Crunch."

"You're real people, then."

"Tell me about your dog," Heisler said, a smile crinkling his face. "And don't say it's a Mexican Hairless or I'll throw you out of my office; that is, if I were capable, which I guess I'm not, judging from the looks of you."

"Female Bulldog. Name of Gotcha."

"You da man!" Heisler exclaimed, laughing with delight and clapping his hands. He offered a fist bump and I responded. "Is there anything else motivating you to snoop around, not that there needs to be. You clearly have sufficient cause."

"People are being paid to kill me," I said. "And it's not my nature to sit around in a defensive posture and hope it doesn't happen. Besides, I have time on my hands. I might come up with something because of how much time, and tenacity, I can bring to the investigation."

I noticed Heisler's merry eyes took on a different tone, a deeper blue and an intensity that would have made me nervous under different circumstances. "I will tell you what I can," he said. "Your face and story give you ownership to the information."

"I'd appreciate it very much."

"It must remain confidential."

"It will."

Carl took a long gulp from his Diet Dr. Pepper, adjusted his weight in the chair, and spoke. "Here goes."

"I'm holding onto my chair," I said, and he began.

Chapter 15

"It is the test of a good religion whether you can make a joke about it."
- G. K. Chesterton

Carl Heisler paused; gathering his thoughts, then spoke. "Hugh Soderstrom was my friend and brother in Christ. He loved life, the farm, Wendy. Oh, man, did he love Wendy. His character was impeccable, and his priorities were solid down the line. However, all was not well in Hugh's life."

"Larry."

Heisler smiled ruefully and nodded. "And Wendy. She was not happy down on the farm. She encouraged Hugh to sell the land to Jurgen Clontz, but he would not, could not. He did not have the authority. So they had a marriage that was not united in its goals and objectives; in fact, they were one hundred eighty degrees out of phase."

"Maybe kids would have given them more in common. People seem to think they were trying to have children," I said.

Heisler got up and walked over to the door to his office and closed it, then returned to his chair. His voice was softer, lower. "Hugh wanted children. Wendy was ambivalent, but it was a moot point. Hugh was sterile. Tests at University Hospitals proved it. He wanted to adopt. She drew the line. Wendy felt as if they weren't supposed to have children, that this was a sign."

"What do you think she'll do now?"

"I imagine Wendy Soderstrom will get on the first thing smokin' and head for a city. Minneapolis, Chicago, St. Louis. Somewhere far from that farm. I don't want to sound uncharitable, but she just never did acclimate to farm life, or this town, for that matter. That's not a condemnation. Not everyone is in love with farm life. And that's fine. I don't think I'd care to live out there, either. But if Hugh had been a C.P.A. or a banker in a city, I don't think you could have found a happier wife. But he wasn't those things. He was a farmer, and happy to be one.

"I can't imagine why Hugh married her, but people do illogical things when they're in love. She went through the motions, attended church with him, pitched in on covered dish dinners and church activities, even headed up Vacation Bible School two summers ago."

"That would make me lose my religion," I said.

Carl laughed. "Me, too."

"Do you know the details of the Soderstrom Farms Estate? You said Hugh didn't have the authority to sell the land to Jurgen Clontz, even though Wendy wanted him to. Who gets what?"

"By the way," Carl said, holding my eyes with his, "the only people who know Hugh was sterile are you, me, and Wendy, so..."

"I won't tell anyone. I don't *know* anyone."

"I know. It just makes me feel a little funny to be telling you all this, but with Hugh in Heaven now, I guess it won't hurt. If Hugh was murdered, he would want me to do everything to help bring the killer to justice."

"So what are the details of the estate?"

"It's no secret. Soderstrom Farms was left fifty percent to Hugh and fifty percent to Larry, but it belongs to the church. It's a Living Trust. Larry rented his out so he wouldn't have to work, but would have a steady stream of income to bankroll his poor choices. Hugh worked his half with the intent to make it productive so he could someday buy the land free and clear, as provided in the Trust.

"If either brother died, the land would be made available to the other brother, not the family of the deceased brother, at fifty percent of the appraised value. A good deal if the money's there. That's where it gets sticky. The Trust becomes quite complicated."

"I thrive on complications."

Carl Heisler smiled. "It's like this: Larry has sixty days from Hugh's death to declare if he wants to buy the land or not. Full discounted price, cash only. If Larry doesn't buy, notices would then go out that the land is for sale, sealed bids and all that. The land must be used for farming only—no developments, golf courses, water parks, or even just left fallow. Has to be a working farm. And the bids go to Doctor VanderKellen and the Deacon Board sixty days from whatever date Larry makes his decision, or not. That clock started ticking the day after Hugh died. If Larry doesn't act, the Trust would appoint an overseer to manage the property."

"Do you think Larry will bid?"

"I have a hunch he won't. Furthermore, the Soderstrom Trust, the church, has the right to refuse sale to any nefarious or questionable sources. Other than that, it's smooth sailing for some reputable person or entity to acquire the land."

"So what happens to Wendy?"

"A cash settlement would be made by the Trust to the family of the deceased brother if either or both brothers were married, that figure to be ten percent of the value of the half.

"This is a large estate, Thomas. Iowa farmland that can yield one hundred and sixty bushels of corn per acre goes for about five thousand dollars an acre, which is up a good bit since the early eighties, the previous high. But there are fewer farmers, with the average age right now being mid-fifties. And the children of farmers don't stick around, so with fewer farms and thirty-three million acres in the state, you can figure it out."

"Farms are getting larger, and I would think, scooped up by conglomerates," I said.

"Over a third of all farmland in Iowa is owned by investors."

"Like Jurgen Clontz, Junior?"

"Yep. And it makes sense. As they say in real estate, God isn't making any more land, so it can only go up. And Iowa farmland is primo stuff. We're not talking sand or red clay," Carl said. "I would guess Soderstrom Farms is worth forty-two million dollars more or less. Probably more."

"So how much will Wendy receive from Hugh's death?"

"From the estate? A couple million, give or take," Carl said, his eyes sparkling as he laughed, the skin crinkling around his eyes in a big smile. "Wendy will be just fine, financially. She will not be left to live under the bridges of Rockbluff County."

"Good for Wendy, especially since she wants off the farm. That much would buy a bus ticket to a big city, and a buck or two left over to purchase a condo and a Beamer or two," I said, Carl nodding his head in agreement. "I have another question."

"Shoot."

"What happens if both brothers were to die in an accident, or they just grew old and passed away? If I understand you, their families would get only the ten percent, but who gets the entirety of Soderstrom Farms should Larry die now?"

"As I said, Soderstrom Farms is what the lawyers call a Living Trust, which means in this case the sons can manage their half of the farm as long as they live, as long as they actually live on it, and it is used for farming. There is a special provision in the Trust that allows either brother to purchase outright the land from the Trust at fair market value, which is what Hugh planned to do with his profits. If he couldn't raise the money he planned to buy other land nearby and work both farms, hiring more men, and so forth. Larry had no interest in that provision, according to Hugh. But if both brothers are gone, and neither has purchased their half from the Trust, the land itself reverts to...?" Carl asked, eyebrows going up as if it were a quiz question.

"Ahhh," I said, slowly figuring it out. "That would be Christ the King Church in Rockbluff, Iowa."

"To appropriate a Roman Catholic term, bingo! Point of fact," Carl said, holding up a cautionary finger, "it does not go to Doctor VanderKellen or Mrs. VanderKellen, or Molly or me, or even wonderful Eleanor Bixby, although she should get it for putting up with us. It reverts to the church, and the assets would then be managed by the Elders. Thirty percent of the interest must go to missions, but that's the only caveat. Missions were very important to the Soderstroms Senior; they were killed in a car accident when they were serving on a short missions trip to Haiti."

"They sound like they were good, tough, smart people."

"I never met them. All that was before I came. But obviously they were good stewards of their assets, and committed to having their wealth put to good use when they were gone. First the land goes to the church, then the proceeds of the sale of the land go to the church, the land itself going to whomever buys it."

I stood to ease the growing pain and stiffness in my body, walked over to the window, looked out at Rockbluff. Carl continued.

"Mr. And Mrs. Soderstrom loved this church, and they wanted Christ the King to always have the very best in facilities and staff as a way of honoring our Lord. So they took time to say so in their estate."

"What would you have to do if Larry Soderstrom were to die tonight?"

"The sale of the land would have to go to the bidder with the highest offer closest to the fair market value of the land, the sale taking place no later than sixty days after the death of the remaining son. It could happen sooner than sixty days, too, because the Trust is so organized and clear. But it might take bidders a while to get together their bids, so sixty days makes sense."

Carl raised his eyebrows again to punctuate what he'd just said. "The Soderstroms did not like to dink around. They foresaw endless dickering over the dissolution of the Trust and took care of it. And you can be sure the big boys are tracking the farm so they can put together a bid quickly. Clontz, of course, is on it, as well. There's nothing he would like better than to get his hands on that land."

"What are the parameters on price?" I wondered. "I mean, what if the closest bid to fair market value is a rigged deal for, say, twenty percent of the value of the land?"

"It's got to be no less than ninety-five percent of the fair market value, which is, as I anticipate your next question, arrived at by independent licensed appraisers every six months. Pricey, but that's..."

"In the Trust, too."

"You got it, Thomas. And by the way, there would be no problem selling the land."

I finished my Diet Dr. Pepper and just held the empty can in my hand. "Would you sell the farms to Jurgen Clontz?"

"I'd rather sell it below value to keep him from getting his hands on it. At the same time, to be candid, there probably aren't many other individuals out there who could come up with the cash. Corporations can do it, of course. Anyway, we are required to take the best legitimate offer from a reputable source."

"Why would Harmon Payne be afraid of Jurgen Clontz?"

Carl Heisler's blonde eyebrows went up again. "Is he?"

"In confidence?"

"Of course."

"He told me Jurgen Clontz gives him the willies."

"Did Sheriff Payne fill you in on the Clontz family history?"

I nodded.

Carl said, "Jurgen has significant wealth and, therefore, power and influence. People like that can get a little carried away if they're not careful."

"Human nature. Behavior probably reinforced time and again over the years."

"Darn tootin'. Jurgen is used to getting his way and, if he doesn't get it, well..."

Heisler's voice trailed off.

"It's called a pre-extinction burst," I said. "If you're used to getting your way, and then you don't for some reason, you escalate behaviors that worked before until they work again. Of course, if they don't work, you modify your behaviors, such as becoming more pleasant, or conciliatory, or maybe killing the person who denied you what you wanted, to use an extreme to make my point."

"Are you a psychologist or something?" Carl asked.

"Behavioral health guy."

"So you know why people act like they do?"

"Sometimes."

"Me, too. It's usually called 'sin nature,'" he laughed.

"I couldn't agree more," I said. "I thank you for your time and information. My eyes are opening fast."

"It'll be a while before they open completely, I think," Carl said, rising to his feet. "Say, would you like to go home with me for lunch? Molly's a great cook, and I'm sure she'd like to meet you under better conditions than the first time."

"I would, but I have someplace I need to be. I appreciate the invitation. Rain check?"

"Of course," Carl said, smiling, his eyes merry again. "Why don't you come and worship with us on Sunday? Do you have a church family yet?"

"No, I don't. I still belong to a church in Belue. My pastor down in Georgia keeps nagging me to find a body of believers, and I know he's right. I've just been a sluggard."

"And the sluggee," Carl pointed at my face.

"Are you preaching this Sunday?"

"No, actually Doctor VanderKellen is, and will be for a while. Then he'll be gone on vacation in early September, and the pulpit will be mine for three Sundays."

"Maybe then," I said, turning to leave.

"Long way off. One more thing," Carl said, and we both stopped walking. He looked at me, his glacier-ice blue eyes peering into my brain. "Maybe I talked too much. Just now. I know the details of the Trust are public knowledge, but the other things really aren't. I don't trust many people, but I trust you. Don't let me down, Thomas."

"I will not," I said.

"I know this is nosey, but where are you off to that has you declining sweet Molly's culinary arts?"

"I'm going by The Grain o' Truth to get some takeout lunch, and then I'm going out to Hugh's place to have lunch with Wendy. Of course, she doesn't know it yet," I said, and then I left, Carl Heisler's eyebrows elevating once more as I headed out.

In my truck I wondered why Carl continually referred to his fellow pastor as Dr. VanderKellen, instead of Ernst. I turned the key in the ignition, the engine came to life, and I headed for The Grain o' Truth Bar & Grill.

Chapter 16

"As a ring of gold in a swine's snout,
So is a beautiful woman who lacks discretion."
- Proverbs 11:22

Lunatic Mooning had elevated eyebrows, too, when I told him the two Loony Burger Specials and a pair of Diet Cokes to go were for Wendy Soderstrom and me. Moon said, "Is this something I should know about? Is this the time for you and me to go into steaming tipi, sit naked and stick eagle claws into each other's chests and beat the tom-tom? Then wrestle and plunge into cold stream?"

"No, oh chatterbox Ojibwa. Save that for the year the Hawkeyes win the College World Series, Rose Bowl and the Final Four."

"Not much chance soon of eagle claws in chest."

"Just fill the order, put it in a bag, please, and I'll be on my way. I want to talk to her and see how she's doing."

"The boys from Dubuque put a hurting on you." He peered at my face, then turned to toss the burgers on the grill and start the fries. He returned. "Your face is larger than when you dropped by this morning. Not good."

"You should see the other guys."

"I know what the medical reports say about last night's miscreants."

The small town was growing smaller. "What were the damages?"

"One man has seven broken ribs, a punctured lung, a ruptured spleen, and will need reconstructive knee surgery to elevate his mobility status to 'crippled for life.' He will always play golf from a cart. The other is blind in the eye you popped out, although, for cosmetic reasons, they were able to reposition it. The other eye is badly damaged and he may be blind in that one, too. It's fifty-fifty. He also has a broken nose, fractured cheekbone, and several teeth that are probably downriver by now," Lunatic said, looking at me with deep regard. Then he said, "Nice job, white eyes."

"I didn't think a forearm up under the chin would have been enough to discourage them. Heck, I'm just an aging behavioral health consultant seeking peace and quiet while trying to walk a reasonably straight and narrow path, and people keep interrupting my progress."

"If you didn't ask so many questions, people would leave you alone, Irishman." Moon turned to the grill and flipped the burgers, pulled the wire basket of French fries out of the hot oil, shook them, and dropped the basket back into the cooking vat.

"You'd do the same thing," I said.

Lunatic returned from the grill. "Yes. You have not asked, but let me advise you. I would take precautions. I would invest in better weaponry."

"My weaponry is fine."

"It is not enough," he said. And then he reached under the bar and brought out Chief Justice and held it out to me. "Take it. Six shot magazine, fully loaded."

I stood silently, stunned. He set the shotgun on the bar, reached back under with one hand, and brought forth a box of shells and set them on the bar.

"I can't take Chief Justice."

"Do you think I have only one weapon such as this?" He strode back to his office and came back out with an identical shotgun: pistol grip, pump action, Mossberg. "This is Associate Justice," he said, and slid it under the counter.

"You're serious."

"As Little Big Horn."

"Thank you," I said, taking the shotgun with one hand and the box of shells with the other. The Mossberg was surprisingly light, even fully loaded.

"I guess I need to find Larry as soon as possible. What do your sources tell you?"

Moon pulled the fries from the deep-fat fryer and assembled the Loony Burgers, placing them in white Styrofoam containers and sliding everything into a large, heavy-duty brown bag turned on its side. He turned back to me, took my money, and said, "He has disappeared. But he is still in the Rockbluff County area. Be careful."

"Thanks, Moon, I will. I did not get to this advanced age by being careless." Then I left, increased ordinance in hand, and headed for my truck. I stashed Chief Justice and the shells on the floor behind the seat and fired up the engine.

Wendy Soderstrom did not look well when she came to the door of her farmhouse. She was pale and her forehead looked sweaty. But she still looked good. She was wearing snug low-cut jeans that emphasized her flat belly and long thighs, and a short green halter-top that was cut low enough to be distracting. Her exposed middle was tan, and there was a little hoop piercing thingy in her navel.

"Hello! Mr. O'Shea, isn't it?" she said through the screen door, her eyes fixed on something over my right shoulder.

"Yes it is, Mrs. Soderstrom, and I apologize for not calling first, but I brought out lunch from The Grain o' Truth Bar & Grill with the hope that you'd join me," I said, feeling a bit awkward. I mean, I'm a single man at a young widow's home in the country, and there is no one else around. I should have arranged to meet Wendy in town, perhaps at The Tenderloin Tap or The Grain. It was not appropriate for just the two of us to be at the farm right then, and I suddenly understood my mistake. Too late. At least I had told two people where I was going, so when the lawyers showed up I could prove I wasn't being sneaky. I stood on her front porch while, inside the screen door, Wendy looked curious, but friendly.

"You're very kind," she said, her voice now low and husky. "Won't you come in?" she asked, her gaze dropping to my feet.

"I think I'd be more comfortable out here on the porch, if that's okay with you. It's a nice summer day."

"That's fine. The fresh air might do me some good."

Her comment struck me as peculiar. "Are you ill?" I asked.

"You might say that," she replied vacantly, pushing open the door and emerging onto the big porch. Then, finally noticing my face, she said, "My God! What happened to you?"

"Actually, I had a difference of opinion with a couple of rude individuals. We worked it out."

"Have you seen a doctor?"

"It's not necessary. I'm a quick healer."

"Won't you sit with me at the table? I'm feeling better already, especially compared to how you're probably doing," she said, putting one hand on my shoulder and gesturing with the other toward a redwood patio set on the porch. When she spoke, I detected a hint of mint mouthwash.

We sat and I handed her a Diet Coke, withdrew the Loony Burger Specials, and slid one across the table to her. She opened it, and her face turned a rather subdued shade of seafoam mist, a color I had seen in one of the clothing catalogues that had frequently appeared in my mailbox in Belue, when I had three females in the house who had educated me about the nuances of hue.

Wendy Soderstrom's hand flashed to her mouth and she lurched from her chair, knocking it over backwards, and rushed for the house. The sounds of her throwing up did not contribute to the rural peace; you know, the lowing of cows, the sweet "tue-a-lee" of bluebirds, the satisfied grunting of hogs. I rose and returned her chair to its upright position by the table. I sneaked a peak at her food, expecting to see a bug or a worm or something else moving there, but everything looked fine. It smelled good, too, with the cooked beef melting the sharp cheddar cheese slice inside the Kaiser roll.

I was hungry: Wendy, apparently not. A few moments later she reappeared, even mintier than before. She had tidied up, and looked much better. The tan had returned. We both sat down again.

"Are you all right? I'm sorry about bringing this kind of food. I thought it would be okay. Lunatic Mooning said that you and Hugh used to come in for lunch, or sometimes in the evening."

"I'm fine, and I appreciate it," she said, eyeing her lunch. She reached out and, with the fingernail of her right index finger, closed and delicately latched the lid to the Styrofoam package. I noticed that her longish fingernail was not the fingernail of a devoted farm wife. The dark purple polish was freshly applied.

She said, "I love Loony Burgers normally, and I'm starving. Hugh and I were more or less regulars at Moon's place, of course, but I'm fighting a nasty bug. Hugh's death has weakened my defenses, I think. But thank you so much for thinking of me, and thank you even more," she said, looking at me with her large, lovely blue eyes, "for helping me that day, when Hugh...well, I just never got to thank you before, except briefly and impersonally at the funeral. Had you not come by when you did, I might have lost my mind. I needed another person there, and then, there you were. Molly said you were an angel. Anyway, Doctor VanderKellen's exhortation to honor my privacy has been taken to the extreme by the people around here. I've been nearly out of my mind."

I had been a bumbling oaf, but if that was a comfort, so be it. "You mean no one's come by to check on you since the funeral?"

"Oh, there have been several. Molly came by twice, and she brought food, and some others have called, and Rachel Schoendienst and Olivia Olson stopped by, but that's been about it. Pretty lonely out here," she said, looking around and hugging herself.

I could feel my stomach growling, grateful it was silent. I opened my Styrofoam box. Wendy eyed the contents briefly, then looked away and took a deep breath. She said, "Please, go ahead and eat. I'm fine."

I closed the lid and shoved both boxes back into the brown paper bag. "I was just wondering how you were doing and what you were going to do with the rest of your life. You're young, you're lovely and bright," (*and have a gorgeous figure*, I thought but did not say), "and you still have a long future ahead of you, God willing. Will you be staying on and managing the hired hands?"

Wendy paused, picking at the edge of the paper bag as if there were a rabid gerbil inside, ready to lunge for her throat. She said, "What do you want me to call you?"

"My first name is Thomas. Please call me that."

"Thomas, Thomas O' Shea," she said in a singsong voice. "Irish," she said. I nodded. "Well, *Thomas*, just let me say that I love this land! I love the way it looks and feels and smells. I love what it does—how it produces so much to take care of us and thousands besides. I love the way it changes over the seasons, as if it were a living thing with a mind and a spirit and a soul. But," she said, looking down at her hands, "I cannot stay. There are just too many memories. I could not bear to look out our bedroom window and remember the joys of our marriage bed and then see that place in the yard light where it was taken away from me forever."

"What will you do?" I asked, wishing she hadn't mentioned "the joys of the marriage bed." The woman was distracting me from my altruistic agenda.

Wendy Soderstrom, widow, looked out over the land that she said she loved and said, "I will take my time to sort things out, and then make plans. Hugh's parents made provision for me in their estate plans, so I have no complaints there. I will just, well, leave. And live."

Wendy looked at me and smiled a brilliant, white-toothed smile made all the whiter in contrast to her suntanned skin. She was a beauty when she smiled, and she knew it, and I found myself longing for Karen and envying whoever ended up with Wendy, except for the fact that she was lying through her perfect teeth. My stomach growled. Wendy ignored it. I did, too.

I pulled the paper bag to myself. "Well, I'll leave you to your travel plans and packing. I wish you well," I said, standing. She stood, too, brushing back her blonde hair from her forehead. "Let me know if I can help you in any way at all," I said, escorting her back to the front door. Even if she was a liar, and she was, there was no reason to be unkind, uncharitable, as C.S. Lewis would have put it.

"Thomas, I know about your own losses, it's a small town, you know, and the fact that you thought about someone else's pain when you have plenty of your own speaks well of what a decent man you are, and I appreciate it. That's very special."

"You are kind to say that," I said, turning away.

At her screen door she said, "Thomas, have you traveled? You look like a man of the world."

"I've been in thirty-seven countries, all of Canada's provinces, and all of the states except South Dakota, which I plan to drive to this summer to see Mount Rushmore, just to say I've visited all fifty," I said, forcing a smile.

"I would love to be able to say that someday. I guess, now," she said wistfully, "I will be able to go anyplace I want, any time I want. As Dr. Seuss would say, 'Oh, the possibilities!' And which place did you think was the most beautiful of all the places you've been?"

Wendy Soderstrom's wistful, artificial interest in my travels were quickly rubbing me the wrong way, despite her kinds words, so I said, "Oh, I'd have to say either Sale City, Georgia, or Calcutta, India."

"I shall go to those places then," she said theatrically.

"Have a good time," I said, moving toward the porch steps. She followed me. "And as I said, let me know if I can be a help to you in any way."

She stepped very close to me. Her breasts brushed against me. Wendy looked up and said in a low, husky voice, "You have already helped more than you know, Thomas. I will never forget you."

I said nothing. Too much drama for me. She was, after all, a new widow, and had spent a lot of time by herself. Of course, I was a widower, which complicated things. Widow and widower. Sounded like a spider convention. With Wendy weaving her web.

I know, of course, that I'm irresistible to women, but I am also roughly a quarter of a century her senior.

While I was wondering what was so unforgettable about my vague, abstract offer of assistance, Wendy reached up with both of her hands and placed one on each side of my throat and stood on her toes and pulled my face down to hers and kissed me, her minty little tongue running lightly along my lips, teasing and hot. Releasing me, Wendy Soderstrom, grieving widow, brushed her hand against my zipper, turned and disappeared into the old farmhouse, screen door slamming shut like an exclamation point.

I stood for a moment on the porch, surprised by a new hunger, and then grabbed the paper bag and hurried to my truck, slid in behind the wheel, and started the engine. I headed home, her scent on my face, her taste on my lips, her caress teasing my id. And also with the sudden and clear revelation that Wendy Soderstrom was suffering from morning sickness.

I was glad I'd left the two Diet Cokes behind. She was going to need the carbonation more than I.

Chapter 17

"Thou art to me a delicious torment."
- Ralph Waldo Emerson

The heat of the day backed off a "tad bit" as they would say in Georgia, when I stepped out of my car in The Grain's packed parking lot. The first evening in July, and the long shadows were cooling things down. But not much. In other words, 95 and humid.

Two weeks had slipped into eternity since I'd dropped in on Wendy, two weeks gone quickly and quietly, but finding me no closer to proving who ordered the Dubuque dipsticks onto me at the bridge. My face healed and my teeth tightened. I stayed home most of the time, worked out regularly at Mulehoff's, running every day now, even inviting Liv Olson for a casual stroll one moonlit night, capped off by a long talk down by the river at Rockbluff High School.

"I love summer nights like this," she had said, "moonlight on the Whitetail River, occasional breeze to pull the heat off my skin, peace and quiet and the sound of those frogs in the shallows downriver." She sat on a bench near the water.

"From my perspective, the company's not so bad, either," I said, sitting next to her.

"I was going to say the same thing. Thanks for asking me to go for a walk. I just finished a book and hadn't picked up another, and it's not so warm outside that I'll miss the air conditioning."

"What book did you just finish?" I asked, stretching my legs out in front of me, grateful that my hamstring had pretty much healed. Just an occasional twinge when I leaped over tall buildings in a single bound. I wore hiking shorts, and I must admit, my quads looked hard and defined. Good workouts at Mulehoff's.

Liv sat Indian-style on the bench. She studied my legs for a moment, then said, "I just put down Cormac McCarthy's *The Road*. I've been putting it off."

"Grim book, but it does end on a bit of an upswing."

"Such loss, such devastation. I don't know how I'd cope with all that death." She turned quickly, facing me, twisting in her sitting position. "I mean, Thomas, in the book. I didn't mean to remind you of...your losses."

"It's okay. I remind myself every day."

"How do you cope?"

"I don't, not really," I said, surprising myself that I would talk to such a new acquaintance. I mean, if I'd thought about it, and then talked about it, that would be redundant. Inefficient. But I felt comfortable with Liv and, besides, it wouldn't hurt to answer a simple question.

"I drank quite a bit. Still do. I prayed a lot, but not so much anymore. I overate. I watched every movie available from NetFlix and Blockbuster, lifted weights, and ran until I nearly blacked out. I drove at high speeds down country roads day and night. I worked eighteen hour days. I fended off well-meaning widows bearing casseroles."

A little chuckle from Liv. "What about friends, people you trusted?"

"The only people I trusted were Karen, Michelle, and Annie. That's it. I know lots of fine people, including my pastor and my former business partner, but when you talk about trust, you're talking about keeping a secret, knowing you can rely on that person to be true to their word. People who would uphold the DNR statement on my medical records; people who would not give in to emotion and guilt. Those people all died south of Atlanta when that truck driver crushed their car."

We listened to the river for a while. I was not angry, not upset. I was just providing information. Data. Observations and interpretations. I looked away from Liv. I could see she was edging toward "Emotion World," the favorite pub of the X chromosome. Moonlight shimmered on the soft water of the Whitetail River, light and lambent and lovely. We had picked a good spot.

Liv put her legs down, turned and put her arm on the back of the bench behind me. Her sleeveless blouse afforded a good look at a well-toned upper arm and shoulder. She smelled nice. *Nice lady overall*, I thought.

"And how do you cope now?"

"I don't cope now. I just bumble forward day to day. Beer buttressed with a bit of prayer helps. And don't forget Gotcha, crazy as it sounds. Great dog. Empathetic. Loves me unconditionally."

"Then thank God for Gotcha."

I looked at her to see if she was messing with me. She wasn't. "Indeed."

Time now to shift the questions from me. She knows too much already. "So, how did you get into teaching, Miss Olson?"

She looked at me and smiled as if she had figured out my conversational defense mechanism already. "Well," she said, scooching closer to me, but not touching, yet quickly patting my leg above my left knee, "let me tell you."

And so she did.

Her love for her work and her students was obvious, and I found myself not only liking her, but respecting her, too. It really mattered to her how her kids turned out, and I was confident she not only presented herself as a great role model for them, but also an excellent teacher. She spoke of new strategies to engage her students, and her fervor came through. I noticed that I liked the sound of her voice up close.

I walked her home. She said she enjoyed walking, hiking even. Then, halfway to her house, she said, "Maybe we could go hiking someday, if you're interested."

"It's been a while," I said.

"We could take a five-miler up at Busted Druggie State Park."

I stopped and looked at her. She stopped, too. "Busted Druggie State Park?"

She laughed, a short burst of joy, and I liked the sound of her laugh, too. "Actually, it's Backbone State Park and not all that far from here. Rockbluffians call it 'Busted Druggie State Park' because there was a big drug bust up there a few years back."

"I like your name for it better."

"Me, too," she said, and she casually took my hand as we started walking again. I had liked that even better than the sound of her voice, or the tan on her legs.

I had that evening with Liv on my mind as I pushed through the doors of The Grain into the cool darkness, and the soft rhythms of Marvin Gaye, asking the ecologically-naive, yet musical, question, "What's Going On?"

I recognized a few faces, nodded, received a couple of head nods in return and a raised hand or two. Arvid Pendergast and Harvey Goodell, proprietor of the motel where I stayed my first few days in town, waved. The Grain was not exactly a place where everyone knew my name, but a place where I liked the people who made it their neighborhood pub. Those looking for a drunken evening, a fight, big-stakes pool games, or a random sexual encounter frequented Shlop's, or smaller, private joints scattered here and there; some across the Mississippi River in Wisconsin.

But The Grain remained my favorite, although I had every intention of becoming a regular at Blossom's Bistro, especially if I might bump into Liv again. I eased up to the bar and plopped down on a barstool. Rachel glided over and said, "Hello, Thomas. What can I get you?"

"A Corona, please, and keep 'em coming, dear."

"I always do. It's getting into dinnertime. Anything from the grill?"

"No sushi bar tonight?"

Rachel laughed. "How 'bout grilled chicken breast on whole wheat?"

"That'll do."

"Side order?"

"Fried cheese?"

"On its way," she said, pouring my beer from the tap and setting the pint on a coaster.

"Moon around?"

"Sure is. He just stepped into the back for a minute to pull something out of the freezer. Here he is," she said, nodding her head toward a back door.

"Thanks, Rachel."

She nodded and left. Moon approached, reached over the bar, and offered his hand for the first time. Surprised, I took it, and we shook hands, strength into strength. The big Ojibwa said, "Good to see you, O'Shea. I understand you've been dating Liv Olson."

"Nearly every night, but I thought it was surreptitious. I keep forgetting this is a small town. We were secretly wed in Lost Nation last weekend." I took a deep drink from my beer. It was cold and crisp. God, I love beer.

"Just as I thought. You have done the right thing. She is a beauty."

"She is that."

"Actually, I did hear that a while back you had lunch with her downriver at my competitor's. It does not hurt my feelings, since I have none. The only part that bothers me is that she no doubt told you about what she perceives as my act about being a stoic Indian and all, that in reality I crochet and write haiku in my spare time, when I'm not delivering meals on wheels to shut-ins and raising Chihuahuas."

"She did say you're not the person you present yourself to be during introductions."

"I will make her pay," Lunatic said. "Aren't you curious, white eyes, as to why I shook your hand just now, given your understanding, now ruined, of my basic attitude toward humanity?"

"Sorta."

Lunatic grinned. It was a huge grin, white teeth against dark skin, an encompassing grin that made me feel good just for having seen it. The first time is always special.

"I think you're okay, possibly even a good guy, probably a good guy, and I just wanted you to know I'm glad you're here, in Rockbluff, now. And I hope you stay. Especially if you continue as a regular here, strengthening my nest egg."

"Does this mean we can forego the smoking tipi and the eagle claws in the chest?"

"Yes, but that's not to say I won't slip into my anachronistic mode from time to time as a form of respect and reverence for my roots. Also, I expect you to allow me full play of that particular Ojibwa persona from time to time with any new pilgrim who might wander into this den of dissipation."

"Your secret is safe with me."

"Too bad Liv could not keep it. I may have to put a big, fat diamondback in her mailbox tonight, just to remind her of the sacredness of our understanding."

"That'll work," I said, finishing my beer just as Rachel came by to pour another and assure me my food was on the way.

"To what do we owe the honor of your presence?" Lunatic asked. "You look as if you are not here to spend the rest of the evening in convivial fellowship, replete with friendly pool games, stimulating conversation, and interaction with the beautiful people."

Peggy Lee was singing "Fever" over the jukebox speakers. The comfortable, casual beat of the song and the velvet voice of Miss Lee fit my mood. "Actually, Moon, I did come here with an agenda."

"Looking for a job? I could use a good barback this summer. Tourists, more and more locals wandering in, the ever-increasing clientele hoping to get a look at the new celebrity, the brawler from down Georgia way."

"Actually, I was wondering if you could provide me with some information."

Lunatic lowered his voice and leaned over the bar. "You mean what do I know that might help you figure out the death of Hugh Soderstrom? If I knew anything, I would have already told you."

Rachel brought my order. "Thanks, Rachel," I said. She winked and moved on to another customer. Man, it makes my day when good-looking women wink at me. The food smelled wonderful, the fragrance of the grilled chicken and the secret mustard Lunatic used, along with the rich aroma of fried cheese combined to jumpstart my appetite. I turned back to Lunatic.

"Here's what I think, my Anishinabe bud," I said, bringing him up to date with my observations, but without the Wendy pregnant - Hugh sterile twist. "Now, is there anyone else, other than Larry, who might gain from this whole stinking mess, anyone else I might need to be alert to, any details you can think of that might help me figure out what's up? Historical stuff you know from living here that I wouldn't know as a newby."

"I'll be right back," Moon said, turning away from me to go around the bar and say hello to three couples who had come in as a group. They were in their 40's, all six looking pleasant and prosperous, decent and solid. Lunatic escorted them to a big booth by a window, shook the men's hands, touched the ladies on their shoulders, and returned behind the bar. Moon exchanged glances with one of his waitresses already on her way.

"Regulars, more or less," he said. "Anyway, before we were interrupted, you were wondering what I could provide to help complete the picture surrounding Hugh's death?"

"Precisely."

"I don't know anything more. You're already operating with a valid 'heads up' on Clontz, but I'm not sure he's your guy. He might be greedy about land, and he might operate on the edge of the law from time to time, and he clearly bullies people into selling their land, but I just don't think he would kill somebody."

"Well, somebody *would* kill me, and it's all connected."

"Your curiosity is the fly in the ointment to the bad guys. And I must say, this is cool standing here talking to someone marked for death. A celebrity. By the way, did you know that your attackers' combined age is less than yours?"

I shot Lunatic a faked smile. In the background, Elvis was singing "I Can't Help Falling In Love With You." For a moment, I was back in junior high, slow dancing at the Clinton YWCA Summer Dances with pretty girls who made me dizzy with the fragrance of their hair. I tried to cling to the memory a tad longer.

"So, what's your plan, oh marked man?"

I looked at Moon, jarred from my reverie. "Find out the truth. Get to the bottom of it."

"You're not alone, you know. Payne's doing some pretty thorough snooping. I'm guessing it's personal with you, but it might be smart to just let the law catch up to the truth. And the consequences." Moon looked over my shoulder, recognition in his eyes. Almost immediately, I felt a tap on my shoulder. I rotated on the barstool.

A diminutive woman stood there. She radiated happiness and peace, energy and intelligence, as if a small piece of the sun had been placed inside her ample chest. She had very dark hair, pale blue eyes, and a lovely face with minimal makeup and a fetching smile. Obviously pregnant, she leaned a little bit aft, her hatching jacket a plain, white, cotton piece embroidered with flowers. Spring and summer.

"Are you Thomas O'Shea?"

"Yes, and you must be the Goddess of Fertility."

The woman clamped a powerful hug on me, standing a little sidesaddle, rising up on her toes, burrowing the side of her face into my chest. The hug grew tighter, then she let go and looked up and crooked her finger for me to bend down. Totally under her command, I did so, and she kissed me on the cheek. Then she stepped back.

"I'm Julie Schmidt. Gunther is my husband. I just wanted to thank you," she said.

Her voice cracked and she swallowed hard, her hands darting to her eyes. She clapped me hard on my shoulder, engaged my eyes with hers, nodded vigorously, and turned away.

"Wait a minute!" I said, and she stopped and turned back. "It's my pleasure to meet the beautiful wife of a real man. I have great respect for Gunther, and admiration for his skills, not to mention his wisdom in choosing a wife. By the way, were you Snow White at one point? I mean your black hair and blue eyes and pale skin, well...?"

Julie Schmidt blushed. I could not believe it. I didn't know people still blushed in this world. "We should have brought you a housewarming gift by now," she said. "I make a wonderful tuna casserole that you would like, right Moon?"

"Ugh."

She grinned. "But I will someday, and I'll bring it over."

"You won't need directions."

"No, I know your home well. Are you happy there?"

I paused, silent. "I will be. It's a fine house. Where's your husband?"

"We're over there, by the pool tables. We just came by for a night out. Gunther didn't see you, but Moon caught my attention and pointed, for which I'm grateful. I wanted to meet you, but didn't feel like I could drop by, although I'm sure you'd say I could. Anyway, a delight to make your acquaintance. Would you like to join us?"

"Only briefly," I said, turning to Moon and saying, "keep me informed, okay?"

I picked up my beer and dinner platter and joined the Schmidts for half an hour, then moved on, swinging by the bar again to enjoy another pint.

"I just thought of something," Moon said.

"What?" In the background, Leslie Gore was carrying on about being able to blubber at her own bash.

Moon said, "Do you suppose someone at Christ the King is involved in any of this?"

"I wouldn't rule anyone out, although I must say, I really liked Carl Heisler."

Moon peered into my eyes. "There are others at that church."

"Something to consider," I said. Moon shrugged.

It was early dark when I drove away. I wasn't quite ready to go home yet, so I cruised down the street and over the bridge and parked, then roamed through Blossom's Bistro, where a decidedly slow night was expiring. Recognizing no one, I left, disappointed Liv was not there.

Over the next few days I kept asking around, trying to glean some scrap of useful information. I worked out at The Earthen Vessel and talked with Mike, who complimented me on my set-to with the two men on the bridge. "I would have paid good money to see that little debate," he giggled, rubbing his hands together, making the muscles in his arms and chest jump. For the first time, I wondered if he was my little helper. Certainly capable.

"I wouldn't recommend it for entertainment," I said. "To tell the truth, I wasn't sure I'd survive."

"One bit of combat in life is quite enough, eh?"

"I guess you could say that," I said.

"I wish I had stumbled onto that scene. I would have been happy to help you out, but it doesn't sound like you needed it."

"Did you forget how this face looked a couple weeks ago?" I asked.

"I remember it well. What did Liv think when she saw the results of your set-to?"

"What?"

"You two are an item, aren't you?"

"I think she's a very fine person. I am now deliberately changing the subject, Mike. Do you know of anything that might help me find out who's behind the hired muscle who met me on the bridge that night?"

"Larry, but I can't prove it. If I think of anything, I'll let you know."

"See ya," I said, leaving.

"The invitation for Bible Study on Wednesday nights at seven is still open," he said, picking up a pen and tearing off a piece of paper from a pad on the counter where the nutritional supplements were sold. He scribbled quickly and handed the paper to me. "My address, e-mail, and telephone number."

I accepted the note and left.

As I cast about for information, I talked to Bunza Steele, John Aldrich and Gene Schumacher from the EMS team that had responded to Wendy Soderstrom's 911 call, and Gunther Schmidt. No one could help me draw any closer to the money behind the thugs. Everyone had hunches, but not one scrap of new information.

And all the while, in the back of my head, there was the warning from Moon to take precautions. I did not sleep well that night, even with Chief Justice on the floor beside me.

Chapter 18

"My mama always told me never put off till tomorrow people you can kill today."
- attributed to Wyatt Earp

I stopped asking questions for a few days, focusing instead on lifting weights, running and reading. My workouts at The Earthen Vessel were effective and I found myself growing into a good routine. My body responded to the regimen, and I grew stronger, with more stamina. The man in the mirror was in much harder condition than just a month ago. All that beer obviously agreed with me.

One early evening when I was reading one of Robert B. Parker's *Spenser* novels, enjoying the repartee between the protagonist and Hawk, Gotcha stared at the door, then made soft little crying sounds, and barked. For her to demand a walk, rather than just accompanying me on a stroll, was a rare thing—it had been a couple of months—so I decided to give in and reinforce exercise for my brindle-and-white Bulldog.

Putting down my book, I grabbed Chief Justice and dumped a handful of shells in my pockets. I looked at Gotcha.

As a puppy, she had enjoyed being outdoors in the summer heat of central Georgia, but when she came in, she always hurried to the cold air register on the kitchen floor, flopping down on it, pressing her pink speckled puppy belly to the cold air pumping through the metal grate. One day, Gotcha came in and dropped down on the register only to discover there was no cold air bursting forth. The thermostat was just about ready to kick in because the house was getting warm again.

That would not do. The little Bulldog puppy had stared at the register, and when nothing happened, she barked at it three times and the heat pump kicked in. This coincidence strengthened her self-esteem, and she has been confident ever since.

"You wanna go out, for sure? It's still hot out there."

She returned my look, did a little dance with her corkscrew tail wiggling, and looked again at the door. "All right, off we go."

It was just a little past twilight, and still steamy despite the cover from the trees. Gotcha led the way toward a favorite path, ranging a dozen yards ahead, ever alert to bear, cougar, or assassins.

We hiked longer than I expected. As we retraced our steps, it was now flat out dark. I looked up through the treetops and saw stars, and Venus. I realized later it was a good thing going out on such a long walk because, by being out in the woods that late, I was not in the house when the men came to kill me.

We were less than fifty yards away when I heard the front door being kicked in. Gotcha tensed immediately and growled, low and deep in her chest. Her ears pricked up and her muscles bunched as I leaned over and placed my hand on her big shoulders, ran it across her blunt muzzle and said, "Still!" in a hushed voice. She grew silent. I could feel the dog's tension without even looking at her. We moved forward together.

As Gotcha and I approached the house, I saw a tall rectangle of light shining from the open front door. I did not see anyone or hear anything. I conducted quick reconnaissance around the property and found nothing. No other visitors. Knowing there had to be a car, we cut through the woods and emerged on a low hill looking over my private drive.

A dark Lincoln Town Car with Iowa plates, Woodbury

County/Sioux City, pointed back down the road, engine running. Behind the wheel a man smoked a cigar. The window was down about four inches to let the smoke out. *Confident dude*. I wondered how many more were in my house as I chambered a round into Chief Justice.

We went back to find out. I stationed Gotcha in shadows near the front door and gave her the hand signal, palm open and passing before her face, to "Stay." She was twitching, but she would follow instructions. She gets edible rewards for following instructions. Little Smokies are her favorite.

As I slipped around the broken door and into my living room I heard voices coming from upstairs as two men descended the steps from the upstairs bedroom. I was calm as I edged farther into my house.

"His truck's here," one of them said as I watched feet and legs slowly appear on the stairs. I took a deep breath and brought the weapon up. Both men came into full view on their way down. Each had a handgun at his side.

They both saw me at the same time I ordered, "Put' em down!"

Before I could say anything else, they turned on me, pistols coming up. So much for following instructions. No Little Smokies for them.

I centered the Mossberg on the torso of the second man, who was ready to fire, a big blond with a brush cut, wearing a teal t-shirt. I squeezed the trigger, the shotgun blast loud and reverberating against the walls.

The pellets went true to the man's chest, banging him back against the wall. He bounced down onto his partner, a man about my age, dressed in jeans and a dark blue knit shirt. Blondie's gun clattered off the side of the steps, onto the floor as I chambered another round. I swung a few degrees to my right and aimed at the partner and said, "Don't do it!" He had lost concentration fighting against the collapsed body of his partner. He used his forearm to shrug off the younger man's body and brought up his weapon.

I squeezed the trigger again. The man snapped off two quick shots that I ignored. A long time ago I learned that, in a gunfight, the one who stands calmly and returns fire is often more accurate than the enemy in a hurry. Both slugs from my adversary's booming handgun missed, but not by much. I felt the first slug whistle by my ear, and the second was only marginally farther off. Under the circumstances, pretty good shooting.

I fired before he could get off a third shot.

Chief Justice's spray struck the man in the shoulder, slamming him sideways as he dove down the stairs and disappeared behind the sofa. I realized I was a little rusty. The man should have been killed with one shot at that range, even though he had been moving fast down the steps before tumbling out of sight. I chambered another round and dropped down behind the corner of a bookcase, grateful for Moon's shotgun and the double-ought buckshot. My Stevens would have been a handicap and I would now be hurrying to reload.

From behind my sofa, the man cursed me in a low voice edged with pain. He was hurting, but as long as he breathed, he could kill. I stood ready and moved forward. No wisdom in waiting for something to happen. It already had, and now I had to clean it up all by myself. On rare occasions privacy can be a bitch.

I moved forward, weapon shouldered. The smell of gun smoke, one of my favorite fragrances, filled the room. I stepped around the edge of the sofa and swung the barrel of the gun around and down. We saw each other at the same time, expected each other at the same time, and as the man on the floor aimed his big handgun, I fired, the buckshot whomping into his gut. He made a whimpering sound and collapsed as if all his tendons had snapped. I watched his handgun tumble from useless fingers.

There was no need to fire again. The man couldn't lift his hands, but I wasn't taking any chances. I'd seen too many movies where the monster appeared to be dead, then came back to life. More importantly, I had learned through experience to make sure that a downed enemy was down to stay.

Blood oozed from his shredded shoulder, but the gut wound was hemorrhaging, and I realized he would bleed out before I could stop the bleeding, even if I tried. I kicked the gun away. We both understood. Still, he had the glare, the hatred in his eyes. *Sure, go right ahead and take an attitude when you go before God.*

I picked up his handgun by the barrel, a .38 Police Special, and set it on a table by the door. The man looked up from the floor and said, "I'm hurt bad." That stopped me for a minute. The truth can do that.

"First things first," I said, and left the house. The first thing is my life, and I intended to preserve that before thinking about helping him as he slipped all alone into death.

I pulled the front door shut, muscling it into place to make sure it closed tightly. No point in getting any more bugs in the place. I hate bugs more than I hate cell phones. I released Gotcha from my order and we set off.

Had the driver heard the gunfire? Maybe. But even if he had, he probably just figured it was a bit more trouble than his partners had expected, but nothing they couldn't handle. Or, maybe, he wasn't overconfident, and was on his way to help kill me. I *ka-chunked* another shell into the chamber and focused on the business at hand. Three rounds left. I fumbled in my pockets, withdrew three shells and reloaded.

When I peeped down over the edge of the small hill overlooking my drive, the big car still sat there in the dark, engine running, the man still smoking behind the wheel, dash lights on. He looked at his watch, then puffed on his cigar.

Gotcha and I slipped down the bank from bush to bush until we hunched down twenty-five feet behind the car and to the right, out of sight of the rear view mirrors, motionless. I waited a few minutes, and when the wheel man tossed out his used-up cigar and lit another, I ducked down and came up fast, together with Gotcha, on the driver's side.

He exhaled a pleasant plume of rich cigar smoke and I stood up and rammed the butt end of the shotgun into his window, shattering it into a shower of safety glass. Startled, the man turned toward me. I chopped down hard with the butt of the gun onto his left collarbone, breaking it. As he cursed and turned in pain, slumping toward me, his right collarbone was exposed, and a second chop broke it, too. The driver screamed, hands dropping to his sides. I like it when the bad guys can't lift their hands. It's a great start toward their understanding the balance of power.

Of course, feet are still available as weapons from the trained individual, but this guy was sitting down. I opened the car door, grabbed the man by the back of his flowery, Hawaiian-style shirt, and dragged him screaming in agony out onto the white gravel. As he exited the car, the man made a point of kicking at the steering wheel, sounding the horn, the noise loud and useless in an otherwise pleasant July night.

He looked like Danny DeVito on Dianabol, dressed in tight white slacks to go with his Magnum PI shirt. He wore too much cologne. From his position on the ground, he tried to kick me, cursing and crying out at the same time. That's when Gotcha lunged and clamped her jaws onto his right calf, then jerked her massive head left and right, tugging violently on the muscle. I could have kissed her. Biting is out of character for English Bulldogs, but Gotcha made me proud.

The man shrieked. I caught Gotcha's collar and ordered her to sit and stay. She let go, but with great reluctance.

"Good dog," I said, over and over again. "Good dog!" Gotcha wiggled her hips in happiness.

"Damn dog'll be dog *meat* when we get through with you!" the man on the ground shouted, grimacing as he tried to touch his calf with a dangling arm.

"There is no 'we,' pal. Your friends are dead. Didn't you hear this?" I asked, holding up my shotgun.

"They're both dead?"

I nodded, glad to know that only three men were sent to kill me. Information is power. I asked, "Who are you and who sent you?"

"Right, like I'm gonna tell you."

I tapped the man on the mouth with the tip of the gun barrel, not enough to break his teeth, but enough to loosen the front ones a little and guarantee a fat lip in the morning. The man flinched and glared. I was not encouraged. No, these guys were definitely not from Dubuque.

"Again?" I asked. The man's response, rich with Anglo-Saxonisms, suggestions to perform naughty acts upon myself requiring a gymnast's flexibility, and various imaginative heresies shocked me. I broke his cheekbone with the stock of the gun, which still did not produce any information. He stopped speaking. I stopped hitting.

"Come on, Gotcha," I said, grabbing the man by the back of his shirt and pulling him to his feet. He kicked at me again and, in a way, I admired his toughness. But Gotcha nailed him again, the other calf this time, tearing the flesh. Creepy, wet sound. I didn't know the old girl had it in her, but I had suspected. Most dogs will defend their families. The man screamed and I ordered her off and the driver thereafter did not attempt to kick anyone. I felt sorry for him. Gotcha's 400-plus pounds of jaw pressure per square inch had to have hurt.

Reaching inside the car, I shut off the engine, not touching the end of the key, but just twisting it. Fingerprint potential.

I used the gun barrel to prod the bleeding driver forward, up to the house. He struggled to walk, moaning and limping, the jarring of each step no doubt agonizing. At the front door, I slipped around in front of the man, holding the gun on him, and shouldered open the damaged door. "Go in," I said. He did.

Inside, he saw his two pals; both shooters dead now. The wheel man merely looked angrier.

I suddenly realized that, if Gotcha had not insisted on a rare walk, I'd be dead. Gotcha, too, probably.

I could kill the driver right now, I thought. Probably should.

I pushed the barrel of the gun against the back of the driver's head, pushed it hard as the man began pleading for his life. If he somehow got off, or escaped, or served a few years and was released, he would come back. The world would be better without him, and I could make up a convincing story to tell Payne, and arrange the driver's body, with a gun, so that when I shot him in the face, it would look like combat.

One of Ambrose Bierce's four definitions of homicide is "admirable." And in the South, "The man needed killin'" is a legal defense. But Bierce had disappeared into Mexico, and we weren't in Georgia.

I took the barrel of the shotgun and prodded the back of the man's head again, hard, and then lifted the gun away. I said, "I'm not going to kill you." Maybe he had daughters.

The man wept, no doubt filled with remorse for not spending enough time in the library when he was a teen. I duct-taped the driver's hands in front of him, taped his feet, then dragged him in front of the fireplace as his cries filled the house. There was blood all over the tile and the throw rugs, reddish-brown smears everywhere. I put Chief Justice on the kitchen counter and retrieved my cell phone from the drawer underneath, flipped it open, and thumbed Sheriff Payne's number. I waited, keeping an eye on my prisoner. He wasn't going anywhere. He was too busy staring at his dead partners, not to mention the disincentive to flee due to his broken bones and ripped calves. The phone rang at the Rockbluff County Sheriff's Office.

"Payne here. How may I serve and protect you tonight?" Caller ID.

"I have three trespassers out here at the house that you need to gather into custody."

"How many are without injury?" A hint of humor in the Sheriff's voice.

"Two have been released from pain forever and one is broken."

"On my way," Payne promised. The bantering edge was gone.

Exactly twelve minutes later Payne was knocking on my damaged door. I lifted it up at the handle and swung it open. I would call Gunther in the morning and let him provide the expert repair needed. Overnight, duct tape would suffice. "Come in," I said, forcing the door back into place once he passed me.

"Their car?" Payne asked, jerking his thumb toward the road as he walked into the center of the room, contemplating the crumpled man in front of the fireplace. I nodded yes. He carried a small gym bag and set it on a chair. Then he noticed the two bloody corpses. He stared at them for a moment, then looked at me. "What in God's name?"

"They're Yankee fans. We were discussing the Boston-New York rivalry. It got out of hand."

"You okay?"

"My spirit is in turmoil," I said. I smiled. Payne did not.

He pulled out his cell phone, made one call. While we waited for his people to show up, Payne took a camera from his bag and took several pictures of the scene. When he took a photo of Chief Justice, he paused for a moment and then looked at me. "Is that whose I think it is?"

"It is."

Payne paused for a moment, as if weighing a response. Finally, he said nothing, just shook his head and continued to take pictures.

In minutes, I heard sirens and looked out a front window to watch a Deputy Sheriff's car, an ambulance, a County Coroner's meat wagon, and a wrecker crowd into my drive. The ambulance crew came into the house. It was Aldrich and Schumacher again.

I said, "Hey, John, Gene." They nodded. Aldrich said, "Evenin', Thomas" and I wondered about the significance of being on first name terms with EMS people.

They took out the driver and left. A crew from the coroner's office removed the bodies. Deputies Doltch and Lansberger came into the house shortly after. It was like a reunion of some sort, and one I didn't want to experience again.

Payne said, "You men follow the ambulance and assist in the transfer. Do not let that man out of your sight. I'll call some auxiliaries to stand watch at the hospital. Put those handguns over there in evidence bags and take them with you."

The deputies followed Payne's instructions and left, nodding at me. Friendly guys. They seemed stunned for some reason. Too easily impressed, I guess.

The Sheriff and I walked outside together as the various vehicles crept away down the drive, crunching gravel in the otherwise quiet night, throwing trails of red and blue light against the trees. The tow truck was easing the Lincoln Town Car onto its bed, the cable whining softly like a dentist's drill. We went back inside.

Payne crossed the room to the wall where the two slugs were lodged. He studied the holes in the wall for a moment, then took out a Swiss Army Knife. He dug out the slugs, held them in the palm of his big hand, jiggling them, dumped them into his pocket. He folded up his knife and dropped it into his pocket, too.

"Tell me, from beginning to end, what happened," he said, producing a small tape recorder from his gym bag and sitting down on a couch. I took a chair. He pressed a button, spoke into the tiny microphone, played it back to make sure it was working. Then he pushed another button and provided a few details including date, time, location, and reason for his response. After that, he placed the tape recorder on my coffee table and shoved the recorder toward me. I provided my narrative. It took less than five minutes.

I pushed the tape recorder back across the coffee table and Payne picked it up, punched the "OFF" button, and returned it to the bag. He rose to his feet. I did likewise. Payne clapped me heavily on the shoulder and said, "Glad you returned fire, Thomas, just glad you returned fire. Why don't you come down to the office in the morning and fill out a report," he said, and then he left, awkwardly maneuvering the unhinged front door open, then shut.

I looked over at Gotcha, stretched out on her belly on the tile in front of the fireplace, licking a bloody spot on the floor. "Very good dog, Gotcha. I love you." She wiggled her tale without looking up and continued to lick.

I walked into the kitchen. A moth flitted silently in front of me, beneficiary of the kicked-in door. I hate bugs. I reached out and captured the insect, clapped my hands together, and dropped the dead bug into the trash can under the kitchen sink.

Gotcha got up and followed me into the kitchen where I produced a package of Little Smokies. I gave her two, took one myself and ate it. She scarfed hers. I produced a little Milk-Bone from the big jar on the counter, scooped some creamy peanut butter on the end, placed an arthritis pill on the peanut butter, and tossed it to her. Gotcha accepted the goody with a loud, wet opening of her enormous mouth, then looked for more. I gave her a new "Giant Treat for Special Occasions" and she took the rawhide bone back to the fireplace to chew on there.

I opened the refrigerator, wrapped the fingers of my right hand around a Three Philosophers. I hooked a beer glass with my thumb and took the shotgun with my free hand.

Gotcha, highly interested in her special treat, chose not to join me on the deck. So I went out alone, slid the glass door closed behind me, and plopped into a chair. I set Chief Justice on the deck next to me, within easy reach. I was weary, but not too tired to drink my ale.

A few minutes later, something occurred to me that I could not ignore. I finished drinking, picked up the shotgun, and stepped inside. I dropped the empty bottle in the trash can under the sink, put the beer glass in the dishwasher, set the Mossberg on the countertop, and looked around.

There was a compulsion nagging at me, a need, several needs, pushing at me relentlessly, tenaciously. I cleaned up the blood from the tile in front of the fireplace. I studied the bloodstains on the area rugs and steps and wall, and decided to replace everything that had been bled on. I sprayed 409 on the wall and wiped the paneling clean.

It was only 9:30. It seemed like midnight. I wished it were midnight, then I could just collapse. It felt like the very center of darkness. I stood silently for a long time in the middle of my living room in the middle of July in the middle of northeast Iowa. I had just killed two men in my new house, and busted up another. *Jesus.* Talk about a non-traditional housewarming. I would have traded it for a Tupperware party any day.

I stood silently. Gotcha's snoring resonated from the master bedroom. What I'd give to have the peace of mind of that Bulldog. Door kicked in, strangers cursing and tramping about, biting a man twice, gunfire, shouts, blood, bodies hitting the deck, sirens, more strangers in the house, and still, able to go climb on her tuffet and conk out in minutes, maybe even seconds. Pure admiration from me.

I strolled over to the kitchen counter, looked at the shotgun I had placed there, then picked up my telephone and set my thumbs to work. When Olivia answered, I said, "Hello, Liv, this is Thomas, and I was wondering if I could stop by for a few minutes. I need to talk to you."

I could not read the tone of her voice other than the fact that it was pleasant, maybe a little surprised, curious. "Of course. Please. The house is a mess, but you are welcome," she said softly, her voice trailing off.

"I'll be right over," I said, dropping the phone back in the drawer and sliding the drawer shut. I turned out the lights except for the one over the stove, grabbed the shotgun, and left the house, making sure to pull the door tightly shut behind me, Gotcha snoring, her pigeon coo softening the edge of darkness.

Chapter 19

"The happiness of a man in this life does not result in the absence but the mastery of his passions."
- Alfred, Lord Tennyson

I knocked once and Olivia opened the door. I said, "Thanks for letting me stop by on such short notice."

"You are very welcome," she said, gesturing for me to come in. I could not help noticing as I brushed by her that her blouse was unbuttoned four down, lush flesh visible. No bra. She wore baggy walking shorts with her blouse on the outside. Her feet were bare. I also noticed her fragrance without wondering what it was other than something very feminine, very nice. Subtle. Soft. Even better than gun smoke. She said, "Won't you have a seat? May I get you something?"

"Oh, no, I'm fine," I said, walking to the sofa and standing, realizing I didn't know what to say now that I was in her home.

Milton jumped down from a wing chair and stared at me, his tail wagging.

"Please have a seat, really, it's okay. I was just getting ready to have a glass of wine. Won't you join me? I have a wonderful bottle of Pinot Grigio chilled."

I paused. The idea of a cold glass of wine with Liv Olson was appealing, rating far ahead of gunfire, blood and death. I said, "I would like that."

"I'll be back in a sec," she said, ducking into the kitchen after scooping up Milton. I heard a door open and close and I thought of the shotgun in my truck. "I just put Milton in his crate on the porch," she called from the kitchen. "He likes his crate."

I looked around. Books everywhere, everything from Hemingway to Ivanovich, comfortable furniture, and a stone fireplace all spoke to the essence of the woman. I heard a cork pop from a bottle, then the sound of wine splashing into glasses. She reappeared and handed me a big wine glass half-filled, set hers down, and darted back into the kitchen, re-emerging with a wooden bowl filled with almonds and cashews.

She said, "Please sit down, Thomas," and I did. Liv placed the bowl next to me, then plopped down on the sofa, the bowl between us. She pulled her legs up under her, leaned forward with her glass in hand. She raised it and said, "To summer, and friends."

"And to the spontaneous hospitality of a beautiful woman."

"And to a good man unafraid to call a lady and ask if he could see her just before Rockbluff's ten PM curfew."

Our glasses touched, and we sampled the wine. It was crisp, cold. "This is very good," I said.

"Help yourself to my favorite snack," she said, nudging the bowl toward me, scooping up a small handful of almonds, tossing them one at a time in her mouth. She sipped her wine again. She watched me, waiting.

I set my glass down on the coffee table next to us, shifted my weight so I faced her. "Three men came to my house tonight to kill me. They were professionals." I stopped and watched her try to maintain the grip on her wine glass, some of the pale liquid slipping over the lip of the glass onto her hand. She licked her hand without taking her eyes off my face. "And two of them are dead."

"You said three men came to *kill* you tonight? And you *killed* two of them?"

"Yes."

"Oh, God, Thomas! I am so sorry! What happened, I mean, that's *awful*!" she said, leaning toward me in absolute interest and focus. She took a deep breath, a deep drink, set her glass down on the coffee table, and sat back, looking at me differently than she ever had before. There was a little touch of horror there. Her eyes were darting all over my face, looking for something, I guess, to calm her.

I told her what happened.

Olivia stared at me, reaching for her glass. Her hand found it and she took it to her mouth, but just held it, staring at me. She spoke over the lip of the glass. "End of story? You just escaped your own murder and you tell it like a narrative, like washing your car, or picking out two videos at Mulehoff's. I need *details*, Thomas! First, are you okay? Did they hurt you?"

"No, I'm fine. Gotcha and I came through without a scratch."

"Thank God! Look, Thomas. I think I'm going to cry, but don't worry if I do, it's just emotion. For you. *Me!*" she said. She bounced her right palm off her forehead. With her other hand, she put the wine glass to her lips and drained it.

Liv said, "I need more wine." Her hand reached for my glass, and I handed it over. She drank. "You think they were professionals? Sent to kill you?"

"I guess they didn't think there would be much of a problem, so they were careless. If they were less confident, they would have set up a two-point ambush, an angled crossfire from perfect cover, catching me from each side as I came out of my house or returned from someplace, like a walk. They would have studied my habits. They would have known where I was when they got there. It couldn't have been easier. Have their colleague drop them off a couple miles down the road, hike in to the house, split up, get hidden, wait. Waste me when I showed up. Pick up their shell casings. Disappear. Job done. Destroy their weapons, go back to what they were doing before they were hired for the hit. No one would ever know."

That brought the tears. Go figure. She began making gulping sounds, shaking her head vigorously, nose dripping, eyes staring at me in something like wonder. “How can you talk so coldly about how these guys *goofed* when they should have killed you? Are you giving out *grades*? My God, are you crazy? I don’t believe this!” she said, and then her hands were all over my face, my chest. “You sure you’re unscathed?”

“I’m the same as I was before they dropped by.”

“Dropped *by*? How can you be so calm when three men just tried to kill you? I don’t get it! Let me see you,” she said, and she pulled my t-shirt up and away from my body and peeked. I let her. She said nothing, but her mouth formed the word, “Wow!”

“Good genes, lots of beer,” I said, stifling a laugh that felt very, very good.

“Oh, God, I can’t believe I did that,” she said, and she actually blushed. First Julie Schmidt, now Liv. A local thing, I guess. “Oh, I’m sorry, Thomas. You must think I’m demented. Here’s your shirt.” She let go. It dropped back down. “I just can’t believe you don’t have any wounds. And how can you say they just dropped by?”

“It’s the Y chromosome, I guess. And Iowa upbringing. No emotions,” I said, a smile slipping out in spite of myself. Olivia pushed both of her hands onto her face, rubbing her eyes. Then she looked at me. “Wait! What about the person who hired them? Who is *that*?”

“Now that’s the question of the day.” I stood. I took a few fat cashews from the dish, popping them into my mouth, and not one at a time, either. I reached for my glass and stopped, realizing it was empty. She had drained it.

Liv looked at the empty glasses and looked stricken. “Whoops! I guess I got a little flustered. Did I just drink your wine, too?”

“You didn’t drink all of my wine, Liv. Honest,” I said. She looked relieved. “I got a little bitty sip before you snatched it out of my hand.” She slumped against the pillows on the sofa where we had been sitting together.

She laughed, made a little fist, shook it at me in mock anger. “I’m going to hurt you for teasing me, and blame the bruises on those three guys,” she said. Then she jumped up and hurried into the kitchen and returned with the Pinot Grigio bottle. She set it before me and sat down.

She took a deep breath. "And yes, I would like another very small amount of wine. You must help yourself to something comparable to your first serving that I gulped down. Good grief, what must you think of me?"

"That's easy," I said. "I think you're a fantastic woman, a beauty, and extremely attractive when you're excited, and that's not the Pinot Grigio speaking, either."

"How could it be? I drank it all!"

"I've had some, too. And I meant what I said." I refilled our glasses.

"You are very, very sweet. And obviously in shock to make such a statement, but I accept it, with much gratitude. So," she sighed, "who do you think hired these men tonight?"

"I don't know," I said, standing and walking over to her fireplace, turning back to her. "I've been asking around, trying to figure out what's going on in Rockbluff with the death of Hugh Soderstrom, and I'm sure now that it was murder, not just another fatal farm accident. There are theories out there, floating around, but nothing to hang my hat on."

"Tonight's the result of your questions," she said, taking her wine glass to her lips. I walked back and sat next to her and picked up my glass. Then her eyes went suddenly wide. "Wait! You never told me about the circumstances on the bridge with those two thugs, those guys who tried to beat you up. I had to hear it from Lunatic Mooning! Why didn't you tell me?"

"It just didn't seem that important. Just a tussle," I said, using Bunza Steele's description. "Not worth mentioning."

It didn't fly. "Two guys try to beat you up, with some success I have been told, and it's not worth mentioning to me? I'm your friend, Thomas, and I would have appreciated your telling me. You told Lunatic, Harmon knew about it because he was there, it was even in the news."

"I didn't want you to worry." It was quiet for a moment as we sampled more wine.

She just shook her head. "We can discuss that later. I'm just thankful you're okay," she said, unfolding those glorious legs from beneath her and lounging over next to me, moving the wooden bowl to the coffee table, out of the way. "I'm glad you called me tonight. I'd hate to go through something like that and have no one to talk to. I'm flattered, actually."

"I have Gotcha to talk to, but she decided to go to bed."

"Sometimes going to bed's the best thing."

"Gotcha swears by it."

Olivia laughed. "Well, I'm glad you called. I am just amazed that you were able to survive that attack. Grateful, but surprised."

"They were in unfamiliar territory, I wasn't. They did not respect their adversary; believe me, I did. And I also had the element of surprise. Huge advantage."

"Oh, geez, I'm so sorry, Thomas. How terrible for you." And then she leaned toward me and kissed me, holding my lower lip in hers for just a second. *Oh.*

"Ummm. You taste good," she said. She snuggled up next to me and threw one tanned, shapely, nude leg over mine. "Will the one guy who's left spill the beans?" Her hand slid up under my loosened t-shirt.

"So far, he's not talking."

Her fingertips drifted across the skin of my chest. "Are you okay?" she whispered.

"I guess. Now that I've come over here. Really felt like I needed to talk to you. Sorry I upset you."

"I was reading a book when the phone rang."

"I'm sorry, I..."

"Don't be sorry, Thomas. I'm glad you called and happy you survived, apparently without a scratch, any physical ones anyway, but let me take a closer look," she said, her voice going husky. She removed my t-shirt, tossed it behind the sofa, and kissed my chest.

"I want to kiss you," I said, no longer afraid. My heart was doing its best to break through my ribcage, but I was willing to risk the fractures.

"I wish you would," she said. "You know, Shakespeare said that action is eloquence."

Liv closed her eyes as I took her into my arms and pressed my body to hers, and then my kiss softly explored her mouth. She moved against me and raised her hands and I pulled her blouse up and over her head. She kept her hands high and arched her back a little, and I kissed her breasts, my lips loving her there. She moaned and dropped her arms and held my face to her bosom. And then we rose and she took me by the hand and led me to her bedroom, turning out the lights as we went, stepping out of her shorts just before she lit the small, red candle on the bureau.

She was wearing a thong, but not for long.

Chapter 20

"Don't accept your dog's admiration as conclusive evidence you are wonderful."
- Ann Landers

I drifted somewhere between slumber and awakening, vaguely happy. The dreams were of a sweet-scented woman who had let me kiss her and had kissed me in return, a fragrant female who had molded her body next to mine, skin to skin, and held me and said nothing between kisses.

From the thick, warm fog of sleep I could hear her soft breathing, was aware of her weight in the bed next to me, her body shifting and drawing closer to me as I edged back to wakefulness. I felt her soft, warm breath on my face and I smiled at the luscious remembrance of the hours before. But my senses drew me back to the present and the warm body next to me, a morning kiss on her lips.

I reached out and caressed her floppy, silky ears and the dream began to fade, and then my hand slipped down to the twenty inch neck and the amorous chuckle in my throat stopped.

I opened one eye. I was face to face with a *face,* the bowling ball head of Gotcha, who had slipped into my bed in the middle of the night, when I was still remembering Olivia.

I laughed in spite of myself. "You booger!" I said, and the Bulldog pounced. In an instant she was on top of me, smushing her wet mug into my face, pinning me with her strength, hunching her shoulders, playing with her master. I tried to push her away and escape under the covers, but she was too strong, and the fact that I was laughing out loud and growing weaker worked against me. Finally I said, "Have your way with me then, my dear, but do be gentle."

Nothing happened at first. And then she pounced again, this time going airborne before her fifty-five pounds landed on my chest. I laughed and rolled over onto my stomach, trying to protect my neck, but that left my ears exposed, and quickly Gotcha was slurping my ears, and when my hands covered my ears, the Bulldog went after my neck.

It was hopeless. When Gotcha paused, I slithered out of bed and onto my feet, the Bulldog right behind poised on the edge of the bed. She tensed, then launched herself. I caught her in mid-leap, roughed her up, then tossed her back onto the bed, where she quickly gathered herself into her pounce position, butt in the air, chest on the bed, eyes wild and playful. "You lose!" I said and ran into the bathroom, Gotcha right behind me. I slammed the door shut and laughed as I heard her butt her head against the door. She would be waiting for me. Or she would be sleeping on the bed.

Sleeping on the bed...that was how I had left Olivia. I was what the psychologists call conflicted, wanting to stay with her until morning, perhaps to revisit our passion from the night before, but also needing to leave, to get home, to avoid her neighbors, to try to squelch gossip before it got started. Liv was a native, and I didn't want to cause any more harm to her reputation than I may have already.

When I left her bed and began dressing, it was three AM. "Love 'em and leave 'em, eh?" She was on her stomach, and she rolled over toward me onto her back, only a sheet half-covering her in the dark room. The candle still burned.

She said, "You have interesting scars."

"And those are just the ones you can see."

"*Feel*, then see. What's that puckered thingy on the inside of your thigh?"

"Gunshot. Eastern Europe."

"And the long, thin one low, very low, on your tummy?"

"Knife. Jordan. Ashamed of that one. I'm not supposed to let them get that close."

"Did you Mirandize this rude person?" she asked, using her toes to push the sheet further down her body.

"Let's just say that, after we met, I made the decision for him to remain silent."

"Tell me more."

"I don't think so."

"Okay."

"Come with me. You still haven't seen my house. I'm serious. Just slip on a robe or something."

"Soooo tempting, but I need to take care of Milton, and you need to take care of Gotcha. I understand. One day I'll get my mom to keep Milton for a weekend and then, who knows where you might find me? Besides, if you leave now, I can say you did not spend the night." She'd stretched her arms over her head and I had gone to her, pulling the sheet away, kissing the point of each hip, then her belly, her breasts, her lips.

"My engine is starting to purr," she said.

"I was hoping I'd have that effect," I replied.

It was still dark when I forced my front door open. I heard Gotcha snoring, then stop, then start again as she realized who it was coming in so late. Or early. I went to bed, only to have my Bulldog wake me later.

When I emerged from the bathroom, Gotcha was asleep on the bed. I dressed in a pair of faded jeans, a royal blue and gold Narnia College t-shirt, socks and running shoes. I called Gotcha and let her out into the front yard, closed the damaged door, and turned to the kitchen.

I fixed breakfast and thought about Liv. But that joy was nudged aside by guilt. I should never have called her. For a moment, I felt like I had taken advantage of her. For weeks I have suspected that she was attracted to me. So what was she supposed to do after letting me in and hearing my story? What had I wanted to happen?

And then I just let it go, said my standard, heartfelt prayer of, "Lord, forgive me, a miserable sinner." I added a caveat, "And God bless Olivia Olson." I did not add anything more, other than thanking God I was able to respond to her. There was that. Sometimes I surprise myself.

The microwave clock read ten twenty-nine. I let Gotcha back in, gave her meds and breakfast, filled up her water bowl, and sat down to eat. I ate breakfast, peanut butter and honey on real bread for a change instead of from a spoon, cleaned up, grabbed the shotgun and walked down to the mailbox, realizing my stroll made me vulnerable to an ambush. I watched the woods and hustled down the drive.

The air was still cool. I could hear birds calling, and the wind roughing up the topmost leaves in the tall trees along my driveway. At the blacktop, I picked up my copy of the *Des Moines Chronicle*, and retraced my steps.

Back indoors, I tossed the paper on the coffee table, set the shotgun next to it, found my cell in the drawer under the computer, and punched in Gunther's number. Julie answered, we chatted briefly, then she agreed to give Gunther my message that the front door needed some adjusting.

"He'll be there today," Julie promised. "I'll give him a call on his pager and get him over there during his lunch break, if not sooner."

"Where is he?"

"Working on another house," Julie said, and I could sense her smile through her voice. "And he has a potential buyer for the house he built last year up in Allamakee County. Thanks to you, Thomas."

"Shucks, missy, I didn't do nothin'," I drawled.

"You're a nice man, Thomas."

"No, I'm not. Sometimes I do nice things, though."

"You are a piece of work," she laughed. "I'll give Gunther your message as soon as we hang up."

I picked up the Mossberg. No more waiting around. Time to do a little in-depth searching for the one person on the planet who could unravel this mess. Time to find the snake and cut off its head.

After I stopped by the Sheriff's office to write my report, I would snoop around, see if there were any inspirational hunches that might surface as the day unfolded, do a little legwork. "You wanna go for a ride?" I asked Gotcha. Her ears perked up and she jumped down from the recliner. "Let's go, then," I said.

On the way, I hung my arm out the window, opening my hand wide to feel the air through my fingers and along my fingertips. I thought about Olivia. I had never expected to ever again sleep with a beautiful woman, resigning myself to bitter, pouty celibacy for eternity. Another element of my grief. Liv had changed it all in just a few days. I wanted to see her again.

Once in town, I turned down First Street. A leg was sticking out of the lilac bushes at the edge of Arvid Pendergast's property, and I honked the horn. I think I saw the leg wave in return.

I turned right on Bridge Street, crossing the bridge, and then pulled into the parking lot at the courthouse. Gotcha and I got out. I put the shotgun on the floor in the back, locked the doors, and then Gotcha and I sauntered over to the steps leading down to the courthouse basement and the Sheriff's Office. We went in. Payne was there.

The Sheriff looked up from behind his battered desk and said, "The Angel of Death and Injuries walks among us. With his fierce protector. What's his name? I didn't catch it last night while I was investigating some routine trespassing out in the woods."

"Her name's Gotcha, and she bites dangerous men," I said. "You're safe."

"Come 'ere, Gotcha, defender of the daffy," Payne said, rising from behind his desk and going to the dog. Gotcha wiggled her little warped tail. Payne was grinning.

I said, "See what I mean? That dog'll bite."

Payne said, "She only bites dangerous bad men."

I changed the subject. "I'll bet the chauffeur from last night's simple trespassing spilled his guts once he realized he was in your custody, didn't he?"

"Won't tell me a thing," Payne squatted, stroked Gotcha's head, and rubbed her ears. "The car was, surprise, stolen. As for the immediate news, there are no fingerprints on anything, including the two incompetents you plugged and the guy Gotcha chewed up."

"You mean no record of their fingerprints?"

Payne continued to play with Gotcha, rubbing her spine at the base of the tail. The Bulldog was licking her chops in obscene bliss. "No, I mean there are no fingerprints because all three of those guys have had their fingertips surgically removed, sandblasted, acid-dipped or something. They are as smooth as a baby's butt. That can be a tip-off that one is dealing with those who have found a previously-rewarding career in opposing the goals of law enforcement. I do not think they were acting on their own. Also, I do not think we will ever know who hired them."

"Dammit. I'd like to know so I can get to the root of the problem and deal with it. I'm getting impatient."

"These guys probably don't even know who's behind it. They couldn't tell you if they wanted to. They got cash from some guy they might know only by reputation and first name, who got the money from another guy, and so forth. Nothing in writing, no real names if any names are given. You could put a gun to our boy's head and he might be inspired to let you know who was behind the hit, and still couldn't tell you."

"Dammit!'

"You already said that."

"But not as fervently."

"I did some thinking last night, before I went to sleep, Thomas, just to turn over a new leaf in my career, you understand, and I was wondering just where you learned to shoot like that. I mean, with them firing at you in close quarters and there being two of them apparently having done this sort of work before..." Payne said, not looking at me, scratching the deep rough at Gotcha's throat, "it might make one think you have some kind of training, perhaps a bit of experience in such activities." He massaged Gotcha's shoulders. She looked as if she might fall asleep.

"Oh," I said, "I've had bits and pieces here and there, over time. I used to hunt a lot as a kid, target practice, qualified as 'Expert' in the M-16 in Basic. Occasionally shot with a friend of mine outside Georgia. On a shooting range in Belue."

Payne rose slowly to his feet and looked at me. "Last night, Thomas, you killed two professional shooters and wounded another. According to you, two had weapons drawn and were looking for you in your home. I assume it was an unexpected visit."

"It wasn't in my Blackberry," I said. "You seem tense, Sheriff."

"I am intensely curious, yes."

"A quality crucial to law enforcement. I congratulate you! Now, if I can just do my statement and press charges against the last of The Three Stooges, I'll get out of your hair. I intend to conduct a search for their employer."

"I have a cousin high up in United States Naval Intelligence," Payne said, "and yes, I've already told him that's an oxymoron. I need to tell you I had him check out your service record."

"Oh?" I said, gathering new respect for the Sheriff. Lunatic Mooning was right.

"I can see that you're merely interested, as opposed to concerned, because you know I didn't find anything you haven't already told me. Correct?" Payne said.

"Why didn't you just ask me? You know military records have a way of disappearing if one knows the right people."

"I suspected that, oh object of curiosity. So what did you do in the Navy? "

"Some of this, some of that," I offered.

"Were you in Special Forces? Were you a SEAL?"

I said nothing.

"Okay, have it your way. But, Thomas, you need to know I'm not buying your line of bullshit."

"I never once thought that you did," I said. Time to move on. "Have my buddies from the bridge debacle fessed up yet?"

Payne jammed his hands into his pockets. "Nope. But I think they will. Whether that person, or persons, will turn out to be the same source behind the dudes from last night, time will only tell. I suspect a connection."

"There have been clues," I said.

Payne made a face.

"So, let's do the paperwork, and then I'm on my way. Call it morbid curiosity, but I don't intend to sit around anymore. Come on, pupper," I said, and Gotcha was instantly at my side, saving Payne from an Alienation of Affection lawsuit.

"You better not get out of bounds with Larry if you find him. Give me a call. Sit on him. Then let me handle it. Let the system handle it."

"I know you can handle it, Harmon, and I have some faith in the system, even if you refuse to waterboard. It's just that I don't know if it will happen in my lifetime or not. After last night, the definition of what constitutes my lifetime is a little vague. Have a nice day. Call me if you hear anything."

"I did hear something," Payne said, a little smile on his face.

I looked at the Sheriff.

"I heard you dropped by to say nighty-night to Olivia Olson last night, after the shooting. I'd encourage you to watch your step."

"What does that mean?"

"It means she's a mighty fine person who doesn't need to get hurt, Thomas."

"Duly noted."

"Good."

"I gotta get out of here," I said, and as soon as I finished the paperwork Payne handed me, I was, Gotcha at my side.

Chapter 21

"These newspaper reporters...ever since Sullivan versus New York Times...have got a license to lie."

- *Edward Bennett Williams*

Gotcha and I rode around a while that Saturday, found nothing, and by late afternoon we meandered on home. A blue Toyota 4Runner waited in my driveway. A young lady sat on its hood. I glanced quickly around to see if anyone else decided to visit. Nope. I parked and got out, retrieved Chief Justice. Gotcha bounded out behind me, sniffed the air, then wheeled and joined me as we headed for the house.

4Runner Woman, maybe thirty years old, dressed in Levi's and a navy blue t-shirt, jumped quickly to her feet. She wore Rainbows, I think they're called. Her hair was thick, black, long, and braided down her back in a single pigtail. Her pale blue eyes revealed intelligence, inquisitiveness, and a smattering of arrogance. A beautiful woman. All the more reason to be careful.

She clutched a purse in her left hand. *So*, I thought, *right-handed*. If her hand dipped into the purse, I would bring the shotgun up.

I glanced around, walked slowly, and thumbed the safety off

Chief Justice as I slipped my finger alongside the trigger guard. This person would not be the first attractive murderer to fool a man. I had seen *The Sting*.

"Don't shoot!" the woman said in an artificially high voice, raising her hands in mock terror. "I didn't come to kill you!" She gave Gotcha a skeptical look.

"Who are you and why are you here?" I asked. "You may put your hands down."

She arched one eyebrow. "I'm Suzanne Highsmith. I write for..."

"The *Des Moines Chronicle*. Columnist. Good technical writing skills, given to overly-dramatic hyperbole in human interest stories, and Marxist slant better left to the editorial pages. Nice job writing about the family that drowned at Lake Okoboji. A little lachrymose."

"'A little lachrymose'? What kind of a man uses the word 'lachrymose' in conversation while holding a rifle on a woman?"

"It's a shotgun, and would you please present your press card and driver's license? Slowly." I tapped the Mossberg against my leg.

"Aren't we a little paranoid?" she asked, slowly reaching into her purse.

"Do you have a tapeworm?"

"What?"

"You said 'we' and you appear to be by yourself. What do they teach you in college these days?" I brought Chief Justice up, butt against my right thigh and the business end pointed vaguely off to my right. A few quick degrees to the left and she would be a target. She noticed, fished out her wallet, and produced the documents.

I approached, took the Iowa Driver's License and Press Card with my left hand, stepped back, and glanced at the cards. Neither photo did her justice. I pointed the weapon at the ground, clicked on the safety, and handed back her identification. She took them abruptly; jerking them from my fingers. I avoided fainting.

"Paranoia is an illogical fear, an unsubstantiated anxiety. I have had a total of five grown men try to kill me in the last few weeks, and two more who merely intended to put me in the hospital, so you'll forgive me for being cautious, Miss Highsmith. If men can't get the job done, why not send a woman? I'm sure you'd agree with those politics."

"I'd like to ask you about the shootings out here," she said. "Shall we go inside?"

"No."

"Your idea of Southern hospitality? I hear you're from down South."

"My version of honesty. My home is private. And I'm from Clinton. Iowa."

"Whatever."

Gotcha ambled slowly over to Highsmith and sniffed her shoes, then looked up and snorted once. Highsmith took a step back.

"Does it bite?"

"Only once."

Highsmith shuddered.

"Chill, Gotcha," I said, and she looked at me with her big, sad eyes, turned away from the reporter, and came over to my side and sat.

"Nice dog." It sounded as if the young woman was commenting on something gooey at the side of the road.

"She is that, truly. Her name's Gotcha, and she won't bother you, but she does like to have her goozle scratched. It's a good way to win her affection."

"I fear to ask, but a reporter's curiosity is insatiable. What's her 'goozle'?"

I reached down and began scratching and massaging the pendulant, soft folds of excess skin under her chin and covering her throat. Gotcha's eyes closed and her tongue flopped out. "She has all this extra skin, her goozle, in case she gets in a fight and the other dog, or whatever it might be, grabs her by the throat. All they get is thick skin, not the jugular or windpipe. Tends to discourage them, especially when the Bulldog turns and bites *them*. And won't let go."

"Is that a pit bull?"

I sighed deliberately to show impatience. "No, she's a Bulldog, known to the unsophisticated masses as an English Bulldog.

Wonderful creatures, really. If you have an interest, I can provide you with a history, and fascinating facts as to why they look this way. For example, that thick wrinkle across the bridge of her little nose is called a stop wrinkle, and it's there to divert an adversary's blood flow from her eyes so she can see clearly while locked on. And her short muzzle and underslung jaw is like that so she can breathe, also while locked on. But, I don't think you're interested, are you?" I looked at Miss Highsmith, who appeared to be suffering from heartburn.

"No, but thank you ever so much all the same. I'm interested in you, and what's been going on relative to your being here in Rockbluff."

Highsmith fished a spiral notepad and ballpoint pen from her purse. She flipped the cover of the notepad, shifted her weight, looked up and said, "I'll call you Thomas if you'll call me Suzanne."

"I'll be happy to call you Suzanne, and you may certainly call me Thomas, but if I am ever in a situation that requires an introduction, I will introduce you as 'Miss Highsmith.' I do not recognize Miz, and I never will. Trash English."

"Now, aren't we being language elitists?"

"We?"

She shifted her weight to the other leg.

"You need to understand that anything we talk about is off the record," I said.

"Why? What difference does it make?"

"I like my privacy. I don't want to be bothered. I don't want my answers to your questions in the public domain."

She stared at me, her blue eyes cool. She looked back down at her notebook. "I understand from reliable sources," she began, "that several weeks ago you called in a nine-one-one from a farm where a woman's husband, Hugh Soderstrom, was killed in an accident." She looked up. "Is that right?"

I looked back and said nothing.

She gave her head a little negative shake, as if to say, "I don't believe this," and looked back down at her notebook. "A few weeks ago you beat up two men in a barroom brawl; later, you fought two more men on the bridge downtown, and you put them both in the hospital, where they remain." She looked up, received no encouragement, and continued from her notes.

"And last night, three men came out here and there was an exchange of gunfire. You killed two men without sustaining so much as a scratch. The third was badly injured and is now hospitalized." Suzanne looked up at me. "Wherever you go, people get hurt or killed. Like, monthly. Am I too far-fetched here?"

"Off the record?"

The young reporter rolled her eyes, glared at me, then put the cap on her pen and flipped her notebook shut. "Okay, everything's off the goddamn record. Jesus."

It was fun messing with the press. "So, what do you want to know?"

"Everything that's happened since the accident at the farm."

"I wasn't at the farm when the accident happened. It was a coincidence that I was driving by right after the situation occurred. I was just getting used to being back in Iowa after a long time, enjoying the look of the land. By the way, if you're interested in accuracy, I did not phone in the nine-one-one call. That was done by Wendy Soderstrom, the dead man's wife. So much for your reliable sources."

"I stand corrected. I will speak to the person. Now, why did you get in the fight in, um..." she checked her notes, "the delightfully named 'Shlop's Roadhouse'?"

"I was asking questions to discover the whereabouts of an individual who frequents the place. His friends took exception to my inquiries. They jumped me as a mode of discouragement and I defended myself."

"And the incident on the bridge?"

"Those men were hired by someone to kill me, at least that's what they said. Before I was forced to defend myself. That's how I got a puffy lip and loose teeth, an abrasion over my cheekbone, a cut over my eye—all nicely healed."

"You seem to be pretty adept at defending yourself. Are you a martial arts guy? Ex-Special Forces or something like that?"

"I'm just pretty lucky, along with having read a little bit about a lot of subjects, taken the time to observe other things, listened and learned." I could tell she didn't believe me.

"So tell me about last night. Things seem to be escalating."

"Three men came by to kill me. I happened to be walking in the woods with Gotcha when they kicked in the front door. I caught two of them by surprise inside the house. The third, who was waiting in a car, incurred superficial injuries as a result of participating in a negative peer group."

She laughed. It was a brief snicker, but genuine. "God, I wish I could use this stuff. This is a helluva story. And you are really a load, Thomas. Now, I have one more question. Do you know what that question is?"

"You've already been told who, what, where, how, and when. You're probably intrigued, as am I, about the why part of the equation. I mean, why are all of these people trying to kill me?"

"Wow! You went to college, didn't you?"

"And graduated, too, even though it was a public institution."

"Well?" she asked, moving her head side to side in anticipation, "What's the answer? Why did the muscle with guns try to take you out? Why did the men on the bridge try to kill you? Why did the dolts in the roadhouse try to rough you up?"

"Another question! But one I'll answer. Yes, I think I know the why. I'm going to find out, beginning as soon as you go back to Des Moines and don't write your story."

"One last thing. When this story is finished, assuming you live through it, I would like to have the exclusive. Deal?"

"Nope."

"Why not? This doesn't make sense! I'll respect your privacy, but when it's over, what's the harm in giving me the exclusive? You'll be famous, and with your attitude, a media darling. Might even get your own talk show. And I'll get the Pulitzer Prize." She smiled a dazzling, white, charming smile.

"That's why no one gets the story."

"You don't want me to win the Pulitzer Prize?"

"I don't want anyone to know any of my business."

"But if you get killed, and I hope that doesn't happen, of course, seeing as how we're on a first name basis and all, I will do the story. And if you give me information now, I'd do your story justice, and, if you're dead, it won't matter to you then anyway."

"Good-bye, Suzanne."

She walked out and started for her trendy wheels, then stopped and turned. "If you change your mind, will you call me first?"

"Say goodbye, Suzanne."

"So long, Thomas. You've been one repressed, impolite, uptight, illogical, mildly amusing and inhospitable pain in the ass. May you fall down in a crowded pig pen and not be able to get up," she said, hurling the ultimate Iowa insult, flinging open the door to her Toyota, flouncing in behind the wheel, slamming the door shut, gunning the engine, and spinning gravel as she left. My visitors like to spin gravel.

There was no way I would have given her an interview. Even if she had been polite, professional, and avoided cursing. Not only was she rude, she paid absolutely no attention to, and acted afraid of, Gotcha. Anyone with such a deep and enduring chasm in their social skills, anyone with such a lack of discernment did not deserve any special favors until they repented.

I walked back inside, set the shotgun on the kitchen counter, and dropped down to the floor and roughhoused with the big Bulldog, who loved it. It was her favorite group activity. A few minutes later, when we settled down, we fell asleep on the floor in front of the cold fireplace, shotgun nearby, Gotcha snoring sweetly at my side.

Chapter 22

"The man who reads nothing at all is better educated than the man who reads nothing but newspapers."
- Thomas Jefferson

For the next two days, I searched for Larry Soderstrom. No one had seen him, and the clock was ticking with regard to the Trust. It was July 18th, two days before the deadline for his decision about whether or not to buy the land left by his brother. No decision from Larry would lead to bids for Hugh's half of Soderstrom Farms, and a fresh 60-day timeline. I hadn't heard a word. Carl Heisler would have let me know.

Payne called me. He had a search warrant and asked me if I'd like to go with him out to Larry's place. "Are you kidding me?" I said.

I met Payne at the courthouse and followed him deep into the country, down a blacktop road that became a dirt road. On a curve, Payne turned into a gravel driveway leading to a soaring A-frame that looked almost new. There were no vehicles.

"Don't touch anything," Payne said as he knocked on the front door. No answer. He tried the door, found it unlocked, and we went in.

The house was well furnished. I figured maybe Wendy, as a helpful sister-in-law, had helped him out on that. Nevertheless, it was a mess. Clothes were scattered. A pair of boots lay toppled over on the floor. Stained area rugs, crusted dishes and filmy glasses in the sink next to an empty dishwasher all pointed to a pig. The refrigerator held plenty of cold beer and the cabinets revealed a few canned goods. Tuna, Spam, green beans. An unmade, king-sized bed with black satin sheets and pillowcases and a giant plasma TV dominated the master bedroom. A mirror looked down from the ceiling over the bed.

Harmon found nothing connecting Larry to his brother's death or the attacks on me. He did find enough cocaine, pot and alcohol to keep Congress supplied for a fortnight, several flimsy female underthings and hygiene products, an extensive pornography collection (both print and video), proof of staggering gambling losses even though he did not bet on the Cubs, and a tardy slip from 7th Grade Home Room. I touched nothing.

"Whether he killed his brother or not, whether he ordered the hits on you or not," Payne said as he finished bagging evidence, "we still have enough to put his butt in prison—not jail—for quite a while. It's not against the law to gamble and drink, but he's crossed the line with drug possession. I can't wait to find him."

"I'm not so sure anymore that you will find him," I said. "Maybe he's just bugged out forever. Maybe his bookies lost patience. Maybe he's even now living in Sri Lanka and laughing up his sleeve at us while he dallies with heroin and pretty brown women."

"Maybe your harsh treatment of his alleged hirelings cast dread over his existence, too," Payne said, "and he decided his long-term prospects were better elsewhere."

"On the other hand, abandoning fifteen to thirty million dollars of prime Iowa farmland doesn't make much sense. Does he have any priors on the drugs?"

"The only priors are misdemeanors. Speeding, public intoxication, public urination, disturbing the peace, minor assault, stuff like that."

"If Larry got himself a superior attorney and faced those drug charges, what would happen to him?"

"Larry would get himself a superior attorney. What would happen to him? I'd guess a heavy fine, long probation, maybe some community service. Seriously-dirty looks from his fellow citizens on the streets of Rockbluff, but he already has that. Maybe a busted nose from a fed up citizen. Stern warning, for real, from the court that if it happened again, he could start his orientation to the new Fort Madison State Penitentiary."

"Then he hasn't bugged out. So, where is he hiding?"

"It's embarrassing to admit, being a law enforcement professional and all, but I haven't a clue, other than to say he's here and there, and the trail isn't getting any warmer, even if the weather is," Payne said as we walked together out the front door of the A-frame. The Sheriff closed the door behind us. There were woods on three sides of the house, and a hay meadow across the dirt road. Everything was green and smelled fresh.

"Well, I'm going to keep looking," I said. "I guess I'll just try being random and unpredictable. Might work. Just missed him twice at Shlop's."

"You're already random and unpredictable."

I smiled. Some people like to be noticed. Not me.

"May I offer a piece of advice as a life-long investigative type?" Harmon asked.

"Sure."

"Why don't you just get away from all this for the time being? Do something different. Let your mind take a deep breath. Might help your perspective. Sometimes I've gotten great insights when I wasn't specifically focused on my most important issue at the time."

It was a little after five-thirty. Good to be in the boonies, missing the growing push of rush hour traffic that I knew had to be converging on the bridge in Rockbluff right about now.

I looked around. Damn hot. Upper 90's for sure. Iowa in July. Hotter than Belue, Georgia, but those people would never believe a state up north could be hotter than a city in the heart of Dixie.

I turned to the Sheriff. "Maybe I'll take your advice. Maybe I'll drive to Des Moines or Minneapolis and have a fine dinner someplace."

"You might sample the wares a little closer to home. Try Whistling Birch. It's been written up in the *Des Moines Register* and the *Chicago Tribune* as one of the best eating places in the Midwest. And it's right here in Rockbluff."

"The Whistling Birch Golf and Country Club?" I had seen their ad in the phone book, and heard it on the radio, but tossed off their bragging about their chef and wine cellar as small town pride in having a guy who did the serious preparation of corn dogs. And twelve bottles of Boone's Farm on their sides in the basement.

"The same," Payne replied. "You have to be a member, or the guest of a member, to play golf there, but the dining room and bar are public. They prefer reservations and plenty of cash. The last time I went it was forty-five dollars for dinner. For me. By myself. I went to the bar, not the lounge, afterwards for three quick brewskis and that was another eighteen bucks. You can spend more if you go early and have a drink in the lounge before dinner, or linger afterward and listen to their piano player while drowning your sorrows that come with the numbers at the bottom of the check."

"I'll give them a call when I get home."

"You'll enjoy yourself. And that piano player isn't too hard on the eyes. She also sings well. College girl. Local. Only works summers and Christmastime."

"Thanks for the tip."

"By the way, Thomas, don't let your guard down until Larry's accounted for. He's a mean man, and he does carry a grudge."

"I am ever vigilant," I said, climbing into my truck, turning the ignition, and enjoying the sound of immense horsepower coming to life. That's almost as good as instant air conditioning. I drove away.

When I got home I made a reservation for two the next evening at the Whispering Birch Golf & Country Club, prepared a dinner of cheeseburgers and Zesty fries and watched the Red Sox defeat the Blue Jays in Fenway Park in a slugfest, 11-8. After that, on a hunch, I grabbed the shotgun and got in my truck and drove by Larry's house, hoping I just might catch him sneaking back. Nothing there. No lights in the house and no Corvette in the drive that circled around behind the house.

So I drove home, drank five beers, and went to bed and slept soundly, eased into dreamland by the rhythmic snoring of Gotcha at the foot of the bed on her tuffet. Nice to have a peaceful constant in my life.

In the morning, I let the big Bulldog out and back in, took the shotgun with me down the lane to pick up the morning paper, and hiked back up to the house. I placed the paper and the shotgun on the kitchen table, fed and medicated Gotcha, poured myself a tumbler of orange juice (with pulp), read the Sports Section, cleaned up, read the *Boston Herald* website articles on last night's baseball game, and tidied up the joint in deference to Ernie.

Out on the deck I watched the morning light spread higher into the sky. It was cool out there, and I enjoyed the morning chill, knowing it would be hot soon enough.

Back inside, I plopped down at the kitchen table and picked up the *Des Moines Chronicle* and checked out the front page. In a box at the bottom left, sections of the paper and their stories were highlighted. Movies and Entertainment, Sports, Classifieds, and so on. I scanned through the list and something in the Op-Ed section caught my eye. "Violence comes to Rockbluff as..." it read. I fished out Section E and there, above the fold, a column by Suzanne Highsmith screamed the headline, "Violence Comes To Rockbluff" with a secondary line going on to state, "Bizarre Happenings Accompany Stranger's Arrival." I put the paper down and stared out the window. *Son...of...a...bitch!*

The article, along with a photo of the double-arch limestone bridge in downtown Rockbluff, read:

Thomas O'Shea, an Iowa native returning to his home state after two decades in Georgia, is a rugged, close-mouthed stranger to Rockbluff, a newcomer who carries a loaded shotgun with him everywhere he goes.

Since O'Shea moved into his pricey hermitage south of Rockbluff in May, he has been involved in several violent, and tragic, events. He was "coincidentally" first at the scene on May 20th when Hugh Soderstrom, 28, was killed in what is being called, officially, a farming accident. O'Shea told this reporter he does not think Soderstrom's grisly death under the blades of a rotary mower, the most gruesome fatality in decades in quiet Rockbluff County, was an accident. O'Shea thinks Soderstrom was murdered, although he would not say who he thinks the murderer, or murderers, might be.

A few days later, on June 1st, O'Shea was allegedly attacked in a local bar, Shlop's Roadhouse, by two men, allegedly friends of Larry Soderstrom, brother of the dead farmer. O'Shea allegedly subdued the men in the name of self-defense.

On the morning of June 15th, at approximately 1:00 AM, two men from Dubuque attacked O'Shea on the town's historic double-arch limestone bridge in the center of this picturesque village. According to O'Shea, the men said they were sent to kill him. Both men were seriously injured and are still hospitalized, one after being thrown by O'Shea from the bridge into the Whitetail River. As if that were not enough to concern Rockbluff's citizens about their new neighbor, on the evening of the 15th of this month, while O'Shea was walking his dog in the woods surrounding his remote retreat, three more men, armed with untraceable handguns and driving a stolen car, broke into his house with the intent, according to O'Shea, to kill him.

O'Shea shot and killed two intruders. The third was critically injured. All three men remain unidentified. The survivor is hospitalized under Sheriff Harmon Payne's protection. So far, the wounded man is refusing to cooperate. And Thomas O'Shea is refusing to talk. Sheriff Payne said that, in each instance, O'Shea acted in self-defense. The Sheriff would make no other comment except to say that the Rockbluff crime wave is under investigation.

This reporter was successful in finding answers to many questions, but others go unanswered. Who is Thomas O'Shea, and why are all of these people trying to do him harm? Was Hugh Soderstrom's death a homicide? Where is Larry Soderstrom? And, most importantly, when will this sleepy, beautiful little village in northeastern Iowa's rugged hill country be able to go back to being the idyllic place it was before Thomas O'Shea moved in and people started to die?

I put the paper down and decided if Suzanne Highsmith were to show up at my front door at that moment, there would be another violent death in Rockbluff County, but not likely as quick and merciful as those previous. I might just set Gotcha on her and let it go. I looked at Gotcha, sleeping with her big tongue hanging out and becoming all dry and papery, the chunky dog relaxed on her recliner.

My first thought was to call Highsmith's editor, maybe even the publisher, but I decided against it. The damage was done, my privacy compromised. Time to move on to better situations.

So I called Liv Olson. When she picked up her phone, I said, "How would you like to go to dinner with me tonight? I would be happy to pick you up at seven."

"Oh, is this that violent guy who never goes anywhere without his shotgun? Should I be seen with someone who has brought so much death to our bucolic little village?"

I groaned. She laughed. I said, "Go ahead, take a chance. Custer did."

"I'm not sure that's very encouraging."

"Don't you want to know our destination, should you decide to take a chance?"

"I'm all ears."

"I know better."

"You've been peeking," she said.

"And it's been productive. So, are you interested?"

"I'd love to have dinner with you, Thomas. What would be the appropriate attire?"

"I guess professional casual would do it. Curious?"

"Surprise me," she said, her voice lowering.

"I thought I did. Very recently."

There was a sexy chuckle, and then Liv Olson said, "Surprise me again."

"See you at seven."

"Yes, you will," she said, and the conversation ended.

Chapter 23

"The character of a man is known by his conversations."
- Menander

I hoped dinner with Olivia might help me calm down, regain my perspective, prevent me from strangling Suzanne Highsmith. I dropped the phone in a drawer, then noticed the e-mail light was blinking on the computer.

It had to be Ernie. No one else had the address.

The e-mail read:

Neat-o article in this morning's Corn Belt Bugle! Perhaps you've read about the madman who's moved into this idyllic village somewhere in Iowa and precipitated mayhem and death. Could you maybe get back to me on the real story, preferably before the sequel? Please?
Shalom,
Shotgun O'Shea's Pastor

I got the phone back out and called Ernie. He answered on the third ring. "Shotgun O'Shea here," I said.

"What's going on up there? I thought everything was going well, almost boring. Now this article. I'm having trouble concentrating. Given the media, are there any inaccuracies in the piece?"

"I don't carry a shotgun everywhere I go. I shower without it. I am not 'secretive.' I am 'private.' I am not 'refusing to talk.' I am just refusing to talk to reporters, especially that one. I'm a regular chatterbox with everyone else, including the Sheriff."

"You've been throwing people off bridges? You shot two guys? Both dead?"

I brought Ernie up to date and filled him in on Hugh and Larry Soderstrom. He asked, "Do you think maybe one brother killed the other? There's biblical precedent, you know."

"I'm pretty sure. And Larry's disappeared."

"So what are you doing now?"

"I'm going out to dinner."

"I was asking what you are going to do now with regard to the guy who is getting people to try to kill you," Ernie sounded exasperated.

"Keep looking."

"But for now, he's still loose and after you?"

"He's still loose. I would like to think he's losing interest in me and seriously considering seminary. Try not to worry, Ernie. I'm pretty good at taking care of myself, and there are some people here who are watching out for me, too."

"Yeah, people named Lunatic Mooning and Bunza Steele. I am not comforted."

"I'd appreciate your prayers. Guardian angels would be nice."

"I will pray, but I'm thinking I need to come up."

"Ernie, if you want, you may worry in itty-bitty increments, just to feel better and meet the worry requirement, but that's it."

Ernie said, "I'm wondering if getting rid of criminals glorifies God. If you think you need a little backup, I'll be there."

"I will not hesitate to call for reinforcements, but I'll be fine," I said.

"God is sovereign," Ernie said.

"Tru dat, yo," I said and hung up. I looked at the clock. Time to get going. I cleaned up and dressed in tan slacks, a blue shirt, and an impressionistic flowery tie Michelle gave me for Father's Day three years ago. Sign of healing, I think, wearing it. I left Chief Justice on the kitchen counter and took off. Born to be wild.

I picked up Liv at exactly seven. She was wearing a simple black dress that, on her, wasn't so simple. She greeted me with a brief kiss and a longer one when I asked how to get to Whispering Birch Golf and Country Club, and then we were on our way.

The place looked like it fit into the property, as if it had been coaxed from the environment. Giant oaks abounded, but also red and sugar maples, and a plethora of white and yellow birch trees flourished everywhere. The club looked old and well maintained. Green before green was cool.

We pulled into the parking lot among a congregation of fancy cars, including a Rolls Royce with Wisconsin plates. My big Ford was the only pickup in the lot. I parked, got out, and fetched Liv. We walked together on the brick sidewalk leading to the clubhouse, admiring immaculate flowerbeds lining the approach. She identified the different flowers. I immediately forgot their names, the kind of exchange Karen and I often enjoyed. A brief shadow of guilt flitted across my psyche, but I let it go.

The blue granite clubhouse emerged in a stand of white birch trees at the end of the winding sidewalk. Inside at the maître 'd's station, I gave my name and "Walter," according to the discreet little nametag on the breast pocket of his light blue blazer, smiled and led us to our table in a far corner of the dining room, adjacent to a window that looked out over the 18th green. I liked our spot and said so, surprised that the maître 'd was the one who seated us.

"Thank you, Mr. O'Shea," Walter said. "Grace will be with you to take your order."

"Grace is always with me."

Walter tipped his head to the side, said, "Indeed;" then, "Here is the menu for this evening. I hope your dining experience is most enjoyable." Then he left.

"So, what do you think so far? Surprised?" Liv asked.

"I'll reserve judgment until I've sampled the Thunderbird and Milk Duds."

"They're both excellent, although I can't speak from personal experience, having never tried them. Harmon Payne told me once they were superior."

"Speaking of Harmon, what's his story?"

Liv leaned forward and I enjoyed the modest display of cleavage the neckline of her black dress afforded. "Harmon's a good guy. A good cop. But his wife left him a few years back because his job seemed to be more important than she was. He loved Pam, but he was shot once, injured a couple of other times, and lost for two days in a blizzard. She couldn't take it, and left. She's living in Ohio someplace now, remarried, children."

"Does he have any children?"

"No. Sad story all around, but I think he does find fulfillment in his work. I think he deserves a bigger role in a bigger place, but he loves Rockbluff. Born and raised."

"Does he have a girlfriend?"

"Rumors to that effect. But not from around here. I think she lives in Cedar Rapids, but that's hearsay. He should have a girlfriend, fine man like that. I love the guy, if you want to know the truth. Known him for years."

Grace, mid-twenties and tall, appeared and greeted us by name. Like everyone else, she was dressed in light blue and white. White blouse, light blue bolero jacket, dark blue skirt with a conservative hemline. We ordered; the chicken cordon bleu for me and filet mignon for Liv ("I'm in the mood for red meat."). I also ordered a carafe of domestic white Merlot.

"Planning ahead," I said to Grace as she wrote our orders, "what do you have for dessert tonight, realizing that dessert is the key to my dining experience?"

Grace replied, "Tonight we have New York cheesecake, amaretto cheesecake, Cherries Jubilee, Chocolata Comatosa, and peach, apple and pecan praline pies, which are all available a la mode."

"Well, Grace, tell my lovely companion about the 'Chocolata Comatosa'."

"The Chocolata Comatosa is the creation of our pastry chef, who is from Belgium. It is a double-chocolate cake, seven thin layers with intense dark chocolate icing between each layer, another icing, from semi-sweet chocolate, on the outside with a special chocolate liqueur poured over the top, and dark chocolate-covered maraschino cherries spilling off the top of the cake. In addition, shavings of very dark Swiss chocolate adorn the exterior of the creation. You may not order Chocolata Comatosa unless you have proof of legal age and a bodyweight of at least one hundred forty-five pounds."

I laughed. "That leaves out Olivia, who won't touch one hundred forty-five pounds holding my Bulldog."

"We make exceptions for people who have twice won the Iowa High School Teacher of the Year Award," Grace said, smiling at Liv.

"Wow. Then, by all means, bring Olivia Olson the Chocolata Comatosa after the entrée. Good for you, Liv," I said. "I didn't know you were famous."

"Thank you. So, what will you be looking forward to for dessert?"

"I'll go Southern with the pecan praline pie. Sounds healthful."

Grace nodded. "A wise and excellent choice."

Big tip for Grace coming up.

Just as she turned away, a gentleman strode into the room, which had been filling up quickly. He appeared to be in his late 30's, maybe five-nine, about 160 pounds and dressed in cream slacks, a pale blue shirt with a bright yellow tie, and a navy blue blazer with gold buttons that glittered even in the subdued light. Sandy-colored hair cut short, and a good, but not overdone tan completed his appearance. His eyes scanned the room intensely while Walter seated him in a booth on the opposite side of the room. Which made me feel less special.

When the man's eyes found mine, he paused briefly, as if he were retrieving and storing data, and then looked away. I had the distinct feeling I was expected to drop eye contact first. I did not. I never lost a staring contest except three or four times with Karen, who cheated by unbuttoning her blouse.

"Liv, who is that man who just came in?"

She twisted in her chair and glanced about. "The man in the lemon tie and blue blazer?"

"Yes."

"That's Jurgen Clontz, Junior. Businessman, millionaire, member here. He's on the Board of Governors, too."

"So that's the man with the Jaguar."

"You know about him?"

"Harmon filled me in. He looks cold."

"He creeps me out, but he can be pleasant."

"How?"

"He's given money to the school. New band uniforms three years ago; completely new, cutting edge computer system and smart boards for the high school classrooms."

"What's the quid pro quo?"

"Maybe none. Some people say he's not Satan incarnate," she said, "but there is lively debate on the topic."

Dinner was delicious, flawlessly served, and excellently presented. Dessert, even better. Liv finished the Chocolate Comatosa all by herself. She looked proud. I called for our check, paid Grace in cash, including an appreciative tip, and started for the door with Liv, determined to complete the evening with entertainment and maybe a cold beer or two in The Embers. Before we could exit the dining room, Grace intercepted us.

"Mr. Clontz told me to request the honor of your presence, Mr. O'Shea, Miss Olson."

I looked across the dining room. Clontz twisted around in his booth so he could see us. The man shrugged his shoulders as if to say, "Why not? Can't hurt."

"Liv, if he hits on you, pound your palm into his nose and shove up."

"You're a crazy person," she said. We crossed the room.

"Thank you for joining me, Mr. O'Shea, and good evening to you, Olivia, always nice to gaze upon a beautiful woman," Clontz said as he beckoned us to sit. We shook hands. Clontz's hand was small, narrow, and cold, as if there were a circulation problem, but his grip was strong, business-like. He said, "I appreciate your joining me, although, judging by the article in this morning's paper, you are already an obvious risk taker."

"As you know, I always carry a shotgun to minimize those risks."

"So, where is it?"

"In my truck," I lied. "I can get to it in about two minutes."

"Might not be soon enough," he said. "But actually, I thought I'd buy you people drinks. I've finished eating," he said, gesturing at the dishes he had pushed to the edge of the table. Much of the food was uneaten, an affectation I never learned to tolerate, growing up poor. America will someday have to account for all the food that she throws away.

"For future reference, what did you have, and how was it?" Liv asked.

"Lamb! I do so enjoy eating the flesh of little lambs," he said, then laughed, "and it was excellent, as is everything on the menu."

"I heard you had significant appetites," I said, "but my sources say it's land instead of lamb. Apparently, it's both."

Clontz looked at me. He ignored Liv. There was no humor in his pale eyes that projected intelligence and purpose, but no appetite, no heat. The look in those eyes reminded me of how a shark's eyes looked, constantly searching for data and food, but without emotion.

"Let's go into The Embers," he said. "I really would like to buy drinks."

"My land is not for sale," I said.

"Not yet," he said evenly. Then he laughed.

"Why are you so eager to plunk down your dough to buy us drinks?"

"Just being neighborly," Clontz said. "I thought a little Northern hospitality might offset the injuries you've suffered here, and help expedite the healing of your wounds, physical and emotional."

"Let's get that drink, then," I said, sliding out of the booth and helping Olivia to her feet. Following Clontz, we left the dining room and padded down the deeply carpeted hallway, past walls with hunting prints every few feet. Faint piano music beckoned to us.

The Embers Lounge was cozy and dark, built on several different levels no more than one or two feet higher or lower than each other, effectively providing privacy. One solid glass wall looked out over the golf course and the woodlands and bluffs beyond. Gleaming, walnut-paneled walls on each side of the glass added to the dark intimacy. Oil paintings depicting golfing scenes, thoroughbred horses, and Formula One racing cars, all enhanced by small spotlights, decorated the walls.

Opposite the big window, a solid stone wall rose from floor to ceiling, with a fireplace in one corner and a Baby Grand piano in the opposite. A young girl played the piano and sang "Blessed Are the Believers." Her voice, sultry and sophisticated beyond her years, caressed each note effortlessly.

"Maureen Maloney," Liv said, "one of my students a while back. Good kid."

We slid into a booth. I made sure Liv and I were facing the Maloney girl. She was much more pleasant than Clontz to look at.

A cocktail waitress in a mildly revealing black dress appeared.

Olivia said, "Hello, Melanie," and the waitress replied, "Oh, hi Miss Olson. Nice to see you." Liv beamed a smile back.

I deferred to Clontz, who ordered a double Chivas on the rocks, then turned to us and asked, "What may I order for you two?"

I said, "I have heard the Pinot Grigio is excellent." Liv's thigh rubbed leisurely against mine, and I momentarily lost concentration.

Clontz smiled and ordered Melanie to, "Scoot along now."

"Coming up," she said, leaving behind a small silver bowl filled with salted cashews, almonds, and macadamia nuts.

Liv and I watched as the young woman finished her number, demurely accepted the applause that followed, and began, "Just Another Woman in Love." *Must be Anne Murray night,* I thought. *Fine by me.*

Clontz twisted in his seat and followed my gaze, smiled grimly as he turned back to face us and said, "Sings like an angel, and with the morals of one, too. What a waste of fine flesh," he muttered.

I could feel Liv tense. She said, "Maureen's a fine person, and her morals are well grounded. Good family, good kid."

Melanie appeared and Clontz stared at her chest while she bent over and placed the orders on little coasters. He pushed a fifty down the front of her uniform and when she startled, she bumped his glass, spilling some of the scotch, leaving a potent puddle.

"Clumsy!" Clontz hissed under his breath.

"Oh, I'm so sorry, Mr. Clontz!" Melanie said, quickly soaking up the spill with a stack of cocktail napkins from her apron.

"It's hard to imagine someone being incompetent at such a menial task. Please, Melanie see if you can keep the next one in the glass."

She finished wiping up the spilled drink and left, her face flushed. In short order she returned with another double Chivas. Clontz said, "Take that out of the fifty, Melanie, and give me back the change. You can kiss your tip good bye."

Melanie nodded, completed the transaction as demanded, and left. I pushed the silver bowl to Jurgen Clontz. He waived it away. I pulled it back, scooped out a handful of nuts, and began popping them into my mouth, using a sophisticated technique I had learned in the finest Irish pubs. The smoothness of the action relied on a precise wrist movement. Then I found a thick, rich-looking whole cashew, picked it up with my fingertips, and bounced it off Clontz's forehead.

"That's for Melanie,"I said.

Clontz looked incredulous. Then he regained his composure like someone used to having nuts bounced off his forehead. "You take more risks than is wise," he said tersely. "Are you finished?"

I ignored him and touched my glass to Liv's, said "To another time," and sipped, enjoying how clean, cold, and good it was. She smiled at me, which redeemed the entire evening.

Clontz took a sip of his drink, the small ice cubes clicking together in the glass.

"Last guy I knew who drank Chivas Regal on the rocks was lined up against a wall in Kosovo and shot as a mercenary," I said, and the conversation began in earnest despite Liv's knee bumping hard against mine.

Chapter 24

"I know God will not give me anything I can't handle. I just wish He didn't trust me so much."
- Mother Teresa

Clontz said, "Is that projecting, or wishful thinking?"

"A friend of mine who served three years in the Middle East as a consultant once told me to never ask the question if I couldn't stand the answer."

"Oh, please stop, Mr. O'Shea, even before you start," Clontz said, waving his hand limply in the air and fluttering his eyelids. "I can't stand the thought of you criticizing me. I will absolutely perish if you continue."

I smiled at Clontz's display, which he dropped.

"I can stand anything you can, Mr. O'Shea," a bit of a challenge in his voice and a look meant to curdle milk. But I'm not milk.

"Perhaps we can field test that assertion someday."

I could see Olivia shaking her head. She said in a sing-song voice directed at us, "Oh waitress, may we have some more testosterone over here, please? I'm afraid we'll run out."

I sought her hand under the table, but she pulled it back, shot me a false smile, and drank some wine. I did, too, only in greater quantity.

"Go ahead, O'Shea, get it off your chest, whatever it is that's bothering you," he said.

"I don't like you," I said. "You stumbled out of the gate when you dumped on Miss Maloney's character, and you went flat on your face with your treatment of Melanie. And that's just tonight."

Clontz's eyes had gone as cold as the ice in his Scotch. He said, "I think it is a waste for a young woman with the face and body of Maureen Maloney to be a priss. Silly girl turned down an opportunity to spend time with me in exchange for all that I can do for her. I have been wildly successful financially, Mr. O'Shea, and I could do much to make her happy. You see, I know something that Freud couldn't figure out."

"Which is?"

"I know what women want."

"Are you kidding? Please, let me in on it! What is it?" Olivia pleaded.

"They want money and the security it brings. Women live for *things*, Mr. O'Shea, and they're all alike. They are all motivated by financial security. The ugly old rich man with the young, alluring wife is not so much a cliché as it is a fact of life."

"This great insight of yours might have come as a surprise to Mother Teresa," Olivia said, jabbing at the silver bowl's dwindling supply of nuts.

"If Mother Teresa didn't have the body of a whooping crane and the face of a horse, she'd have been like all the rest of the broads. Give her beauty and boobs and she'd have left Calcutta for North Beach in a heartbeat. I understand she questioned her faith the last twenty years of her miserable husk of a life."

"We'll have to discuss Elisabeth Elliott and Corrie ten Boom sometime," Liv said. There was enough heat coming off her words to cook kabobs. She finished her wine.

"Never heard of them," Clontz said.

"Of course not," Olivia responded.

I said, "So tell me, Mr. Clontz, since you know what women want, and you can provide it, why aren't you happily married?"

"I assume this marriage would be to the woman of my dreams?"

"Something like that." I caught Melanie's eye and she brought us another bottle of wine. I poured for Liv and me. Then I loudly slurped the wine for Clontz's benefit.

"I am not married, Mr. O'Shea, because I do not need to be married. Women need to be married. As long as I am wealthy and remain single, I can take from women what I need. Married, I lose my leverage, because her incentive to please would be gone. You must be some romantic, hopelessly stuck in a developmental time back in fifth grade when you could be made happy by a special Valentine from some pre-pubescent cutie."

"How did you know about Joyce Berkowitz?"

Clontz sighed. "I corrected our clumsy waitress because, as a Board member, I want to make sure the Club continues as the four-star establishment that it is. Spilling drinks is unacceptable."

"In my book, you were just being mean, and I have little regard for mean people."

Clontz shrugged. Olivia sipped. I slurped again. Olivia's knee smacked mine. A little too hard, if you ask me.

"Changing the subject, tell me, Thomas, did shooting those two men at your house make you happy?"

"I can tell you that when the shooting stopped and I was still breathing, I was positively gleeful."

Clontz finished his drink and looked across the room. Melanie appeared. Her hesitation was fleeting, and quickly overcome. "Melanie," I said, "would you please bring another round for Mr. Clontz?"

Before she could answer, Clontz said, "Make mine a triple Chivas on the rocks, which is fifty percent more than a double. And see if you can be less messy this time. Now, give me my change."

She did. I smiled at Melanie. She left quickly, returning almost immediately with the drink and a larger bowl with abundant mixed nuts. I gave her a one hundred dollar bill and told her to keep the change.

I looked at Clontz and said, "Reparations." Liv's hand sought mine and I took it.

Clontz fished in his pocket, withdrew a handful of change,

extracted two pennies, placed them side by side on the table, and returned the rest of the coins to his pocket. "My tip for ovary brains."

"As long as we're engaged in such a delightful repartee, perhaps I could seek your wisdom on another topic involving capital," I said.

"What? Investment advice?" Clontz sneered. "How 'bout, let me see now, land?"

"I already have some, thank you. What I'd really be interested in is your take, being local and all, on who the hell's trying to kill me. What have I done to deserve such a rude reception in this beautiful village?"

Clontz said, "Follow the money trail, Mr. O'Shea, follow the money trail."

"What?"

Clontz paused, as if waiting for my feeble mind to catch up. Then he said, with obvious fatigue from apparently having to put up with a lesser intelligence, "Money is the greatest motivator there is. I admit it. It's greater than sex, because if you have money, sex is a cinch. So follow the money trail and you will find out who is trying to kill you. I think even the Bible says that money is the root of all evil."

"You're almost right. But it says the *love* of money is the root of all evil. You should know that."

Jurgen Clontz waived his hand, as if to shoo away my observation. "Whatever, but, as I said, in your situation, someone's after money."

"I don't have any money to speak of," I lied.

"That's bullshit, and you and I both know it, but to the point, you are likely impeding someone from acquiring money. I know you are poking around into this Soderstrom situation. Maybe someone is getting nervous. Otherwise, they wouldn't be taking the extraordinary steps to remove you from the equation," he said, lifting his drink to his lips and chugging the rest of it. *That's a lot of hard liquor all at once*, I thought. Clontz looked at his glass, then set it down.

Maureen Maloney was singing "Proud Mary" in a rendition antithetical to Tina Turner's style. I liked Tina's better.

"So tell me," I said, "what would you do if I were impeding your acquiring eight thousand contiguous acres of prime northeast Iowa farm land?"

"It's eight thousand five hundred and twelve acres, to be precise."

"That, too."

"You mean if I were a person without ethics, professionalism, acumen, restraint, or class? A lowly crook?"

"Yes."

"I would take you out."

"Would you do it yourself, or would you hire someone to do the dirty work?"

"There are advantages both ways," Clontz said, his eyes no longer just cold. They were intense, oddly enthusiastic. Discussing business was right in his wheelhouse. He pounced. "If I did it myself, and this is purely hypothetical, you know, I would be assured of success. It is a truism that one simply cannot get good help these days—observe Miss Slop-and-Mop who has so ineptly waited on us tonight. But if I did it myself, I would chance some aberrant risk factor rearing its ugly head with the end result being my capture, conviction and incarceration, although another truism is that rich people aren't usually convicted. The alternative is to hire, one-on-one and very privately, a quality professional, so that if he is ever caught, or decides to try blackmail later, it is just his word against mine, which is flimsy stuff when trying to get convictions. No direct contact is critical. Use a middle man, or better yet, several middle men. Nothing that would link me to the event. Nothing in writing. Everything in cash. Conversations at random locations to avoid eavesdropping, human or electronic."

Clontz was tipsy now, but the land hog seemed caught up in the topic. I disliked Clontz more by the moment, but I had a grudging admiration for the way he went at a hypothetical. There was something vile, something downright odious about the man as the veneer of sophistication evaporated like the trace alcohol in his glass.

"So," I said, "given the scenario I just presented, which of the two ways would you do it?"

Liv squeezed my hand hard, but when I looked at her, she was staring at Clontz. I think she was seeing the same thing creep out from under his thin patina of civilization.

Clontz leaned across the booth. "Given those factors, I would take you out personally, for the satisfaction," he said, jamming his finger into my chest.

I considered grabbing Clontz's finger, pulling him forward, and then breaking the man's forearm against the edge of the table, but fought off Mulehoff's Initiative.

"And if I were you," Clontz continued as he started to slither out of the booth, "I would be ever vigilant until your adversary is neutralized."

"Thanks for the tip."

He shook his head, squirmed out of the booth, and stalked erratically out.

"You really know how to bond with the big shots," Liv said. She studied her wine glass, took a drink, then another, finishing it off.

"It's a gift," I said, then I took her hand and we left.

Chapter 25

"You lust and do not have;
So you commit murder."
- James 4:2

Liv, I think that went pretty well, as far as romantic evenings go, don't you?"

I helped her up into the truck, went around, and got in behind the wheel. I turned on the ignition and adjusted the a/c to fight off the thick, hot night. I turned on the headlights and looked at her when she touched my right arm.

She said, "Well, you captured my heart for sure tonight. I would have preferred a little more intensity with Clontz, especially when he jabbed his finger in your chest. I'm surprised you didn't break it off."

"I don't know, Liv. I kinda like the guy. He's certainly on the money about the function of women in society." Liv's punch on my shoulder was only a glancing blow, so I was able to stifle my cry.

"What a piece of work," she said.

I headed out of the parking lot and stopped at the exit. "Enough about Clontz; heck, the night is still young. What might we do for some fun?"

"Let's go find Larry Soderstrom."

"I've been trying," I said as we pulled onto the blacktop. "So has Harmon. In fact, last night I took a chance and drove out by his place around twelve thirty. No luck."

"Where does he live?"

"Not far from here."

"It wouldn't hurt to go take a look-see. We just might catch him, and how cool would that be? Besides, I'd like to see the place where he takes all those wild women."

"That would be fine, but I don't have Moon's shotgun with me. I left it at home. I could go get it, then we could come back out. Larry's A-frame is only about five miles away."

"Let's go right now before I chicken out."

"Okay, but not until I get Chief Justice."

"That'll take too long, and I suspect you'll want us to stay at your place once we get there, and who knows what carnal caperings could ensue?"

"Carnal caperings?"

"Oops."

"So now I have wonderfully lurid pictures in my head. Your fault. Your words," I said.

"Thank you."

"But we still need a weapon," I said.

"There's no need to go get a gun. We are not unarmed." And then Olivia Olson reached daintily into her glittering little purse and extracted a small pistol. "Look what I found, Thomas. My God! Is this one of those firearm doohickeys you big boys talk about all the time?"

I just shook my head and we took off as she placed the pistol, a double-barreled, pearl-handled .22 derringer, back in her purse.

Minutes later, maneuvering around a corner on the dirt road leading to Larry's house, I noticed with sharpened interest that some of the lights were on in the A-frame.

"Can we be this lucky?" I asked. Liv smiled and patted her purse.

I doused my headlights and rolled my truck to a stop out of

sight of the house. I shifted into park and secured the emergency brake.

"What are we going to do now?" Liv whispered.

"Go see if he's in. Quietly scout the house, apprehend him, if possible. What do you think we should do?"

"Shoot the sucker in the croakies, ask questions later," she said, then she started giggling. "It's fun talking tough. Nice to slip out of my schoolmarm persona."

"This is sooo disappointing, Liv." She stopped giggling, but a smirk remained.

I pushed the switch for the dome light to "Off," then eased out of the truck and quietly pushed the door shut. Liv came around to my side of the truck. She took my hand and said, "That was way cool, neutralizing the dome light. You are sooo hot!"

I put my finger to my lips, and Liv whispered, "Oh, really, you think we should try to be quiet?"

She followed me as I approached the house, darting from tree to tree. The night had cooled, and a fine mist drifted in the air. I smelled earth and plants and rainwater, and I heard the corn growing in the fields across the road from Larry's house. The moon, nothing more than a vague disc gliding through a batting of wispy clouds, offered little light. As we waited, we heard the velvety call of a hoot owl from a tree behind the house.

Then we heard another sound, definitely not natural, a big handgun going off. We froze. I waited for three or four minutes without hearing another shot, then took off, sprinting low, keeping trees between us and the house until we were at the front door.

I inched my way to a window with a curtain partly drawn across the glass. By the light of a single lamp on a small table, I saw Larry Soderstrom slumped in a big chair, blood slipping from his mouth, and something odd about the shape of his head. His right hand draped over the chair's armrest, a handgun hanging from his fingers. I watched as the weapon fell to the floor. His left hand dangled out of sight.

I could not see anyone else. The sorry sucker had committed suicide. I rushed to the front door and tried the doorknob. It did not turn. I stepped back and kicked in the door, grateful the lock gave way and not my knee or hip. The wood splintered and the door swung open, banged against the rubbery tip of a doorstopper, then swayed slowly back toward me. I pushed the door back and rushed inside the room, Liv right behind me.

She saw Larry, muttered, “Oh, Jesus,” and grew silent.

I held my hand up and she nodded her head. She looked like she was going to be sick. I turned and approached the chair. Larry Soderstrom was dead. Shot in the mouth, and I knew a thorough examination of the scene would find bits of skull and brain behind the dead man, perhaps on the ceiling. A half-empty bottle of Wild Turkey lay tipped over on the floor. Good taste in hard stuff, I guess, but then, I don’t touch it. I just ooze virtue.

A door closed in the back.

I stopped, completely silent, listening. Liv tapped me and I turned. She had her pistol out, and when she nodded toward the back of the house and raised her eyebrows in a “Shall we go?” expression, I nodded back, and we crept toward the sound. Another sound could be heard, the rumbling of a powerful automobile engine cranking up.

We burst through the kitchen and out the back door onto a terrace and saw Larry’s silver Corvette parked in the driveway. But we also saw a Jaguar sedan speeding rapidly down the driveway, lights off, tail lights flashing once as the driver negotiated a turn in the dark, and disappearing around the house and out toward the road. When the taillights flashed, the license plate was revealed—MYLAND. Like there was any doubt about who else might be driving a Jag in rural Rockbluff County. They’re all over the place, farmyards filthy with them.

Liv and I rushed around to the front of the house to my truck, me babying my leg so it wouldn’t go south on me again, Liv hobbling along in her high heels. “I’ll get in myself! Hurry, hurry!” she shouted, pushing me to the other side of the truck. We jumped in and I got the engine roaring, flipped on the headlights, backed into Larry’s driveway, turned around, and floored it, fishtailing down the dirt road while Liv fumbled briefly with her cell phone.

"Pick it up, pick it up," she chanted softly, then, "Harmon, this is Liv. I'm with Thomas. We just left Larry Soderstrom's house. He's dead and we just chased off someone and we're in hot pursuit. Is that how you say it? Hot pursuit?"

"It's a Jag with the MYLAND license plate," I said.

"Harmon, it's a Jag with the MYLAND license plate. Yes! Yes! He's going north. I'm following now in Thomas's truck. Got it?" A pause. "I won't do anything foolish, believe me. Can't speak for Thomas, but I'll keep an eye on him. Bye." She pushed a button, exhaled loudly, and tossed the cell phone over her shoulder into the backseat. Flamboyant crime fighter.

"Can't speak for Thomas?"

Liv shrugged and smiled.

"Larry didn't kill himself. Clontz just murdered him."

"Ya think?" Liv said as we flashed down the country road, green fields of corn streaking by us on both sides. "He's not going to get away from us, the stinkin' misogynistic creep!"

"I love it when you use big words," I said, pressing the accelerator harder and delighted I had a big V-8 powering us down the road. "Turns me on, woman."

"Just don't let that sucker absquatulate!"

Five minutes later, following the Jaguar's dust clouds in the misty night air, we swooped down upon the car nosed into a deep, soft ditch beside the road. A Rockbluff County Deputy Sheriff's car stood twenty yards farther down the dirt road blocking the way, headlights lighting up a green cornfield. I recognized Deputy Sheriff Doltch walking toward the Jag, flashlight in one hand, Glock nine millimeter in the other.

I braked hard and pulled over, blocking the road from our direction, but the way the Jag nosed into the scenery made any escape unlikely. The car was stuck in a soft dirt bank and wouldn't be getting out without a tow truck. Too much Chivas on the rocks.

I scrambled out. Liv jumped out of the truck on her side, hand in purse, rushing forward. I caught up to her, put my hand on her shoulder, and said, "You're a helluva woman, Olivia, but I want you to stay right here, okay? No need to go down to the car."

She saw I was serious and stopped. "Be careful, Thomas."

I hurried to reach Clontz slumped over his steering wheel, my mind already made up to punch the man in the face when I got to him. "Don't let him be dead, Lord," I muttered. "I want a piece."

But as I drew near, I saw that it wasn't Jurgen Clontz, Jr. behind the wheel. It was a woman. Doltch stopped, then moved forward, his gun hand dropping.

"Watch her, Stephen!" I shouted, and the Deputy brought his Glock up again. We slid down the bank side by side, arriving simultaneously at the car. I wrenched the door open.

Wendy Soderstrom sat behind the wheel, staring straight ahead into the milkweed and long grass on the bank, headlights muffled into the vegetation, the green weeds white in the glare. Her head rested on the collapsed airbag, a fine white powder sprinkled across her lovely chest, along with dark spots here and there I could not identify, but suspected. She'd suffered a small cut over her right eyebrow, and a thin line of blood trickled down alongside her nose and onto her cheek and lip. She held a cell phone in her left hand.

Doltch said, "Would you please step out of the car, ma'am, if you are able?"

Wendy started to move but her seatbelt snagged her. She released it with her right hand, dropped the cell phone on the floorboards, slipped out from the seatbelt, and emerged from the downward-angled car. "I'm okay," she said as she struggled briefly, and then squirmed up the bank with Doltch on one side of her and me on the other, each gripping one of her elbows, assisting. Doltch delivered her Miranda rights. She cursed briefly. He patted her down. She cursed some more.

Wendy looked at me. "So you're the asshole back at Larry's. Christ. Talk about timing."

She preceded Doltch to his cruiser, turned around, and leaned up against the car's grill. She wore designer sweats, dark chocolate brown with orange piping, and a dark headband in her tangled blonde hair. Even in the bright headlights of my truck, disheveled and banged up, she was beautiful. But no longer appealing as I realized the dark spots on her front were blood splatter.

A rising siren wailed over the fields of corn and soybeans in the drizzle of the black night. The four of us in the Iowa countryside waited silently and, in a moment, Sheriff Payne pulled up behind my truck and parked, leaving the blue lights flashing, but killing the engine and the siren. He got out and strode to the bleak gathering.

"Looks like everything's under control," he said, staring at Wendy, then looking at me. I shrugged my shoulders in response to the unspoken question.

Wendy said, "I waive my rights to an attorney. I give up. I did it. What do you want to know? Anybody got a cigarette?"

No one had a cigarette. Payne said, "Evening, Mrs. Soderstrom. Would you like to go down to the office with us and answer some questions?"

"Hell, no. I want to answer questions here and now. I doubt I'll ever be so free again as I am here in the middle of this God-forsaken vegetable bin you call a state. I'll tell you every goddamn thing you want to know, and I'll do it here, if you'll allow me. If you won't, you'll never, ever, get another word out of me."

Doltch holstered his Glock, turned to his car, reached into the front seat, and emerged with a tape recorder. Wendy watched, leaning against the cruiser. The cut on her eyebrow had clotted and the bleeding had stopped. She rubbed away the congealed blood from her cheek and lip. And then, in the mist growing heavier, she spoke.

She waived her rights against self-incrimination without threat or coercion from anyone. On tape. "I just want to be clean of the truth," she said firmly. The mist became a sprinkle, but no one moved, fixed in that place where the criss-crossing shafts of cold headlights and the blue staccato flashing from Payne's car converged on the widow, the murderer.

Liv came to my side and put her arm around my waist. I looked at her, and her sad eyes looked back at me, then to Wendy.

Wendy took a deep breath and began.

"I loved Hugh Soderstrom from the moment I saw him on the campus in Ames. He was tall and blonde with an athlete's body, and he had brains and the quiet confidence of someone much older. A man among boys," she said calmly, slowly. "He knew who he was and he knew where he was going, and when he asked me to go with him, I didn't think twice. I was a girl and he was a man. It was a no-brainer. Him, too, as it turned out. He liked my boobs. When we returned from our honeymoon in Bermuda, we went into the military for Hugh's two years' active duty. We lived in Hawaii and it was exciting. Then he got out and I found myself on the farm, and most of the time the only human being for miles, unless you count the hired help. The contrast between Honolulu and Soderstrom Farms was extreme. The contrast between Ames and Soderstrom Farms was extreme.

"I liked it at first," she said. "It's kind of pretty, you know, the expanse of land and field and crop and horizon, and I loved it because Hugh loved it so much, and I loved Hugh. Still do," she said, raising her eyebrows as if surprised by her statement. "He didn't lie to me. He was a farmer and a businessman, and that's all he wanted to be. Over time, though, I realized there was no hope of ever leaving the farm. None. I was crushed, pounded down, and flattened by the truth. And then I thought I could persuade him to consider a farm managing position in Rockbluff, then Cedar Rapids, as the promotions came from corporate farming CEO's he would be working for, and perhaps then to Des Moines, and eventually Chicago. Or Minneapolis. I thought approximations to farming would entice him, but Hugh wanted to work the land directly. He liked the black dirt under his fingernails, for God's sake."

The sprinkle eased back to a fine mist, drifting this way and that like a flimsy curtain in a breeze, then stopped. No one else seemed to notice, certainly not Wendy. She did not seem concerned as she delivered information without emotion. There was no remorse.

"I am a fairly quick study," she went on, taking a deep breath, then exhaling loudly, "and I finally understood that there would be no moving anywhere. I became restless. Then Hugh made me believe that children would change everything, and I talked myself into half-believing that they would, but it wasn't going to happen. Hugh was sterile, and in a way, I was glad." She looked at Liv. "You were smart to not have children. You look terrific for your age."

Liv remained silent, gently squeezing my hand, keeping her eyes on Wendy as if the murderer was an exhibit of some kind, and I guess she was.

"So, with no chance of children, I was back at square one. Back to no hope. My mind began to wander, to suppose," she said, and she smiled half-heartedly. "I became what the romance writers call a desperate woman thinking desperate thoughts. All kinds of 'What if?' ideas slipped into my mind.

"Larry noticed. He had been coming on to me at different times, and I always turned him away as gently as I could. Then he came by one day and I didn't turn him away. Surprisingly, we talked afterwards. At the time, Hugh was in Omaha at a conference of swine producers," she said, laughing a brittle laugh. "There was a kind of shallow pleasure, an irony, in bedding down the substance-abusing brother of my perfect husband while he was at a conference to help learn more about raising pigs. I liked it. Anyway, after a while, Larry told me he could arrange for Hugh to have an accident, that he wouldn't suffer, and that I would end up free and with a couple million bucks, certainly enough to get me started in the direction of my fantasies, if not take up actual residence in them. We were together a lot after that. Larry called himself The Two Million Dollar Stud, and I had to agree."

Wendy stopped talking for a full minute, maybe two. No one spoke or moved. Payne and Doltch just stared, transfixed. Wendy was looking beyond the headlights of the cars into the cornfields in the distance, as if she were searching for meaning out there.

I looked at Liv. She looked as if she wanted to strangle someone. Then she said, "Wendy, I have a gun and honestly, I'd like to shoot you."

Payne shot her a quick look. I didn't. I knew she wouldn't shoot Wendy now, too many witnesses, but her emotions were valid.

"Save your bullets, Olivia. Let me finish, then you can shoot me. Girl, I'm just getting warmed up."

And then she started talking again.

Chapter 26

"Confession is good for the soul, especially if it's someone else's confession."
- Anonymous

The contrast between the hushed countryside with its rows of corn and soybeans flourishing in humid warmth and the grisly tale of cold-blooded ending of human life was not lost on me. Listening to Wendy's song held a strange fascination, and I wasn't the only one. All four of us stood, transfixed, as she continued her confession that sounded more like bragging than remorse.

"So I agreed to Larry's plan and we killed Hugh. Larry had never much cared for anything about the farm, or upkeep, and so when he asked Hugh to show him how to operate a tractor pulling a rotary mower, Hugh was surprised. Happy. Larry was operating the tractor with Hugh standing up there alongside him, a little back of him, just pleased as he could be. Cutting the grass of that big yard with his little brother. So sweet. So special.

"I came out and walked beside the tractor as it was cutting and started talking to Hugh, which distracted him. That was Larry's signal. He pushed Hugh off the back of the tractor and the mower ran over him. Then Larry jumped clear and shortly after, he bugged out."

Wendy stopped for a moment. Her face made little movements, like false starts into emotions she couldn't sort out all at once as she remembered. "It was worse than I could have imagined. The sounds. God!"

She looked away again into the cornfields, gathering herself in. After a while she said, shrugging her shoulders, "Anyway, Hugh was dead, and it looked like we had pulled it off. I don't regret it." She stopped for a moment, alone with her thoughts. Her eyes might as well have been fine blue porcelain instead of sclera and iris and pupil, because those eyes looked dead. "You must remember," she continued, "that I loved Hugh, but there was nothing there for me except the things he wanted. I could not die on the farm, an old woman who never really lived."

I had never seen selfishness personified before. Up until then, I thought I was the most selfish person I knew.

Wendy shifted her weight, looked directly at me and said, "That's what happened just before you came by that day. Larry grabbed me by the shoulders and made me look at what used to be my husband, then pushed me down into the...stuff. That was the horror. You might have thought Hugh's death was the reason I was screaming, but that wasn't it. It was being pushed down into it. And that's my story," she said lightly, tossing her hands into the heavy air, as if releasing her words into the sky. "Take me away. I want to be executed."

"Not in Iowa, you won't," Payne said. "No death penalty. Surely you knew that."

Wendy smiled.

I said, "Why are you driving Jurgen Clontz's car, and what happened back at Larry's?"

"Oh, hell yes! I should have known there would be questions! You better sit down, boys," she said, actually grinning. She looked like a demon with a smile. Liv noticed, too, and her hand clamped harder on mine.

"I went over to Larry's to kill him, of course. I told him to meet me there. It was supposed to look like suicide, and it probably would have worked. But," she said, turning toward Liv and me with pure hatred and ferocity in her face, "you two had to show up, didn't you? Christ! I wish to God you had died in that wreck with your stupid family, Thomas. You completely screwed up everything!"

"Good," I said.

Wendy shook her head as if to realign her thoughts. Her hand went to her forehead, her fingertips touching the cut. Her gaze returned to the dark cornfield. "Anyway, Ernst talked me into killing Larry and making it look like suicide."

"Reverend VanderKellen!" Sheriff Payne blurted.

"We've been having what you would call in polite circles, serial assignations. A discrete affair. When he found out I was pregnant, he freaked, absolutely convinced it was his, the ego-meister. I guess it could have been his, or Larry's, or Jurgen's for that matter."

Payne whistled. "You were sleeping with Jurgen Clontz?"

"Five Hour Energy Drink junkie," Liv whispered in my ear.

"We were hardly sleeping," Wendy said. "Trust me on that one. He was attentive, gave me diamond earrings and cash I had to hide from Hugh, and promised me that if certain things came together, we could travel and enjoy each other's, um, company, without any strings. Sounded good to me. Anyway, our plan, I mean the one Ernst and I had, was to kill Larry and then leave for Europe together. He was going to leave Ruth behind, of course, the prude, and have a sweet chunk of change of his own."

"'A sweet chunk of change' from...?" Payne asked.

"Oh. Yes. I didn't tell you about that. This is sooo cool! I've realized this really is an interesting little community, and just as I'm leaving it, too," Wendy said, smiling. "Anyway, Ernst and Jurgen had worked out a little deal with regard to the sale of Soderstrom Farms, which couldn't take place with regard to the entire property, unless both brothers were dead. Of course, Larry and I took out Hugh, and I took care of Larry.

"See, when the land goes up for sale, Ernst was going to find out what the sealed bids were so he could tip off Jurgen, who would, naturally, come in with the highest bid. Ernst told me that Jurgen would pay a ten percent kickback, which we estimated at around four-plus million bucks, which we'd split. That would put my total take at, let me see, oh, I guess figuring in my two mil from the estate, right around four million dollars, give or take—widow's recompense. Course, I'd ditch the good Reverend VanderKellen after a couple of thank-you tumbles in a five-star hotel in Paris. He'd manage, and I'd be on my way."

Sheriff Payne just shook his head. Stephen Doltch's mouth had been hanging open for quite some time. I feared bats might be attracted, thinking it was a cave. "So Jurgen Clontz had nothing to do with the death of either of the Soderstrom brothers?" I asked.

"Nah, he's a scuz, but I think whacking someone is a little beyond his repertoire. Don't get me wrong. He's a greedy little shit and wants the land, but I don't think he did anything wrong. Just a little old-fashioned affair with me and insider trading. Nothing you can prove, unless Ernst confesses, and then it's just a he-said, it-said."

"So who's been trying to kill me? You?" I asked. Wendy looked at me. She actually grinned.

"Larry hired those two idiots from Dubuque, and when that didn't work, he dug a little deeper and went with the so-called professionals from God knows where. Which I thought would work. We had no idea you were such a man," she said, wiggling her eyebrows. Liv's hand tensed in mine. "You've got a hottie there, Olivia, if you know what to do with him."

Payne said, "What happened tonight, Wendy?" His voice was soft, sad.

"Oh, that. I went over to Larry's to take him out. Loose lips sink ships, and man, did he have loose lips. Anyway, I got him drunk and he passed out. Then I took his gun, stuck it in his mouth, and pulled the trigger. I wiped down the gun, put it in his hand and left when I heard Mr. Ubiquitous over there," she said, jerking her head toward me, "fiddling at the front door. I could not believe it. No one would have doubted Larry's suicide and I could have been long gone, the grieving widow and sister-in-law, with my treasure, disappearing into happily ever after. Except for you, Thomas."

Wendy glared at me. "Why in God's name did you show up tonight, of all nights, at that house?"

"Actually," I said, "it was Olivia's idea. Something to do after dinner. Random."

Wendy's head dropped until her chin was on her chest, then, quickly, she looked up and said, "Why couldn't you just mind your own business? And you, O-liv-ee-a, why couldn't you have just taken Sweet Thomas back to your tacky little bungalow tonight, of all nights, and sweated up some sheets? All this would've worked. Damn!"

I returned her look, saying nothing, then, "Wendy, tell me about your baby. How does he, or she, fit into your fantasy?" I needed to know about the child.

"That baby is no more," she said. "I took care of it ten days ago in Iowa City. Ernst paid, thinking he was the baby-daddy, the egocentric phony."

Doltch finally spoke up. "Why are you driving the Jag?"

Wendy turned and looked to her left, at the questioner, as if she'd forgotten Doltch stood there. She looked surprised. "Another county heard from! To answer your question, Jurg and I had met earlier this evening at his place. He said I could take it, that driving the Jag would give me a taste of the possibilities if something were to happen to Larry, like, for instance, he killed himself because he lost his brother. Said he'd take his Mercedes over to the club when he went out for dinner."

"And what Jurgen Clontz gets out of this situation is a guarantee he'd get all of Soderstrom Farms now that both brothers are dead. Tidy," Payne said. "Did Clontz have anything to do with Hugh's death? Anything at all?"

"No, he didn't get involved until after. He saw an opportunity. But it was Ernst who got me to thinking about taking out Larry. He knew what had happened out at the farm that morning."

Payne said, "So you murdered Larry at Doctor VanderKellen's suggestion?"

"You are sooo brilliant. May I touch you? Ernst never directly suggested I kill Larry. He'd just say things like, 'If Larry wasn't around anymore' or 'If Larry had an accident like Hugh.' Stuff like that. Subtle. And he'd say things like, 'Of course, murder is wrong, but still, things do happen.' And it was obvious that, until Larry was pushing up daisies, there was no way Jurgen and I would ever bed down in a spiffy hotel on the continent. I mean, nothing was going to happen for me with Larry alive.

"This afternoon I swung by Ernst's office for some pastoral counseling, which took all of ten minutes, and, while we tidied up, he reminded me of those things about Larry. I guess I was just inspired to act on what needed doing. He wasn't man enough. Oh, by the way Thomas, he says you're the kind who'll sniff around until you get what you're after and, if he'd been Larry, he'd have set you up and killed you himself before you wised up. I believe him. You should, too," she said.

"You think Doctor VanderKellen will try to kill me?"

Wendy snorted. "Look, O'Shea, once it gets out what happened tonight, Ernst will know that you know. And maybe the courts could never convict him of anything, but he'll be afraid you'll be on him like a fly on a cow pie, and mess up his little scheme with Jurgen. Not to mention the public humiliation and probably losing his cushy job at the church."

"Wendy, how did Ernst find out about what happened to Hugh?" Payne asked. "You said he knew. How? How did he know you two conspired to kill your husband?"

"Larry told him, for God's sake! Can you believe that moron! Which proved Ernst's point about Larry spouting off, which Ernst made clear to me later. Ernst got Larry looped several times out at Larry's place after Hugh's death, not a tough task, by the way. Finally, motor mouth had to blab about what a criminal wizard he was, what a great criminal team we were. In less than forty-eight hours after Larry spilled the beans to Ernst, the good Reverend let me know he knew everything, and told me what he and Jurgen had cooked up. That's when he started in on the idea about killing Larry."

"Let me get this straight, for the record," Payne said, glancing at the tape recorder. "You got restless on the farm, began an affair with Larry which led to killing Hugh so Larry could continue his affair with you and you could acquire the money in the provisions for widows in the Trust. You and Doctor VanderKellen were also having an affair, and when Doctor VanderKellen started getting suspicious about Hugh's death, he got Larry drunk and found out about the murder conspiracy. And then he encouraged you to kill Larry and make it look like a suicide?"

"Spot on, I say," Wendy replied with a British accent.

Payne went on. "You were pregnant by Larry, Doctor VanderKellen, or Jurgen Clontz, and Doctor VanderKellen paid for your abortion, thinking the baby was his. Doctor VanderKellen and Jurgen Clontz have a kickback scheme on knowing the bids for Soderstrom Farms. Doctor VanderKellen was going to take the kickback money from Clontz and split it with you, and you two would go off to Europe. Clontz had nothing to do with either murder or the abortion. Larry hired the boys from Dubuque and the three gunmen to kill Thomas because he was snooping around and getting close to the truth of the fraudulent sale of Soderstrom Farms. Is that it?"

"Pretty well sums it up," Wendy said. "For what it's worth, Larry said he'd have first dibs on Hugh's land, but he wasn't too excited about it. He didn't need the money. Besides, he wouldn't have been able to come up with the cash down payment. Too much money up his nose."

The cloud cover broke up into little, individual puffs after the drizzle stopped, and moonlight worked its way through the breakup, flooding the countryside with soft light pouring through the brief, dark blue clouds scudding across its face.

Liv suddenly spoke up, breaking the heavy silence. "Wendy, why didn't you just divorce Hugh, or simply walk away if you were so unhappy? God almighty, look what you've done!"

Wendy sneered at Liv. "You are so naïve I can't believe it. We had a pre-nup. If I divorced Hugh, I would come into the staggering buyout of fifty thousand dollars. If I just walked away, I would get fifty thousand less than that. I know you teach English, but do the math."

Olivia looked like someone had just dropped a baby squid down her front.

"Wendy Soderstrom, I am arresting you for the murders of

Hugh and Larry Soderstrom," Payne said, handcuffing Wendy, who put her hands behind her back when he began speaking. "You have the right to remain silent," he began, and she cut him off.

"I know my rights, Barney, and I've waived them twice. Pay attention. Are we done now?"

"You are, young lady," Payne said, and he motioned Doltch to take her, which he did, escorting her to his cruiser, opening the back door, and motioning her inside. He forgot to place his hand on her head as she got in, and Wendy banged herself hard, but did not react. Doltch thumbed off the tape recorder, slipped it inside his pocket, closed the door behind Wendy. Then he got in behind the wheel and waited for the Sheriff.

Payne climbed down the shoulder of the road to the Jaguar, reached in and turned off the headlights, took the keys, and slammed the door shut. He climbed back up the slippery embankment and approached Liv and me.

He said, "Since we have murder here, I'll need to call the DCI and State lab people, then I'm going over to Larry's place to secure the crime scene. After Lansberger comes out, I'm going to have a chat with Doctor VanderKellen." Payne waved for Doltch to leave and he did, the big cruiser edging away into the night.

"Trouble is," Payne said as the car's taillights faded into the mist, "I don't think we can prove anything beyond Wendy's killing Larry. Everything else is just her testimony against Clontz, against VanderKellen. A good defense lawyer will laugh us out of the courtroom, and Jurgen and Doctor V will be on their way."

Payne looked older suddenly, and I felt sorry for him. His quiet little picturesque town on the banks of the Whitetail River had gone sour, and it started with me. Payne looked around, up at the sky and across the deep black fields and then, finally, back at us. "It's pretty out here, isn't it?"

"Yes, it is very pretty," I said.

The Sheriff looked at me and said, "Come on by in the morning so I can get your statement. You watch your butt in the meantime." He turned to Olivia. "Good night, Liv. Sorry you had to be involved in all this." He kissed her cheek and she pulled him to her and hugged him, then hugged him again. Payne ambled over to his cruiser, got in, executed a perfect reverse turn in the narrow road and eased away, quickly picking up speed.

Liv and I got in the truck and just sat there in the dark on the side of the lonely dirt road in the vast Iowa countryside in a night that was beginning to finally reveal a star or two after the mist and rain, all alone with our thoughts and the events that were consuming us.

I looked around at the emptiness, looked at Liv, leaned over and kissed her mouth. And had my sorrowful kiss returned. I turned my key in the ignition and executed the same turn Payne had performed, and drove away toward Rockbluff.

Chapter 27

"But Thou, O Lord, art a shield about me,
My glory, and the One who lifts my head."
- Proverbs 3:3

We drove in silence for a few miles, then Liv said, "Would you think less of me if I told you I'm afraid?"

"Of?"

Liv looked over at me as I drove, then back on the road stretching away in the headlights. We approached Rockbluff, passing farmhouses with darkened windows, yard lights standing sentry over sleeping people, in bed hours ago. It was past midnight, and as we entered Rockbluff, the little town seemed at peace.

"Evil," she said, answering my question.

"We saw it tonight, didn't we? And no, I don't think less of you. I might if you were chipper, unaffected, wanting to go home and watch your old *American Idol* tapes."

"I don't watch *American Idol*, much less tape the damn thing."

"You have just risen in my estimation."

"Thank you for trying to maneuver me off the subject."

"You're welcome."

"I'm still afraid," she said.

"Why don't you come home with me?"

She looked at me for a long time, looked away. We came to the point in Rockbluff where we had to go left to cross the bridge to get to her house, or go right and head south toward mine. I stopped.

"Hang a left, kind sir," she said.

She was crying. I reached over and brushed my hand against her hair, her cheek, wiping away her tears with my thumb. She looked beautiful in the faint light of street lamps. I turned left, crossed over the bridge. No other cars.

At her place, I turned off the headlights and the ignition, got out, and skirted around the front of the truck. Liv had her door open. She took my hand, sliding gracefully from the tall truck, pistol-packed purse in her other hand. I pushed the door shut and escorted her up to the deep shadows around her front door. She had forgotten to turn her porch light on when we left earlier in the evening.

There, I embraced her, holding her to me, hunching down, my hands dropping to the hem of her simple black dress, inching it up until it was at her hips.

I smoothed my hands inside the back of her bikini panties and spread my fingers on her warm skin. She moaned, murmured, "I thought I'd be too exhausted."

"Me, too, but sometimes I surprise myself. You just look so drop dead gorgeous, sexy, edible. And you feel luscious." I caressed the well-rounded flesh of her fabulous butt, wishing my hands were bigger.

"I am so tired. I just want to sleep. With you. That would be enough tonight."

"No, it wouldn't," I said. She chuckled.

"Maybe we could wait until the morning; I have a hunch we'll both feel frisky then."

"Good reason to get up in the morning."

"I love it when you talk dirty," she said, bumping her forehead into my chest.

"Oh, you English teachers," I laughed. "Just remember, joy comes in the morning."

"Lots of sex in the Bible."

"I'm just trying to boost flesh up onto a spiritual plane," I said.

We kissed again, and then she either trembled or suffered a petit mal seizure. I'm pretty sure it was a tremble. I leaned down and kissed her throat, her collarbone. Her perfume was making me dizzy. She leaned back a little and pushed my head down to where my lips brushed her breasts.

That's when her cell phone rang. God, I hate cell phones.

"I have to answer it or it'll wake up all the neighbors."

"I thought my breathing was doing that."

She retrieved her phone, flipped it open, touched a button smaller than a flea's navel, said "This better be damn good." She listened, handed me the phone. "It's for you."

"Show me how to work it."

She rolled her eyes, indicating I should simply hold it to my ear and speak. I took the phone and said to the caller, "This better be damn good."

It wasn't. The voice was Harmon Payne's. He said, "Thomas, I hate to call you at such an obviously inopportune time."

"You have no idea."

"Yes, I do, but there's a situation you need to know about."

"I'm listening."

"I'm at Christ the King Church. Come down here as quickly as you can," he said, his voice tired but alert. There was an edge I had not heard before. An urgency. Like he was pleading with me. "And make sure you bring your weapon," he added.

"Why? What is it?"

"It looks like Doctor VanderKellen has committed suicide."

"Oh."

"Just come on down as soon as you can. We'll be here."

"We?"

"Me, Doltch, and Aldrich. Ruth. Carl and Molly Heisler. And Thomas, don't bring Liv with you. She's seen enough for one night. One lifetime, really."

"I'm on my way." I snapped the phone shut and handed it back to Liv.

"What's up?" she asked, scooching her dress back down.

"I'm going to church."

"Thomas."

"Harmon wants me down at Christ the King, and he told me you absolutely could not come with me. It's a Men's Fellowship meeting."

"If you try that, you don't know me. I'll just hop into my car and follow you."

"You've had more than enough for one night. I'm telling you to stay here. I'll touch base with you in the morning."

"You're telling me? That's bullshit. I'm going with you. I'm a big girl, Thomas."

"Liv, you need to go inside, lock your doors, and go to bed. I know you're a big girl. I will keep you posted if I can. Do not go with me. Do not follow me. I am dead serious. This is not some movie."

"I said I'm going. Who the hell do you think you are, Thomas? This isn't your town; it's my town. I've come this far in this whole stinking mess, and I intend to see it through. And smart guy, I'm fully aware we're not in some damn movie. Don't patronize me."

"Please, just keep your distance for a little while. Stay here. I'm going. And if you decide to follow me, I'm sure Harmon will be more than happy to have one of his deputies keep you away."

"You're serious," she said, incredulity in her voice. "Even after tonight!"

"I am not messing with you by any definition. I'll see you in the morning."

"No, you won't. You need to just stay away from me, Thomas. This is just wrong, and I thought *Clontz* was the sexist."

Liv was steamed, but I knew she would get over it. She could be mad at me all she wanted, even if it was Harmon's idea to keep her behind. I respected his advice.

I said, "Good night," turned, and hurried back down to my car.

Liv said, "Up yours, O'Shea." I heard her open the door, go inside, and slam the door shut. Feisty. *Up yours?*

A few minutes later, ignoring Payne's advice to get Chief Justice, I pulled into the parking lot of Christ the King Church, alongside other cars and an ambulance. A few lights on in the church, windows outlined in the dark, made the big stone church look like some kind of deranged jack o' lantern.

I went straight to VanderKellen's office. The good Reverend Doctor slumped back in his chair, head to one side, mouth slightly open, tiny trail of inglorious spittle slipping down into his trim beard. He was pale. Dead. Room temp.

Ruth VanderKellen, or at least the woman I assumed was she, sat on a loveseat to one side, with Molly Heisler next to her. Carl Heisler and Harmon stood between the pastor's wife and the dead pastor. Deputy Doltch helped Chuck Aldrich move the body onto a gurney at the far side of the large, luxurious office.

"Thanks for coming," Harmon said. "I think you know everyone here."

"Not yet," I said.

"Molly, this is Thomas O'Shea," Carl said. "Thomas, my wife Molly." We nodded.

"I haven't met Mrs. VanderKellen," I said, and Carl introduced us. When Ruth VanderKellen looked at me, hot tears stabbed my eyes when I saw the pain in hers, tangible there in the middle of the night. "Mrs. VanderKellen, I am so sorry," I said.

She smiled forlornly. "Thank you."

Ruth VanderKellen was a fine looking woman. Early fifties, black hair with streaks of silver, strong features, half glasses, light blue eyes, and dressed in matching dark blue slacks and top. No makeup. No tears, either.

"What happened?" I asked, turning to Payne.

"Looks like a mega dose of pills washed down with booze," Aldrich said before Payne could answer. An empty pint bottle of Canadian Club sat in the middle of the immense desk. Empty brown-orange plastic prescription containers with it, white caps scattered.

Harmon took me to the side and said, "Ruth woke up an hour ago and realized Doctor VanderKellen wasn't home. From the manse, she saw the light on in his office. Checked it out, found him like this, called me."

Aldrich and Doltch lifted the body onto the gurney. VanderKellen was wearing a summer weight light blue suit, white shirt, and floral pattern tie. His shoes were shined and he wore navy blue socks, these things I noticed as the two men wheeled the body out of the office. *All dressed up and no place to go*, I thought. *At least not in this world, unless you count the graveyard.*

I didn't like VanderKellen, but I didn't want him dead. Prison, yes; dead, nope. "Why did you call me here, and ask me to bring my weapon?"

"Because you need to read this," Payne said, moving around behind the desk and pushing a piece of paper toward me with his pen. "Pick it up at the edges, please."

I could not fathom what was on the handwritten note that I needed to see. Probably a suicide note, but why did I need to read it? I went ahead, every eye on me.

It is the night of July 19th, the end of the last full day I shall live on this earth. Wendy Soderstrom just called me with a message that forces this act. She has murdered Larry Soderstrom and she has been caught. She is going to tell all. I will not live with the ignominy of her disclosures; further, I know now that what I have done is so terrible I cannot be forgiven by anyone. To make a clean breast of it (speaking of Wendy)*, my sins are these:*

- *I had an affair with Wendy Soderstrom.*
- *She was pregnant by me, and I convinced her to abort the child.*
- *I persuaded her to seduce Larry Soderstrom, kill him, and make it look like a suicide.* (What irony in that!)

• I had an agreement with Jurgen Clontz to let him know what the bids would be on the Soderstrom Farms property; in return, he would provide me with a gratuity of $4,000,000 which I was going to split with Wendy.

• I have been embezzling small sums from the church for years because my salary was inadequate and I hated the house that was provided.

• I am beyond redemption. I do not know if Hell really exists, unless it is the absence of Heaven. I hope that is all there is to it, a bleak nothingness separated eternally from God. So I send myself there by my own hand.

Larry Soderstrom hired the men who attacked Thomas O'Shea on the bridge, and the men who tried to kill O'Shea at his home, so don't blame me for that.

One last thing, and perhaps this warning will ease my eternal fate: there is one more killer coming, a professional. O'Shea will be killed in Rockbluff in July to keep him from interfering with the sale of Soderstrom Farms on or before September 19th. I hired this person through intermediaries I never saw. He cannot be called back. I cannot find the first link of the chain *that led to the hiring. This was as planned. With Larry dead, the only thing between Wendy and me escaping was O'Shea stumbling onto our plan. So, O'Shea had to die.*

I hate Thomas O'Shea for his relentless, do-gooder nosiness. Everything would have worked if he had never come here.

I will be thinking of Wendy's body as I fall asleep.

The letter was signed with a flourish,

Ernst VanderKellen, D. Div.

I did not realize I had been holding my breath, but after reading the suicide note, I exhaled loudly.

"Now you know why I encouraged you to be armed," Harmon said, carefully taking the note from me and sliding it into a plastic evidence envelope.

"I am so sorry about this," Mrs. VanderKellen said, standing and coming to my side. She smelled good, and I wondered what was wrong with me that I noticed her fragrance right after learning someone was coming to kill me. Gallows hypersensitivity? The guy stepping up to the guillotine realizing the grinning peasant in the fourth row has an abscessed tooth? That there is a ruby-throated hummingbird darting from flower to flower five hundred yards in the distance as the trap door falls away?

"Nothing to apologize for. We'll catch the guy and then all of this will be finished," I said.

"Except for living with it the rest of our lives," she said.

"Obviously, we need to keep this note as quiet as possible," Harmon said. "I let the state Division of Criminal Investigation know about Larry's murder and they're on their way right now. They have resources for gathering evidence that I don't. I'll bring aboard a few more part-time people to keep their eyes open for strangers. Doctor

VanderKellen said the hit is supposed to take place in Rockbluff, so that helps." He looked around, said, "Well, we better go." He gave Mrs. VanderKellen a brief pat on her shoulder and left.

"You two can go ahead and go home," Mrs. VanderKellen said to the Heislers. "I want a word with Mr. O'Shea, in private. Thank you so much, Molly, Carl, for coming to my side at this time. You two are blessings, and I am grateful for you."

"You are more than welcome to come over to our place, at least for the night," Molly said. "We love you, Ruth."

"Thank you. You are so kind, but I'll be fine in the manse. I love you, too."

When the Heislers left, Mrs. VanderKellen took me by the arm and escorted me out of her dead husband's office and down the hall to the foyer, where she sat next to me on a large sofa upholstered in green silk fabric adorned with peacocks.

"I regret that we have met under these circumstances. I have heard a great deal about you, Mr. O'Shea, from both of the Heislers, some from my husband, and quite a bit from people in the community. Mike Mulehoff, others. I feel like I know you a little bit."

"Please call me Thomas," I said.

"Please call me Ruth. Thomas," she said, shifting her weight, "did you notice anything odd about that note Ernst wrote, other than the rather unusual length? I apologize for my attitude, but right now I'm not only hurt, but angry. His sermons were often too long, and now this," she said, shaking her head, a furtive smile coming and going. "Anyway, did you notice anything else peculiar about his note?"

"I noticed several things about that note, besides the implications in it for me."

"What did you notice, other than the deeply disturbing revelation about Ernst's business relationship with Jurgen Clontz?"

"I noticed, and I don't mean to hurt you any more than you've been hurt already, that he never once mentioned you, or any children."

"You are astute, especially under the circumstances. How interesting," she said, looking at me with a slight smile. "It's true.

Well, he wouldn't have mentioned any children because we didn't have any. I wasn't able to give him a child. The fertility experts said it was me. That was not as big a problem for him as it was for me. I wanted to have children, could not. Ernst was not interested in adopting, either, so that subject was dropped." She looked at her hands, folded them in her lap, looked up, went on. "They say a woman knows when her husband is straying. I knew.

"You see, about three years ago, Thomas, I had a radical mastectomy. Ernst lost all interest in me, at least in the sense of physical intimacy. It started with that. He made up nicknames for me, cruel nicknames, and we grew very much apart. Separate bedrooms. That was painful. I had no idea it was Wendy. Makes sense. She has youth."

Ruth shrugged her shoulders. "So, our marriage was no longer complete, and that's why he didn't mention me in the letter. He didn't care about me anymore. He did, obliquely, get in one last dig."

"That last line was unspeakable."

"Not as unspeakable as other things he mentioned. Now, did you notice anything else unusual in his letter, other than not mentioning his wife of twenty-nine years?"

"He made it sound like he was beyond redemption, but that last bit made me think he was finally hopeful."

"You are a lovely man. I believe that is what I will hold onto, instead of my anger. God bless you, Thomas! Molly was right: You are an angel."

"As unlikely as it is that I am an angel, I would be foolish to try to disabuse you of that notion. My pastor in Georgia suggested maybe God put me here to help bring all of this stuff to the surface. But my pastor in Georgia is a nutcase. What can I say?"

Ruth smiled, then took my hands in hers and looked into my face. "Ernst was a fine man, committed to the sharing of the Word and this flock, at least initially. But he made mistakes, all driven by pride and resentment. You heard his comments about salary and the manse. I can't imagine. His salary was generous. The manse is a beautiful, big house with wonderful views from every window. I wish you had known him when we were first married. He was so in love with his faith and life...and me."

"But Ruth, this is also an opportunity for you, for new life, for freedom. Beauty for ashes."

Her face brightened, then, quickly, impulsively, she stood up, as did I. She gave me a hard hug, and then she released me. "You are a blessing, Thomas. Now, I need to let you go. Please, please, Thomas, take care of yourself. I am worried about you."

"Thank you, but don't worry. I can take care of myself," I said. "Now, may I walk you to your door?"

"Of course. I'd like that," she replied, and we walked out of the church and across the sidewalk that led to the manse, dark and cold.

At the front door, she turned and faced me. In the half light in the shadows, she was even more beautiful than she appeared in the office of her dead husband, a mean man gone totally down the drain. I felt a surge of compassion for Ruth VanderKellen, and I said, "Would you like for me to come inside for a while?"

Her eyes went soft and moist and she stepped forward and put her hands on my shoulders and said, "Yes, and that's why you should not. But thank you so much for asking; you have done wonderful things for my heart."

And then Ruth VanderKellen came to her tiptoes and kissed me softly on the cheek, more of a light touch than a kiss, then turned away saying, "Good night, Thomas," disappearing inside her empty manse. I heard the door lock.

I stepped back toward the church and looked at the stone house and saw lights go off downstairs and lights go on upstairs, and I turned away. For a moment, just a moment, I had seen her not as a new widow, scarred by a mean man, but as a beautiful woman all alone. It flickered in her countenance briefly, then fled, as did she. But there was hope for her, peeking out from the pain.

Not so much hope for me, though, ashamed of myself for my thoughts. Again. I turned around, walked to the parking lot, got in my truck, and drove to my house in the darkness of a very dark night.

Chapter 28

"That's the secret to life . . .replace one worry with another."
- *Charles M. Schulz*

Driving back to my house in the middle of the night, I realized that, since I had arrived in Rockbluff, multiple murders, two killings by my own hand, suicide, abortion, fraud, greed, lust, and several physical assaults on my delicate self were keeping boredom at bay. And that doesn't include Bulldog bites on a scumbag. I had to believe property values in Rockbluff sucked. Jurgen Clontz had no choice other than to hate me.

I passed Arvid's house, no lights on in any of the windows, no body draped over the wrought-iron fence. I guess he only fakes his death when he's sure to be found. Or maybe he was practicing in the kitchen, face down in a batch of chocolate chip cookies, glass of milk tipped on its side, white puddle spreading, spreading.

I drove on.

All that remained to clean up the mess I started was to avoid my own murder while catching the professional paid to put my lights out. No sweat. Clarity is one of my favorite words, and I was about to achieve it. Muddy water I did not even know about rinsed clear with Wendy's confession. People wanted me dead because I kept asking questions, and the fact that $42 million was part of the equation probably ramped up their motivation to have me move on into the next world.

If the hired gun were successful, someone else would have to deal with it all. I'd be in Bonhoeffer's "true country," and I could find out whether the streets of Heaven really are paved in gold, and, if so, if that indicated how worthless gold is in Paradise, or just represented a little beatific bling.

The hit was going to happen in Rockbluff. In July. And this was already the night of the 19th, the morning of the 20th. Valuable information, and I thanked VanderKellen for the tip. Not at my house, not in the country, not in Busted Druggie State Park. Rockbluff. Theoretically, if I avoided Rockbluff for the rest of the month, the trouble would just go away. Something I maybe should have done back in April.

But did the hired gun know why he was going to knock me off? Was he paying attention to what was going on in Rockbluff? Would he realize that VanderKellen was dead, Wendy was blabbing, and Clontz was exposed? If so, would he just shrug his shoulders and go away? Or was I just a target to be hit? I suspected the latter. Hit men just do the job, no questions asked, I am told. It's just business.

I wanted what the therapists call "closure," and so I would have it. No confronted hit man, no closure.

So the hit would happen in Rockbluff, and the most logical time would be during the upcoming regional gala that put every Olympiad to shame—The Annual Rockbluff County Pork Festival, three days of fun, food, and soaring cholesterol levels. And that would begin in just eight days. In ten days it would all be over, one way or another.

I drove on home through the dark, interrupted Gotcha's sleep enough to give her goozle a good kneading, then ambled into the kitchen and retrieved my cell phone out of the drawer where I had last thrown it. I knew he would still be up, so I gave Payne a call and told him what I thought about getting shot during the Pork Festival. He agreed with my analysis, then he said he would double his patrols and give me a bodyguard at the festivities.

"What good would a bodyguard be?" I asked.

"Well, he could, um, guard your body?"

"And keep the hit man from making his move until some other time. Harmon, I appreciate the gesture, but the idea is to get the bad guy to make his move so you can snatch him up, give him a Dutch rub, and put him in the slammer. I respectfully decline. Use my bodyguard to step up surveillance."

Payne reluctantly agreed, and I went to bed.

I woke up at ten-thirty with Gotcha snorfeling my neck. She wanted to go out. I got up and let her rumble into the edge of the woods.

I took care of my morning ablutions, let Gotcha back in, and left to go have lunch. On the way, I wondered about Liv. I had done the right thing telling her to keep away, but I still didn't like having her angry with me. I thought about Ruth, too, as I drove into town. Like all sinners, there is a thorn in my flesh, but in my case, it is me. And it is flesh. When it comes to attractive women, I tend to confuse the creation and the Creator.

Pulling into Moon's parking lot, I thought about other things of more immediate importance. I felt secure knowing I would only have to be on edge for the three days of the Pork Festival, maybe just one if I got lucky, so the next few days might turn out to be okay.

The usual lunch crowd was keeping Loon Moon in high cotton. I spied Horace in his favorite booth, wearing a bright yellow t-shirt with "Jesus Wants Me For A Sunbeam" across the chest in block letters. A head shot of a leering Paris Hilton was directly under the lettering. Horace's thin hair was combed straight back. He looked like a demented television pitch man or a college football coach, I couldn't decide which. Same basic profession. We acknowledged each other as I sidled up to the bar.

The joint had gone noticeably quieter when I entered, and now, at the bar, I looked around to see that just about everybody was looking at me, some whispering, others just looking. A few people I knew smiled and waved. I waved back, then turned around to look for the bartender.

Moon came over and placed a pint of something dark in front

of me. "You just missed your columnist girlfriend. Suzanne what's-her-face."

"She was in here?"

"Yeah, looking for you. Said she might go up to your place, but didn't seem too eager to actually do it. I told her these days you just shot anyone who approached. She wanted your angle on last night's unpleasantness. She's already talked to Harmon. You've certainly been a busy boy lately, Thomas. What's wrong, did your satellite dish break?"

"I've been a little busier than I would like, Moon. I'll be glad when things get back to normal, or is this normal in Rockbluff?"

"This is a small town, and the whole story's out already about Wendy, and Doctor VanderKellen's suicide. Man oh man it's getting interesting. Everybody in here right now is talking about it. You're quite a newsmaker. No wonder what's-her-face is after you and, by the way, she's quite a looker."

"Her last name is Highsmith," I said, taking a slug of cold Three Philosophers. "I was right about Hugh's death not being an accident. Hugh was murdered by Larry and Wendy, Wendy murdered Larry, and Doctor VanderKellen killed himself. Clear as can be. If Wendy had just turned Larry away when he started to hit on her, none of this would have happened."

Moon said, "Oh, those girls from Davenport."

"Yeah, that's the core problem, Rockbluff girls wouldn't do what Wendy did. Clinton girls wouldn't either. Or Dubuque girls, for that matter."

"So, it's all over now? Does it end with the sealed bids being opened?"

"I sure hope so." Astoundingly, for a small town, he didn't know the details of the suicide letter, and I wasn't going to tell him. No point.

Moon gave me a look that had just a tinge of skepticism in it.

"What?" I asked.

The look fled. He said, "There's a lady sitting alone back in that corner booth. Just got here. You might go over and say hello." I looked. It was Liv. I took my pint in hand and said to Moon, "Much obliged," and tipped an imaginary Stetson. I strode back to her booth and sat down across from her. She looked up and smiled and I felt that little flutter in my chest.

"Hey, big boy," she said in a sultry voice, "wanna have a good time?"

"I've got Hershey bars and panty hose in my truck, babe. What could be better?"

She batted her eyelashes at me and said, "You have a very limited concept of 'better.'" She reached her foot under the table and rubbed her arch against the inside of my thigh. My pulse took off.

"It's good to see you," I said.

Her smile grew. "Thank you. Thomas, I am so sorry about what's been happening to you. Last night..."

"Was awful, wasn't it?"

"I enjoyed dinner, and your little repartee with Jurgen. And I enjoyed our side trip to Larry's. Exciting beyond the definition of the word. But what we found was horrible, and Wendy's capture and confession were, too. And then, before I could even get ready for bed, a friend called me about Doctor VanderKellen's suicide. I had nightmares. Specific ones. Icky. You sure know how to put together an intriguing evening."

"It's not easy orchestrating all that stuff."

"I liked how you orchestrated your hands on my bare ass."

"Too bad the cell phone sounded off."

"Ummm. I'm beginning to hate cell phones, too. Still, I can't imagine what Ruth is going through, and Carl and Molly. My God, it just goes on and on."

"I think all of it's going to be over pretty soon," I said, and Liv seemed to relax. "I have felt like a lip reader at a ventriloquist's convention since I got here, having all this stuff happen and not knowing what in the world was going on. The old 'Why me, Lord?' syndrome was in full flight, but last night, hearing Wendy's confession, then Ruth finding her husband dead at his desk helped wrap it up for me."

Liv said, "Some good things might come from all this now that you've lived through it. I am happy you came by that night after the men tried to kill you. I thought I would faint when you kissed me. I did not want you to stop. I'm glad you didn't. Truth? I never thought I would ever be held again by a man who was tender and gentle and warm." She looked down, then looked up at me again. Her eyes were soft, blue, deep, intelligent.

"Me, too," I said.

"You mean you never thought you'd ever be held again by a man who was tender and gentle and warm?"

I made a face. "Let me revise my statement. I didn't think I would ever again be with a wonderful woman who wanted to be held by me, who wanted me to kiss her. I thought those things were over for me. I guess I was just numb to that part of my life."

"Did I un-numb you?"

"Indeed, you did. You were the light at the end of the tunnel beneath my wings."

"You did that on purpose, mixing your metaphors, trying to get me to rise to the bait."

"Yep."

"You have better bait than that," she said as Rachel arrived to take our order. When Rachel left, Liv's face grew serious. She said, "I need to tell you something about me, my past, that you need to know."

I kept the smart comeback to myself. I could see she was serious.

"I was married, once. His name is Preston Myers. We went to school together here. He was the star quarterback, I was the cheerleader. All that stuff. I loved him, and when he asked me to marry him, I jumped at the chance. I had everything planned out for us, the usual—three kids, growing old together in productive lives right here in Rockbluff."

"Sounds good."

"It did sound good. But it didn't last long. Very quickly he found fault with me. My breasts were too small, I didn't cook well enough, I was lousy in bed, being a teacher was too important to me, I cared more about my students than I did about him, and so on. Nothing I did would please him. Nothing. I won't go into the details, but let me just say that he is now a life partner with another man. He lives in Baltimore, last I heard."

"I can't imagine someone being mean to you."

"The marriage endured two years. I've gotten over it, but for a long, long time I didn't want to be around any man who seemed interested in me. Small town," she said, smiling ruefully, "but for a while the word was I was a lesbian and had driven Preston away because of my sexual preference. Ironic. That rumor died out years ago as the truth gradually surfaced, but not by my lips."

"So how did the truth find its way?"

"Moon took a little trip to Baltimore, then he came back."

"God bless Moon."

"Amen."

"I'm glad you told me, but you didn't need to. Sometimes it hurts a lot and doesn't solve anything to dig up old wounds," I said.

"I just wanted you to know. It's important. I care about you, Thomas. You are good and decent and brave, and most importantly, you know when you mix your metaphors."

We both laughed. It felt good to have that in common after last night's freak show. She went on, her voice even softer. "And last night, what I said after Harmon called you out to the church, please forgive me."

"Of course. I just didn't want you to see what I saw. Harmon didn't, either, and it's good that you stayed home."

She looked at me. "You pissed me off."

"I must have. You said, to me, 'Up yours.'"

"But that was yesterday."

"And yesterday's gone."

"So, good looking, do you have a date to the Pork Festival yet?" she asked.

"I do not."

"By coincidence, neither do I. If you don't mind me being a brazen hussy, would you like to go with me to the Sixty-Third Annual Rockbluff County Pork Festival next week?"

Under the circumstances that she did not understand, I did not. Stray bullets and all that. But to turn her down would start Liv asking questions again. So be it, I thought. Time to compromise the truth again to protect the innocent. That noble stuff can be tiring. "I'd love to go with you, but I think I'll take a rain check. I have no interest in the Pork Festival. Seriously. I'm thinking about heading down to Iowa City for a few days, give Coach Ferentz some tips for the football team, visit some old neighborhoods. And then I'm thinking about heading out to West Des Moines to touch base with an old friend."

Liv's eyes went hard, suspicious. "You know that old saying about Hell hath no wrath like a woman scorned?"

"Yeah, my dad told me when I was twelve."

"You didn't listen." She stood up abruptly, bumping the edge of the table with her hip. "Thomas, I cannot abide a liar." And then she stalked out.

I knew that, with time, she would recover. Better to have her ticked off than wounded by a random bullet. I returned to the bar, ale still in hand. I sat down.

"So," Moon said, "did you say the wrong thing again?"

"Yes. Now, how about one of those Specials of yours? And two more cold ones."

"Coming up," Moon said, and turned to prepare my order.

I laid low the next few days, sticking to my house, taking short walks with Gotcha and Chief Justice. Nothing suspicious popped up. I read a lot of newspaper accounts of what was going on here in Rockbluff. Nothing from Suzanne Highsmith; just straight news stories from several local and regional papers. I declined interviews with reporters. I ran some, watched a couple of movies, worked out at Mulehoff's, shopped for groceries, took a couple of long drives farther northeast and back. Surfed the net. Waited.

The first day of the Pork Festival began with its beauty pageant, won by a breathless and beaming Tiffany Swartzendruber, a recent graduate of Rockbluff High School, who would reign over the festival for three days and retire, then present her crown to next year's Miss Pork. But that wasn't all that took place the first day. The "Farnsworth Brothers' Carnival & Midway" at the Rockbluff County Fairgrounds, and the "Taste of Pork" exhibit under the big tent just inside the gate at the fairgrounds lured many a festival-goer into their domains.

The "Taste of Pork" provided over 150 recipes, many of which I tried in my ongoing attempt to be a good citizen. My favorite? A simple serving of roast pork. Worst recipe? Poached pork loaf with butterscotch glaze on a bed of pork rinds seemed the least appealing. The usual festival food enticed as well: funnel cakes, soft drinks, cotton candy, caramel corn, hotdogs, hamburgers, bratwurst, curly fries, and homemade ice cream. The "Suds Tent" turned into a gold mine in the high heat of the day. Prediction? According to the Weather Channel, it was going to hit 98. On July 29th, what did they expect?

I made a point to keep moving, never staying at one exhibit or another more than a few minutes, constantly watching, looking for unfamiliar faces. There were too many of those, so I tried to focus on anyone who seemed to be watching me too closely.

No face told me, "I am a hardened hit man and I am going to shoot you dead."

The faces I did recognize I saw over and over. Everywhere I turned I saw, or bumped into, Mike Mulehoff, Horace Norris, Arvid Pendergast, Gunther Schmidt, Carl Heisler, or Moon, who rotated supervision of The Grain o' Truth Bar & Grill with Rachel.

The shadows grew longer paired with a faint backing off from the heat and humidity as the first day of the festival wound down. I made a tour through the carnival rides, barely watching the activity in the Ferris Wheel or Tilt-a-Whirl, more interested in the people than the activity.

Lots of unfamiliar faces. None of them sinister or overly-interested in me. People whose faces I did vaguely recognize as citizens of Rockbluff seemed to notice me, say something under their breath to their companions, and kept moving. I did not see Liv Olson, and I rejoiced. Maybe she decided on her own to go visit her aunt in Oelwein.

Shortly after dark, I went back to the house and found a Red Sox game on the tube. I got out Gotcha's beer bowl, poured her a cold Sam Adams Boston Lager, and started drinking one for myself.

I fell asleep in my recliner; Day One was in the books. One day closer to being a target.

Chapter 29

"I'm not concerned about all hell breaking loose, but that a PART of hell will break loose...it'll be much harder to detect."

- *George Carlin*

The morning of the second day of the Pork Festival dawned, and I realized it was even more likely than the day before to be the last day of my life. That worked better than caffeine to get me started.

Sometime during the night, I had awakened in the recliner, noticed the game was over and *Baseball Tonight* was on, and went to bed. So this morning I just eased out of bed, took a shower and shaved, and dressed. I took Gotcha and Chief Justice and poked along down to the mailbox, retrieved the paper and returned to the house.

I debated having a roast pork sandwich for breakfast down at the festival, decided against it. I wanted to be alert, so I fetched a box of waffles from the freezer, nuked them, slathered butter on each waffle, stacked them, and drenched them with Aunt Jemima's Maple Syrup. A good breakfast washed down with Diet Coke to keep me sharp. If I were going to be shot to death, I wanted to have my eyes wide open. Might as well experience fully the last occurrence on this earth, I thought. Such a philosopher, not going gentle into that good night.

I gave Gotcha a leftover waffle with a little raw hamburger and some grated cheese on top of all that before I left. After all, she saved my life, sort of. She was breathing in her breakfast when I left.

I drove into town and parked in the lot at Christ the King, then walked over the bridge and joined the crowd, finally deciding to hang out downtown with a multitude in front of Kathy's Kuntry Krafts Korner. It was already hot.

I heard bands warming up nearby, and found myself waiting for the heavily-anticipated "Grand Parade." Who could resist? I watched for the person who had been paid to kill me. The size of the crowds worked against me, and as I, through sheer willpower, forced myself to forget about Liv, and even Ruth, I began searching faces.

The parade started and the Rockbluff High School Marching band approached playing the mandatory-in-Iowa "76 Trombones." I noticed Lansberger passing by. He wore street clothes, a loose shirt covering his weapon tucked into his waistband, barely bumping out the back of his shirt. We made fleeting eye contact and he moved on, watching the crowd. Five minutes later, the marching band passed by in front of me playing "Thriller." Across the street, between passing rows of musicians, I saw Doltch, in uniform, chatting with a young lady, facing her, but with his eyes scanning the crowd.

I turned my attention back to the band. They looked sharp in their green-and-cream uniforms, their performance stellar. And while I was thinking about her and her love for everything connected to Rockbluff High School, Olivia appeared at my side, wearing white shorts and a pale pink, sleeveless blouse.

She said, "I thought you were headed for Iowa City and Des Moines, Thomas."

"Change of plans. People I planned to see weren't going to be home," I lied. It was getting easier.

"Uh-huh," she replied, skepticism oozing out of both syllables. Time to change the subject.

"I'll bet you know every kid in the Rockbluff High School band."

"Damn betchum," she said.

"Probably every kid in the whole school, too."

"Right again," she said as the band passed, followed by several individual kids on bikes with red, white and blue crepe paper intertwined in the spokes and bright, Day-Glo orange streamers hanging from the grips on their handlebars. Several of the juvenile bikers wore cardboard tri-corner hats.

Three more bands passed by, followed slowly by five convertibles filled with various dignitaries, including the Grand Marshall, a corpulent local politician I had never seen before. Then a series of floats passed, including one with an enormous papier mache' pink pig. Then another band from Strawberry Point High School. "Grand Parade" indeed.

I don't know what it was that made me look back around to the people on the sidewalk. Maybe a boring float, maybe an unusual sound, maybe good instincts. Or God nudging me to wake up.

I did not notice anything unusual, but Liv, who turned back to the crowd at the same time, did. A girl in a Rockbluff High School Marching Band uniform and wearing wraparound blue mirror sunglasses was walking directly toward us.

At that same moment Horace rollerbladed by in the street, zipping toward the girl. Horace did not look at me or speak, instead, he fixated on the band girl. He jumped the curb, plowing into the pedestrians on the sidewalk, scattering them left and right, keeping between me and the girl. *What the…?*

Then Arvid showed up and cut in front of the girl, a determined look on his face. At the same time Liv said, "She's not one of ours. Why is she wearing that uniform?" even as Arvid clutched his chest and fell to the ground in front of bandgirl, even as she reached inside her tunic and withdrew a handgun, stepping over Arvid without looking down, continuing to stride toward me, the gun now down at her side. The crowd did not notice anything except Arvid on the ground and Horace on his rollerblades, quick-striding toward the girl.

In an instant she brought up the weapon, sunglassed eyes fixed on me, right arm extended, pointing, aiming. And ever since VanderKellen's suicide note, I had been looking for a man. *Oh, God,* I thought, *how stupid!* Profiling gone bad, and now the real shooter closed in, stopping just a few yards away, bringing her left hand up to steady her aim, knees slightly flexed, arms extended in classic shooter's stance, the pistol point blank at me.

Everything that happened right then on the hot sidewalk in front of Kathy's Kuntry Krafts Korner took only a few seconds in real time. In my mind, it was all in slow motion, took minutes, and will never leave me.

I remember crouching and starting to surge toward the girl, my hands in front of me to deflect or accept slugs, determined to feint left and right. But action exploded around me, simultaneous decisions by several people that stunned me, marking me and the town and people of Rockbluff for the rest of our lives.

First, Liv, suddenly ferocious and strong, grabbed the front of my t-shirt with both hands, spinning me away from the woman, slipping between the shooter and me.

I heard pistol shots, felt a sharp slap at the side of my head and, at the same time, something mountainous and dark looming to my right and a deafening, thunderous explosion. Lunatic Mooning brought his backup Mossberg, pistol-grip shotgun into play as the shooter continued firing.

I began to totter, my legs curiously wobbly, my eyes still on bandgirl whose creamy-white tunic top was driven back into her chest from the shotgun blast. An enormous splash of blood burst through her torso as the impact of the shot lifted her up off her feet and onto her back on the sidewalk. I remember the acrid smell of cordite and the sound of her skull cracking like a brittle melon on the pavement.

In the background, far, far away, I could hear screams, lots of them. I saw Gunther, Mike, and Carl rushing up, and then Arvid's face as I slipped down, too heavy for Liv to keep me from going down, dragging her with me as she held on to me, stretching my t-shirt. Then Liv was on top of me, spreading her body over mine; a blanket, a blessing, a shield. The crowd surged back, pressing in, staring, horror on their faces.

"I'm okay," I said, not sure if I was telling the truth. "Help me up, someone."

Then Gunther and Mike had me up and were propping me on a bench, and I was aware of a steady stream of warm stickiness on my face sliding down onto my chest and shoulder. And there was Liv's white face, filled with fear. She said, "Oh, God, Thomas!" and sat down quickly next to me.

"Ain't nothin' but a scratch, ma'am." Which I knew to be true. I'd been shot before. I forced a smile, then, "You stepped in front of the shooter."

She nodded vigorously, tears in her eyes, forcing a quick smile.

Then there was Moon's big face as he squatted down next to Liv, the man in black serious. "If you two palefaces, and your faces are really pale, can skip the John Wayne clichés for a minute, maybe we can get you over to the hospital and take care of that little scrape."

Moon was still holding his shotgun in one hand, the short, lethal barrel pointing down at the sidewalk. I heard sirens. I heard Arvid say, "Hiding behind a woman. Sheesh. What a stud! I guess I couldn't interest you in a whole life policy about now, could I?"

I said "No," then, "that was a pretty convincing heart attack."

"Pure inspiration. When the muse intervenes in the lives of mortals, one must obey. Thought it might throw her off a bit."

Moon said, "That it did, but it was still close. She got off shots, but you'd be dead, Thomas, without Arvid's collapse or what Liv did. Helped me, too. Extra second made a big difference. Got me closer, surer."

I was feeling drifty, people appearing to be far away, then up close without their moving a muscle. I laughed at that. Carl Heisler's face appeared. His hands and face were covered with blood. His eyes were tormented. "You okay, Thomas?"

I nodded, the movement of my head bringing on a fresh rush of dizziness. I heard an ambulance stop far away nearby. I was hoping it wasn't for me. Rides in ambulances years ago didn't leave a desire for more. I looked past my friends and saw Schumacher and Aldrich rushing to someone on the sidewalk. *Who? What?* "I'm fine," I said to Carl, "but you got more blood on you than I do."

"Not mine," Carl said. He struggled, swallowed hard, started to speak, finally did. "Horace took a bullet, Thomas."

Everything under my skin stopped, frozen. Horace had told me once that he had my back, that he could be counted on. Inwardly, I had scoffed, had humored him. Now he was shot. "Where?" I asked.

"Upper chest," Carl said. He looked over his shoulder, then back at me. "You better get some help quickly. You're bleeding a lot, Thomas."

"The scalp is extremely vascular, Carl. It's not as bad as it looks," I said, my dizziness dissipating. "What about the shooter?"

"Dead," Carl said. "I went to her, lifted away her sunglasses, looked into her eyes. She cursed me with her last breath. She was just a child."

"That's okay, man," Moon said, setting his hand on Carl's shoulder. "Let it go. Sometimes you just gotta flush the toilet."

"Let's get you to the hospital," Liv said. "Enough talk."

Gunther said, "I'll drive you, buddy."

"Actually," Mike said, "I'll take him. My car's right here."

"I was here first," Gunther said.

"You forget I work out with weights," Mike said.

"But I work with my hands, steroid breath."

Another voice. "But it's my job," Harmon Payne said, pushing through the crowd. "And I've got the uniform to prove it. Now step back. Come on, Thomas," the Sheriff said, offering a hand. I took it and came quickly to my feet and felt woozy again, tried to mask it, succeeded. To buy time, I said, "Come on, Liv."

But Liv didn't say anything. I turned around and looked for her, then saw her propped up there on that bench, slumped as if she didn't have any strength, and I noticed blood on her pink blouse, and the perfect bullet hole between her right shoulder and her throat. Still bleeding.

Chapter 30

"There is no safety in numbers, or in anything else."
- James Thurber

The shooter got off four shots before Moon's blast stopped her. One. Liv Olson was struck with the first bullet. The nine millimeter round had gone completely through her right trapezius muscle, entering the front and exiting cleanly on the other side. The wound produced considerable bleeding and would leave a scar for discussion when she wore tank tops or summer dresses, or nothing at all. She was shot just as she turned to grab me.

Two. The second round deflected off my head and ended up in a trashcan twenty feet behind me. Lansberger found it. A miracle he found the slug, a bigger miracle no one else in the crowd was struck by it. The damage? Nothing a long string of stitches couldn't repair. Minor crease in the bone of the skull. Serious headache that, after a couple of intense days pretending to be a migraine, began to fade. Good drugs.

Three. Four. The last two shots killed Horace Norris. Two bullets, not one, had pierced his chest. One in the heart, another just below. He was dead before he hit the ground, as they say. I am not ashamed to say I wept when I heard. I am ashamed to say it was my fault. That will not, ever, go away. It would have been better for me had one round gone into my heart. Less pain. The truth hurts more than any other wound. I understand that more than ever.

Because people scattered from the shooter almost immediately, and he was so close to her, stray pellets from Moon's shotgun blast struck only one man, a superficial wound that was treated on site.

They took Liv to one treatment room, me to another. Later, during the day, a steady parade of visitors went from room to room until nurses ran them off.

Because she had moderate blood loss, even though the wound was clean and relatively small from the 9 mm the shooter carried, Liv was encouraged to stay overnight, then see her personal physician for follow-up. As for me, they suggested I stay overnight given my brief period of disorientation at the scene. They wanted to monitor my mental status for concussion or other brain injury. There'd be a CT scan if I wasn't clear in the morning.

So the medical staff kept us both overnight for observation, but not very close observation. Sometime during the late night or early morning Liv made her way in to see me. "I am here to comfort you, Thomas," she said. And she did. We whispered words. I thanked her, said I was sorry my situation had gotten her shot. She said no problem. See you later, alligator.

They released her first thing in the morning. "How do you feel?" I asked as she came into my room to say good morning. Rachel and Molly were with her.

"Very, very sore," she said, rotating her shoulder and yelping. "I chirp a lot, grimace, mutter meaty Anglo-Saxonisms. They say I'll be fine, shouldn't have any complications. Groovy scar, no pun intended. How 'bout you, Thomas?"

"They're letting me go after lunch. Headache's still shouting at me. I'm going to have to let my hair grow a little longer to cover up my body art. Should get my stitches out quickly. I feel tired." I did not say I felt like shit because of what I had brought to the sleepy little town of Rockbluff. I had begun calculating the damage done by my presence after Olivia left my bed hours before, and I wanted a drink more than anything.

"Get some rest at home, then give me a call when you feel better. I want to know how you're doing," Liv said, then she came over to me and kissed me full on the mouth, but it felt like goodbye. Molly and Rachel smiled and looked at the ceiling. Then they were gone.

After lunch, Mike came by, brought me clean clothes, and gave me a ride home. He told me Gunther and Carl retrieved my keys and took my truck home yesterday, leaving the keys under the doormat. *Original idea*, I thought. But then, I didn't have any more killers to worry about, did I? They also fed Gotcha last night and this morning and aired her out twice, then dropped off my clean clothes at Mulehoff's Earthen Vessel Barbell Club and Video Store. And Mike brought them the rest of the way. Such good men.

We didn't say anything on the drive out to my place. When we pulled up at my front door, I asked about the shooter. "Who was the girl, Mike? Did Harmon find out anything?" Mike looked ahead through the windshield. He took a deep breath and I felt sick to my stomach. Could the news get any worse?

"Thomas, the shooter was a runaway who disappeared eight years ago when she was fourteen. Milk carton kid from California. No idea how she turned into a professional hit man, hit person, whatever. Her work history is not traceable. Her family's coming to claim the body today." He stopped talking, his gaze focused on the thick stand of red maples, oaks, and birch trees to the north.

"And?" I asked. Then it hit me. The band uniform. "How did she get the damn band uniform, Mike?" Chills jumped out all over my body.

He turned his head from the woods and looked me in the eye. "I'm sorry, but Stephen Doltch found the body of one of our band kids behind the McDonald's two blocks from the shooting. The ice pick was still in her ear."

"Oh, Jesus," I said, suddenly without strength, and without strength to stop the tears. I could do nothing but weep. Sob is more like it. No strength. Nothing left. Mike was silent. I summoned resolve. "Who was she?"

Mike swallowed hard. "A good kid. Maggie Rootenbach.

Fifteen. Sophomore. Only child. Parents have a farm north of here. Solid folks. I'm awfully sorry, Thomas."

I had to get away from Mike, from everyone, before I heard anything more that I was responsible for. "Thanks for the ride, Mike. I appreciate it. Tell Gunther and Carl thanks for me, willya?' I put my hand on the door. Mike put his hand on my shoulder. It felt like an anvil. I could not look at him.

He said, "I know you don't want to hear squat right now, Thomas. I'm not going to lay any platitudes on you, but I am going to say please let me know if I can do anything to help you. You did not do anything wrong, and I'm glad you're here and I, for one, thank God you're among us. ."

"Thanks, Mike," I said, and I got out, shut the door quietly behind me, strode to the front door, took the keys out from under the mat, and went inside, where the cold beer waited. And Gotcha, of course.

In the middle of a community where my presence had brought devastation, death and disaster, Gotcha came up to me, her little corkscrew tail wiggling, trying to grin against the great grip of gravity pulling on her pendulous facial folds. What I got was a grimace, but under the circumstances, I took it. She didn't know I was about to lose my mind, and just maybe her face would be enough to keep me from it.

I got down on one knee and petted her massive head, massaging the heavy rolls of loose skin around her skull and under her chin, kneading her goozle and petting her and rubbing her chest. She toppled over in delight, and I rubbed her belly. When I stopped, she emitted her soft growl of encouragement to continue, and I did, and then I surprised myself by weeping again.

To my credit, I stifled the tears when a couple spilled onto Gotcha.

My next stop was the refrigerator. I took out two, then three, Fat Tires and grabbed a pint glass I had bought from The Dirty Duck, my favorite pub in Stratford-upon-Avon. Then I went out on the deck in the heat of the day and took a seat in one of my Adirondack chairs. Gotcha chose to stay in the air conditioning, and I couldn't blame her.

I filled the pint glass and drained it, filled it again and drained it, got up and went inside, retrieved a cold four-pack of Three Philosophers and took it out on the deck. Hell, it was the last day of the Pork Festival. Time to celebrate. Last day in July. Time to celebrate. Last piece of the puzzle with the shooter dead. Time to celebrate.

"Wait!" I said out loud. The shooter wasn't the last piece of the puzzle. Poor Maggie Rootenbach was.

Time to get drunk.

I knocked back another pint and was grateful for the way it took away some of the ragged edges of my mind, which felt like it had been ripped by a crosscut saw.

Now that it's over, I thought, *I guess I can count the cost to Rockbluff, the cost to the people who welcomed me into their midst when I was trying to get over losing my wife and daughters.* Now it was their time to lose family.

I topped off my Dirty Duck pint glass and held it up to the sky. And then I drank and called out names of people who died since I came to town, beginning with Hugh Soderstrom and continuing through Maggie Rootenbach, calling the dead hit person "Shooter," like the guy in the basketball movie, just so she'd have a name.

"I'm hungry," I said to myself. Drinking always makes me hungry. I struggled to my feet, thinking about a can of smoked almonds and three stale raspberry-filled doughnuts in a box on top of the refrigerator.

Although I was a bit wobbly, I managed to keep my balance. I banged my right knee hard against a chair, skidding it a few inches. And then I let it go, a string of filthy language that came and came and came, erupting from the pit of my being, every curse directed at myself. When I finished, I just stood on my deck overlooking the distant Mississippi River valley, breathing hard, woozy, ashamed of what I had said, more ashamed of what I had done. Most ashamed of what I was.

I thought of Karen and Annie and Michelle. *If they could only see me now*, I thought. Karen could see me in bed with Liv, and the girls could see me drunk with a bullet wound in my head. A husband, a dad, they could all be proud of? If you can't stand the answer, don't ask the question. I remembered.

Every now and then, since my family was crushed to death, incinerated, I speak their names out loud, just to be saying them. Oddly, it helps a little. It's like if I say "Karen," or "Annie," or "Michelle," they aren't so far from me. So dead. Sometimes I even say things to them, like, "How 'bout those Red Sox?" or just, "I miss you, girls."

It always messes me up inside but, at the same time, it's like I'm keeping the memory of them alive. That helps. I look at their pictures, too, and I wonder what they'd be doing now, if they hadn't died.

I know that, years from now, I'll wonder what Annie would have been like as a mid-30's something woman, or Michelle as a recent college graduate. Or especially, what Karen would have looked like with streaks of gray in her hair. And I know that I will never, ever know. When we had been married just a few years, I told her one morning before we got out of bed, "You know, some morning you'll wake up and look over and see that you've been sleeping with an old man." She had just smiled and whispered "Good" and kissed me. It will never happen. Now I wake up, alone, and the first thing that comes to mind is that part of my heart and soul has been carved out of my life.

Now, because of me, the Rootenbachs would get to go through the same thing. *God help me.*

I stumbled back inside the house, banging my stitched-up head against the sliding glass doorframe. There was pain, but mild. Nothing like a little liquid anesthetic taken orally to numb the discomfort. And get a start on the other kind of hurting.

I was sweating from the heat and my cursing fit and wiped my hand against my face. It came back bloody. "Probably plopped a few stitchers," I said out loud, then laughed at my mumbling. I touched my head again, my fingers finding the place. I looked at my fingers. Blood. "Fuck it," I said, then banged my head again, hard, on purpose. It hurt. Good.

At the refrigerator, I swung the door open, steadied myself, looked inside. A fresh four-pack waited for me, and I pulled it out, almost spilling one from the cardboard caddy. I set the ale on the counter, put my hand on top of the refrigerator, found the half-empty box of doughnuts, dragged it down and pushed it next to the beer.

At the cupboard over the sink I retrieved the can of smoked almonds and dropped it into the flimsy doughnut box next to the three desiccated treats. Taking the box in one hand and the ale in the other, I started for the door. Through the kitchen I could see Gotcha on her tuffet. "Wanna celebrate my accomplishments with me?" I asked. She lifted her big head, then put it back down on the double pillow, watching me.

"I don't blame you, girl. It's not a very nice party," I said. I went back outside. I was glad to be alone on my deck in the woods in the country, deserved to be alone on the big deck of the beautiful home.

Why in the name of God, did I have to stop for Wendy that time?

I stood and finished off another Three Philosophers, then decided to put the rest back in the refrigerator. Any more and I would be sick. I didn't want that. I turned to go back inside, and fell over a chair I had forgotten about. And cracked my skull again. This time it really hurt. I sat down in the chair for just a minute, bottles skidding all over the deck.

When I woke up, it was late twilight. My head hurt through and through. I shuffled inside and went to bed, my last thoughts on the fact that Liv Olson had been shot trying to save my pathetic life.

That was the last day of the Pork Festival.

I awoke in considerable pain a little after noon the next day. Experience got me out of bed and into the shower, blood washed away. I shaved and ingested aspirin. I could feel the crease where the stitches had popped, then shrugged it off. *So what?* I put my bloody pillowcase in the washing machine, cleaned up the blood on the tile floor and the side of the sliding door frame. I fed Gotcha and let her out, went out on the deck and cleaned up my trash, let Gotcha in, then drove to town to buy more beer, my silent, non-judgmental friend.

On the glass door of the Hy-Vee Supermarket, a memorial service for Maggie Rootenbach was advertised. It would be tomorrow at the high school. I went inside, bought a case of Corona and two packages of bratwurst and took them up toward checkout. I expected a dirty look. Rockbluff is a small town.

One of the three cash registers wasn't busy, so I set my purchases on the conveyer and walked up to the cashier. I got the classic double take. She rang up the total and told me the tab and I paid for it with my debit card. She kept glancing at me as the machine buzzed and spit out my receipt, which I stuffed in my pocket. She tentatively told me to have a nice day.

I drove home and drank all day and grilled and ate one of the packages of bratwurst. I played towel tug-of-war with Gotcha, spinning her until she was airborne, locked onto her end of the towel, but it made me dizzy, so I stopped. I did not turn on the radio, television or computer. I thought about calling Olivia as she had asked. While I thought about that, Ernie called.

"It stinks that I have to have FOX NEWS tell me someone put a bullet in your head," he said. "Other than that, how ya doin', man?"

"I had it coming."

"We all do, Thomas. But if you kill yourself over this, I'll never speak to you again."

I took a deep breath. "I'm not going to kill myself."

"Why not?"

"Because I'm too damn tired, and there's a chance the Hawks will play in the Rose Bowl. Don't worry, Ernie."

"Yeah, well, I do worry. I know about the shooting, I know about the local girl who was murdered, I know about your lady friend, and I'm thrilled that you have a lady friend. I know about Horace Norris. That's a terrible burden for you to take on, Thomas."

"How'd you know about Olivia and me?"

"Lunatic Mooning, who else?" I raised my eyebrows. "I called him. I told Lunatic who I was and, once he accepted that, he filled me in. Lots of people are worried about you, but also sensitive to your wanting to be alone."

"A blessing."

"You want to be alone so you can just drink until things get better?"

"Yes."

"Well, I'd be a lousy friend if I expected you to go through all this alone. Olivia told me you haven't answered your phone for three days. She's doing better, by the way, and thanks for asking."

"You called Olivia Olson?"

"Yup."

I stood up and walked outside. The day was cooling down, to my surprise, to the point of being comfortable out on the deck. A strong breeze stirred the treetops and filtered down to me. "You're pushy, Ernie."

"Tough. So, what's so important you can't pick up the phone when a fine woman wants to talk to you? Never mind calling me, your friend and pastor for nearly two decades. That's okay. No big deal."

"I hate cell phones, and this one's going off the deck down to the bottom of the bluff this house was built on as soon as we conclude our conversation."

"Got a guest room available?"

"I have two guest rooms, but they're not available to anyone. I need time alone. I'll be all right. I have not lost faith in God, Ernie, so you don't need to buck me up. I believe Jesus was a man of sorrows, too. We can relate."

"I'm not unpacking my car until I am convinced you're not going to put that damn shotgun in your mouth and pull the trigger."

"Job 13:15, Ernie."

"'Though he slay me, I will hope in him.'"

"You got it. And somewhere in Habakkuk."

"The Lord God is my strength, and so forth..."

"You must be a preacher or went to seminary, or both. Very good."

"Okay, I'll leave you to your ruminations," Ernie said, "but you're drinking too much, like you did after you lost your girls."

"I don't need the reminder. You know me pretty well, friend, but you don't *know* me. I'll be okay. Someone once said that all the world's problems are caused by, and cured with, alcohol."

"That alcohol quote is a load of bull. And what have you done, anyway? Where have you screwed up?"

"If I had minded my own business, there would have been a total of one murder, and this town would have continued on believing it was a farm accident. You know the rest. So, any way you cut it my involvement caused a bad situation to expand beyond belief, certainly beyond understanding. And please don't tell me God will use it somehow for good."

"You think you should have ignored what looked like a genuine appeal of a hysterical woman for your help? You think you should have kept going, focused on your own pain, your own depression?"

"Indeed."

"Then I'll hang up, now that I know you're not going to kill yourself, and now that I know you've decided not to be a human being. I may not know you, as you claim, Thomas, but I mostly know you, and this isn't right or good or excusable. So stop whining in your beer. Your life is worth more than that."

"Say hello to the family."

"I shall, Thomas. We all love you."

"See ya," I said, and that was that.

Chapter 31

"If you haven't forgiven yourself something, how can you forgive others?"
- Dorothy Huerta

Over the next two days I made another beer run, avoided eye contact with people in the Hy-Vee, and began to eat more. Toward the end of that second day, I was fixing myself a nice lunch of bratwurst and potato skins with cheddar cheese and, bless me, a glass of whole milk, when a knock on the door interrupted my preparations. If it was Ernie, I was going to bloody his nose.

I opened the door to Olivia Olson.

"You need to shave, put on a shirt and tie and come with me. Horace Norris, who died for you, is being buried today. Funeral at Christ the King, Carl Heisler preaching, burial at Rockbluff Cemetery. Get going."

"You look nice," I said. "How's your gunshot wound?"

"Get going. I'll wait out here."

"It'll be a long wait. I'm not going with you. I can't."

"You skipped Maggie's memorial service, you're holing up like some sort of damn hermit, and you're making Heineken's stock skyrocket."

"I'm not drinking Heineken at the moment. Three Philosophers is my beverage of choice."

"What the hell is wrong with you? Come on! Get going. You owe Horace."

"He'll never know."

"That's rich. Now, let's go. Don't be gutless."

"I'm not going. Run along. I mean it."

Olivia glared at me, shaking her head. "You are one sorry sucker. You should be ashamed of yourself. And if you don't show a little respect for a man like Horace, and all your other friends in this town, and for me, I'm not so sure I want to see you again. You're better than that."

"No, I'm not."

"False humility makes me want to spit up."

"Go," I said. And I shut the door in her face. She left.

I wasn't hungry anymore. I felt nauseated. If I stayed home, I would hate myself more than I already did. If I went to the funeral, I would be the object of others' hate. But at least I could face myself. I strode back to the front door and opened it, but the only evidence of Olivia's visit was a soft cloud of powdery white dust settling back in the road where her car had sped away.

Back in the kitchen, I got out a juice glass and retrieved a bottle of Myers Rum, only for special occasions, from a cabinet. I filled the glass, downed it, put the bottle away. I brushed my teeth, gargled with blue mouthwash.

I dressed in a pair of dark slacks, white shirt, dark blue tie, and the only jacket I still owned, an old navy blazer I was married in. Sentimental slob.

I arrived half an hour early, in searing heat on August 2nd, big surprise, but the parking problem replicated Hugh Soderstrom's funeral, a ceremony that seemed like five years ago. I parked as close as I could and walked quickly to the church, up the steps, and into the narthex. A man I didn't recognize looked at me, handed over a program, and continued to look at me as I slouched inside and sat in the last row. In five minutes, there were people standing in the back. Timing is everything.

I couldn't see Olivia, but I knew she was there. Her force field is obvious.

The closed casket waited in front of the altar. The church choir filed in and settled themselves. I looked around and recognized everyone I knew in Rockbluff. I offered up a silent prayer of gratitude for the rum.

A few minutes later, Carl Heisler, dressed in a dark suit and tie, entered and took a seat next to the pulpit. The choir sang, "Shall We Gather At The River," and several people in the congregation were nodding their heads and smiling, no doubt thinking of Horace, as did I, in his inner tube, floating down the Whitetail.

Carl rose, then read: "For I am already being poured out as a drink offering, and the time of my departure has come. I have fought the good fight, I have finished the course, I have kept the faith."

I liked the part about a drink offering.

Carl went on to say, "Our friend, our brother, has fought the good fight, literally dying during a fight, giving up his life for his friend, my friend, Thomas O'Shea."

I felt like someone jabbed me with a cattle prod. Carl could not see me, so what he said was not meant for my ears. He went on, "I am confident that Horace, who died a hero's death, would have preferred it this way, rather than wait out the ravages of cancer. Horace loved life, and he loved it so much he gave up his life for another's.

"But the Devil is a liar, and I believe, I *believe*, he is telling Thomas O'Shea that Horace's death is Thomas' fault. It is not. Don't believe that, if Thomas O'Shea had not come to Rockbluff, everything would be fine, that there would not have been so much death and heartbreak. I tell you, do not go down that path. It leads to bitterness and destruction.

"I implore you to reach out to Thomas. He is a man who does the right thing. He has done nothing for you to forgive. And that is all I will say about the man Horace Norris gave up his life for."

Carl started, stopped, swallowed hard, struggling. And then, thankfully, he moved on to a stirring eulogy. He spoke of Horace's faith, his commitment to the children and youth of the community, his zest for life that manifested itself in tubing down the river, sky diving, roller blading, and helping others.

People wept. I did not. Dry well.

The ceremony ended and the pallbearers moved to the sides of the casket on the rolling platform. Lunatic Mooning, Mike Mulehoff, Arvid Pendergast, Gunther Schmidt, Harmon Payne, and Chuck Aldrich. They rolled the coffin down the aisle and outside to the hearse waiting to take Horace to his grave. I slipped out behind them, drove to the ABC store, bought three bottles of Kendall-Jackson Pinot Grigio, and went home. *I am not man enough to stand by and see Horace lowered into the rich, black earth of northeastern Iowa. I am not.*

I hit the Drive-Thru at McDonald's, behind which they found the murdered Maggie Rootenbach's body, and ordered two double cheeseburgers, a giant order of fries, and a fried apple pie—all gourmet delights especially created for chilled Pinot Grigio. You can look it up.

I headed home, nibbling on the hot fries. I drove over the double arched limestone bridge, remembering my confrontation with the amateurs from Dubuque, remembering how much I enjoyed beating the hell out of them, wondered about that. I drove by Arvid's house, its inhabitants at the burial. I doubted Arvid would fake his death there, urging of the muse or not. I drove out of town, toward the house, eventually motoring up the white gravel driveway to the front door.

Inside, I gave Gotcha half of one of the double cheeseburgers, then took out a big tumbler, decanted one of the bottles, and poured the glass nearly full, then dumped a handful of ice cubes to top it off, spilling a little. My gauche treatment of a fine wine would horrify some people, but I don't care.

I am a sorry sucker most of the time, and I accept that. Like Horace, we are all afflicted with a terminal disease. It's just the playing out of the details that is different for each of us. I glugged down some wine and found myself envying Horace, instantly dead in the midst of his heroism. Does it get any better than that?

Gotcha, having wolfed down her half sandwich, followed me outside, begging silently for nibbles with her large, brown, liquid, intelligent eyes. “No deal, Gotcha,” I said, and she rumbled back inside the house, forgetting to close the door. I love my dog. She is clear and good, devoted to sleep and food and me in that order, a hierarchy we both respect for its honesty. She is brave, and always does her best. I wish I could say that about me.

I finished the wine before I reached the deck furniture, so I set the McDonald’s bag on the arm of the Adirondack chair and went back inside for a refill. I put the two remaining bottles in the freezer, hoping I would not forget about them and be reduced to enjoying Pinot Grigio Slushies later in the evening, or the next day. Sliding the door shut, I went back outside with a full glass.

By now the sun was slipping down through the trees, a red disc taking with it the heat of the day, leaving behind humidity, fatigue, and hope for cooler weather. In the remaining light, I found myself regretting my behavior toward Ernie. I am such a jerk sometimes, but in my own defense, I am a solitary person who prefers to be alone now that my family is long gone. As I told Moon, what I had only happens once, and it died in Atlanta. I sang softly to myself, “Na na na nah, na na na nah, hey he-e-y, say goodbye.”

I took another satisfying sip. Briefly, I wondered why indulging in something pleasurable brought with it a penalty—hangover, remorse, and guilt. Not fair at all.

Guilt overwhelmed me for a while, but I didn’t have the stamina to maintain it for more than a couple of minutes, but while it was in my neighborhood, I felt guilt for dragging so many people into my self-righteous, fervent search for the truth. I felt guilt for sleeping with Olivia. I felt guilt for drinking too much. I felt guilt about everything except the sinking of the Lusitania. I reveled in it. I knocked back more wine. I finished the food.

Once, after being in the Middle East, mostly Israel, for nearly a year, I spent thirty-three dollars at the first McDonald’s I saw upon returning to New York. That was before golden arches sprouted in every country, behind every pyramid, next door to every mosque, and when thirty-three dollars went a lot further.

I went inside and got myself another glass of wine, tossing the empty bottle into the trashcan under the sink. The glass shattered on another bottle.

I am afraid to leave the house, afraid to go into town. I remembered Carl's moving appeal for me, that I had done nothing to deserve their condemnation. I will thank Carl someday. But there are serious "reaching out" behaviors I wish he would have mentioned, like sex. I thought about Liv, beautiful in bed—passionate, erotic, sweet, almost innocent. I loved being with her, having her hands on me, the sounds she made, the murmurings and the slumber when the lovemaking was over.

When I was with her, I forgot about everything. Simple as that. I even forgot about Karen, God forgive me. I never expected to have that kind of intimacy again, and then, there it was. I drank some more and wondered if hope had an address that would show up on a GPS.

Oh, pathetic man that I am, I thought. *I do that which I should not do, and I do not do that which I should. And if that isn't a legitimate appeal for some more wine, Dolly Parton can see her toes.*

I shuffled into my kitchen, refilled my tumbler, and wondered why in the world the doorbell was ringing, and so far away.

Gotcha stayed on her tuffet, boofing briefly, refusing to budge. I answered the door. It was Liv. I stared at her, unable to speak.

"You're drunk again," she said.

"I like to think of it as chemotherapy. 'Drunk' is a pejorative term that is an affront to those of us who are connoisseurs of the fruit of the vine. Nevertheless, it is a blessing to see you. May I kiss your luscious lips?"

"You may kiss my ass," she said, sweeping by me into the living room.

"That's even better," I said. "Won't you please denude that delectable surface for my affections?"

Instead of slipping down her slacks and panties, Olivia turned around and said, "I understand you were at Horace's funeral service this afternoon."

"Your understanding is founded on fact."

"Thank you. That was a good thing to do."

"May I remind you that Horace had no idea I was there. I simply went because my guilt would have been stronger if I stayed away than if I attended. I can thank you for that perspective."

"You had it coming, Thomas."

"Yes, I did." That stopped her. "Won't you have a seat?"

"No."

"Why not?"

"You might persuade me to stay."

"No, I won't, but you are welcome to stay as long as you want. As long as you want," I repeated. She looked at me. She came in. She looked around. First time inside my house.

"Very nice," she said.

"Gunther is an artist," I said, stabilizing my uprightness by placing a hand on a door frame.

She said nothing. She stopped walking. Liv Olson was frozen in front of the bookshelf with my family pictures. *Oh.* Time for *me* to say nothing. Tough to do when one is half in the bag and Irish.

Liv was slowly shaking her head. She stood there a while, just looking at photos of Karen, Annie, and Michelle. When she turned to look at me her face was tear-streaked, her mascara melted.

"Are you okay?" I asked.

"Your family was so beautiful, your wife, your daughters. Oh, God, I am so sorry you lost them, Thomas. It never really struck me before. How in the name of God are you able to keep from losing your mind?"

"Sex and alcohol. But lately, mostly alcohol, regretfully."

"That doesn't even begin to be funny, Thomas. I can't do this. I can't compete with them," she said, gesturing back toward the bookcase. "I need to go right now."

"I want you to stay. Overnight, beyond. I want to kiss your face in the morning."

Liv shook her head. "Can't do it."

"Why not?"

Olivia looked at me. "Your family, for openers, and because

you're starting to spook me a bit, Thomas. Are you the kind, funny, considerate man I welcomed into my bed? Or maybe something else, someone with a past you can't leave behind, that bumps up into your life from time to time? You don't think any of us are buying your 'I read a lot' line, do you? That's insulting." She walked away from me, toward the front door, put her hand on the doorknob. "Harmon says you've got background, training, experience he can't get to. What is that? Tell me the truth about those things, Thomas."

"I could tell you, Liv, but then I'd..."

"Don't go there, Thomas! That is not funny. What's wrong with you? Why do you have to make a joke about everything? Why can't you just tell me the truth?"

"You want certainties."

"I want you," Olivia said, and my heart soared like the hawk, "but I don't know who you are. But I do know you are a liar, and there's nothing to build on there."

"Oh."

"See what I mean? You are an enigma wrapped in a conundrum. Who is Thomas O'Shea?"

"That's easy. I'm just a guy who reached the midpoint of his life and got derailed, and now I have to make some adjustments at the half, as they say on *Monday Night Football*. I'm just trying to get to tomorrow a little stronger. As for tonight? I want you to stay. Who am I? How 'bout someone who needs you, Liv."

"It's not possible," she said. "I have to go. Thanks for going to Horace's funeral today. I heard what Carl said, and I accept it. You have done nothing wrong other than lie to me over and over again, but I must say, to be honest, if you had never come here, life would be easier. And quieter."

"So you would ignore the truth in favor of peace and quiet? That's what my pastor asked me."

"Oh, Thomas, I don't know! Give me a little room, won't you?"

"You're the one who came out here."

"Good night, Thomas, and thanks again for coming to Horace's funeral."

"Where does that leave us?"

"To tell the truth," Olivia said, "I don't think there's any 'us' anymore, Thomas. I'm afraid of you, I'm afraid *for* you, and I'm afraid to be with you," she said, her hand drifting to the mark on her body near her neck. "And you lied to me. Besides that, which is not easily overcome, violence, dead bodies, broken people are attracted to you like shadflies to streetlights."

"Nice simile, but all of that's behind us now, Liv."

"I don't think it'll ever go away. Good night, Thomas, and have a good life."

"That doesn't sound very encouraging for tomorrow."

"It isn't," she said. And she left, reneging on her order for me to kiss her butt.

I closed the door once the car's taillights disappeared around the curve of my drive. I returned to my bedroom and looked around. My Bulldog was on her tuffet on the floor at the foot of the bed.

"And there is no joy in Mudville, Mighty Thomas has struck out," I said. Gotcha wiggled her root, I went into the kitchen and opened the freezer. I transferred one bottle of wine to the refrigerator. I opened the other one and took it with me outside.

Chapter 32

"They who wait upon the Lord shall renew their strength;
They will mount up on wings as eagles,
They will run and not be weary,
They will walk and not faint."
- Isaiah 40:31

Harlan Clontz, Jr. quietly withdrew his bid on the Soderstrom Farms property. He provided no information about his decision except that it was irrevocable. He insisted no one know except members of the Board of The Soderstrom Trust, and received their solemn assurance that his condition would be honored. Forty-seven minutes later, it was common knowledge in Rockbluff.

On a chilly September 25th evening, in a public meeting (as called for by the provisions of The Soderstrom Trust) in the Fellowship Hall at Christ the King Church (as called for by the provisions of The Soderstrom Trust), an agricultural conglomerate out of Minneapolis bought the land for $44,500,000. Everyone felt joy, I guess, except Clontz, who was not in attendance.

At the announcement of the winning bid, the crowd in the Fellowship Hall burst into cheers and whistles. No surprise. I was sitting by myself in the back when the good news broke forth. After the bid was certified and accepted by Mike Mulehoff, Senior Deacon of Christ the King Church, the burly schoolteacher asked for the attention of the noisy gathering.

His announcement that the Ruling Church Body offered the position of Senior Pastor to Carl Heisler, and he accepted, brought forth a burst of spontaneous applause. Ruth VanderKellen, seated with deacons and elders and the Heislers at a long table facing the crowd, dabbed at her eyes and kissed Molly Heisler on the cheek.

Other than that, it was just another routine, boring night in Rockbluff, Iowa. I tried to slip out the back during the backslapping and male hugging, two activities I detest, but Arvid Pendergast came up behind me, grabbed my arm, and said, “A bunch of us are heading over to The Grain o’ Truth for a little celebration. Won’t you join us? Only the elite have been invited.”

“So, why are you inviting me?” I said, faking a smile and moving toward the door.

“Just slumming, I suppose,” said another voice. It was Gunther. “You need to come back into the community, Thomas. It isn’t good for you to stay out in the sticks all the time. I haven’t seen you in weeks and weeks.”

“I don’t stay out in the sticks. What do you think I’m doing now? Hey! I’m being sociable, dudes! I’m hangin’ in the ‘hood, groovin’ on the vibes of Rockbluff! This is, like, awesome, what just went on here. I’m happy for everybody, like, gleeful.”

Another voice, softer, behind me. A woman. “Thomas, we’d be more than happy if you’d just come along and bless us with your company,” Ruth VanderKellen said, putting her hand on my shoulder. Dirty pool. How could I resist the invitation of the woman my actions had turned into a widow?

“Okay, okay. Hard to resist that,” I said. I smiled at her. “I’ll drop the smart-ass persona and just, like, you know, go along with the crowd, or whatever.”

“You ooze wisdom,” Ruth said, “but I’m sure it’ll be tough not to be a smart-ass.”

We all laughed. Ruth saying “smart-ass” didn’t go with her subdued good looks and simple dignity.

A crowd lined up five deep around Carl and Molly Heisler, so we decided to congratulate them later, when they joined the party at The Grain, as they had promised. It's hard enough to congratulate somebody, but I'm not into standing in line to do it, especially when it can be deferred to a place where multiple grains of truth are served. So the "elite" split.

Ruth started to leave, so I said to her, "Do you need a ride?" At first she didn't hear me, drifting toward the double doors leading from the Fellowship Hall foyer back into the big meeting room. So I reached out and tapped her on the shoulder. She turned and looked and smiled. I said, again, "Need a ride?"

"It'll save me a walk over to the manse to get my car, and I'd like your company. Thank you."

"Let's go, then." I offered her my arm and she took it. We started walking together.

"You know," she said, "at first I was just going to 'melt back into the night,' as they say, but being with people tonight seemed like a good way to, you know, kind of come out of seclusion, if you can call it that."

"I understand," I said, but I didn't agree. We walked out into the nippy night air and over to my truck. I opened the door for her and she smiled and said, "Thank you, Thomas" as if she really meant it. I helped her up and in, then hurried around and got in behind the wheel.

"This truck has an excellent heater," I said. It should kick in just about the time we get to The Grain."

"That's almost a mile. Maybe a little more. I think I can withstand the chill, though," she said. Then, as if she were unsure of what she was saying, she said, "I'm tough."

"Yes, you are, Ruth." I started the engine and turned to her. "You know, you did absolutely nothing wrong, no one blames you for what happened, and I don't think anyone wants to see you withdraw. Besides, you're good looking, and hiding out deprives us menfolk the opportunity to gaze upon you imaginatively."

"You do have the Irish gift of flattery without foundation, but I do like it. It's just hard. I have always loved it here, even though Ernst did not. But I think it might be better if I went away."

"Where?"

"Oh, I don't know, back to my roots maybe, just until I get my feet back under me."

I flipped on the heater, directing the flow to the floor. I don't know about women getting their feet under them, but I know about women's feet in cold weather. "And your roots are where?"

"Southern California. Santa Ana, to be exact," she said softly, putting her hands near the blast of warm air pouring onto her feet.

I began humming "I Wish They All Could Be California Girls" and pulled out of the Fellowship Hall parking lot. Ruth laughed. "What about you? Have you decided not to be a recluse? No one seems to have seen you much since you were shot. That's a long time, Thomas."

"Tonight's a big step for me. I didn't want to miss the opening of the bids, but I hoped to slip out and go home, but Arvid and Gunther nabbed me."

"They are good guys. You told me I needed to understand nothing that happened here at the church was my fault, and I think I believe you. Now you need to understand that what you think was your fault was not your fault, either. God knows you did nothing wrong. "

"Good to remember," I said, glancing over at her as we approached the bridge. I must say, she looked particularly fetching in a cashmere sweater and slacks. Both clinging affectionately to her topography. And bottomography, too. I notice things like that. So sue me. *Ernst, you were so dumb*, I thought.

"I'm being truthful. Evil was here before you ever showed up in Rockbluff, Thomas. You had a purpose here. You got rid of the infection and corruption and stink so that this place could be whole again. I know it was a terrible price for you to pay, but it needed to happen. I am grateful for you, and I thank God for you."

I said nothing as we crossed over the Whitetail River and continued up the slight hill to The Grain o' Truth. I didn't know what to say. If Ernie had inferred that God had used me, I probably would have popped him one. Wrap up all the world's trials and tribulations in a "God Used You!" knapsack and then go out for the buffet at Pizza Inn, appetite sharpened on sanctimony.

I pulled into the parking lot and shut down the truck. And sat there. Ruth said, "Are you going to leave Rockbluff and go back to your roots? I heard you were from downriver. Clinton. Before you answer, let me tell you, Thomas, that I hope you'll stay. It would be terrible if you left, if you let all that's happened to you since you got here drive you away from so many people who really, truly, care about you. You have no idea. You won't let yourself understand, and you should."

"It would be terrible if you left, too, and headed for California," I said. "Same thing."

Ruth smiled an impish smile, leaned across the floor shift and looked me directly in the eyes, her face less than a foot from mine, and said, "I won't if you won't."

"Okay," I said, "but don't expect me to become the bon vivant partymeister of Rockbluff. I'll ease back into a regular life, slowly but surely."

"I imagine Liv Olson will help with that easing. She's a wonderful woman and a fantastic teacher. I understand you've been an item these days."

"Not anymore. Nothing to build on once you've been called a liar and gutless. Nooo, I don't think there's anything left there."

"I'm sorry."

I got out and escorted Ruth to The Grain o' Truth Bar & Grill. Inside, we were met with the competing fragrances of Loony Burgers on the grill, French fries in the bubbling vat of canola oil, and pizzas in the ovens. Harry Belafonte was singing "Banana Boat Song" and several young couples were dancing to the music that was recorded decades before they were born. I took Ruth's hand and bulled our way up to the bar, edging by people who took the hint and made room.

"I'm sorry your bid for Soderstrom Farms came up short," I said to Moon, now looming up before us.

"Life is a trail of tears," he said. Then he noticed Ruth, edging her way to the bar from behind me. "Good evening, and welcome, Ruth. Good to see you." Moon turned to me and said, "By the way, white eyes, where the hell have you been? I haven't seen you in days, and my personal economy has suffered a recession. If you had been a regular like you were before, my bid might have won."

"I've been pouting. I've been sucking my thumb. I've been feeling sorry for myself. I've been feeding a pity party. Okay?"

"That won't hold up if you keep the present company," Moon said, nodding at Ruth. "The woman's a wonder. Now, what do you people want to eat? Remember, everything's on the house this evening. Rachel's paying."

Hearing Moon's remark, Rachel sidled by, holding a tray filled with pints. She beamed when she saw Ruth, and the two women performed a sidesaddle hug, Rachel balancing her tray. "He's telling the truth about everything being on the house tonight," Rachel said. "But he's a lying dog about who's paying. Truth is, he's paying. He just doesn't want to take credit, so order big, you guys, you'll never see this happen again." Before disappearing into the crowd, Rachel patted me on the butt and said, "Good to see you again, Thomas." I love it when women pat me on the butt. Or give me a long hug. Or even a quick kiss on the cheek. And then there's those winks.

We ordered Loony Burgers and a pint of Heineken's each. As we turned away from the bar, Mike Mulehoff came up to us, put a big hand on each of our shoulders, and said, "We've pushed a couple of tables up next to a booth in the back corner. The usual suspects. Join us in our celebration?"

"On our way," I said. When we arrived, there were cheers for Ruth and me both. Maybe there was something to what Ruth said about these people and their attitude toward me. I looked around.

Mike squeezed in next to his wife, Gabby, a diminutive, almost matronly woman with mischievous brown eyes; Arvid and his wife Clara, a stout woman I believe would have fit right in waiting tables during Munich's Oktoberfest; Gunther and Julie, and Liv Olson and Harmon. A little shot to the heart for me, an averted glance from Olivia.

We drank and ate and told stories on each other and laughed a lot. I drank quite a bit, sitting just a few feet from a woman I'd slept with and never would again. Ah, flaming youth!

Then, as the noise died down and The Grain began to slowly empty, Moon joined us.

"I have a question," I said, "and I know the answer is right here among us."

"I am not gay," Moon said, and everyone laughed.

"I'm serious. It's painful to be serious, but I want to know how Horace and Arvid knew the shooter was a woman. Come on, guys, 'fess up. You wouldn't have looked at the shooter twice if you didn't know to look for a female. I just want to know how you knew."

"We know how to look for a female," Moon said, and everyone laughed.

I said, "Give it up, Squanto."

Arvid looked nervous and adjusted his weight in the booth. His wife gave him a look and an elbow. He looked at Moon, who took a deep breath and put both of his hands on the table. Harmon looked particularly interested, so I knew he had no foreshadowing. Liv studied her hands, perhaps a torn cuticle, snagged while groping the Sheriff?

Moon said, "It would have come out, anyway, Thomas, but you're pushing the timing a bit."

"Go ahead," I said. Ruth moved closer to me and I felt her hip against mine. I briefly lost concentration.

Moon addressed the group. "A few nights ago I got a call from someone who said they wanted to talk to me about the person who had been hired to kill Thomas. This person told me to meet with him at Bloom's in five minutes, and I did.

"Here's what he told me. He had pulled in favors, made some threats, distributed money; whatever he could to find out whom to look for. He came up mostly empty, but he did find out that the shooter was a woman. So I got together with Horace, Arvid, and Mike to hang around Thomas at the Pork Festival and be on the lookout for a female who would be acting suspicious and approaching Thomas. So we did what we did. But it cost us Horace, and I'd like to offer a toast to him and to his memory. God bless Horace Norris!" And with that, we raised our glasses, and I said, "So say we all!" And everyone answered in kind.

Then I noticed Harmon was about to come out of his seat. "I don't believe this! You weren't fortunate, Moon, you were flat out damn lucky! Why the hell didn't you tell me this, and who was it that told you to watch for a woman? I could have used that information and maybe Horace wouldn't be in the ground now, but sitting here with us! I want to know, Moon!"

Lunatic and Harmon engaged in a staring contest, then Moon said, "It was Jurgen."

"I don't get it," Ruth said. "I mean," she said, shifting around in her seat, "How would Jurgen know? I don't know, it just seems out of character, is all."

Moon snorted. "He told me all the violence had the potential to mess up land values, and another murder in Rockbluff would cost him millions on paper. But he also told me that, even though Thomas was a pain in the ass, he didn't want him dead."

There was a significant buzz at that point, with Julie Schmidt saying loudly, "We don't want you dead, either, Thomas!"

"And so say we all!" Arvid shouted, raising his glass.

"And so say we all!" everyone replied, except for Harmon, who was still angry at Moon.

Harmon said, "Okay, Moon, you and I go back, friends, and I appreciate your good intentions, but you still haven't explained why you didn't tell me. I'm the professional here, and I might have been able to step in and not only protect Thomas, but keep Liv here from being shot, Horace being killed, and the shooter alive to stand trial."

"Fair question, my friend," Lunatic Mooning said, "but you had your hands full of responsibilities only you and your men could have handled officially—directing traffic, those two assaults with the participants having to be jailed, the stabbing, drunk and disorderlies, people from Minnesota..."

The reference to Minnesotans draw a couple of faint laughs as Moon tried to cool down Harmon. It didn't work. Moon continued, "So we felt like it fell to us to try to intervene."

"You made a big mistake, Moon. I'm sorry to have to say this, but you were wrong. I know you meant well, and you kept Thomas alive, but you ended up with one of our old friends dead, Thomas and Liv wounded, and the shooter dead. Not to mention where the blame might fall on Maggie Rootenbach's murder."

"You better not go any further, Harmon," Moon said, standing, "or I'm afraid we might have to take this out into the parking lot. That's a cheap shot bringing Maggie's death into the conversation. I resent it."

Harmon stood up quickly, his chair skittering behind him and tipping over. Liv reached down and righted it, fear on her face. Payne said, "I resent you and your Barney Fife approach to law enforcement, and if there's any way I can charge you with anything, obstruction of justice, interfering with a police investigation, discharging a firearm in the city limits, I will. Now, I better leave before we both say things we'll regret."

Harmon reached out and Liv took his hand and they left together. I manned up and looked in her face as they passed by, but she kept her eyes straight ahead.

It grew quiet in The Grain, the festive nature of the gathering leaving like air from a soufflé. "Well, that went pretty well," Rachel said, appearing behind Moon. Nervous laughter bubbled and died away.

"I haven't had so much fun since the hogs ate my brother," I said, and the level of laughter upticked a tad.

Just then, Carl and Molly Heisler showed up, and when the cheers started up again, the tension and anger fled like April snow.

Chapter 33

"Oh, life is a glorious cycle of song,
A medley of extemporanea;
And love is a thing that can never go wrong;
And I am Marie of Romania."
- Dorothy Parker

I drove Ruth home that night, again walked her to the front door of the stone manse that stood behind the church, as welcoming as a giant tomb. Lights shone in two rooms downstairs, and the porch light glowed as well. The upstairs remained dark, like the thoughts going through my head.

"Aren't you going to invite me in?" I asked.

"That's your beer talking, Thomas. I had a nice time, despite the little spat between Moon and Harmon. Did you notice the point of contention did not involve you, except as a secondary casualty?"

"I did notice, and it's a blessing."

"Good, I'm glad you were listening, not talking. I don't think you can count too much on your words at this point in the evening."

"Aren't you going to invite me in?"

"See what I mean?" she said.

"I should probably check out the manse to make sure some

psycho serial killer isn't waiting inside with a meat cleaver in his hand."

"You should probably not. But thank you for inviting me to go with you tonight. I enjoyed myself, and your company. You have no idea what a fine man you are."

I didn't say anything. I had a world of words I wanted to say, but I didn't. Sometimes I surprise myself. The September breeze picked up a bit into a gust, a chilly gust. *Good. Autumn on the way. Best time of the entire year.*

"I had a nice time, too, Ruth," I finally said. I put my arm around her waist and drew her firmly to me and kissed her and immediately woke up inside. I wanted to kiss her again and again, and that was not my beer talking. It was as if my soul had been touched by her lips, and I wanted more. My heart surprised me by wanting to cheer. I did not understand anything other than kissing Ruth was a good thing.

"Here we go again," she said, pulling away with a rueful smile. "I'm going inside, now," she said. "I'm afraid I am not feeling very strong at the moment, and I know you aren't, so I guess it falls to me to make the decision." And with that, she was gone again inside the blue granite home. I heard the locks click and the porch light went out.

"Thomas?" A muffled voice from behind the solid oak door.

"What?"

"Did you hear the locks on the door clicking?"

"Yes, I did. And I am filled with remorse, yet grateful you are a woman of fortitude. That doesn't mean I'm not wishing you were a woman of significant moral weakness."

"That clicking was the locks to the door, not the lock to my heart. Good night, I'm going upstairs now and I won't be able to hear you say another word. Sleep well, and thank you for being nice to me."

"It's easy!" I shouted as first one downstairs light went out, then another, casting everything on the ground level into darkness. In a moment, upstairs, a light came on. I wondered what she slept in, then chastised myself for the thought.

I wobbled my way to my truck and drove home.

In the morning, Gotcha woke me up with snorfles in my neck just under my right ear and, when I looked up, she pounced, her weight knocking me back. Then it was her game of "Don't Let The Master Get To His Feet."

She won until I said the magic word that always makes her stop whatever she is doing and pay attention to me, the King, the Source of Her Joy, the MASTER. I asked, "Eat?" and she leaped down from the bed, ran to her bowl, turned, and gave me the look.

I know how to follow instructions, so I got up, fed her, listened to her wet vacuuming of the porcelain dog dish, opened the front door for her to go out. It was chilly. Imagine.

My hangover was minimal, testimony to a growing tolerance for the brewer's art and, after a shower and change of clothes, I felt good and strong. And hungry. So I let Gotcha in, watched her plop down on her tuffet for her morning nap, and drove in to town to grab some grunts. It was 2:17 PM when I got to the Grain o' Truth Bar & Grill. My stomach was growling.

I ordered two Loony Burgers and a pint of Diet Coke, a double order of fries, and fried mozzarella cheese sticks, a nod to the memory of Bunza Steele and the cuisine of Shlop's Roadhouse. While I ate, Moon and I talked about the Cubs and Red Sox, both hoping for an "official" World Series with those two teams. We talked about the break in the weather and football, and he commented on my "GEORGIA" sweatshirt I had pulled on when I noticed the chill after opening the front door for Gotcha.

"Why Georgia?" he asked.

"Because they're the Bulldogs, Moon, and I used to live in Georgia, and I have a Bulldog. Connect the dots."

"I do not believe you have a Bulldog, but I wish you did. I admire the breed."

"I have a Bulldog," I said, finishing my meal. "I'll prove it to you sometime and bring her in. She is well mannered unless I am threatened, and she would add ambiance to this joint, something it could use."

Moon smiled. "Bring her in. I'll buy her a beer. Does she like beer?"

"Is she my Bulldog?"

We both laughed. A rare thing. I said, "After I dine, I think I'll go pay a visit to a lady."

Moon's face shifted, the humor slipping away like oversized boxers on a Kenyan marathoner.

"She stopped by earlier this morning. She left this for you," Moon said. "She knew you'd come by, creature of habit and connoisseur of good taste."

He reached under the bar and brought forth a small, gift-wrapped box and a lavender envelope, *Thomas* written across the face in a delicate hand.

My stomach hurt. Moon's eyes did, too.

I took the gift, the envelope. A little puff of pain went off in my chest. I knew. "Thanks, Moon, I guess I'll be going," I said, thinking of my precious privacy and a refrigerator stocked with beer and wine. Rum in the cabinet.

"Don't be a stranger. And bring that Bulldog in with you next time you're headed this way. I'll buy her that beer."

"Imported?"

"Is she your Bulldog?" Moon looked as if he had received bad news, not me. I guess he knew, too. After all, he had actually seen Ruth.

As I was leaving The Grain, someone played "Mother and Child Reunion" on the jukebox. When I arrived at my truck I got in, sat quietly, reminisced, and wept. Then I wiped my face and started the engine. Time to suck it up. Again.

I went by the bank, chatted up the girl teller who was nice to me. I stopped by the Hy-Vee. People inside were nice to me, too. One woman gave me a little hug when she saw my face, probably thinking something else was behind my expression other than run of the mill sadness. I looked in at The Earthen Vessel, but Mike wasn't there. I drove around town, over the double arched limestone bridge, out to Shlop's Roadhouse, back by Christ the King, down by the high school, back across the bridge, and home.

Back home, I put away the groceries and grabbed a pair of cold

Three Philosophers and trudged out onto the deck with Gotcha. I opened the envelope first and read the brief note.

Dear Thomas,

I'm off to California to take care of some details and afford myself some time. I will avoid another Iowa winter, yet come spring, I'll come back to stay. Then we can talk. The phone is charged and paid for, so give me a call at first snowfall and tell me how lovely it is from your place. Just push "1" on the cell. And make sure you give Gotcha a good rub for me now and then.

The note was signed,

Yours, Ruth

I unwrapped the box. It was a nice cell phone.

For a while I gazed to the north at the Whitetail River valley, and beyond, to the northeast, at the Mississippi River valley, and thought about "Yours, Ruth."

Wisconsin never looked so good. Or Iowa, for that matter.

Well now, I thought, *I've got some time to make myself acceptable for Ruth's return.* Cell phone and note in hand, I ambled back inside. I said to Gotcha, "Let's get started, girl. A lady is waiting."

She wiggled her little corkscrew tail and sneezed. I laughed.

I set aside the Belgian Ale, took a deep breath, and punched in the numbers for the good Reverend Dr. Ernest Timmons back in Belue, Georgia, confident if I invited him up for a long visit, he'd come.

Sometimes I surprise myself.

Author's Acknowledgements

I would like to thank the following people for their help in my writing life in general, and/or this novel in particular: Carol (Cook) Kaufman, who inspires; Joe Badal; Brad Steiger who encouraged me as a fledgling writer; the late Vance Bourjaily, who helped get me into the Iowa Writers Workshop (where I learned it's okay to be a writer); Charles Poteet of the *Morganton* (N.C.) *News-Herald* who gave me my first job as a newspaper columnist; Larry Franklin of the *Clinton* (S.C.) *Chronicle* for freedom to write whatever I wanted in that fine newspaper; the "novelistas" critique group (Melinda Walker, Melissa Lovin, Sarah "Mustang" Cureton, and Kevin Coyle, fine novelists in their own right) for all their careful reading and feedback on this novel; Nancy Koesy Parker for encouragement; Dr. Jodi Peeler for her network that was key; and my old friend Doug Brown of Maquoketa, Iowa whose expertise was critical in the building of my story; Joe and Donna at Neverland Publishing, who guided me through this entire process with patience, professionalism, and a sense of humor; Author Ron Rash for his thoughtful review.

The greater acknowledgements go to my daughters: to Rowe Carenen Copeland for cheering and editing support; and Dr. Caitlin Carenen for showing the way to publishing a book with her own, and her enthusiasm for this project.

And maybe my dog...

CPSIA information can be obtained at www.ICGtesting.com
Printed in the USA
LVOW11s0919121014

408392LV00006B/904/P

9 780982 697160